This story is about a relationship between a child and eventually a woman and her Shona maid, in the lowvelds of a war-torn Zimbabwe. Seen through the prismatic eyes of Joanna, this is the source for a multifaceted and captivating story of people, culture and personalities. The story means a lot more than black and white. A raw and romantic perspective that can only be provided by someone who grew up in the midst of it all and who is able to brilliantly paint the picture in the language of her African heart. As brutal and beautiful as the reality of the wildlife and her roots – The Save Valley Conservancy, 3442kms squared in size and world-famous stature, her playground. Crazy parties, sad events, hate, love, motherhood and murder, lions and liars, the cowards and the courageous. Tears and laughter as loud and as beautiful as the backdrop of the African bush itself.

Dedicated to:

Nyika

My daughter, Kate Nyika,

and

All the women of Zimbabwe.

Master Sun: "*Therefore, those who win every battle are not really skilful, those who render others' armies helpless without fighting are the best of all.*"

Alice Vye Henningway

NYIKA, I LOVE YOU

AUSTIN MACAULEY PUBLISHERS™

LONDON ∗ CAMBRIDGE ∗ NEW YORK ∗ SHARJAH

A CIP catalogue record for this title is available from the British Library.

ISBN 9781398435377 (Paperback)
ISBN 9781398435384 (ePub e-book)

www.austinmacauley.com

First Published 2022
Austin Macauley Publishers Ltd®
1 Canada Square
Canary Wharf
London
E14 5AA

For my parents, siblings and my family.

Mom and Dad,
Chooks, Russell, D and Belle
I love you!

We are able, simply, because, of the way in which we were raised.
We have true grit. Thank you for instilling that in us Mom and
Dad. It is one of the greatest gifts you could have given us as
your children.
When I visit The Save Valley Conservancy, it is where I hear your
voices. "*Do it the Henningway*" comes across really clearly and
makes me smile. No shortcuts in life, Doobs! "Chishakwe": "The
Place of the Lions," may no longer belong to us, but we will
always belong to Chishakwe! Our childhood was second to none,
despite the challenges and confrontations. They only prepared us
perfectly for the road ahead.

"Aan mijn Van Maanen familie ben ik veel dank verschuldigd
voor alle aanmoedigingen en het geven van een thuis gevoel.
Dikke kus."

"THE MIRACULOUS RANCH in southeast Zimbabwe was the wildest land we ever lived on, the least scarred. It wasn't a complete cure for what ailed, for the shocks and the aftershocks of the war, and for all that had come with the war, but I think it was the beginning of the cure or the cure was ours for the metabolizing, if we knew it or not." - Page 62

AND words from her father who had worked on the ranch,

"That was the wildest place we have ever lived, Bobo. You could really fall off the map out there." - Page 64

-in Alexandra Fuller's own words from her book Travel Light, Move Fast-

Chapter One
Dear Joe, Love Dad

Dear Joanna,

When you came into this world on the twenty-fourth of June 1972, we, your parents, Herman Marcus Hagen Snr and Claire Joy Hagen-Reagan owned our own ranch called "Ngwane" which in the local language of the Southern part of Zimbabwe (South-East Africa) being Shona means "Crown." It was situated in the Lowveld. Joe, you asked for a letter from me describing the first ten or so years of your life, as a Christmas present. Your life: an adventure from the get-go, so here you go "Merry Christmas"!

Altogether we had five children, Susan Ellaine Hagen, Jonathan Russell Hagen, Herman Rudd Hagen Jnr, Samantha May Hagen and you, Joanna Vye Hagen. Sadly, we lost Jonathan at the age of 15 months when he was searching for sweets in my office desk drawer. He came across a bottle of toxic tablets and, mistaking them for sweets, swallowed one which unfortunately proved fatal. Being so far away from a hospital we were unable to make it to the nearest small town in time. Jonathan died in your mother's arms, in the car on the way to the hospital. As you may be older, reading this now, you can well imagine how heartbreaking this was for us as his parents. You never get over the loss of a child. One exists as though you have lost the use of a limb.

We had decided to raise four children so you, Joanna, came along as a welcome addition to the family. Having gained considerable experience raising four children, you proved to be relatively easy to raise as you soon showed your independent spirit and we had to employ a maid called Nyika to watch over you as you were so unfearful of the African Bush. The African Bush in Zimbabwe can be very dangerous at times for adults, let alone little children, so your tendency to explore alone had to be supervised carefully. You became extremely attached to Nyika. Joanna, you were born in a very small hospital in Chiredzi, which served family communities, in not only Chiredzi but also Triangle and Hippo Valley which were huge sugar cane estates. I helped in your delivery, due to the fact as a rancher, assisting in a birth was not new to me.

I had delivered many an infant, young mothers from the neighbouring communal lands were bought to me to help with the delivery of their babies. One day as such arrived at my cattle dip, a mother in a wheelbarrow. Being pushed by her rather overwrought husband. The delivery had already started and since the hospital was some 100 kilometres plus away on bad roads, perhaps the worst roads you had ever born witness to! Strip road, on gravel with potholes, half of it washed away by heavy rains. I was left with no choice but to do my best, so I assisted the new arrival into the world. The parents named him after me. This happened a couple of times so there were a few Herman's from the communal lands.

However, dark clouds hung over Zimbabwe. Little did we realise the extent to which we would be affected and that our lives would change not only completely but forever!

Joanna, you were but five years old when we were first attacked by heavily armed terrorists (terr's). I am going to let you draw your own conclusions on what you would like to call them. To try and negotiate with them was impossible no matter how open-minded one was or how hard you may have tried. When you are actually *involved* in a war, pick a side, it is as simple or as complex as you choose to make it, simply because there are no other

10

choices. Do or die. However, people coming to kill my family and their own tribal people were not freedom fighters in my opinion. We were good people and we certainly did not deserve this, along with many breadbasket providers and tribal people in communal lands.

Our home was only two kilometres from the communal lands where the bulk of the tribal Shona population lived and who had been converted into supporting the Mugabe Brigade ZANU PF. With little to no choice of their own. One fact that so many people do not realise is that both armies had both black and white soldiers in them, but as propaganda is sold, it was turned into a war of race, greed and the colour of your skin. Fuelling the intricate need of human beings' desire to be part of a group. Wanting desperately to belong somewhere.

It had been said, that there were many Shona and Ndebele soldiers in the Rhodesian Army. The Rhodesian Army was the ZANU PF and ZAPU Party's opposition during the civil war known as the *"Independence Struggle"*. There were not only white soldiers in the Rhodesian Army. Stats imply for every one white soldier there were two black soldiers. The two black tribes in Zimbabwe, after the *Independence Struggle*, went head-to-head in their own war called The *GUKURAHUNDI MASSACRE*, with the new President Robert Mugabe (ZANU PF party) killing an enormous amount of the Ndebele (ZAPU Party-Joshua Nkomo's people), from 1983 to 1987, it was the most horrific mass murder operation we had ever witnessed as a country.

It strikes me as incredibly vicious to turn against your comrades after they have stood by your side in an *Independence Struggle*. There were further rumours that certain Asian countries had a helping hand in this too. Where is the comradery in that Mugabe? Where is the world's hype about that? I didn't see it splashed across news screens or in newspapers or on the news, period! I do recall this information being almost a "secret", swept under the rug. It just wouldn't sell newspapers, would it now? The

Shona Tribe used the Ndebele Tribe to win the *Independence Struggle* and played on the colonial card, as soon as the war was won by the ZANU PF Party (which was all Shona & Robert Mugabe's Party). Even if the ZAPU party had helped them. No credit was given when credit was due. ZANU PF won, end of story! Comradery? Nowhere in sight! The whole relationship changed with the ZANU PF party turning on the Ndebele Tribe and the *ZAPU Party*, just three years after the *Independence Struggle*. The leader of this party fled the country in fear of his life. In 1987, he controversially signed the Unity Accord allowing *ZAPU* to merge with ZANU to stop this genocide. That was his only choice. Joshua Nkomo the leader of *ZAPU,* then became the Vice-President of Zimbabwe and ZANU PF party, from 1990 – 1999 eventually passing from this world in 1999. Robert Mugabe then raped the country solely for his own good, his own pockets and for some of his cronies. Once again, a country in Africa with a dictator. The country's soil drenched in blood. That's a simple outline of politics for you, Joe. It is always more complicated in real life.

I had built a tower adjoining the house with its only entrance being from inside the house itself. It extended upwards about two metres above the rooftop, giving me a 360-degree view of the area surrounding the house. So, I could see terrorists approaching. I was equipped with an automatic rifle, and I raced up into the tower at about 10 p.m.

Your mother had always told me to keep my F.N rifle alongside me when I was taking a bath, thank God I had taken her advice, as on this particular occasion I happened to be taking a bath. I leapt out of the bathtub and I wrapped just a bath towel around my waist grabbed my gun and bolted up the stairs. I opened return fire on them, an important part of survival. The object was to show my attackers that I was no pushover. I felt totally vulnerable on this occasion, as you and your siblings were just too young, and your mother, whilst trying to get you all to safety, was also radioing for help. Numerous attacks followed on our home and on the workers. All of you children became tougher, the workers became wiser. We all became soldiers, some of us too young for that type of experience.

To be one soldier, protecting your family against a group of terrorists, is gut-wrenching. I was scared. However, that fear was replaced by survival and the inherent knowledge, that if those terrorists got hold of my daughters or the female farm workers, they would suffer as no woman would want to suffer. The torture tactics of the terrorists on white people and black people alike were sick. Plain and evil, from cutting out tongues, cutting stomachs open to remove growing babies, rape and a number of other torture practices. These tactics leaving you cold.

All farmhouses were equipped with the radio communications keeping in touch with one's neighbours, the police and the Military Operations Centre, was effective, but not easy when you are fighting a group of attackers, trying to fire. Hoping your family is doing alright, as this was their first experience of an attack. I had also managed to trip up the stairs, bumped my top lip and dislodged some of my front teeth. Whilst running up my tower I mentioned earlier.

The battle raged on for some two hours with the house being peppered with small arms fire, including automatic machine guns as well as being rained upon by mortar bombs. Mortar bombs are fired from a close range as mortars do not have long range. A mortar round has a very steep arc while the artillery round has a flat trajectory. Mortars fire rounds at slower speeds than artillery, that is why they are fired at a higher angle. Leaving devastating splash-damage in their wake. We definitely had our fair share of those. There was no military help available at the time until the early hours of the following morning by which time the attackers had broken off the attack and made their way back into the communal lands.

At 4 a.m. I heard a voice calling from the radio receiver, 'Christmas, Mr Hagen.'

It was the army arriving at our house using the call sign your mom had given them over the radio receiver. We used to call it an agric alert.

When the sun came up the following morning, there was no bird chatter, it was dead still and the damage was easily visible. All the windows in our house were smashed, there was a large hole in the wall about a foot above our bed, (you, Joanna, shared our bedroom during the war years), making it clear that we were lucky enough not to have already been in bed, and rather in the bath and in the lounge. We would have been killed, if we had been in bed already, your mother, you and I. The walls were full of holes and a thick layer of dust covered the house floor. The roof too was full of holes and the length of the tower wall above the house was similarly a mass of holes. The amount of damage was ruinous. It was obvious that the tower had saved our lives. I later added a wall around the house, to protect us further. A type of maze of sorts. Joe, you often got lost in this.

About a month later I flew to JHB South Africa to watch rugby. On my return I found that our security fence around the house had been tampered with, an obvious sign of a further attack was imminent. When I went to watch rugby, my wife Claire (your mother) guarded the house and family. Two bright lights (soldiers) came to look after your mom and you kids. There were only a few failed attempts of attacks in my absence. Your mother is no longer my wife but I have yet to meet a braver woman, in the face of war, she was phenomenal, so were you and your siblings … you all held your own. Your mother was also an amazing shot.

In the house, I had installed a concrete slab over the bathroom, a safe cover from mortar bombs and you and your siblings were taught that at the commencement of another attack you should all take cover in the bathroom. Your mum made sure that all of you knew exactly what to do, you "practiced a terror attack," by your mother signalling a ratatatatatatat (improvised by Blessing), until the motions became second nature, no matter where you were,

14

you had to drop to the floor and leopard crawl as fast as you could and as quietly as you could to the bathroom. Find a position inside the bathroom. Joe, you always climbed into the wash basket, and you were told to be silent. You all did so extremely well in this, never once did we have to remind you that this was for real. As children, you had absorbed that reality. I had moved the radio and installed it into a position just outside the bathroom door where your mum (Claire) positioned herself and kept the security forces (as well as keeping an eye on you lot) in the know as to our well-being.

Since I was sure that another attack would take place that night, I was ready. Sure, enough at 9 p.m. they opened fire on us. You kids were wonderful, taking cover and following the security process as you had all been taught. Your mum reported the attack immediately and I shot up into the tower (that I had built alongside our home), and opened fire against the attackers. The muzzle flashes gave their positioning away.

Prior to this attack, the army had given me a few hand grenades, smoke bombs, lighting grenades and extra magazines for my rifle. When I began shooting back, I came under enormous fire, the sound was deafening. I immediately threw a lighting grenade which instantly lit up the entire area around our house. I had ten magazines each holding twenty rounds and I used eight of these in the first two hours or so in the battle to save us. To save you guys. The din was indescribable and I know, to this day, you cannot stand the sound of gunfire. Be it in a film or otherwise, fireworks even make you antsy! This is to be understood. You tend to shy away from guns completely. Having taught all of you to shoot, to strip a gun and put it together again, in the case anything happened to your mum and I, you had to be prepared to fight for your lives as a collective and alone. With all this noise I thought the family would be terrified, but no, you were all marvellous, shouting encouragement to me and screaming threats at the terrorists. After realising being quiet in this din made no difference.

There is a very strange feeling that comes over you, knowing that people are specifically coming to kill you. War, such a senseless concept.

Using the radio that day for your mum was difficult because of the tremendous noise, but she managed to keep in touch with the security forces who were on their way, but had to first clear the road to us, from land-mines, a slow and demanding job, another "game" I had taught the children to play, was how to recognise a land mine in the road, before it was too late. This job takes an enormous amount of concentration and diligence, so we did not expect the security forces until the following morning. The attack stopped as abruptly as it had started. Another enormous silence followed, not a sound from the surrounding bush for hours, as though even the insect world was taking cover.

Then I heard the low-pitched voices coming from the direction of our road into the housing area. I immediately commenced firing again, this time at the voices. This was followed by an agonising scream, and then running footfalls which soon faded away. Sometime later I heard an accidental discharge from a terr's rifle up in the hills, which could only have meant that someone had omitted to engage his safety catch and had pulled the rifle trigger accidentally. This was the first indication we had that the terr's had left our farm. It came as something of a surprise that my watch indicated it was now past midnight. Attacks of this type were fairly common, commencing at 8 p.m. or 9 p.m. in the night so that the terr's had enough dark hours to disappear back into the bush and communal lands. We experienced our fair share of these attacks.

I was proud of my little family, not a tear anywhere, just quiet anger that we had been attacked. We were not racists; I guess the war turned some people that way. Not you, Joe, in fact, quite the opposite. We were good neighbours to the people living a few kilometres away, always giving them farm work, food, running water, boreholes, schooling them, driving them to hospital when they needed help and dosing them with medicines we could administer with the permission of the Nyanga (witch doctor & traditional medicine man). This gave them the hope of surviving the long walk to the hospital and perhaps the opportunity of surviving.

Two nights later just as the sun was setting at around 5:30 p.m., I heard two shots emanating from the communal lands. I radioed the security forces (no mobile phones in those days), who got back to me at 10 p.m. (keeping in mind that demining lands mines is a very taxing and lengthy job). The six soldiers and I set off to investigate the shots I had heard earlier. You, Joe, were in charge of doing my camouflage, which was collecting grass and shrubbery for my helmet, and rubbing shoe polish on my face. You used to joke about it being my make up for the attackers. We set off in our army uniforms, equipped with weapons and waved goodbye to my family. Your mum had her rifles with young Herman Jnr (all of 15 years old), positioned in the tower, the girls in the bathroom and our eldest, Susan, close to the Agric-alert (radio), with her firearm. In the case of another attack, whilst we were out. Living daily by the mantra that it is better to be safe than sorry.

Our arrival at the compound was not well received as now they would have difficulty explaining to the terr's about our presence. Not everyone wanted this war, but everyone was forced into it and involved, whether they wanted it or not. However, I spoke the local dialect fluently and a mother and father recognised me, as their daughter worked on the farm, so they relaxed. The mother began crying telling me what happened, their 16-year-old daughter had been raped repeatedly and then shot by the terrorists. Who kills their own people? Her crime? She was engaged to a local white government policeman. They had not had time to bury her, so what happened was abundantly clear. She had been such a hard worker, I remembered her, and her earnings helped the family tremendously, they would have a hard time without her salary. I gently told the mother, that she could come to work when she was ready if she would like that, we would cover expenses for the funeral. For the Shona's, a funeral is a very important event, going on for up to a week, where every family attends even in a war. We helped them bury her. Such a stupid murder, with an additional vengeance that would achieve nothing. What kind of men do this? Trained to murder and trained to rape as a punishment to the local tribes from which they came from. I wept in privacy that evening. Even for a man such as myself, who has seen his fair share of revolting, this was too much.

October 1977 came and went, and then again in November another attack on us took place. A sloppy affair, lasting 15 minutes, but I am convinced the rapid response of my son and I convinced them that we had now become a dangerous opposition. Then there was a quiet period of about five to six months, until May the following year. I suspected our neighbours turned up for the annual cotton-picking event that takes place every autumn on our farm, as the cotton bolls dry out and open.

I had worked out with the foreman Chowadi (meaning Truth), that if he had picked up on the fact, that the terr's had perhaps accompanied the pickers, to our fields he should talk to me in an aggressive manner with a cigarette between his lips. Every morning I would attend the weigh-in of the cotton picked by each individual picker from the day before. Our pickers numbered some 300 individuals, so it was easy for terrorists to pretend to be a part of the pickers. Not all terrorists were men.

It wasn't long before Truth did his thing so when he did, I climbed back into my Land Rover and shot home having loudly informed Truth that I had work at the house, in the local Shona dialect, so the terrorists would understand. It took a lot of nerve to go through this every morning, not to know if you were going to get outright shot or tortured first, which was their favourite pastime and I had four women to keep in mind and a teenage son. The picking session lasted some three months and towards the end I could feel the pressure. The terr's held their firearms and just watched me some days. I laughed and joked with these young men, not knowing which was friend or foe.

I learned that the pickers had persuaded the terr's not to kill me and my family, but once again this turned out to be nonsense. Once the wages were paid, I was ambushed twice alone in my Land Rover, but it was also mine-protected so I was fortunate. They opened fire on me in my Land Rover, a hail of bullets, I sped home, they had been hiding in the high grass waiting for me to get home, it was about 5 p.m. they were firing high and were facing my response with my F.N. on fully automatic.

I managed to get from the car to my house without being shot. I checked on my family. All good. Ran up to the tower only to see a terrorist firing at Nyika and you, Joe.

This time I received a real fright, as my wife Claire, Nyika and especially you, Joe, had been in real danger. You had been playing on the front lawn with your nanny Nyika, on the swing, when all this happened, they had fired at the two of you. It was this incident that changed my mind about where we were living and I decided that I could not carry on indefinitely as my luck would certainly run out. I also saw how it had affected you. You were only about five years old, when this occurred.

I put out some feelers and heard that a nearby Sugar Estate Mkwasine was closing down and its outlying sections of irrigated lands were available for hire. Mkwasine, was still in the region we were living in. Probably about two to three hours from Ngwane. My application to hire from the company some 300 hectares of irrigated land was fortunately successful. I also discovered that the workers were not sleeping in their houses at night because terrorists were holding brainwashing meetings many nights a week. They were sleeping in the bush. After arriving at work drenched through from the morning dew. We could not live like this. This was a further reason to leave. I asked if they wanted to relocate with me. They agreed, leaving behind their ancestral burial sites; for Shona people this gesture is massive and the biggest compliment you can receive as a farmer. They would return home when this war ended.

We packed up and left, escorted by an army mate of mine. I had to abandon my farm and left with nothing. Everything I had worked for was lost. Every cent. When I say we left with nothing, I mean every word of that sentence. We did not have the time to pack, neither the trucks to move all the furniture. We left with pretty much the clothes on our backs to start a new life. I was amazed and touched that my entire workforce would be standing by me and leaving to continue to work with me, this is virtually unheard of. I was moved by this. It said everything. My family made no complaints either. We packed the little required and departed.

The new farm and farmhouse came with a good three-bedroomed house as well as more than enough accommodation for all the workers. Here, I was able to continue with my irrigation cotton and wheat program, but not with my cattle and wildlife which was my passion. All my cattle had actually been stolen: 1200 of them. The terr's forced the local people to assist them in stealing cattle, they had no option, if they did not, they were killed. Their plan worked as follows; stealing 50–60 head of cattle on a moonlit night, run the cattle some 15 or 20 kilometres into the communal lands, dropping off four to six herds of about ten cattle each, as they passed each compound until the whole herd they had stolen was totally depleted. The locals were then under the threat of death ordered to slaughter the cattle, bury the hides and hide the meat. If any local did not co-operate he or she was shot immediately in front of their families including their children. Many ranchers became victims of the same fate, as I did the math in all, many 1000s of heads out of the National Herd were stolen. One of the ranchers which I later became the MD for lost 19,000 head of cattle out of a total herd of 26, 000 cattle.

The picture of the irrigated cropping of cotton and wheat is very different. I had hired 300 hectares and cropped the whole area first with summer cotton and followed with winter wheat for three years. The plan worked well, as by the end of the three-year period I had resuscitated my financial position and even saved a penny or two. The company then indicated that they needed their land back.

Joe, you loved picking cotton, you would pick cotton with the cotton pickers and Nyika, singing along with them, you would be so proud of your bale of cotton when you were old enough to begin picking. Before that, you were positioned on Nyika's back, wrapped in a bath towel, I also had to pay you accordingly for the bales of cotton you picked.

During the wheat season, you would sit in the combine harvester with me or Truth (our foreman) or "Chengetai," which means, "To Protect – The Mechanic" who you were friends with, and steer the combine harvester while it gathered the wheat. Sometimes you would sit in the trailer where the wheat gathered, barefoot might I add, playing with handfuls of wheat. You also assisted me every year in hanging the plastics to scare away the deer along the perimeter of the fields. The movement and the flapping of the plastic frightened the birds and the deer.

During this time, you also accompanied our great friend nicknamed Goblet, for his love of wine, in his crop sprayer. He would zoom low over the fields to spray the crops and you found this ride thrilling in his airplane. He and his wife Mona were a brilliant couple and great friends. They were building a yacht at home, to leave Zimbabwe (being a landlocked country) and sail the world together, which they eventually did.

Living here in Mkwasine was relatively safe, but we still had huge metal reinforcement blinds on our windows to deflect gunfire in the case of an attack. We still had curfew and all lights were to be out by 6pm. Absolutely no lights on. Only candles or paraffin lamps. Mkwasine came along with that expat lifestyle, the country club, with all the sports, golf, tennis, swimming, bowls and squash. This was not only for white members, there were many black members and golfers. Zimbabwe did not have Apartheid. Colonialism not being the answer at all either. However, during this time my marriage fell apart and your mother and I separated permanently. She moved to Masvingo, formerly known as Fort Victoria or as "Mas Vegas", your nickname for the town. She had grown up there. I placed a deposit on a house, for you children and your mother. You and Samantha went to stay with your mother in Mas Vegas and Susan and Herman Jnr had already left school. Susan was nursing in Harare (the capital of Zimbabwe) and Herman Jnr went to agricultural college in England.

You and Samantha shared school holidays between your mother and I. I remarried in December 1982 and was offered my dream job, to move back into working with cattle and wildlife. I moved with my new family. You visited during school holidays, when you weren't in swimming galas or tennis tournaments, to Devuli Ranch/The Save Valley Conservancy and became the MD.

There we turned 3442kms squared from a cattle ranch into a wildlife sanctuary. Now called The Save Valley Conservancy. You grew to love the ranch, it didn't take much time till you were knee-deep in saving all the animals you could. To the point that all animals found wounded or parentless, were brought to our kitchen door, where you nursed them back to health, sometimes lucky and sometimes not. I would say you flourished in the African Bush; it was your natural habitat. God knows how you live in a city these days, but being a deep child, you would survive anywhere and make the best of it! You spent most of your time riding your horse, which was unfortunately, killed by a pride of lions. After all Chishakwe had many lions, and it meant "Place of the Lions"!

All the kids, including you, learnt to drive from the age of 12 or 13 as one does living out in the wilderness. You asked if you could fix up one of the old Land Rovers, you did along with our mechanic, and that was your vehicle for years. You used it to transport sick animals that you found in the wild or when you released animals back into the wild.

The Save Valley Conservancy was once known as Devuli, we always called it *The Ranch*. Our section was called, *"Chishakwe – Place of the lions."* I managed to save 6000 head of cattle from being stolen which went some way to restoring the breeding herd to the 10,000 cows which the available grazing could support.

The company in support of the new government's policy of acquiring farming land to supplement the over-populated communal lands was sold at a fair price.

The owners of the company decided to invest the subsequent financial realisation into a development program in order to make use of one hundred percent of the available grazing on the whole ranch for a carefully calculated breeding production program.

These owners, who had lost so much in the war, were still willing to invest while many people were trying to get their money out of the country. The company was under the chairmanship of an incredible Rhodesian/Frenchman, who had worked timelessly during the war years to save the ranch for the benefit of the younger generation. Joe, you became firm friends with the Frenchman and your love of nature and wildlife impressed him tremendously, as you had knowledge and good ideas for a young girl. You spent many a night at their rather eccentric home, eating snake even, listening to very loud jazz music and discussing the future of the ranch. Yes, my girl, it was in your blood. When he died you were devastated. He was a big influence in your life. He was a tremendous personality, larger than life in all ways. Always pushing the envelope, always finding a solution together. He was very much a father figure to me, and a grandfather to you.

This led to you becoming tribal, spending a lot of time with Nyika in the compound, eating and sharing with local tribal people, the Shona's. Learning all about tribal ceremony, whether it be rain dancing or getting rid of an angry spirit. You wore no shoes for years. You were an African, and you will always be an African, Joe, it goes without saying.

At the end of the war, the Frenchman's son and I decided to realise his dream and brainchild for the benefit of the younger generation. You were thrilled by this prospect. We were to turn the ranch back to its original state. It was to become a conservancy for wild animals. The speech from the new President Robert Mugabe gave many people hope, that even under a new leadership, our Zimbabwe would not become like the other countries in north Africa. How naïve we had been.

My son, Herman Hagen Jnr, joined me to partake in this procedure. To have my son working alongside me as his father was what most fathers, dream about. Hagen Jnr, proved to be one of the best partners if not the best partner I have ever had. Son, I love you and I am so very proud of what we accomplished together. Along with many other men and woman joining us to achieve our goals. Your sister and her husband, as well as her in-laws moved to Chishakwe and helped us enormously in realising this dream!

Our ranch life was what people only dream about. The ranch abounded with all species of wildlife in its natural habitat. There were many stories I shared with you, Joe, that I hope you will share with your family one day. As you may remember most Sunday's after a hearty brunch, the whole family would pile into the Land Rovers, drive around the ranch spotting the wildlife, watching the birds and checking the crocodile pools in the river beds that we would walk along. I taught you which spoor belonged to what animal, your tribal people taught you how to track an animal and shoot with a bow and arrow, to kill an impala for meat and a meal, how to skin it, hang it to bleed and how to prepare it into your favourite biltong.

Our home was always full of people from all walks of life, and you got to socialise with some very important people, some not so important but in all, very interesting characters, full of life. I can imagine you find normal people quite dull. You even met a chap who was walking up Africa, who knocked on our door one evening as we ate dinner, out of the blue. His name fails to come to mind. This chap was remarkable.

You naturally learnt a lot about the bush and developed a natural knowledgeable sense of how it operated. During your high school years, I would dispatch an eight-ton truck to Mutare where you went to school to pick up teenagers, who came to spend holidays on the ranch. There, these youngsters would learn to track animals, observe the outdoors and wildlife, read, listen to music, talk around campfires and hunt for their food. You cannot imagine how fortunate you all were, and us as parents not having to worry too much about teenage shenanigans. There is something very special about sitting around a campfire, just talking to your friends and relating stories. A welcome break from city or town life, with the odd lion or leopard growl or roar, jackals calling to each other, and hyenas with their uncanny laughter.

Often you would go out at night in your Land Rover using the bright spotlight to see various game that you could not see during the day, sighting the odd leopard. You were part of helping approximately 500 elephants find a new home on the ranch. You babysat along with your brother Hagen, Samantha, Susan and Happiness, (the herd's boy), four baby elephants that had arrived parentless. You all raised them successfully and introduced them back to their natural habitat in the wild, with a lot of tears at goodbye time. But remember an elephant never forgets. The largest translocation of wild elephant in history of its kind ever carried out and it was a major success!

There had been a drought in the area in where the national parks were situated, the park was overpopulated with elephants so we gladly accepted them. The conservancy was formed due to the result of a major drought in our area with which the cattle could no longer cope. They were transported to cold storage.

So then, twenty-three ranchers joined together to create the conservancy, of which I became the chairman and managing director, my ranch was called Chishakwe, meaning place of the lions. All fences were taken down and one fence surrounded the property.

We hired three thirty-ton trucks complete with enclosed containers and each carried five to six elephants. We hired a gentleman, who was an expert at translocating elephants to do the capture onto our trucks. Considering the enormity of this project it went more than well, the exercise went incredibly smoothly. All the 11 little ones got the utmost care. You, Joe, being so in touch with the translocation, checked on them daily when you were home and even slept the odd night in the boma. The elephants prospered. We kept them for a couple of years before releasing them into the wild. The exercise was enormously successful and by 2013 there were over 2000 elephants on the conservancy. 1,300 are progeny of the number of elephants relocated from national parks. Hagen Jnr, your older brother, supervised all your schedules and encounters. Hagen Jnr was very attached to the elephants as he lived on the ranch, so he was in contact with them daily. He would take them for walks with you like most people walk dogs. Tiny the elephant being his favourite. The one with the most attitude!

The conservancy went from beef production to wildlife management (conservation) and tourism; however, this is not a zoo or national park. This is a sanctuary where the animal comes first and not the tourist. They operate at their migration pace and if you are fortunate enough to spot some animals as every species is there, you have spotted them a hundred percent doing what they would be doing without human encroachment. Each rancher built safari camps and some built luxury lodges as accommodation for tourists, employed guides and created a considerable number of jobs for local people in the area. It was a win-win.

Today The Save Valley Conservancy is world-famous, bursting to the seams with large numbers of wildlife including the big five and an abundance of bird life.

As you can see from the synopsis of your life, Joe, you had an upbringing which was arguably the envy of any number of people. War and all.

A world full of adventure, excitement and enjoyment. Your, cup truly overflowed in many respects and I am confident that you have very few regrets. Your love for Africa, particularly. The Save Valley Conservancy will always be in your veins.

Love, your dad.

Chapter Two
Ngwane

When I think back to when I was a child, tears can come hard and fast, but laughter can come just as hard and just as fast. I was fortunate to have been given an adventurous life and I have always bitten off more than I can chew.

The sunrise and sunset are my two favourite times of the day. Both have a special meaning for me – in one you can prepare for the best and expect the worst and in the other you can reflect on the best or lament the worst. However, the sunset has always been the one I prefer. Something about the screeching and angry bells which sounded every morning (every day for all those years) at boarding school took away most of my love for the mornings. The sunsets on our farm were breath-taking – a myriad of colours joining for one last finale, before taking their bow and allowing the darkness to take their place.

Have you ever wondered how a sunset is made? That work of art, free of charge especially for you. Air molecules scatter away the shorter wavelengths of light the violets and blues and the only light which penetrates through the atmosphere are the longer wavelengths of light the yellows, oranges and reds which produce these dazzling and colourful sunsets. Just like people, in a way, the ones who never give up, survive and shine through. If the sunset is more pinkish then more blue light has made it through.

How luminous the world can be, sitting on the kopje (hill) top at the edge of my garden on Ngwane Ranch in Zimbabwe, South-East Africa, close to my swing and in the shadows of the Shepard Tree known as the Boscia Albittrunca. My swing a discarded John Deere tractor tire, gently swaying in the warm breeze, the brilliant colours of the Bougainvillea (Glanbra Choisy), tumbling over another "kopje" behind me. Rubbing my feet in the dirt, chewing a piece of grass, the sound of cricket's chatter, and the call of the nightjar bird coupled with the piercing cry of the fish eagle. We had a dam close to our home, where the fish eagle perched on an eternally leafless tree; a group of these trees pushed up above the water, appearing as if skeletons or hands grappling to grab the sky whilst bodies were sinking, in the fading light.

Our farm was called "Ngwane," which means "Crown" in Shona. Shona is the language spoken in the Southern part of Zimbabwe by the majority of the population. We learnt it at school, for our Zimbabwe Junior Certificates.

I had been born at the time of the African Bush War, in 1972, which continued, right up until 1980. The new ruling party – ZANU PF. They gained power over the Ndebele's (the other tribe in Zimbabwe), soon after the independence struggle, which then lead to the mass murder of Ndebele's in another war called, Gukurahundi. When we as a country were still reeling from the first war.

The "Gukurahundi" it was a series of massacres of Ndebele civilians carried out by the Zimbabwe National Army from early 1983 to late 1987. Under the Mugabe rule. It derives from a Shona language term which loosely translates to "the early rain which washes away the chaff before the spring rains"– Wikipedia.

Shadows of Africa pass so secretly in the night, where not a whisper can fall, nor a dream bend. This was savage at its best. The beast of the fat cat rulers unleashed. How did Mugabe ever get away with this? No one really knows the actual "truth" about this all, but one day it will come out. When people are free to speak. When freedom of speech will be allowed in our country.

In parallel universes, he will pay the price. I happen to believe that we have more than one life. Having been brought up alongside an African compound and learning the lessons about listening to ancestors and tapping into that energy stream, it's inevitable that one becomes more in tune with the universe. Sceptics, will say, my she has lost her mind or what an imagination she has. God, forbid you tell them you spent time with what the west calls a ghost.

How one deals with this information is chiefly their prerogative. For me, God or Mwari is a feeling. Enlightenment is just being willing and aware to open your mind to the possibilities that the universe offers you.

Our farm, Ngwane, was situated in the Lowveld of Zimbabwe, back then it was called Rhodesia. We loved our farm; it was our home. I was eighth-generation African. Long before, our German, Irish and Argentinian ancestors had settled themselves here, before the 1850s. We had lost all our German, Irish and Argentinian roots, language and habits. None of us, in my immediate family had British roots. Even though it was generally assumed that all "white" people were British, by the vast majority. It was not the case.

I could hear the drum beats of the compound where the Shona people resided. The beat carries you away to a place of peace and what-ifs. I could hear them singing and praising Mwari, their God. Night fell. A blanket of stars filled the sky. I lay on my back and watched them twinkle. A falling star burnt out and I made a wish. Falling stars were a regular occurrence in my life, having such an open sky above me, free of city lights. The bell for dinner sounded *Brrring*, and the smell of roast beef wafted across the lawn. I inhaled, the delicious scent of a Sunday meal deeply, kissed the stars' goodnight and went inside for dinner. Dinner on a Sunday, was usually a stiff and rather formal affair; white linens and polished silver – candlelit.

Before dinner we were required to bath, brush our hair and look respectable either in our pyjamas and gowns with slippers on or as you became older, something decent. I had clearly missed out on this part of this evening's tradition, lost in my thoughts for a change, I would indeed be scolded. As there was a war going on, no lights were allowed after 6 p.m. so the oil lamps burnt into the night. There was no television, only a battery-operated radio, which was also switched off at 6 p.m. The generator was also turned off and its absent sound stilled the long, nervous wait for a potential attack on our home. Living on the edge of a knife's blade. The feeling of ice cubes that stick to your fingers when you take them out of the ice tray that has been lying in the freezer a tad too long. The relief you feel when you place your fingers under running warm water and the ice cubes drop off. Waiting to be attacked is the same, not getting attacked, one more night, gone by that you have remained alive. Your heart beats in your chest, tick tock, the grandfather clock in the lounge. We all smile. A smile of uncertainty, of love and of deep fear.

Dinner was served by Blessing, our cook boy, beautifully presented in his white chef's outfit. Nyika – our maid was to thank for this. Those chef whites were pressed to perfection by Nyika, not a crease in sight. Nyika and Blessing were best friends, they had been since their childhood days and they were happy to work alongside one another pretty much like brother and sister. Blessing was older, a wise soul, who spent many hours perfecting even the simplest dish.

Blessing, like Nyika, was part of our family. Well, at least that was the way things were in our home. Having said that, how certain people in southern Africa now run their households leaves a lot to be desired. Each to their own so I am told. We had to talk to Nyika and Blessing with utmost respect. As one should. My parents did not tolerate bad manners in any shape or form. It would be dealt with swiftly, usually along with a wooden spoon on a bare buttocks or my mother's Bata "special" slops (flip flops as the Western world knows them). Usually, it only took my mother, lifting her eyebrows sky high, for us to immediately know we had gone too far and that we should keep our gobs shut.

Blessing was rather short and sinewy; he had grey hair early and wore it in a short afro style. He used to show me how he would comb it and put this special gel in it. I was amazed by his hair, so springy and light. Blessing's white chef outfit came with a fancy hat which he took great pride in wearing. Blessing was quite the fashionista. I had my first cigarette with Blessing. He used to roll tobacco up in a newspaper mixed with dried Paw Paw (papaya) leaves. He was rather small for a man, but Blessing was dedicated to his cooking and vegetable garden and he shone at both. His food was delicious. Blessing was the most gentle person, I have yet to meet anyone more considerate, kind and soft-spoken than him. However, put him in a bad mood, which was incredibly hard to achieve, believe me you would feel awful.

Nyika let me play with her hair and she plaited my hair like hers from time to time. It hurt, but any chirp out of me was met with a loving slap on the top of my head. Learn to handle pain, control it, be the master of your mind and not the other way round. I heard this sentence so many times from Nyika. I am surprised that I forgot it until recently I was reminded of it through meditation. Nyika also taught me to brush my teeth with a stick and ash from the fireplace. This tasted awful, although it defied the usual so it was fun of course. Now-a-days I see Colgate with added charcoal for sale in supermarkets and I have to smile. Yes, you got it, that Colgate smile.

I arrived at the table in a heap. 'Calm down, young lady,' said my father in firm measured tones.

His voice commanded respect. It could also conjure tears if it was directed solely at you when caught off guard doing something wrong. We joined hands.

'For what we are about to receive, may the Lord make us truly grateful, amen,' we said in perfect sing-song unison. We never missed grace at meal time.

'I see you did not bath, or change, that you did not bother to brush your hair. You should be sent to bed with no dinner. If this occurs again you will be off to bed with no supper. Am I clear?'

'Yes, Dad. Sorry I got caught up in the sunset and nature's temptations.'

We placed the serviettes on our laps. My father would calve the roast, then hand the plate to my mother who would dish up the vegetables. Cauliflower cheese, with a perfectly crispy crust as if it was heaven in a bowl; golden roast potatoes that I always burnt my mouth on, but still wanted more, and gravy that came from the gods themselves (Blessing prayed daily in the kitchen). Sunday dinners at home were my all-time favourite, strict or not. I enjoyed the food thoroughly!

My brother was always served first; he was the second eldest, but this was the custom. He also sat at the head of the table, opposite my father. I sat next to him, to his right and he was forever stealing my roast potatoes when I wasn't looking. But I loved him too much to make a fuss and settled for merely giving him the "evil eye." My father asked us, one at a time, about our day, and one at a time, we had to answer him back. We were not allowed to interrupt our siblings or our father.

Because of this, I learned to speak on matters concerning exceptional coincidences, that may have occurred during that particular day, and I learned to say what grown-ups wanted to hear, 'I started reading a new book today!' and the like.

My parents were a striking couple. My father, with his hazel eyes, his jet-black hair and good physique; he had been a sportsman at school and mastered the art of professional diving. He held himself well. He was not tall by Dutch standards or Masai standards but he was by no means short. He was a man of challenge and determination. My father wanted to leave his mark on this world and that he did. He achieved such feats as building a theatre, getting his private pilot's license, flying across Southern Africa and being the Chairman of the Lions Club. He was appointed Chairman of the Cotton Growers Association and he created the canvas to build the largest wildlife conservation privately owned in the world. He was instrumental to this project. His only weakness was beautiful women. He was the most charming man in the world, so I am told.

My mother had been a ballerina and dancing had been her life. She had been offered a scholarship in Europe, which she had turned down in order to marry my father. My grandmother was devastated and never failed to remind my mother at family gatherings of her disappointment and her "missed opportunity." My mother was a brunette with dark brown eyes and beautiful olive skin. Her smile was worth millions and it never failed to brighten a room or make her children happy. She had massive dimples and an incredibly contagious laugh. My mother was down to earth but always made sure she was well presented. Even when my brother died, she maintained her standards and dignity. That takes courage. That takes stamina. Even with a gun in her hand, her hair was immaculate, no fingernails chipped. In heels to boot. Never once resulting in gutter language.

For there is nothing worse in this world than losing one's child. The bond between mother and child is unbreakable. Later in my life, I was privileged to work with young, troubled children from the streets. I was always at a loss for words when they cried to return to the mothers who had put cigarettes out on their small helpless bodies. The same mothers who beat them mercilessly and frequently starved them.

My mother filled our house with music and laughter. She was a maestro when it came to baking and cooking and our home was always filled with love and warmth. Her rose garden was a picture of perfection and here she would build fairy houses with me as a child. We would play for hours. She would even leave fairy footprints made with the end of a matchstick, in caster sugar alongside the roses, as proof that the fairies had been there. Sometimes, notes from the fairies appeared on the top of the refrigerator in the kitchen in the smallest of handwritings, where I left cookie crumbs for them, after Nyika, my mother and I had finished baking. My mother fed my imagination and fed my heart with love... pure love and imagination. I have never suffered from boredom. We adored our mother, without question, we were incredibly fortunate to have such a parent, and we are reminded of that daily. Her absence later on in our lives proved to be massive.

We shared the same humour, my mother and I. We just had to look at one another and we knew what the other was thinking. She handled all the financials for the farm. She arranged the accounts and paid the wages for the cotton pickers and planters. In these wages, she made sure that wife number one, because some of the gentleman working on the farm had more than one wife, got just that bit extra. This was the local custom and it helped to follow it if you wanted to maintain peace in the compound.

The African system, where a man can marry more than one wife is allowed if the man can provide for all of his wives and children. Which inevitably never truly works out. Too many children are conceived and there is a shortage of money and of food, because seriously how can one man provide education, food and nurturing for 13 wives and God knows how many children.

Naturally, these relationship structures are rarely harmonious. What is even worse is that, at times, female jealousy can get the best of the wives and houses and husbands have been known to suddenly go up in flames. Or a remedy from the Nyanga (A local tribal Dr), leaves another wife or the husband with chronic stomach cramps and endless hours spent running to and from the thatched hut to the long drop. A long drop is a homemade toilet, basically a very deep narrow hole with a toilet seat on it and that is if you are lucky.

My mother had a unique gift for keeping the peace amongst these women. She would sit and do crafts with them of hand-woven cloths and embroidered table wares, I still have my croqueted blanket that Nyika made for me. It goes everywhere with me. She, in addition, encouraged them to negotiate with the male artists for the most outstanding sculptures.

Later on in life, she opened a shop, where she would sell these local treasures, along with her famous homemade scones and strawberry jam. People were known to travel for up to four hours on roads that seemed to come straight from hell, not because of the tarmac, but because of the drivers. Her scones became famous. Orders were placed from all around the country.

Along with her scones were her equally famous crunchy biscuits. All day long, our home was filled with the delicious and delightful aroma of baking. It was heaven. It came to be that Blessing, Nyika, my mother and I spent many a day baking, side by side, for hours at a time. Though I must admit, I ate more than I baked and preferred the outdoors. I was never a natural cook or baker. I would leave at the first opportunity to escape the kitchen. As we baked, we listened to the endless and fabulous jazz music that played on the old gramophone. We would all dance in the kitchen, smile and laugh. It was perfect. At times, when my father was not too distracted by work, he would play the piano and we would all sing and dance together. I look back at these times now and smile. What a perfect childhood. War and all. It was still amazing.

My parents could dance superbly. They held the floor at all the parties we attended when I was a child. They could dance every dance, from the fox trot to the tango, to the waltz and rock 'n roll. My parents taught Blessing and Nyika these dances and in return they taught us the tribal African dances, which I preferred, apart from rock 'n roll. I revelled in the beat of the drum, it shook my soul and my booty. To wiggle your butt like a Shona woman is a feat all on its own. They make it look effortless. I adored my dance time in the compound. I came alive and felt that anything in life was possible. My parents encouraged dance and music on all levels. Freedom of expression was allowed and I delighted in expressing myself.

My brother Herman Jnr, Susan and Samantha all went to boarding school in a town two hours from our home – Masvingo- or, as it was known then, Fort Victoria. I liked to call it Mas Vegas, due to the fact it was totally extraordinary. They came home every three months or on long weekends. One holiday was called "Gooks and Spooks" (*Gooks* – the name given to terrorists – and *Spooks* – the name given to the white/black Rhodesian Army). They began at boarding school from the age of six or seven and they stayed at our grandmother's house most weekends. She would collect them in her Citroen with red leather seats and wooden interiors donned in matching gloves and handbag, her neck dripping with a long string of pearls. She was the main socialite around town. Her house was a colonial home built by the first settlers. The inside of the house was a Tom Ford wet dream.

Playing bowls and sipping Gin, that was the life. Working hard and playing hard. My grandmother, on my mother's side was known as Diva – Rita, she owned the local take-away and restaurant called Palm Court. It was the hippest place in town. All the town gossip flew through Palm Court. Next door to Palm Court, she additionally opened a dress and hat shop. My mother, my aunt and grandmother were divas in Mas Vegas. In this little town, there were a cascade of colourful characters as if something was in the water. We will come back to some of these characters after I explain one or two things about my siblings and family. My mother lost her father when she was a toddler, he had left my grandmother and mother high and dry. I never met him.

Susan is the eldest of my siblings. She is fourteen years my senior – more than a decade. She could almost be a mother to me and certainly in Africa this would not have been unusual. Some brides are taken at the age of twelve. When people ask me how I feel about such customs and traditions, I am inclined to give a vague and non-committal answer for to fully understand Africa, its people and its "ways," you would have to be born there. Even though I don't like this part of the tradition one teeny weeny bit! A westerner could not possibly understand the intricacies of tribal Africa, just as a tribal African could not possibly understand the mind and motivations of those from the west. My understanding and appreciation of tribal Africa is borne out of respect.

Susan was born with fair skin; the fair skin from my father's side of the family – almost the colour of fresh cow's milk. She was an incredibly talented water skier; however, she suffered badly in this pursuit with sunburn and sunstroke. Failing to smother herself in sun-cream resulted in the most horrific blisters and high temperatures. Sunstroke would cause her severe pain which lasted for days on end. To compliment her milky white skin, she had thick, shoulder length, jet black hair, a sprinkling of freckles across the middle of her nose and bright cherry red lips. Susan is the most diligent of us all. She is also an incredible painter, capturing light at the turn of her brush so effortlessly. Susan was raised the strictest, so her no-nonsense policy is pretty much non-negotiable. Her home is much like my mother's, warm and welcoming always putting her immediate family first. Her wood oven a blaze. However, she has an ability to attract snakes at the drop of a hat, so taking walks with Susan involves one's eyes being peeled open and really, really wide.

She, has a resplendent mandarin plantation and has captivating and talented children. Susan created the essence of family and she protects them as much as any fearless lioness would. Susan is a loving sister, however stern. During the last few years of my mother's life, Susan was a saint. She took care of our dying mother and we will all be eternally grateful for that. She aspired to become a nurse after studying in Cape Town, in the neighbouring country of South Africa. She shares such a deep and endless love with her husband, this was almost tragically stolen from her. During the war, her now husband was badly injured – his life hung in the balance. Susan returned from South Africa to Zimbabwe and patiently and tenderly nursed him back to health. They met in their early 20s and their love never died to this day. For me, their relationship and their story is more romantic than most relationships I have borne witness too. Susan and I have very different views about the world which keeps it interesting however there is enough respect as one should have for their eldest sibling. We do however share a deep adoration and devotion for and to the African Wilderness.

Jonathan was born after Susan, however, he sadly passed from this world at a young age. He had blue eyes and blond hair – an angel; I am certain he is watching over us now. He was said to look a lot like my grandfather on my father's side, his eyes always twinkling with that element of surprise.

Herman Hagen Jnr came next. He was my mother's absolute darling and I think my father was perhaps a bit put out by this. Herman Jnr acquired all my parent's best attributes. He is by far the best-looking of us children and coupled with this, he has the gentlest soul; he became a brilliant farmer, a natural. He is a talented musician with a zest for life and could have turned his talents to anything. Yet, he helped my father from the get-go; being the only son, so much more was expected from him. With his partiality to music, he learned to play the acoustic guitar and composes his own songs for his wife, the gorgeous Mindy. Such a romantic.

At the tender age of fifteen years old, he was already protecting us along-side my father in the tower adjacent to our house, when we came under attack.

Herman Jnr worked with my father developing Ngwane and later The Save Valley Conservancy. My brother was the son that father's dream about. I admired their relationship; it could handle storms. Herman Jnr had chocolate brown hair, warm brown eyes, exactly like our mother. We had our ups and downs, but our brother and sister bond and our respect for one another is rock solid. We have different views on Africa, but he contributed so much to Africa, so I listen to his views with respect, rather than agreement. Being the phenomenally hard-working man that he has become, I truly look to him with an enormous amount of admiration. With their vision on the future of a lack of water in The Save Valley Conservancy they built a dam. Naturally with no experience, except the vision. No dam makers were hired. They researched how to make a dam and did it. It's still there to this day. Fully stocked with fish, crocodiles, hippos and water most importantly. Chishakwe Dam.

Then there is my sister Samantha. I hardly every call her Samantha, I refer to her as Bell most of the time. Bell, is my best friend and she has not once let me down. She is seven years my senior, with hair the colour of wheat and a heart of gold. Her nickname is Bell on account of her laugh, which sounds just like the ringing of beautiful steeple bells. She inherited this laugh from our mother and the two of them together could crack even the sternest of faces when their laughter is in full flow.

Samantha is such fun to be around and we got up to some shenanigans on the farm. Like me, she also has a deep proclivity for animals. In fact, we all do. When Samantha grew up, she travelled the world running around the entire planet from Rio to Rome working wherever the wind took her. I remember fondly the most fabulous letters that she would send home about her new adventures accompanied by a polaroid or two. A dull day did not exist in Samantha's life. Jumping out of bed every morning as if in a race with dawn itself. Her love of cooking took her on to be a sous chef cooking in the countries she visited. She studied beauty therapy, which she never pursued. Not driven by image in the slightest or by material possession, her fondness of the world is sufficient and thus completes her. After giving birth to a healthy boy, the time for settling became apparent, so planting herself in the United Kingdom, she created a world as a single mother which

I admire her greatly for. Being born a natural artist she dabbles in the scene keeping abreast of the crafting trends. Her son was blessed with a stroke of genius and his world is just like my sister's – their own painting and that is priceless.

Last, but by no means least, are a few more characters that are so worthy of a mention and who were intricate parts of mine and my families lives.

Happiness was the garden boy and shepherd of Ngwane. He was short in stature; he was extremely fit and he had unruly hair. He always looked a mess in his mudded overalls, soiled fingers and red eyes, roadmaps from too much weed and alcohol. He was a full-blooded character. Happiness spent hours in the garden with me, explaining how plants, trees and vegetables grow. I have fond memories of us colleting ripe vegetables before dinner time and shelling peas. He was a wizard in the garden. Everything grew and his vegetables bred like pedigrees. There had been occasions where lettuce had been planted up the driveway instead of roses. One too many joints, I guess. This also depended if he had been to the shebeen (the local beer hall) the night before or not. Usually he ended up there, spending his entire salary in one night. The next morning, he would arrive at work with blood shot eyes and smelling like rotten fruit. I would steal money from my mother's wallet to give him a little extra as I was terrified that one of his many wives would burn him alive. Happiness was in my life from the day I was born, until he passed away at our protea farm in the Bvumba mountains of Zimbabwe, which are on the border with Mozambique. In fact, every person that worked with us, stayed with us, until they passed from this world. We were a family, no doubt about it. All the people I mention in this story, were important and impactful in and on our lives.

Happiness was with me the day I almost drove my father's car into our kitchen wall, so I had to leave the car parked where my father had NOT left it, and it would be obvious that I had disobeyed him. I was too afraid to park it again, I was 12 at the time. I had been given specific instructions not to touch the car. They had been my father's departing words, before he flew off to a meeting. Hence Happiness's advice was always simple: pack your bible, pack some food and go. As well as his gardening duties, Happiness was also in charge of chasing the deer, warthogs, guinea fowl, rabbits and larger game, off the airstrip, so our plane could gain enough speed for take-off without killing one of these wonderful creatures or ourselves. Happiness was hilarious and a natural comedian in this specific task. He would have a whistle and his staff or he would ride the moped down the runway shouting, 'Shoo shoo! Bugger off! Get lost! Shoo!' accompanied by a whistle blow every now and then. He later acquired a megaphone. Happiness – although employed as a gardener and animal "shooer" – was very much a part of our family and will forever be part of our family.

Then comes Truth. Truth was our Boss Boy – he was head of the fields with my dad. Truth truly admired my father and vice versa, they had an honest friendship. There was a tremendous amount of mutual respect between them, it was similar to the mutual respect I saw later on between my brother and Sadza on The Save Valley Conservancy. The relationship between Boss Boy and Farm Owner is a salient relationship and the utmost trust is crucial. I learnt a lot from being around them. Watching two different views work side by side, achieving mind-blowing results. Such solid friendships. I am proud to have witnessed these exchanges.

Truth's job was a very important one. He had to make sure that all the workers on the farm were happy and taken care of. He worked alongside my father in droughts so bad that completely wild animals did not, or could not run away from you. They were so weak; you could touch them if you dared. However, we all understood that a man's scent on an animal made them outcasts to the animal kingdom, so out of respect to nature you would never touch them.

Truth was with my father throughout the war; he was never without his green floppy hat. Over the years it became more and more faded. I cannot imagine him without it. As well as the hat, I remember his baggy khaki pants and "veldschoens" (these are traditional Rhodesian and Zimbabwean farmers shoes, made from genuine leather). They are known for being very comfortable but if they are wet and left inside they will leave a stink unrivalled.

Every season I looked forward to spending time with Truth. Between June and September it was cotton picking season and weighing the cotton bales. In spring we planted cotton, after the threat of frost had passed. We checked the soil, with a soil thermometer, it had to be around fifteen degrees Celsius for planting. I had to push the thermometer about three and a half inches into the soil to get a proper temperature reading. I enjoyed the natural texture of cotton straight out of the bud, the pods, bursting open, plush. It smelt of purity and dust simultaneously. The scratchy cotton bales piled high upon one another, providing us with a home-made jumping castle. Watching the cotton bugs called, dysdercus suturellus, Okaloacoochee or simply the Cotton Stainer or Red Cotton Bug, dart all over the bales. Their backs represented African Masks in deep reds and blacks arranging themselves in a diamond shape. I found it fascinating that they mated facing in opposite directions. Separating the cotton from the seeds took many hours, the pods were rather sharp, under a tin roof, sweltering heat and appreciative thunderstorms, with open bales in front of us laden with fresh cotton. Singing at the top of our voices. Only Woman. The ladies were dressed in Ankara fabric with their colourful African prints. Their headdresses and wrap-around dresses bright against the white cotton. I was dressed in a linen pinafore, on more days than I care to remember, with a hat the colour of fawn. I did however like the clothes my mother sewed for me. Linen was the perfect fabric for these climates and it was comfortable. Many of the ladies had babies or small children on their backs. At lunch we would take a break, sharing sweet tea, bread and Sun Jam. I was absorbed by Shona women's song. We sung and swayed. Enjoying our work. The ladies best attribute was their humour, man they could tell the funniest stories. We spent many hours laughing. When these woman laugh, it's contagious! Nyika always by my side. Earlier on in my life, I would be on Nyika's back, wrapped in a towel, whilst she either picked cotton or sorted cotton, until I was old enough to accompany her barefoot.

Truth was a serious man but that didn't mean he could not appreciate a good joke. He was almost polar opposite to Happiness, however, both had green fingers. Truth was short and stout, rather like a tea pot. He also had a big round belly from too much sadza and the local beer Chibuku (the "beer of good cheer"). He had a rumbling voice that sounded like distant thunder and his hands were rough from endless hard farm work. He had a huge mole on his chin and the most perfect white teeth one could imagine.

Truth loved sugar cane and he always kept a stick for me in the combine harvester when it came to mowing the wheat. I always called it mowing the wheat, as for me as a child it looked like a massive lawn mower. Wheat was a winter crop, it can withstand almost freezing temperatures, this is needed for it to produce seed. Our wheat was harvested in spring and summer. Truth encouraged me to learn about the crops, so he taught me how to check for leaf rust, which is the main disease for wheat in our country. An untreated infection could reduce grain yield by up to ninety percent. It is a fungal disease. We would spend the day bird spotting and eating sugar cane. He would test us on the names of birds and the birds individual song. Whether it be "alarm call', "begging call", "chewink", "chirp", "buzz" or "rattle". He knew so many bird sounds, it was incredible. I also got to steer the harvester. It made me feel very grown up. In the trailer accompanying the harvester, the wheat would fall in, as if hard rain. My friend, Kudzai (which is his Shona name), in English means;

"honour", wound dance under the falling wheat and we would laugh because after dancing under wheat grains they give off a golden dust, so he appeared as if he were an albino boy dusted by the wheat. We would try to bury ourselves in the wheat and pretend it was a trailer of gold. We would look for treasures – he was the king and I was the queen. My mother got wind of this one day and hid some sweets and chocolates in the trailer. We were delighted and screamed with unbridled joy. We felt like adventurers who had discovered gold. Kudzai was Nyika's son. Her only child.

Sweets really were a treasure during the war years as there were none. We shared these sweets with Truth, both of us sitting up front in the harvester laughing and watching the last light of day skim over the heads of the remaining wheat fields. Today we were alive. For now, that was enough.

Then there was Zuvarashe (meaning Lord's Son), the deputy boss boy Zuvarashe. He was the world's best storyteller. Zuvarashe had the flattest nose I had ever seen. Kudzai and I would tease him mercilessly. 'Can you even smell that, Zuvarashe?' However, his fingers found their way into those nostrils every chance they got. Kudzai and I would tease him about that too. Zuvarashe carried out most of Truth's orders and was dedicated to his work. He was also dedicated to sharing the Shona Fables with us – his favourite was the Tokoloshe. Even though this fable is not inherently Shona, it was the one he loved best and he adapted it to terrify us.

The Tokoloshe is a little man who lives under your bed and if you don't behave, he will torture you in the night. He knows everything about you and will give away your secrets to your parents. He watches you constantly but you can never see him. Zuvarashe is neither tall nor short. He is neither strict nor funny. He is merely lukewarm and safe. But when he tells a story, that's when he comes alive; his voice booms, shakes and alters to send your imagination to the moon and back.

He always tells the stories around the fireplace and his animal impressions were magnificent – we could all join in with him on those ones. We would make up shadows alongside the fire light, and menacing animal sounds.

Nyika would have to walk me home from the compound when he finished his stories as I was too afraid that the Tokoloshe would grab me out of the bush and whisk me away to the land of evil and no sweets. Nyika, cursed him for this. 'Must you do this to children? The only one the Tokoloshe is looking for is you, Mr Zuvarashe.' Then we would laugh. Zuvarashe's features were all too big for his face. I am so grateful for his storytelling. Under God's blanket with the light poking through, millions of stars were made… Kudzai and I would laugh, scream, stare wide-eyed, but never cry. We were the brave.

I nearly forgot about the mechanic Chengetai, also known as Wine, Chengetai means to protect, what a legend. What a name. I was also too young to even think about it back then. He has to be the kindest man I ever met. He sorted out the car, even using my mother's stockings once as a fan belt, so we could get to Mas Vegas on time. He had an angel face and a voice of golden syrup. He had a deep blue-black skin as taut as the skin on a drum. We all loved Chengetai, he also loved wine and on the very rare occasion when wine came from South Africa, we would save him a box. Then naturally he would miss work the next day. He would blame it on the nectar of the Gods. He was close to my brother Herman Jnr mostly and our sister Susan. He worked magic in coaxing even the stubbornest engines to kick off. He was in tune with not only engines, he was enlightened and took time to explain the meaning of life to me at every opportunity he had. His advice was to love and to do everything with love, easier said than done. I am not the saint, he was. 'Joe, if you treated humans the same way you treated all the animals you try to save, life would be so much easier for you. You do know judgement day is real.' I would smile. The wind would blow and I was off with it.

Kudzai was my best friend. When I had first met Nyika I was overjoyed. I was even happier to hear she had a son my age. We used to joke that we were of the same star. He was so tall and lanky, with feet like submarines and long wiggly toes. He had no eyelashes and hardly any eyebrows; they had been burned off with a gas lighter and had never grown back. He had the biggest smile; it looked to me like an enormous slice of watermelon. His arms were long and awkward – sort of like an orangutan trying out javelin for the first time. His pants were always worn halfway down his ass; he said he was a gangster from America.

'Where is America, Kudzai?' I would ask.

'North of here, Joe.'

Kudzai started school with me in the shade of a Shepherd Tree. School on the air brought to you by the BBC.

Last, but not least, there is or was Nyika. Nyika, was the daughter of the chief of the compound, Chief Marimba. He was an open-minded chief, but with enough old-fashioned values. He never forced Nyika to marry and she never mentioned why and I never thought about it till this line here. Nyika came to work at our home when she was twenty-five. I saw Nyika and I liked her immediately. She took me up in her arms and she smelt of fresh Lifebuoy soap and Vaseline. The fabric she wore on her head was called a douc, it was to protect her from the harsh African sun and soon became part of my attire too. Nyika was tall and reed thin, naturally so; she was an incredibly fast runner and a tireless one at that – she could run for hours. Many attempts were made to try to make me run. It's just not part of my get up. Nyika had beautiful manners and long elegant fingers. Her voice was a steady stream. Her eyes were a jet-bead black, like pools of oil, but they were real and they felt safe. Nyika, also never liked to wear shoes. Nyika taught me so very much about life and how to embrace the real African ways and purpose of life I had been given to by God. She shared all her knowledge with me and there is no doubt in my mind that she was my second mother.

Our day one began with learning some Shona songs under the Shepherd Tree. If I wouldn't sleep when I was younger, Nyika would put me on her back, wrap me in a towel, tie it in front of her body and we would walk like that through the African Bush until her voice mixed with the chatter of birds on the wind rocked me into a deep and secure sleep. Kudzai alongside us in the pram, we used to swop places apparently. For as long as I can remember he was always there. We got our first teeth together, had our first mopane worm together, he walked before me. We saw the Tokoloshe together, convinced about this, our story became an elevated truth. We left nappies at the same time. Kudzai taught me to sculpt a spear head, and make a bow.

We used to walk a lot, past deer, impala and dika; Nyika walked and walked and when I awoke, it was always to look up into a brilliant blue sky or from the pram into her warm expression. No clouds. Just a brilliant clean blue. Sometimes we would share a mealie (corn on a cob) or a stick of sugarcane. Chewing the cane till we had squeezed every drop of the sugars nectar and we then would spit the cud pretty much like a cow. I would ask to compete in how far we could spit the sugarcane cud. I never wore shoes. My first word was "maruva," meaning flower or bloom in Shona. My first word was an African word.

Chapter Three
To Be Hunted

I remember the morning we were being taught how to leopard crawl. This is a crucial, life-saving technique in order to survive a terrorist attack. Mornings, at least most mornings, in Zimbabwe invited you into the day with a beautiful blue canvas of sky. When you looked up into it, you felt as if anything was possible. Strokes of clouds dotted the blueness. Cirrus Stratus appearing as if they were fish scales. When your eyes saw the world this way up, you felt as if everything in life would flow according to your own plan. It offered your imagination a treat, so vast and so staggeringly beautiful. Endless.

'OK, I need all of your attention kids; enough of the buggering around! This is serious! We could be attacked at any time!' My mother's voice was rather shaky, a little tense and for the first time that I could remember, authoritative.

Usually, our mother's warnings fell on deaf ears. It was our father's voice that got our attention; it was his powerful rumbling commands that shook our whole bodies and rendered us tearful and fearful, especially us girls, as it happened so rarely. I guess it was because we heard our mother's voice constantly, and we got used to it. Even as our teacher she was firm but not strict.

Girls don't handle being shouted at by a father very well. My brother had long since mastered the art of not crying; he had been taught that boys were not allowed to cry. That has to be one of the saddest lessons of this world – "Be a man!" Men don't cry? What the hell is that about? It was at boarding school he had learned this; the ability to cry had been whipped out of him.

'Joanna, listen! For once in your life, listen!' snapped my eldest sister Susan, 'this is serious! This is a matter of life and death!' She was always so incredibly bossy. Knowing it better than anyone, even better than our mother. Oh, for the love of God could she just be a sister instead of trying to be my parent.

To be taught the art of listening is an art on its own. A good listener is so rare.

'What is death?' I asked, not knowing what she was so desperately upset about.

The room fell silent. How do you explain to a five-year-old that life may be extinguished in a heartbeat?

'Tonight,' my mother continued, 'all of you begin your AK-47 rifle lessons with your father. This will include stripping the rifle down piece by piece, cleaning it and putting it together again. Susan, Herman Jnr and Samantha you will learn to fire it. Joe, you are a bit young still for a rifle and we would rather remain alive, not be shot by a random bullet from a five-year-old. This is a skill you will all have to learn in order to survive in the unfortunate case your father and I are killed.'

'What is killed?'

'Joe,' my mother faced me on her haunches; I was sitting on Nyika's lap on the floor. 'Not everyone in life is good,' she continued, 'not everyone in this life is bad. Remember, watching the cocks fighting in the chicken run? They fight 'til the death. Death is when the other cock no longer gets up and his chest is no longer heaving up and down. When your eyes no longer have life in them; no movement. Gone. Vacant. That's death.'

'Are you going to die, Mum?' I asked. 'Is Dad going to die? Are we all going to die? Cause I want to die first.'

Everyone laughed; the youngest is always so spoilt.

When you hear the sound of an AK 47 – the "ratatatatatat" sound, like hail on a tin roof but ten times the speed – it takes your breath away. You become desperate.

'This will certainly kill you. Why don't we show Joe what death is?' suggested Nyika.

'Yes,' replied my mother, 'we should do that. Herman Jnr, get your catapult.'

He got up reluctantly and awkwardly; a teenager, resentful of being told what to do. After all he was already performing adult man responsibilities and tasks.

We all gathered outside under a paw-paw tree. In Europe they are called Papaya. They are only called Paw-Paws in Africa. The weaver birds were eating their way through my mother's favourite fruit. Like a cold-blooded reptile, she ordered my brother to kill one of them stone dead.

'Herman, I would prefer to have it stone dead,' she muttered to him, 'so that I do not have to try and explain semi-dead… and recovery.'

Herman, as if in a trance, nodded at her and pulled the catapult back. The stone rocketed from the catapult, made a thud and a weaver bird, with a bright yellow chest, landed at my feet, legs in the air, not a tweet and not a twerp. I bent down and picked up the tiny bird placing it gently into the palms of my hands. Still warm to touch. Just a second ago, it was enjoying the paw-paw and now its legs were up in the air, like two toothpicks. Eyelids shut tight. Pale blue eyelids as if eye shadow had been applied. No heaving chest. I buried it after the explanation.

I have a very cruel family; how could they do this? My mother looked at me suddenly, realising the magnitude of what she and my brother had done.

'This is stone dead!' I shouted, tears dripping from my eyes. 'This is what will happen to me if I don't listen to you, Mum; if I don't learn to leopard crawl. My brother will kill me stone dead with his catapult.'

I certainly got the message loud and clear.

'No, Joe,' Bell said soothingly, 'Herman would never kill you stone dead; but the terrorists will. You are such a drama queen; would you please return from the dream world on occasion?'

'Yes, the terrorists will,' Nyika spoke up, 'they are the enemy and they will kill us tribal people too. They want to take the land and take everything from it.'

'Will you protect me, Nyika?'

'As much as I can,' she replied, 'but your mum and dad are here and the terrorists mostly attack at night.'

'I thought that was the Tokoloshe?' I whispered, looking into her genuine eyes.

That afternoon, Blessing pretended to be the AK-47. As soon as we heard the ratatatatatat, we jumped flat to the floor and using our elbows, propelled ourselves forward and our legs followed suit. It looks similar to a cat stalking a bird. When we had mastered this, we were to leopard crawl from the bedroom to the bathroom. There, we were to remain silent. My mother would monitor the Agric Alert, through which she would request the army, (led by Harris Scott) to come and help us. "Christmas" was our radio code-name. My mother would practice calling it into the radio. It all seemed like a game, a game that could save our lives. The leopard crawl game. 'This is Christmas, come in, we are under attack. Christmas, under attack.' The static of the Agric alert sounded like we were communicating with aliens.

I was kicked in the face by my sister, Bell, a couple of times when we were leopard crawling. After a few harsh exchanges, I decided that in the future I would always try and crawl ahead of her; in front of everyone. When we reached the bathroom, I would hide in the wash basket; mainly because I was the only one who could fit inside. Nyika had made it as a present for my mother. The wash-basket was made of woven reeds and palm fronds known traditionally as (Murara), weaving was a traditionally inherited skill. Many Zimbabweans, in general abound in their traditional artisanal skills. During the real attacks Nyika's wash-basket offered my young self a false sense of security. Peeping through the spaces between the weaves, I watched the apprehension, dread, terror, fright, panic and trepidation play out before me in the reflection of my siblings eyes. As brave as we attempted to be we were still fearful. I heard my breathing, every breathe. At times, when we were really afraid, waiting for the "pause" in the reining gun fire, our breathing was all we heard, accompanied by our heartbeat. Agonisingly loud.

We had a lot of laughs during our leopard crawl practice. Not all of the war was horror, during this period I importuned and harnessed some of my fondest memories. However, I do feel that our lives displayed extremes. One minute we could be enjoying a meal, like a normal family, the next we were cowering and leopard crawling, bullets flying, to hang onto our lives. It was a time when we as a family consolidated and stuck together. We shared such highs and lows, but always had each other and were there for one another. Every situation, every moment, every event both positive and negative, was inevitably followed with the question, "Shall we have a cup of tea?" The world would be coming to an end and I swear to God that would be the question my mother or Nyika would ask us.

Susan turned nineteen, Herman Jnr was fifteen, Samantha was twelve and I was five. My mother had always wanted a big family. The death of our brother Jonathan had affected her deeply. It affected my father too, however, no one spoke of it, not ever.

We finished our biscuits, my mum's homemade crunchies and left the remaining crumbs on top of the refrigerator for the fairies. My mother had work to do – balancing wages while my siblings were up to their ears in studying material. O-level and A-level exams were coming up the following term and my siblings took their studying seriously. Money and success didn't happen by accident – they lived by this mantra. Blessing was going to cook macaroni cheese for dinner and it was time for me to play outside in the last remaining hour or two of the day with Nyika.

Nyika and I had a ritual; we would go to our Shepherd Tree at the edge of the garden about a hundred and fifty metres from the front of the house. I would swing in the tractor tire that Happiness had fashioned for Kudzai and I; Nyika pushing me back and forth, humming and singing all the while. I could lie in it or I could sit in it. It was wonderful! At times Kudzai and I would push Nyika in the swing, trying our level best to tip her out of it, naturally with little to no success. She played along. From the swing you could see the African Savannah stretching out in front of you – endless beauty, where your imagination challenges your mere existence. That endless blanket of greens, golds, yellows, browns and an array of colours blended in a flurry, reminds you just how small and insignificant you really were, and in the end, you are nature's guest!

The tall grass spread out before us grew densely from the earth, appearing as if waves of gold, rustling in the gentle breeze. The air smelt similar to melting butter on fresh hot mashed potatoes, with a pinch of salt. The odd chirp of a cricket. An impala's grunt. The oink of a torpedoing warthog and the stamp of an angry buffalo. As I swung back and forth on my makeshift swing, I would try to identify every call and sound and spot every glorious species. The clash of two Kudu Bulls horns in a battle and the call of the Fish Eagle. What an orchestra! What a show! A show – it seemed – performed just for Nyika and I, from our swing on the Shepherd Tree. Our theatre.

This cacophony of nature – I would drink it in with my eyes; feeling afraid, that if I did not drink every drop, it might be snatched away from me and I would die of thirst, die of misery… of longing. Nyika made me thank God for it every night in my prayers. Now that I knew what dead was, if you were dead, stone dead, you would not see such beauty again. Or maybe, you would, as the tribal people believe, see if from a distance or from above

– and if you were one of the terrorists inflicted on this country, maybe you would listen to it from a furnace down below.

The blue sky was changing into various shades of brilliant pinks and pungent oranges that you could almost smell – as if it were a fruit salad.

'Nyika, imagine you could eat the sunset? I think it would taste like a fruit salad. With strawberries, oranges, blueberries, raspberries, pomegranates and peaches.'

I smiled at her.

'And for the white that is left I would throw in a leachy or two, and maybe some whipped cream.'

Nyika smiled back.

'What about paw paws? You cannot have a sunset fruit-salad without paw paws.'

We both laughed, loud and long. I was lying back in the swing and Nyika was pushing me gently.

'One more hard push, please, Nyika,' I pleaded, 'the push that makes my tummy turn. 'Kudzai had not joined us today as he was to finish his math lessons.

The flock of birds were suddenly disturbed and reached for the sky; their wings beating like hands of the African drummers. They were putting on quite the performance and just as I turned to ask Nyika, "Why are the birds…" I heard the AK-47s open fire. I heard that sound Blessing had made; I thought for a moment how perfect his imitation had been. It smelt like burning metal and rubber, like when you put a horse shoe on a hoof.

They were shooting at Nyika and I; they wanted to kill us. Stone dead.

'Missus Joe!'

Nyika pulled me out of the swing, but my foot caught in the swing's hand rest. I wiggled it out. Looking around, wild-eyed, I saw a terrorist in the bush stand up.

'Leopard crawl to the front door, Joe!' Nyika ordered, a tightness in her voice.

Everything happened as if in slow motion. The man who stood up was dressed in plain clothing – his T-shirt was ripped and he had stone washed jeans on. He was pointing the gun at us, laughing and shouting, "Kill that, Mukiwa!" (Kill that White One!) He sounded like a hyena. I think of him now as pure evil – the thought of shooting a child appealed to this monster. I heard him shout, "Let them get a bit further away! Let's hunt the Mukiwa!"

He looked so deranged; the whites of his eyes dazzling. His teeth had something reptilian about them and the thought of smiling crocodiles passed through my mind. "Kill the Mukiwa!" Surely, he was possessed by the devil himself. Then he disappeared as fast as he had appeared.

I could see my father's Land Rover going hell for leather on the road that ran alongside our home with dust flying up from behind it. I could hear my mother screaming and was gathered helpless with my siblings at the front door behind the concrete walls.

'Joe, crawl!' urged Nyika, 'Dear, God, Joe, move!'

I had completely frozen. Confused. Nyika pushed me to the floor. I bit my tongue and tasted blood in my mouth. Why would someone want to kill Nyika and I?

'Leopard crawl as fast as you can,' Nyika demanded, 'I am beside you.'

The bullets landed around us – hitting the dirt – leaving brief miniature dust tornadoes in their wake. Bullets hit the house; they sounded like a thunderclap. I could hear my mother on the Agric Alert.

'This is Claire. Christmas anyone? We are under heavy attack! Christmas come in, somebody come in, Send troops! Repeat, this is Christmas we are under heavy attack! Armed guerrillas.'

'Nyika, I'm scared,' I spluttered, crawling as fast as I could.

'No time to be scared,' she spat back, 'No time, Joe. Crawl! We're nearly there.'

I felt tears burning the rims of my eyes. I could taste the sand and blood in my mouth. I could feel that my elbows, stomach and knees were bleeding and scratched. I could see Nyika's elbows were bleeding. She was crying and breathing heavily too.

'Come on, let's pray!' Nyika gasped, 'Dear, Sweet Jesus. If you are there and if you do exist, let us make it to the house alive. You are all powerful; you are all glorious. If we are to make it through this, I will make sure Joe knows more about you Lord Jesus. Mwari, help us! Joanna, pray! Gentle, Jesus, meek and mild, look upon thy little child, suffer me simplicity, suffer me to come to thee,' I muttered spitting blood into the tufts of grass.

They just stuck there like hot toffee dripping on a stick.

Then I saw my father and brother up in the tower to the left of the house. They were firing back at the terrorists.

'You guys can do this, Joe and Nyika!' they shouted, 'Come on you guys can do this! Come on, crawl!"

'If you get shot, Joe, I will never forgive you!' screamed my brother, 'No more sweets from me. No more covering for you when you don't eat your Brussel sprouts. Come on! MOVE!'

As we reached the house, we scrambled through the front door and leopard crawled to the bathroom. My mother and sisters by this stage were on the verge of hysteria. Nyika and I lay low in the bathroom. My sister Samantha lay in the bath. I climbed into the wash basket.

Suddenly, out of the blue, Susan bolted upright. She ran past my mother and out of the house into the front garden. Gunfire reigned. How all the bullets missed her, to this day, none of us have a clue. I guess it just wasn't her time. She toyed with certain death, and death replied, *"Not today, Susan. Not today."*

She was screaming at the terrorists, 'What have we ever done to you? You bastards, I hate you all! I hope you all die!'

On hearing her voice, her dog Chico came running towards her. We heard a loud yelp and a deafening scream. The next moment Susan was back in the bathroom, tears streaming down her face and blood everywhere.

Chico had been shot. My mother grabbed him in her arms and quickly found where the blood was coming from. The bullet had not actually hit him and penetrated him but it had grazed him badly – hence so much blood.

'Get on the Agric Alert, Susan!' my mother shouted, 'We need army guys here to help us fight these buggers. And if you ever try a stunt like that again, I will personally shoot you!'

Then there was an almighty explosion. It ripped through the house. A mortar had hit my parents' bedroom. If we had been in that room, we would have been dead. Gunfire carried on into the early hours of the morning. I had to pee down the drain of the shower. We all had too. I fell asleep in the wash basket no dinner, only to be woken by Chico the dog, whining next to me. He had been bandaged up and was looking quite perky.

He pushed at the wash basket with his nose. I could smell his breath and see his eyes. He looked happy, so that must mean good news. I looked around the bathroom. No Susan, Herman Jnr or Samantha, nor my mother or Nyika. I thought for a moment, that maybe they were all stone-dead, that is perhaps why they had left me alone? It was so incredibly silent. I could smell firewood and food. I was ravenous. I clambered out the wash basket and with Chico by my side, I walked to the front door. It was early morning. My family, Nyika and Blessing were sitting under the Shepherd Tree, by the swing. There was not a sound, no birds were chirping, nothing – no orchestra. I hugged my mother and hugged my father. I went to my brother and looked at him.

'I love you very much,' I said, 'and you never help me eat my Brussel sprouts.'`

I rubbed my eyes and went to cuddle Nyika sitting on her lap, Kudzai was with his grandfather the Chief Marimba. Chico lay at my sisters' feet. My mother kissed my forehead. My elbows and knees had been bandaged up, so had Nyika's. My lip was cut open and a large red dot of antiseptic ointment covered my lip and chin, appearing as if a birthmark.

Everything was as quiet as the feeling of melancholy. If you have ever sky dived, you will only hear a rushing of wind at your ears. It was this sound exactly. The wind teased through our hair, whistled and whispered. I looked over at my brother; two tear marks had made rivulets down this face, clearing the dust like two crooked pathways. He looked like he was wearing an African Mask. I guess he was. He was fifteen years old and he had just fought to keep his family alive alongside our father, to save our lives again.... His eyes were dull and I had never seen him so lost. He smiled at me; though his smile – for the first time – didn't completely make it to his eyes. It remained cut off, somewhere, between here and there. Between the truth and what we have to accomplish to survive. War and how it ages the young. Youth snatched from you, finger on the trigger. I personally was relieved to see them all alive, considering my earlier concern.

Our lives had taken a grim turn. The innocence had been wrung out of us, similar to a bath towel in a washer women's hands. That day changed everyone; the sky was no longer a brilliant blue or open canvas as before. It was still beautiful but now a little tainted. I somehow felt bulletproof, yet fearful – sickeningly fearful – of the noise of the gunfire, of the smile on that monster's face as he called me "Mukiwa."

To be hunted by total strangers; strangers you would never meet. You would never have the chance to ask them why, to ask them for a reason; or to argue with them over a heated discussion or debate. There would never be that opportunity to change their minds or for them to change yours. There would only be encounters like we had just endured; or worse – torture – when death would be an answered prayer.

Dear War Puppet Leader and Dear War Puppets led, your beliefs, so full of propaganda, scheming and strangling the very resources you were giving your lives for. The few making the money from war, laughed in the face of child soldiers, raped mothers and daughters. After all, is not war a business too? Die for your country, how absurd. What a campaign. The honesty of Africa lies in its women. Looking into the eyes of the innocent leaves scars unsurmountable. Oh, how fast bad news spreads.

The leaders then never thought to look beyond the borders of their continent or their country. That sort of leadership is dangerous. Boasting the highest inflation rates on the planet. Poverty at an all-time high. Colonialism not being the answer at all either. A democracy a far loud cry from where we are now. Far from it. Why are we all so blinded? By wanting to dominate, to rule and to be part of a group. To fit in; to fit into what exactly? Since when do guests take over a household? Conquer and divide. Divide and conquer. Here we stand rootless, nervous and lost. Zimbabwe a country so rich in culture, mineral wealth and land. Yet, we choose not to change and not to work together to build, to build people! It's too easy to point fingers. Its time. It's time to forgive, it's time to say sorry. I am sorry. I am sorry for our ancestors that caused colonialism. I am deeply sorry. Ndokumbirawo ruregerero zvakanyanya kuburikidza nezvakaitwa nemadzitateguru angu munguva yekupambwa kwenyika ye Zimbabwe ndisati ndazvarwa, ndinokumbirisa ruregerero wese werudzi rwangu asi ndinotanga neni pachangu... ndiregerereiwo! Unfortunately, I cannot speak Ndebele. However, my apology does extend to the Ndebele People in this particular context as well. We cannot change the past, we can learn from it. However, we could make the future a bright one for all. At the current moment in Zimbabwe there is no currency, no jobs, no schools, no medical aid and no freedom... nothing, for most people. This has to change! How can the world just stand by and watch this happen? We need to get up on our bare feet and stand tall, stand proud and make our country a country we can all be proud of!

Dictators who ravaged this country, our country, my country and your country. The all-weather friends of Mugabe infiltrating Zimbabwe as fast as you can say "Bob's your uncle", to take what is rightfully our peoples. Yet, we stand ever so still in dripping fear!

Petrified. Learning their tongue. Just who is the guest here? Africa, the lost continent. The ones that were not able to leave, deer's in headlights, simply because they cannot speak freely. Am I a coward for leaving? No, I can do more for my country out of it, than in it. Let that sink in for a moment. I am a fortunate Zimbabwean, and I thank God every day.

Fat cats and more fat cats. Donning designer garb. Their countries in tatters, their people, our people scrambling for food, dying of thirst, starvation and disease. Promises of education, better times and freedom. All these promises smashed by a fat fist.

You fight for equality. You vote for equality. And what happens? You end up fleeing your country. Fleeing elsewhere, far away, to earn money to send back to the family you leave behind. Miles away from your family, from the familiar, moving at a pace so unfamiliar to you – this is your and our reward for fighting for our freedom. Eating food, you have never heard of and can barely pronounce; sitting in tight spaces, where no one sings or barely talks. Where a smile falls stone dead in mid-air. Yes, there are sometimes temptations – shopping, clothes, tech – but any thought of these is spoiled by guilt. Guilt for those back home who have nothing. The art of forgetting is a tempting mistress in the dead of night.

The Agric Alert was crackling; a welcome glow of hope.

'Come in, Slick (my father's nickname), and Claire. It's Christmas.'

As we looked towards the horizon, we heard a helicopter in the distance. It edged closer towards our house; this huge metal dragonfly. We all jumped up, hugging and screaming with joy. Waving our arms above our heads. Ecstatic. Rivers of relief cascading down our cheeks. We heard the compound drums start to beat. We heard the singing and the whistling of the tribal people. Then we heard the song of the troops: "Oh when the saints; Oh, when the saints; Oh, when the saints go marching in. I want to be in that number; Oh, when the saints go marching in."

At the head of the troops was Harris Scott – the father of an incredibly good friend. Harris, the lead trooper, was known all over the Lowveld region. He was famous for this arrival – leading the troops singing this song while he played his trumpet.

It was incredibly reassuring seeing Harris and the troops – our protector, leading the soldiers up the hill to our house. They were all in their camouflaged uniforms with big and heavy back packs. Guns. The troops arriving also meant it was time for bribery and corruption. Kudzai and I would play games with the soldiers for sweets from their rat packs. A rat pack is a box with the soldiers' food supply. For this I would need my partner in crime, Kudzai, Nyika's son. I went to find Kudzai with Nyika. To Honour. To Nurture, To Respect, that was my best friend. The fun was about to begin, sweets from heaven itself. Sweets, it had been a lifetime since we had, had any. The mere thought of sweets made us dizzy with joy.

Chapter Four
Hijacking the Troops

I felt a surge of energy as I heard Harris's trumpet and the troops marching up our driveway, all of them sounding in good spirits. There is something about humour in desperate times; it sheds light into "personal-darkness". Laughter, high fives and hugs were dished out.

'Harris, I love you, buddy!' said my father, hugging his friend, 'I am so relieved to see you.' "Me too, Slick, tough guy", offered Harris.

I saw tears in their eyes and could see the comfort and security they found in their friendship. To see my father emotional was something I had never seen before, I was grateful to witness this moment, as it made him appear not only venerable but also human, not just a hero. Comradery shared for survival and endurance, lifting spirits and giving one the will to persevere.

It had been a long day for Harris and his troops. The sun was slowly descending into the horizon, a myriad of colours filling the sky. Shadows dancing, as if sunlight would never return, in perfect unison with the drums from the compound beating for life, beating for joy, beating for God, Mwari. There were around eighty troops, including an additional ten from the helicopter following closely behind. The chopper had landed on the airfield in front of our house. I watched my heroes jump out the chopper, ducking below the blades. Dust whirling. We never had a plane at this house but a military airfield ran alongside our house for emergency op's. Our plane came later at the ranch. I ran to the soldiers; I knew Mr Harris very well. He hoisted me onto his shoulders in one swift motion, dropped his backpack and began marching again, playing his trumpet – all of us following in suit and we started singing again: "Oh when the saints, oh when the saints, oh when the saints go marching in, I want to be in that number… oh when the saints go marching in." Kudzai was marching along with them. We were family, all of us. I looked back at Kudzai and we were laughing, so happy. Nyika so proud of her son. She loved Kudzai dearly, he was everything to her.

Mr Harris's trumpet attracted the drummers from the compound. They all recognised this sound and they loved the army. Soon we were singing, dancing, grooving and laughing from our gut. Blessing, Happiness, Zuvarashe, Chengetai, Nyika and Truth all joined in. Huge fires were made and the festivities continued. Kudzai and I helped collect firewood. Even though we all knew lights had to be out by 6 p.m. care was tossed out on the wind. The soldiers drank homemade beer called Chibuku. I watched as some cried, drunk and emotional, recounting loss of life, missing their loved ones, families and children. Not knowing if they would ever see them again. A dull ache.

The soldiers were used to the feeling that each day could be their last. A strange, unsettling and awful feeling. Nothing in life is certain; but in a war, that lack of certainty is even more pronounced – those in the thick of it live day by day.

'Your reality,' said one trooper to me over a bottle of Chibuku, '…is not mine.'

Neil Diamond was murmuring in the background, something about Crackling' Rosie… whatever that meant.

It was bedtime. We had no idea, of what was instore for the compound that night. Nyika took my hand. I looked over my shoulder, where the campfires were dying down. The army were either in their sleeping bags or gathered around fires talking in hushed whispers. I love drifting off to sleep with a party in the background; it's so reassuring to me. Snatching titbit's from conversations to make my dreams take me as far from stone dead as possible. Most evenings, either my mother or Nyika would read Kudzai and I a bible story. I hugged Kudzai goodnight. His fists full of sweets. My sweets under my pillow. Nyika tucked me in. After kneeling to pay our respects.

That night Nyika read the story of how Judas betrayed Jesus at the last supper. We said our prayers kneeling next to my bed as was our custom every night. Nyika's croqueted quilt lay on my bed in bright and happy colours, my security blanket; it has weathered my most challenging storms to date. I loved Nyika's scent. It gave me reassurance.

'I love you,' whispered Nyika.

'I don't love you,' laughed Kudzai.

'I love you too, Nyika.'

'I love you anyway, Kudzai, you are my best friend. Joe and Kudzai, Judas didn't mean to betray Jesus,' Nyika continued, 'God had a bigger plan. Sometimes in life we cannot help betraying people. Sometimes, fear drives us. Goodnight, we said for the umpteenth time, have sweet dreams. Tomorrow will come, with a bit of yesterday and a glimpse at the day after. Stay that soul, child, baby-girl.'

I watched her close the bedroom door and heard my mother's footsteps coming up the passage. I heard Kudzai laugh. I heard his footsteps. To this day I can recognise someone by the sound of their walk. Everyone's step is as unique as their fingerprint. Little did I know that this would be the last time I saw Kudzai.

I drifted off to sleep, listening to the distant chatter like a light rain on a tin roof. My sister Samantha's cat, Wednesday, was curled up next to me and Chico, the dog, lay at the bottom of the bed, snoring. The troops were the best; tomorrow they had agreed that we could be with them for the whole day. I would go haul

Kudzai away from his books to join me. He was such a study head. A good influence on me my parents said. We would seize the chance to swindle as many sweets from the soldiers as possible. Even more than we already had. Oh, and we would bring the lucky beans we had been hiding. Our stash. Our cash.

I woke to a stream of light coming through my window and mesh curtains. The light had caught the dust particles and they were dancing as though in a ballet, pirouetting amongst one another, thousands of them, miniature ballerinas. The cockerel was crowing and it ordered you to get out of bed. I could hear Blessing in the kitchen readying the tea tray. I loved the clink of china and silver. It was almost a piece of music. If you swayed to the clink and the clunk you could build up a little rhythm. I did so every morning – the "China and Silver Sway" I called it whilst I danced with dust ballerinas in the new morning light.

Chico was outside barking. He was probably running up and down the fence, being teased by the deer or monkeys or perhaps a baboon. A group of monkeys spent hours ridiculing him. The vervet monkeys were a particularly mischievous bunch – stealing fruit from the fruit bowl in the house and sleeping in cars if you happened to leave the window open. Many an encounter had taken place. I had even seen my mother negotiating with a monkey over banana's and her precious avocado pears. Whilst the monkey made itself at home on the table and sat there unperturbed, a tad bit mischievously, provoking and tempting my mother to do anything or something to it at all. A bit like a child in puberty. Eyes reading, I dare you! You, naughty monster, cute but naughty, shoo she motioned, with a bunch of bananas, until literally tearing them apart and throwing them at the monkey till it bolted out the kitchen window and taunted her from the tree, throwing back the avocado pips. It was a normal morning one filled with monkey business and china tea sets.

I walked into the kitchen with the wooden stove in full swing. The tin kettle was boiling up a storm. Blessing and Nyika were

66

singing a sad song, I wondered why for a split second while my parents were in the dining room talking in hushed tones. My brother was brushing his teeth; no doubt he had spent the last hour in bed, idly leafing through Scope, his favourite magazine. My sister Samantha was still in bed, which was rare, she usually had a race with dawn daily.

The bell sounded, however, and we all materialised at the table as if by magic. Abracadabra! That's an Arabic word by the way. Oh, the tricks one learns to appear on time and in order.

The first tea of the day is essential to kick start the rough edges of my personality; I prefer not to speak until this daily tradition is completed and probably five minutes after that too. Thank goodness, Samantha was not all perky this morning, her morning animated and happy gestures could drive me nuts. Breakfast was always oats porridge, made by my father. He was so proud of his porridge and we loved it. The fact that it was made by a man who could cook nothing else, made it even more special. Sometimes I thought he was prouder of his porridge than of us. This pretty much spelt it out for me – in his heart, all he craved was to please his family. As a boy, all he wanted was to please his father. Now, as a man, all he wanted was to do his best by us.

As children, we forget that our parents are people too. They are just as prone to making mistakes as we are. However, for some reason we put them on pedestals. Parent relations with children and vice versa are so multifaceted that it's impossible to fathom.

My father was delighted in the dawn of the day. He was an early riser – a man of opera and land. He had already checked the fields and had his morning meeting with Truth. He rose at five hundred hours am daily, rain or shine, vacation, weekend or no weekend. They had already shared their first tea watching the sunrise. Every now and then, I would join them in this ritual, by sheer force naturally, not because I loved to do it, but once up the dawn was welcoming – the curl of the steam, rising from the tea, merging with the morning light and mist, as we enjoyed the whispers of the day. These mornings they discussed the harvest and how much the crop would bring in. They would talk about any problems with the workers and would share the latest about the war.

Their morning tea was brief. My father was given one of the signals that terrorists were watching our farm, our home or our movements. One signal was Truth whistling in a certain pitch. Another signal was a particular song that the ladies picking the cotton in the fields would start singing. Truth might start shouting at my father for no particular reason – that was another signal, a particularly urgent signal. With a cigarette dangling out his mouth. The cigarette being key.

That feeling of someone watching you – such a disturbing feeling. You know they are there, but where? It's similar to the feeling, when people are sitting around a table, where you see an exchange between two or more persons and you are painfully aware, that those exchanged looks were particularly about you. A leaf fluttering, a bush rustling, a soft thud – is it the breeze, an animal, or is it? Paranoia niggles, eating away at you. You try to shake it loose, but it clings to you like your shadow in full daylight.

Breakfast came to an end.

'Is Kudzai in the compound, Nyika?' I asked.

I looked at her, noticing her bloodshot eyes.

'Nyika, is Kudzai in the compound?'

Not a peep. I bolted out the back door down the hill at the back of the house as fast as my legs could carry me. My heart was thumping so hard it was pounding and punching my chest.

Something was off, something was amiss. I knew it, I felt it, in every fibre of my being. Every breath was a heave. My head was spinning and I felt nauseous. I am blessed with a strong sense of intuition. I stepped on paper thorns and devil thorns which would, usually have stopped me in my tracks, feeling nothing more than a prick. Feeling nothing at all really! The sky was its usual blue painted canvas. The weather felt hot and sticky, Mopani flies drank at the edges of my eyes, as if animals at a waterhole, fighting for the moisture, for the last drop of water, dizzy with madness. I slapped them away, irritated. The bush was dry and the tall golden grass stood still, not a breath of wind in sight. Vultures circled up above.

The compound was not far from the house at all probably about two kilometres. It consisted of thatched traditional rondavals, mud walls, grass swept cleanly away from every house. In the centre of the compound was where the fire burnt every night, and ashes sat heavy in the fire pit. African pots and pans stood against each rondaval, alongside the African Drums.

I ran, straight into the compound screaming at the top of my lungs: 'Kudzai! Kudzai! Kudzai! Where are you, Kudzai?'

The world was still for a while. All around, I could hear the muffled sound of tears. Chief Marimba walked towards me.

'Where is Kudzai?' I demanded, forgetting my manners completely.

'My, dear child, sit,' he replied soothingly. 'Listen, my child…'

In Shona, in his deep baritone voice, he was muttering words from a song we had made up together long back. He looked ashen and depleted.

The left side of his face was covered in a bandage. They had burnt his face, with wood and coals from the fire. Whipping signs on his back were clear, made from thin reeds. He could not walk properly. Our strong Chief, looking as fragile as a flame in a gentle breeze. I looked at the rest of the tribe, a few had bandages on to. I found out later that my mother, father and Nyika had been there in the early hours of the morning, stitching up deep wounds, cleaning up burns and whippings. A sadness clung to the air like clingwrap clings to a left-over bowl in a refrigerator. Whilst I had been asleep, my friends had suffered atrocities at the hands of the same people that called themselves freedom fighters. The same tribe. Blank.

As I could not find Kudzai, I assumed he had been killed. The life out of my lungs flung me to the floor voluntarily, no questions asked of me. As if taken over by an imaginary poltergeist. For a while I just lay there and stared into a burnt-out fire pit. Ashes blowing in the breeze. The words of our song never intended for our youth.

May your soul be free
May it fly high
To God's gates
Shimmering golden in light

We release you from our hearts
Brave
Tall
Strong
To another army you now belong

May your soul be free
May it fly high
To God's gates
Shimmering golden in light

You gave to this life of mine
A meaning
Your spirit will be cleansed
Your wings won't need preening
Mind your steps in life
Bullets flying, strife

May your soul be free
May it fly high

To God's gates
Shimmering golden light

Once you were my flesh and blood
You are no longer
I let you go, destroyed, I try not to ponder
One day I will hold you in my arms
Yonder

May your soul be free
May it fly high
To God's gates
Shimmering golden light

Song by Alice Vye Henningway

I sat still. My legs felt numb. My stomach weak.

'Kudzai was taken by the terrorists last night,' the chief had told me. 'They will turn him against his family, against you, against all he knows. If you see him again you can never trust him, do you hear me? Kudzai is now a terrorist against his will. He will become a child soldier. He will hunt you and kill you mercilessly. Mark my words and never forget them because it will mean your certain death.'

I leaned forward and vomited from the pit of my stomach. My head was spinning; I felt like I was drowning, helplessly drowning in the raging currents of the great Zambezi river itself. I fell into the sand, biting my lip and tasting the warmth of my blood. Again, fear in dirt and blood. My best friend, gone. Taken from his mother; taken from his family – to be taught to murder, torture, rape and pillage. I placed myself into the lap of the chief. He put his arms around me. I could see Nyika approaching; she was freeing her heart. Out of her stomach came a melody that resonated with pain.

The same song the Chief had been muttering. Nyika was singing it from the depths of her soul, it resonated with the surroundings.

How can you lose a child like this? Lose a child to a war so pointless and self-destructive.

Nyika's voice encouraged the women of the village to join in her sorrow. Soon they were all singing as one. Nyika's face had not been damaged. She told me later, that she had been whipped on the back and kicked in the stomach. Blessing had received the same punishments. That is why I had not noticed this morning at breakfast. I had noticed the shift in mood, as siblings we all had. No-one spoke of the night before. My parents, had already decided to avoid the topic and just get through breakfast, knowing they would have to deal with it later on that day, they were also exhausted. It was their way of trying to protect us. The army, had not heard the commotion, it was carried out menacingly quietly. They were also professionals after all. Blessing had come and woken up my parents to ask for help. Chico my sisters dog would usually have heard something, slept through the night with not the slightest disturbance, he knew Blessing so Blessing coming to wake-up my parents was a familiar occurrence. Oh yes, their brainwashing session had been planned perfectly, as per usual. The army were only able to help after the incident. Helping my parents administer medical aid. Search the surrounding area.

The people of the compound surrounded the three of us – the chief, Nyika and I – in the middle of the compound. Their bare feet stamped the dust with unforgiving naked anger, full of purpose. The drums began to beat. I joined the dancers to will his spirit to be strong; to be brave to go on. To come home. We escaped into a trance...

It was my first day. I got to smoke the Chief's pipe. This will heal your pain; release his spirit from yours. I choked and spluttered, then felt I was free of my body. My mind followed the drum beats and my bare feet hit the sand in unison with Nyika and the women of the village. Dust rose and clung to me, covering me in another skin – of scales.

Later that evening, when I showered with Nyika sitting on the side of the bathtub, I felt like a snake shedding its skin – shedding a life – as I watched the soap suds disappear down the drain. A deep and complete sadness passed over me and I cried – tears mixed with water and sand; now of mud. My best friend that I had, had for my entire life of 6 years old, was now gone. Poof, into thin air, never to be seen again, and if I did see him, apparently, he would kill me stone dead. My Kudzai, who I had laughed endlessly with, who I had shared nearly every waking hour playing with in our fort in the garden, pretending to make this world a better place. Gone, just like that. Gone. Nyika's son, her only child. Gone.

'The soldiers are outside,' whispered Nyika soothingly, 'we could hijack some sweets.'

'It's not the same without Kudzai,' I replied through stifled sobs.

'He is my son. But I have you and you are like a daughter to me. So, we have to carry on.'

'Nyika, I can't. I feel dead. I feel like I am walking around in an empty skin.'

I offered not knowing about life at all. A mere child.

'If I have to carry on, you have to carry on. God knows best.'

At that, I lost it completely. I began screaming, crying and threw myself on the floor.

'God!' I screamed. 'He knows nothing! Where is he now? This God you speak of, where is he?' Or she or whatever it is meant to be?

'You will see! We do not know his plans, so we must accept his will.'

'Accept?' tears streamed down my eyes, 'Your son – my best friend – is taken and taught the very worst atrocities, and you say it's part of God's plan. Your God is a liar. I hate your God.'

'Child, child. Africa is not for sissies. Africa will eat you alive if you don't stand up and carry on.'

Nyika slapped me across the face to bring me back to reality. I stared at her.

'You hit me! You have never done that. I hate you, too!'

'And don't you dare use that tone with me, who in God's name uses that type of language, hate is too strong a word? I will slap you again if I ever hear that word and wash your mouth out with soap, young lady. Gutter language if I ever heard it, right out the mouth of a babe! I know this one to,' I screamed as loudly as I could, 'your God's a cunt!'

Well, it was definitely too loud, because my mother had heard it. She came marching into my room, slipped off her Bata special flip flop, lifted my dress and paddled my backside. Ladies do not use that type of language ever.

I left the house, with a sore cheek and a burning backside, my ego and feelings in turmoil, I marched over to my kopje and sat on the rock, staring across, into the endless maze of plants and trees. Kudzai was out there somewhere. No doubt being tortured, forced to accept things he knew to be wrong. Alone. Terrified. Confused. In pain for sure, they were merciless to their own. Meanwhile, I was stuck here… completely helpless. A child, who could not even shoot straight if I tried.

Nyika's God was doing nothing at all – sitting there watching us die, as if we were flies, watching this happen to Kudzai. What kind of world was this? A rainbow stretched right across the sky, bowed and landed yonder. I smiled, as much as I could muster. A defeated smile. I had lost. Nyika had lost more. We all had lost in one way or another. Yesterday evening ever so joyous, now the other extreme. A rainbow seeped into the bush beyond the farm. That's where Kudzai is, I thought, he's at the end of the rainbow, bathing in a pot of gold. This thought stilled my mind. And I came up with a plan. I can fix this.

I ran home, straight to the soldiers, the wind at my heels. Down the dusty foot path, no shoes as per usual. It had been a damp cold sitting on the rocks and now the sun melted into my bones and spread hope. I felt like Mary Poppins, but cooler; I didn't need an umbrella. I burst into the middle of the group of troops who were hovering around waiting for their sergeant.

'We have to find Kudzai!' I shouted. 'We have to get Kudzai back!'

They looked down at me.

'Who is Kudzai?'

'My best friend!' I spat back. 'He was taken last night from the village. They're going to turn him into a child soldier.'

'Joe, that's not possible.'

'I heard the sergeant say; "he will be miles from here already". Not to mention we are all exhausted from last night's atrocities. I have in addition also had to split up my platoon to help other farmers, excuse my language, but last night was a shit storm, with titties up,' he said breathlessly. 'The terrorists have not left the area as far as we know!'

'Why are you talking about titties, sir? We have more serious problems,' I said trying to prove I was also tough, all of six years old.

'We have to prepare for the next attack. It could be your farm; it could be another farm. We have to be ready.'

'He is your enemy now!' I shouted. 'He is our Nyika's son. Do you have a son? He's like a brother to me and you say, 'No.' Fine, I'll go myself.'

'You will do no such thing. Go to your room!'

I lay on my bed, pouting… fuming. Knock, knock.

'Joe, it's Dave,' said a voice from outside, 'it's Mr De Braine.'

I sat up and went to my door.

'Yes?'

Forgetting my manners completely, yet again, more on purpose really.

'Joe, we're going to look for Kudzai. But I want you to prepare for the worst. There's a very good chance he's already dead or brainwashed. These are the only two possibilities. Even if he were to, come back, the punishments he would have endured would affect, him for life and he would never be the person you knew before. You would not be the friends you remember. In my opinion, hang on to what you have and let it rest. It's for the best. For all of you and the survival of the tribe and your family. We will search for twenty-four hours. That's all we're able to do.' Then we will have to move on to another area of the lowveld altogether. Other farmers have radioed in needing our help. The troops will radio your mom, if we find Kudzai.

'Thank you!' better something than nothing!!!

I was jubilant. Nyika's face was filled with hope. We hugged for what felt like eternity. The next twenty-four hours dragged horribly. As if I was trying to ride a donkey in a horse race. I felt like a slug in quicksand. It was like a crow was flying above me, casting a huge shadow wherever I moved. I felt smothered, suffocated; and breathing seemed difficult. I fell into a troubled sleep, curled up in Nyika's arms.

My dreams were filled up with nonsense. Kudzai eating the gold at the end of the rainbow – and not wanting to share it. He had black beads for eyes and the whites were red; he was half man and half gun. I woke sweating. Nyika sung to me. My mother had covered us in the night.

Dawn came. Today the blue sky was pitch black.

I walked outside. The mood was sombre. Kudzai had shot Mr. De Braine. He had been rushed to hospital in the chopper. He was badly injured but would survive. Kudzai had crossed the line. He had crossed it against his will, like so many other boys. Kudzai's childhood was already a distant memory; he was now a shadow of the kind; gentle boy I knew. He was a hero now to the wrong side of humanity; washed up on the spill of blood.

Nyika cried in *my arms* this time. Those monsters, those puppeteers who stole my friend; they are damned. When the time comes to show their faces, when they move out of the shadows, no amount of camouflage will cover their faithlessness and their hopelessness. They will see that darkness is attached to their heels and it will follow them everywhere, eternally. My thoughts, rambling around in my head.

I decided to make peace with God, with Christ. After all, I was here; I was alive. My life, could have ended in ways I preferred not to think about. But he had protected me. Have faith, have hope, stay strong. Hold Nyika's hand forever. God willing. Amen. Nyika and I began to sing, because it heals, because to give up is not an option. That quicksand does not ask twice.

We sang loud; we sang proud, this time we sung a different song – "Mamatora." My mother joined us and held us for she knew very well what it was like to lose a son. My brother had died from mistaking tablets for sweets. He died in my mother's arms – she had not made it to the hospital in time. My parents were devastated. They became ghosts for a while – living, but not really – each trying to battle with their emotions. During the worst moments, they would blame each other. During the best moments, they were silent. Eventually, the guilt that wracked my parents came spilling out.

My mother shook with Nyika in sobs of tears. Two women together; neither colour nor war could divide them. They held each other, sharing a loss that only two mothers can understand. Nyika's loss although completely different was still a loss, an unclosed circle. Both dealing with a never-ending sadness.

I watched Nyika walk down the hill to the compound in the fading daylight. She was to take the day after tomorrow off for a while, a week or two. Heartbroken. Unbeknown to us all, at that moment, we were all being watched. A further brainwashing session was to take place at the compound that night, in the absence of the army, the enemy came tiptoeing into the compound and caused silent havoc. I would come to find out much later.

Chapter Five
A Funeral for The Living and an
Unwanted Visit in the Dead of Night

'Nyika,' I began tentatively, 'I think we should have a funeral for Kudzai.'

I watched her for a response.

'Don't you want closure?' I continued. 'Don't you want goodbye?'

Nyika looked at me with her orange eyes, the colour of popcorn seeds half burnt. From crying eternally. Today, she looked lost; confused – like a chameleon on a Smarties box. Today, Nyika looked beaten. A mere ghost of the lady I knew.

'Yes,' she replied softly, 'I think we should. I will speak to the chief tonight.'

'Do you want me to come with you?'

'No.'

I had walked halfway down to the compound that morning and I sat cross-legged on the hill, waiting patiently for Nyika. A bond had formed between us during years together; a bond richer than our country's mineral wealth; a bond that transcends skin colour or culture – a rich, deep and unbreakable bond.

What is freedom exactly? Are any of us ever truly free? Do we dare to be? Or do we just fit the mould and tell ourselves we are free. Some people discuss freedom when it seems fashionable. One moment a concert, the next moment a dictatorship. Music dispelling the wagging tongue. Or is it, the habit, of just a smile, hiding the torture you feel inside. Is freedom a garment, a uniform, that we can betray ourselves in? That we can commit the unthinkable and use it as an excuse; brush it under the mat? Freedom comes at a cost few can afford. Here nobody was free. Everyone was being watched. Throw caution to the wind and things would go wretchedly wrong.

Nyika beat the drum two shorts and three longs (our phone number) on the party line of telephones we used to have with the handle. Sort of similar to an egg beater. I walked down the sandy path, barefoot, kicking at the dust. Watching it rise and land, without a sound. I stood on a devil thorn – cursed – then took it out. Yes, the devil was at play. Horns and tail galore. His little pitchfork raised, looking for comradery and allies. He was recruiting.

The long grass blew gently in the wind and the rustling of the Lucky Bean tree cast its tones – a distant rattle. A pod fell onto the path in front of me – I wondered if it was a message from the gods themselves. I cracked it open. All the lucky beans stared at me, red-hatted and black-bodied. Uniformed. All neatly stacked in a row, ready to march right on out of the seed shell. To grow to prosper in a barren land. I took the seed shell with me. I would give it as an offering. My father's offering, for the goodbye to Kudzai, was to give Nyika a sheep for slaughter.

I had watched its throat being slit open and watched the white fleece turn red. Blood spurting out and spilling down into its wool, its eyes screaming for help. Once, again I was reminded of my helplessness. I was a coward. I watched unable to take my eyes off this revolting scenario, its legs kicked one last time then stiffened. Stone dead, just like the weaver bird. Finally shitting itself. There is no dignity in death. Not even for you or me, nor sheep. I watched the other sheep watching this ritual. I felt so bad for them, they sensed it, all staring death in the face. This sheep had been, a daughter a mother. Was I imagining this or was I going mad? Still feeling like a coward, a loser. Could we not be more humane? Everything was upside down. A death offering for a death offering that was not a death offering, simply because we really did not know if Kudzai was dead or not. We would close the circle making him dead to us, but not in our hearts, there he would remain alive. Nothing was happy or safe anymore. The rituals were ready and the festivities would start that evening.

I was thinking that if Kudzai was alive he would have to be incredibly brave, just like my Uncle Andre (who was the only white man initiated into the Shangaan tribe in a private ceremony) - he was the bravest man I had been privileged to meet. If Kudzai could be like him, he would manage. Unfortunately, Uncle Andre had been shot to pieces about three weeks ago, by a new group of terrorists, who had been crossing the Mozambique Border, into Zimbabwe. Whilst he had been fixing a water pump at a waterhole, they had ambushed him in his Land Rover. Opened fire on him, leaving him in that finale of the bullet dance. So many bullets for just one man. Slumped over his steering wheel. Gunpowder and bird's flutter. Stampede and recede. Africa all too aware of his departure, lying bare the open sky. A huge loss.

Tribal people loved Andre; he was held high with utmost respect. When we attended his funeral, along the kopje that adjourned his home, Chiefs and soldiers alike from the surrounding tribal trust lands stood sombre in full traditional regalia, against the red-hot setting sun and dying light, to pay their final respects. A song in baritone. Goosebumps even on your head. This image burns in my mind, never to go out. An apology was later announced, after some time. That the terrorists that shot him were not of this tribe, and they had made a grave mistake. They too paid the price. His absence in our worlds created an empty void, that was never filled.

He was gone, Kudzai was gone, my dad was very busy with the farm and had a tonne of emotional and financial stress. Having four children and a wife in a civil war is not exactly a walk in the park. My, siblings were off to boarding school soon. At least I had Blessing, Happiness, the chief well sort of he was no longer himself and understandably so. Truth and Zuvarashe, Wine. The male influencers in my life. I would have to be strong for Nyika.

Always try to do what is right. It may not make you popular, but it will help you sleep better at night. What is right? I was losing my compass. Out there in a huge sea of confusion. Listening for my ancestor's guidance, as I had been taught by the Chief. I could hear, nothing. Speak out, dammit. Listen harder. I screamed at my ancestors, I yelled to the heavens. Where are you all? Nyika snapped me out of my ranting at the heavens, reminding me we had work to do for that evening's ceremony.

Taking hold of the machete, I helped Nyika collect firewood from the surrounding bush. I was seven and Nyika had long since taught me how to use a machete. It was painfully sharp and half the size of me. One miscalculated swing and bang there goes a finger. I took my firewood gathering very seriously.

I was just about to take my first swing at some of the narrow branches when out of nowhere a green mamba fell from the branches above and landed opposite me. A green mamba is a snake. Very poisonous. Deadly, I think. My brother collected snakes and he knew plenty about each species – the green mamba is deadly, he had said. Or had he not said. I stood stone still, frozen in place. My mind going at a million miles an hour. I was like the woman in the Bible who turned into a pillar of salt, Lot's wife, Sodom and Gomorrah all around me. I stood silently, almost afraid to breathe, watching the snake, as still as me. We were like this for what felt an eternity.

I could hear Nyika calling and calling me. Surely, she would realise something was amiss. The snake was incredibly striking – a rich, brilliant green that matched the tree's leaves perfectly. I heard Nyika, reprimanding me and getting closer.

'Child,' she cursed, 'you are most certainly deaf.'

I lifted my pointing finger ever so slowly. Then she turned and fled. I could hear her footsteps take her down the hill, shouting for the bow and arrow from the chief.

The snake simply lay there; I stood motionless – I could have been one of the trees. Or a rock. I tried to imagine I was a tree or a rock to help me keep perfectly still. To take the stillness. Joe the salt pillar. My joints were beginning to burn, it was agonising. I finally heard Nyika's noiseless footsteps. She whispered. Do not move an inch.

Out of nowhere, an arrow whizzed past my right ear, landing squarely in the head of the snake. I bolted as fast as I could. Today I actually managed to run, apparently when I need to, I am able. After sprinting who knows how far away, I had the sudden realisation that I had to pee... desperately. I darted behind a baobab tree and watered the grass. As if the day was not going badly enough, I sat to close to a blister beetle, who sprayed its blister fluid all over my bottom. It stung like hell.

I called for Nyika. 'Nyika! Nyika! Help!'

'Not again,' I heard her muttering to herself, just loud enough so I could hear it.

'What have you done to yourself?' she exclaimed.

She yanked me round to discover large red blisters all over my bottom.

'Pull up your panties,' she said, 'let's go to the dairy shed.'

We set off at a fast pace, arriving at the dairy in no time. Nyika squeezed some fresh milk from one of the cow's teats, put me across her lap and rubbed the milk on my blistered bottom. The sting eased.

Then she milked the teat some more, enough to fill a tub with the fresh cow milk and said to me, 'Plant your derriere in there for a moment, and everything will be as right as rain.'

So, there I sat in a large dish of fresh cow's milk. What a day, it was turning out to be and it was not even lunch time yet. The dairy cows ignored me, as if this sort of thing was a normal occurrence.

Their long lashes gazing down at me as if I was a piece of turd. 'I am not that stupid you know, Miss Dairy Cow?' I could not believe I was explaining myself to a cow. Maybe the sting was making my mind tipsy or wonky? I was made to sit there through lunch, munching my mealie cob with my bottom in a bowl of milk. I had also done a bit of reading. My favourite story being *The Land of The Faraway Tree*. My mind in the land of topsy turvy with Moon Face. It was by now late afternoon. Chico and Wednesday had kept me company.

I could still see the compound; the firewood had been gathered and a huge fire was blazing in the centre. The thatched huts with their mud walls were far enough from being caught unawares by a wondering flame, they were scattered away from the centre in an imperfect circle. The chief had put on his finest traditional regalia: he was clad in leopard skin and lions' teeth, passed down from his ancestors. The women looked striking– Nyika the most beautiful of all. They were wearing traditional garments with original Zimbabwean African prints. Sarongs and headgear, bright and colourful. Lifting the mood. Drums were being beaten in a gentle rhythm.

To not embrace another culture and to remain only steadfast in your own beliefs and cultures is to miss out on so many abundant possibilities and incredible occasions. Look at what I was witnessing. I felt alive, so rich. My bottom was stinging, but I couldn't have cared less. The drums began to beat rhythmically; the woman began to sway their hips and then began the singing. The men also joined in the festivities. Their deep baritone voices perfectly complementing the women's polyphonic tones, the melody carried on the wind across the vast horizon.

Blood, bone and flesh gyrated and pulsated in a hypnotic rain of rituals, entangled with generations of exhausted thieving of one's children and women in the dead of night. I watched as a flame drew another participant into the throng of singers. I was mesmerised and grateful for Nyika and thankful to have had Kudzai as a friend even if it had been short lived.

I wanted to dance too. I jumped out of my bowl of milk, said thanks to the cow, pulled up my panties, ran down to the compound and joined the woman. Chico at my heels. Wednesday the cat, just staring distastefully. Not even interested in the milk. 'Spoilt brat,' I thought, momentarily.

Nyika took my hand reassuringly and led me to her hut. We went inside. I had been inside her hut hundreds of times. I had even slept nights in her bed. Her bed was raised from the floor so the Tokoloshe wouldn't get her. Photographs in polaroid squares covered the walls. They were mostly of Nyika and Kudzai, the odd one of all three of us. I met Nyika's eyes. She had removed Kudzai's bed.

'I have a gift for you,' she said.

'A gift?' I replied, 'What did I do to deserve a gift?'

She took a box down from the cupboard and lifted the lid. Inside was my very own traditional dress for tonight's festivities. Beige and green are my favourite colours and this dress was the colour of sands mixed with every shade of green. I was so grateful and putting it on, I felt truly like a princess. My mother and father had given me permission to come to the festivities tonight. They had long since realised that I did not fit the usual mould.

'Now, child, sit,' ordered Nyika, 'I have to braid your hair.'

I sat down in front of her dressing table – something out of a seventies commercial with its huge round mirror and stool to match. My grandmother had given it to Nyika as a gift. The hut was round, so none of the furniture actually fitted anywhere. I sat with my back straight – obedient – and looked at us in Nyika's dressing table mirror.

Nyika was dazzling this evening in her bright purple, gold and green African Sarong and douc. Her douc was wound around her head and her eye shadow was gold dust. Her lipstick was bright red against her coal complexion, while her eyelashes curled up, much like a giraffe's, touching her eyebrows.

Nyika was slim for an African woman. In the Shona culture, the rounder and more robust you were, the more attractive a man would consider you. It's the total opposite of the western culture. Due to the fact that, at times, food can be scarce and also due to the AIDS epidemic, the belief was that a skinny person was sick or necessitous.

Larger women are considered a better catch. Most African men will laugh at you if you ask them whether a skinny woman is attractive. They will diplomatically say that all women are attractive but that something to hold onto is far more attractive. Shona men are some of the laziest men I have ever come across; leaving almost everything to the Shona woman. Planting and monitoring crops, building the compound and not to mention, looking after the many children they seem to produce with no thought for birth control or financial implications.

Shona and Ndebele women have now taken matters more into their own hands. No longer will they accept punishments dished out for no good reason, accepted in the past as part of "tradition." These women too are taking a stand. Maintaining the tradition and mystery of the Shona people is important, but some things belong in the past.

One thing that should definitely be consigned to history is the tradition of punishing married Shona women if they have a wet and inappropriate dream. Such "offenders" are cruelly punished by the hand of the Nyanga, the witch doctor of the region whilst contrary to a man's wet dream which is shrugged off –and taken as – one of those things.

Some Shona woman are inclined to embrace the elongation of the labia tradition, believing that this will tantalise and pleasure their husband, and thus he will not stray. The labia are physically pulled as soon as the young woman hits puberty, so at the age of around 12. At times they rip, but hey, as long as you keep your man, right? Mwari only knows the suffering of woman in tribal Africa. Their endurance is endless; embracing pain like the arms of a long-lost lover and when it surfaces merely biting down on their bottom lip.

The Nyanga is a very important man amongst the Shona people. He practices both herbal and ancestral medicine. The Nyanga is the one who gives you messages from your ancestors. They are the only ones with that power. Nyika's father was not only the chief but he was also the Nyanga. To the Shona people, their ancestors and ancestral burial grounds are hugely important. They are sacred – and rightly so. The ingredients of their medicine are at times "dodgy" and questionable to say the least. There have been whispers and suggestions that human body parts go for high prices and are highly sought after in certain concoctions whipped up by the Nyanga. Rumour has it said that Albino body parts are sold at an even higher fee and that the heart of a baby or an Albino baby is gold for certain spells so to speak.

The Zimbabwean local newspaper is an absolute treat to read. It's mind altering. Ritual killings are a common phenomenon in Zimbabwe, although one can only take all this at face value. Superstition has led to the torment of many a tortured soul, last seen running from nothing that anyone else can see. Penga – the Shona word for mad. Believe me, you do not want to be labelled Penga. Your life will be a misery – isolated, avoided by everyone; treated as though you were contagious.

(ritualkillinginafrica.org) Zimbabwe/Ritual killings and ZHRC Zimbabwe Human Rights Commission) express concerns over ritual killings from newsday.co.za.

Nyika's fingers worked like a large spider spinning a spider web; like a daddy-long-legs – quick, accurate and nimble. She divided my hair into precisely equal parts and each part was a little bundle. Each bundle was then plaited, extremely tightly and painfully. It brought a slight wave of water onto your eyelids, similar to that of cutting onions without opening your mouth. A stinging sensation – your eyes leak involuntarily.

She looked at me – at her handiwork – carefully. 'And now for your dress.' I whipped off and discarded my normal daily clothes in a second placing them neatly on Nyika's bed. I had been taught by Nyika, that scattering clothing on the floor was not what a well-raised child did. My sister obviously didn't have Nyika as a guide.

I felt ecstatic. I was going to join the Shona woman in a tribal dance. It was an official invitation – with an open heart and extended hand from the chief himself. I felt honoured. I stood next to Nyika, each of us admiring the other. A million thoughts of being an African princess raced through my mind. Nyika took my head between her palms and planted a kiss on my forehead. She took me by the hand and led us out of her hut; she ducked so as not to hit her head on the door frame and thatch.

The night air smelt of wood smoke and sheep crackling, it smelt delicious despite my earlier visions my stomach grumbled. The night sky was pitch black, not a star in sight. Two women stood over a huge metal pot with large, long wooden sticks, shaped as if they were holding giant baseball bats, stirring the traditional sadza, Zimbabwe's staple diet, made from maize. They stirred and sang, babies on their backs, also in traditional dress. The full moon appeared from behind the clouds. Filling the bush with a sheen of sorts a dull light on the lowest dimmer switch. You felt as if someone ought to turn it up a tad. A thousand invisible eyes watching you. You waited to no avail. A lion roared in the distance. The sounds of a herd of a family of elephants eating not so far off, breaking down trees. Gently, massive trees fall to the ground, ever so faintly. A hyenas laughter echoed mingled with provocation and distance. Sort of like a bitch in a room. The sound of a herd of wildebeest running along the fences gave my heart a thud. A leopard's meal. A zebra herd snorted whilst their hooves pounded. Down by the dam, the hippo's played; the males honking, asserting their dominance. Bringing the bird, the Night Jar into the mix, can only be described as if, dropping a beat, the DJ of the African Bush, throwing in the final mix ending in pitch perfection. My child eyes wide open at the tradition laid before me, I was grateful and shy all at once.

We were barefoot. The drums were pounding. On Nyika's entrance, the women let out a loud wailing sound of appreciation and high respect. After all, Kudzai had been the chief's eldest grandson and heir. He would have been next in line to be the Chief of the compound and extended tribe. Nyika, the apple of his eye. We joined the circle of women, dancing, prancing, whooping and wailing, butts shaking. Nyika, having acquired a position, through her ancestry, most certainly was not adored by all. Mother of the next heir. Nyika's family had once been part of the hereditary monarchy of the Shona, who reached the peak of their power and influence in the mid-fifteenth century. During the time of Great Zimbabwe when it represented a medieval African empire. Some people are prone to envy, come rain or shine. Would someone do anything to try to challenge her position? With no Kudzai, would Nyika be the one to lead this compound? This tribe? A woman? Under these extremely rare circumstances it could be possible. There is always that one malicious individual looking for the perfect opportunity to disrupt a peaceful chain of events.

We went round and round the perimeter of the fire – flames flicked and licked the night air. The African finger piano called the Mbira or the Kalimba a more contemporary term you may also call it a Sansa, made from a wooden board, which is often fitted with a resonator, with attached staggered metal tines. You play this by holding it in both hands, using the thumbs and forefingers. These days you can also find them made from Coke cans. Cuban music also uses this instrument.

Zimbabwean djembe drums are the centre of traditional Zimbabwean music. When the mbira is being played it is accompanied by rattles or hosho we call it "Kutamba mbira nehosho" the translation being, "playing the thumb piano with rattles". Hosho are dried out gourds with seeds inside them, and they are usually played in pairs, one in each hand. In collaboration with these are the leg rattles called Magavhu, they make the same sound as the Hosho's. These are tied to the ankles or the whole of the lower part of your leg.

All these shakers remind me of the hiss of chips from freshly cut potatoes, when thrown into boiling oil. Then there is the Marimba or Xylophone although not traditionally from Zimbabwe it has worked its magic and way into our music. Marimba clubs are popular in our country. Music has that power, to provoke or intensify a specific mood or feeling. A universal language we all share.

The sheep had been slaughtered earlier that day, bled out and blessed as an offering to the Gods and ancestors and specifically for Kudzai.

The sheep was rotating, slowly basted with a sauce made from garlic, sunflower oil and salt. Next to the spit, a black tin pot was on the boil and mealie meal Sadza (fresh ground maize) was poured generously into the piping-hot bubbling water, this was the third pot in the making. The woman's arms as strong as steel, mixing the sadza. Sweat glided down their forearms, and hung on their brows, and still they continued. The drums had picked up a slight tempo and their hips swayed naturally to the beat, their babies on their backs gurgled, clearly content. One woman had her breast exposed, feeding her infant, her colourful douq pushed out of place, the way mothers sometimes look, when babies come first. The baby's chubby hand was playing mindlessly with the stiff cotton fabric of its mother's traditional dress.

It amazed me to see the sheep's eyes, hooves, ears, nose, tongue boiling in a pot amongst tomatoes and onions. I thought ooh, that takes it a step to far for me. Its skin lay on the floor to the right of the Chief's hut bathed in salt, to absorb all the moisture.

The Shona do not waste any part of the animal – the hooves of the sheep are used to balance the stools they sit on while the skin is used as a mat in huts for warmth. The Mutumbus (the insides of the sheep and balls) are also prepared with onions and garlic and they are prize dishes – similar to Tripe. Eyes, ears, nose, mouth and tongue are all eaten too. Waste not, want not.

Soon it was time to pray and for the chief, Nyanga of the village and region, the ancestor's calling was essential. The chief demanded quiet. Only the crackling of the fire remained and the heavy breathing of dance. We all stood around the chief and the Nyanga. Bones were thrown onto the gravel and the way they fell spelt out the message from the ancestors. The whole tribe stared transfixed. I sensed Nyika stiffen. I could see flames burning in the reflection of the tribe's eyes while sweat glistened on their bodies. It was so intense; so surreal. I stared – hungrily taking it all in.

The Nyanga, after slaughtering a chicken, poured the blood over himself and Nyika. It splashed over Nyika's head running down her face. I felt rather privileged to have witnessed such an intimate occasion. The red blood continued to trickle down Nyika's face and body; it represented her acceptance that her son had gone. That he was now dead to her. Dead to this tribe. Dead to me. Dead to his mother.

The other women gathered around Nyika providing her with emotional support. Without any warning, a spirit took the body of the Nyanga and his voice changed completely. The message uttered by this deep, resonating voice was clear.

In Shona he said, 'Kudzai is lost to us. He has gone. There was that word again. Gone. What does it mean? Stay away from him and his new family. They are nothing but trouble. Drink this potion Nyika and your love for your son will be long forgotten. You may bare another son or another daughter one day. 'Be still woman. Be still.

Soon after drinking the potion given to her by the Nyanga, from a long brown homemade pottery jug, Nyika entered a trance-like state. She closed her eyes and seemed to lose consciousness. The women caught her and carried her to her hut. Nyika was dribbling the last portion of the potion from the side of her mouth. The women laid her gently down on the bed. Now that her mind had been tricked, sleep came striding in holding her hostage. They covered her with a warm croquet blanket and tucked her in at the sides. Later in the night, not only Nyika, but the entire compound would awaken to another tormenting session. Nobody expected this unwanted visit of a wolf dressed in sheep's clothing.

What was in that potion? What was that concoction? To this day I have no idea, but it worked, she had passed out. The festivities continued well into the night. I was escorted back home by one of the other women. Her name was, Isabella. She was a half-sister of Nyika's, from the Chiefs second marriage. She was kind, thoughtful and real. My mother met me at the door of the kitchen. Thanking Isabella warmly, she drew me into her arms, caressed my head planting a kiss on my temple and said, "There you go!" Goodbyes are at times not the easiest.

'Your evening must have been mind-blowing, for a child turning 7, what a tremendous tradition you just witnessed and were a part of, I am so proud of you Joe' she said. 'And I'm sure you have a great deal to share with us. But tomorrow is another day, and I am exhausted after having all those soldiers here, feeding the army, literally actually and bandaging up all the victims of two days prior brainwashing sessions in the compound by the terrorists. Blessing is also bombed out. Shower time, madame, then come and drink your warm milk and honey in the kitchen with the rest of us. I think tomorrow instead of breakfast, let everyone sleep in and we meet for brunch at 11 a.m. We all need some peace and quiet. Nyika will be off for a week or two. Joe, that means no visiting Nyika, at her hut in the compound.'

After showering, I felt a lot lighter emotionally. I would always miss Kudzai. But that had been his funeral. I had said goodbye. If our paths were to cross again, it was Mwari's will.

I walked into my bedroom to find Wednesday the cat on my bed fast asleep. I wondered if she did anything else or did she just sleep. Eat fairies and sleep. Chico was with my siblings. They would be leaving the day after tomorrow, to go back to boarding school. The festivities of the compound had come to an end. The night was quiet.

My mother would definitely insist on an early night tomorrow, so they would be fully rested in time to start school.

We finished our warm milk and honey that evening and went to bed.

Waking up to the sound of brunch being prepared. I had slept way too late!

My mother was a natural when it came to making meals look beautiful and also tasting delicious. The smell of fresh bread and scones wafted through the house. Jars of homemade strawberry jam sat on the table, the smell of crispy bacon hung in the air, the sizzle of French toast played in the background. Fresh glasses of orange juice lined the table. A huge bouquet of roses from my mother's rose garden sat in the antique vase at the centre of the table. My sister's words were lost in the first rumble of my stomach. We all sat down, said grace and tucked in. The atmosphere was pleasant. Blessing had also taken the day off.

After brunch we played croquet in the garden until curfew, which was 6 p.m. We had high tea with cucumber sandwiches and chocolate cake. We buggered around all afternoon.

I missed Nyika and looked forward to her return. It would be a while. Later on, we moved inside our house, meandering through the maze of concrete walls that surrounded it, laughing. My brother and father started to play a game of chess. My mom and I started making tomato soup for dinner. My sisters finished their final beauty manoeuvres. Lastly, we gathered in the kitchen,

Blessing would come in tomorrow to say goodbye to everyone. We sipped our soup elegantly like well-mannered children from our ladles, savouring the flavours. My siblings savouring the family moment. All vaguely wishing that they were already amongst their peers. They adored home and the farm, but they loved high school.

The convoy to Fort Victoria, which was down the road about 5 kilometres from our house, left at dawn. A convoy was the norm during the war, all cars travelled with armoured vehicles. Per convoy, there was one armoured vehicle for every ten cars or so. There was the leopard security vehicle that looked remarkably like a dung beetle, a dung beetle is roundish, with short wing covers, that expose the abdomen. This vehicle looked incredibly awkward, it was landmine proof, so it had roll bars, appearing unstable, just as the beetle was. How it got named the Leopard was beyond me. Imagine a round beetle on wheels with rollbars and bang you have your Leopard security vehicle.

Then there was the Rhino vehicle, used mostly by police, robust and cylindrical with a large front it really did look like a rhino. Last but not least, there was the crocodile. It had a long slender shape as if representing the snout of a croc. It somehow also appeared a tad prehistoric. I am sure I do not have to explain why. All the cars appeared in the usual military camouflage colours. All were bullet proof and landmine proof. I had taken a ride as a kid in every one of these military cars. When you are late for a convoy they do not wait. Missing a convoy could literally mean you live or die.

When you sit in your car in a convoy it's as if you are sitting on cracking ice. You look up into the kopjes (hills) surrounding the roads looking like Dali's Sculptures, rocks balancing uncannily on one another! We in the cars, sitting ducks. Target practice. My mother and I missed a convoy on one occasion and not only that but twenty minutes into our drive we had a flat tyre. I recall my mother changing that tyre at the speed of light Max Verstappen would have put her on his team immediately. Fortunately, we made it home in one piece. My mom put her foot down and we defied gravity. I hung onto the handle above the door for dear life. Finally catching up with the convoy. The army boys gave my mom a loving and partly relieved scolding. They knew my father well. It was very serious and particularly terrifying to miss a convoy. This never occurred to my knowledge again.

As there are a lot of hills in Zimbabwe and terrorists would ambush these convoys regularly from carefully selected lookout points in the hills (kopje's), The mornings my mother and siblings left were always chaotic. Someone invariably forgot something and it was always important enough to come home and search for it. 'How so?' I thought. Surely it was stupid considering you should not be late for a convoy, each to their own: a hockey stick, tennis racquet, wallets and once a trunk. I have heard that sometimes students are locked in these and rolled down the boarding school staircase. "Initiation" they called it – and it became more and more cynical as the years went by. Some adults to this day reminisce fondly over their initiations, it all seems more like corporal punishment as far as I'm concerned. How it somehow shaped them. It terrified me and did not shape me at all. I don't see how pushing a ten-cent piece down a 100-metre-long corridor with your nose, shapes you, it wastes your time and you do not get to keep the ten-cent piece, that used to bother me quite a bit.

Reflecting back on my boarding school days, it was more the Afrikaans bullies that were the problem, not any initiation or corporal punishment. The Afrikaner is a special breed. Thousands of Trumps, it doesn't get more of a nightmare than that!

So, the trunks were packed. I loved watching the packing of the trunks. A trunk is a large black metal suitcase a meter and a half long and a foot deep and a foot wide. With your name in big bold white letters on the lid of the trunk. As an example: for you fortunate readers who never had to brave boarding school and a reminder for those who did, one's address at school, would read as if written on an envelope: Herman Hagen Jnr. House Oats, Falcon

College, Bulawayo. He was leaving Mas Vegas this year and going to Bulawayo.

I would be lying if I said there wasn't an inkling of jealousy – they were off on their adventures with all their friends. They also got something called a "tuck box." Now that was precious cargo. It was a small square box filled with treats. At the boarding school, it was kept in a large room in a cubby hole and once a week, on a Saturday afternoon, you could line up and take one item out of your tuck box for the weekend. The tuck box was filled with such treats as biltong (dried African deer meat from an Impala or a Kudu), tennis biscuits, fish paste, marmite, homemade crunchies, chocolate logs, jelly tots, jelly powder, condensed milk, Fredo bars, Willard's chips (in all flavours) and absolutely no chewing gum – it was against school policy.

The Peugeot 404 was always packed the evening before leaving for Mas Vegas and Bulawayo. My mother always cooked Hagen Junior's favourite meal on the night of the departure because even if the girls claimed to be on a diet, they all found this dish secretly delicious.

Steak, fried eggs and chips served with a hearty helping of pepper sauce. Herman's plate was piled so high, as if the poor boy would never see food again in his life.

My father was secretly pleased that Hagen Junior was going back to boarding school. With him out of the way, there was a possibility he could have his doting wife back again. Herman Jnr never seemed to chew his food – big mouthfuls would fly down his throat. Then the cheeky bugger would steal from my plate, pretending to distract me.

'Hey, Joe' he would start, 'look at the spider over there, behind you.'

'Where?' I'd reply, looking over my shoulder.

Two mouthfuls nicked.

'Over there. Don't you see it?'

Steak gone.

'I'm looking. Where?'

Last chip… taken.

This would be Susan's last year of school. Hagen Jnr had his O-levels coming up and Samantha had nearly been expelled last term. She had been caught sneaking out after lights out at her hostel. All of her classmates had been gossiping about it over the holiday and the scandal was still on everyone's lips. I heard it on the "party line," the old telephones we had. Bit of eavesdropping every now and then didn't hurt anyone.

When you are at a boarding school you are not allowed to leave the school premises without proper permission. If you are to visit a restaurant or a shop, you needed a parent or relative or a friend physically signing you out on a register and agreeing to take full responsibility for you whilst you are under their wing. Samantha and our cousin had decided they needed some cigarettes. A further crime. My father detested cigarettes. Now this further ruined Samantha's chances of avoiding expulsion – smoking was definitely not allowed and certainly not in school uniform in public. It was shameful.

Samantha and our cousin climbed out of their dormitory window in the middle of the night. They ran down to the kiosk, four blocks from the boarding school's hostels, bought cigarettes (Madison Reds) and four jacks of whiskey. On their way home they had the misfortune to bump into the headmistress – she happened to be going to the kiosk for cigarettes too. Goodbye to the all-girls school. Who wanted to be there anyhow, uptight bunch! Queen something or other the school was called. After some sort of royal family name, that quite honestly in Africa made no sense at all and screamed colonialism. No one except the odd few gave a damn about queen and country.

Samantha was also no longer in Harare, she was in Mas Vegas. The drive for my mom was pretty long. She had to drive the length of the country, not missing any convoys and then on the way back she had to drive alone. Ngwane to Mas Vegas was a 3hr 11 minutes roughly 229.3km. She would stay the night with my grandmother then she was off again, and then finally to Bulawayo which was five and a half hours and about 500km. She would spend a week shopping in Bulawayo and then make the same trip home.

But back to my sister's little charade, getting herself expelled, both sets of parents were called; both daughters were reprimanded. In those days you were given choices for punishment. Firstly, you could get three strikes on your bottom with a sham buck (sort of whip) from the headmistress; this left welts on your thighs and buttocks and stung like hell. It was sore and unpleasant, no doubt about it. However, it was appealing compared to the other punishments, as these went on for weeks. The second option was equally as silly. One could clear stones off the sports fields, every breaktime during your school day for the duration of the school term. You were handed a bucket and under the sweltering sun you placed stone after stone in it. This was to be done no matter the weather and it was tedious and ever so boring. A term was three months on average and this punishment felt like a lifetime. Finally, option three, was writing lines. To me, this punishment is entirely stupid and a complete waste of time and energy with no benefit at all. Let alone a complete and total waste of paper from our precious trees. Every break time you would go and write lines in a book, which was especially assigned with your name on it and the lines were related to your punishment. Samantha's would have been, if she had chosen this punishment: "I will not bunk out. I will not smoke. I will behave like a lady." She would have repeated these lines in writing of course, over and over again, for half an hour every day for a week or more depending on the head teacher's mood. You had to at least have a minimal of two A4 size papers at the end of the time scheduled for this nonsense.

Samantha and our cousin both chose option one. It indeed was sore and unpleasant, but it was over there and then. Next, they were asked politely between tight-lipped expressions of a nervy headmistress to leave the school. As young ladies do not behave as they had. Toodaloo... you are expelled. Remember to pass go... sort of like Monopoly. Simply because smoking in school uniform was reason enough to expel you. Simple as that.

At dinner that night before, they would all be returning to boarding school; Samantha was given a bit of a talking to. She would finish the term in Mas Vegas this year and then she would also go to college in Cape Town the following year to study wellness. Susan, the model student, was told she should look after her siblings better. She was the eldest and the responsibility fell on her shoulders, seeing that her parents were miles away.

It was not as if she had all the responsibility however, our grandmother also helped a lot. Madame Palm Court. Madame Citroen; Madame String of Pearls and Gin and Tonic. Red cherry fingernails and no gutter language. Bowls on Sunday mornings in fresh whites matching hat. Such a charming sport.

The following day came all too soon. Nyika was still not coming to work as she was having some much-needed time out; "bereavement time" almost – time to come to terms with things.

After we stacked the breakfast plates in the kitchen, my mother went back to the cleared large oak dining room table and began to take her AK-47 rifle apart. She needed to clean it before her trip to Mas Vegas and Bulawayo with Susan, Hagen Jnr and Samantha. If she missed the convoy, she would really need her gun and the assault rifle for Susan to use in the case of an ambush.

The dimensions and shape of AK parts vary depending on where the model was bought. Not all AK parts can be used with all AK rifles. My mother had to clean the gun, so she took it apart piece by piece: recoil spring, dust cover, bolt carrier and trunnion. She, cleared the 7.62mm x 39mm rounds, hammer, trigger assembly, magazine catch, Shepard's hook, double checked the energy point for the fire selector, cleaned the gas piston, wiped out the front sight and finally cleared the muzzle. Each piece was spotless. This exercise had been taught to all of us – my siblings had it down to a tee. My sister and brother, Susan and Herman Hagen Jnr, could do it blindfolded, Samantha had no problems either, but we were a lot slower and giggled too much and my mother was an expert. I hated it – the cold feeling of steel in my hands always creeped me out. The gun was nearly as tall as me anyway. When it was time for these "lessons", I would hide in the wash basket. Although, this never worked and I was forced to practice like everyone else. Just not shoot. That would start the following year. I would be eight.

After finishing with the AK47, my mother moved onto the assault rifle. She cleaned the slide, checked the take down notch, checked the slide top notch and the slide stop (on both sides of frame). She slid the rotating take down lever forward and backwards, wiped the trigger guard and filled the magazine with bullets – each one making a distinctive clicking sound as it found its place. Then she put it all back together with one clean swoop. That was good to go. May I add she did this in heels and a summer dress looking like she was off to the horse races and not a convoy that may or may not warrant an ambush. It would be placed in the cubbyhole of the car – a quick and easy reach for Susan if need be.

The magazines were loaded in both guns. Herman Hagen Jnr also kept a shotgun. He had already cleaned it, loaded it and had stocked up on ammunition. He was all set. Safety catches set and double checked.

The following morning everyone was up and as bright as larks. The food basket was packed, along with flasks of tea and freshly boiled eggs, wrapped in tin foil and sprinkled with salt. Clean cold water sat in bottles having been freshly made the night before. No water from our taps was drinkable and had to be treated. We could not drink any of our water without boiling it first. The cock was crowing extra loudly; it seemed to be talking to us – saying goodbye perhaps.

Susan and Herman were, for their age, brilliant. In the absence of our father for this trip, they were going to protect our family all of nineteen and sixteen years of age. Herman Jnr and Susan handled weapons as if they were professionals. Everyone piled into the Peugeot 404. I took a look at my mother – I couldn't believe she was wearing heels. She was dressed so elegantly in her summer dress. Her nails were freshly painted, fingers and toes in matching colours, cherry red and her hair was up in bun, with tendrils of curls hanging loosely down. She was truly beautiful. I'm sure most girls think this about their mother but, in my case, it was actually true. My sisters and I fall short of this particular elegance. That's being blatantly honest.

With the AK-47 beside her, our mother started the car, climbed out the car again, checked the luggage one more time, everything was there. She planted a kiss on my dad's cheek, leaving red lips there. She gave Blessing his final meal plans, again, as if he did not know what to do by now. My mother always held me a bit longer than necessary she told me later in life that she was so afraid it would be the last time she saw me. In reality, that was totally feasible. She climbed back into the car, let off the handbrake and bounced down the driveway. We watched them drive through the front security gate. The fencing that surrounded our isolated home was three meters high, with barbed wire along the top of it. We watched them fly down the road in front of the house. My father mumbled; I don't know why she always has to drive like a bat out of hell. Then they disappeared around the corner.

The shotgun was beside Jnr and the pistol was in the cubbyhole for Susan. Samantha had already put her headphones on – no doubt listening to Kris Kristofferson or Barbara Streisand. Susan and my mother had their music ready too – ABBA.

I was standing next to my father at the doorway, his arm around my shoulder.

'Off they go then,' said my father, and we said a short prayer together to keep them safe.

My father had to go down to the fields, so I would spend the day with Blessing, Chico and Wednesday the cat.

I walked inside. It felt empty and quiet.

'Joe,' said Blessing, 'Your brother left you a surprise. This surprise may happen today or maybe tomorrow... African time!'

We both burst out laughing.

'But for now,' he continued, 'Jazz and scones. Are you ready for some jazzy baking?'

'I have a question, Blessing,' I replied. 'What am I going to do now? Kudzai is fighting for the other team, Susan, Jnr and Samantha are gone, Nyika is resting and even my mum is away now.'

'Joe, we have a plan for you.'

'Who is we?'

'Your brother, Happiness, Truth, Zuvarashe, Chengetai, Chief Marimba and myself. Nyika, had to agree and so did your parents.'

I was bursting at the seams to know what was going on.

'First, jazz, nothing can take place without jazz. Then scones. Then at teatime, you should find out.' I watched Blessing light his massive joint, which he only did when all the cats were away. My father would be out on the farm all day. He took a huge drag and said 'Jazz baby girl, jazz.' I loved the smell of weed.

He looked through the records.

'How about a bit of Chet?'

We baked, danced and sang *Look for the Silver Lining.*

Chapter Six
Soul Saving

Tea – with Nina Simone. Seriously, who else? I'm feeling... a bit sorry for myself. Her voice has gotten me through many a moment, many a hiccup.

Our tea party consisted of Blessing, myself and Nina Simone. Good company. It was 4 p.m. Scones with homemade strawberry jam and whipped cream straight from our home dairy. Unbeatable. No TV – simply because it had not made its unwelcome presence to our part of the world. I gave some cream to Wednesday and a bowl of milk to Chico. We just sat and enjoyed the peace and quiet. Two extra soldiers were arriving later on that evening, in case we were attacked and they would join us for dinner. They were known as bright lights.

Out of the blue, there was a loud knock at the back door – there stood Happiness beaming the biggest smile you have ever seen with two Impala lambs under each arm. Chico went berserk. I got him to relax while Wednesday just licked her paws and looked at us. The security one finds in souls that never change, that absolute, guarantee of consistency and predictableness. Whether you gravitate toward them or not. She always lay on top of the refrigerator with that look – she should have been called Sloppy Chops instead.

And that is how Bambi and Guru, arrived at our back door. It would become a habit of mine to collect injured or orphaned animals. I would bring these back to the house and look after them until they were well enough to be set free. When Happiness had found those two – scared and afraid – he knew just where to bring them. The other animals I had rescued were merely birds, snails, a frog and the odd grasshopper. However, now, we would start with impalas.

Bambi and Guru – I fell in love with them right off the bat. In addition to my promised "surprise," Happiness and Blessing had secretly built an enclosure for Bambi and Guru at the back of the house. It was so cute. They had even roofed it so that in rainy weather they would still be protected. There was fresh cut grass on the ground – their version of hay. A water tin stood in the corner and by the entrance, they had placed two big milk bottles brought straight from our home dairy. My sister, Susan, being the incredible painter she was had painted a mural in the impala's sleeping quarter of me lying down with the impalas snuggled up against me. I suddenly felt really bad that I had given her so much grief. It was beautiful. I would write and thank her. I remembered that over the years she had made me quite a few things: my "Pookie" Blanket, my poncho in rainbow colours and when I was a baby, she croqueted me booties and a jacket. Maybe I should do more from my side too. I had drifted off again. Happiness cleared his throat, 'Joe, earth calling Joe!'

'What happened to their mothers?' I asked Happiness.

'Eaten,' he replied, 'eaten by the chief.'

He sort of swallowed the last words.

'Oh,' I said, 'both of them?'

Happiness nodded.

'Please ask him not to do that again. There must be something else he can eat.'

Mothers are just not an option.

We walked to their enclosure and I gazed lovingly at the two impala lambs as they got a feel for their new home.

'They must be hungry,' I said to Happiness and Blessing, 'let's feed them!'

Guru sucked hard on the teat of the bottle. Milk directly from the dairy, still warm, and full of goodness. I chugged on a glass myself, I was a big fan of the milk from our dairy, warm and fresh. Delicious.

'When did the Chief kill their mothers?' I asked Happiness.

'This morning.'

I was relieved that they had not missed too many feeding times. They were beautiful – so trusting and so gentle. Their eyes, at first fearful, became fearless. They drank every drop. I refilled one more bottle for them to share. They finished that too, though this time more slowly. I could see their eyes becoming heavy.

I lay back on the grass in their enclosure; Bambi and Guru were huddled in close next to me. Their breathing became steady and their eyes closed. I felt needed and less lonely all of a sudden. I wanted to be there for them when they woke up – I knew they would be disorientated and wondering where their mothers were.

I opened my eyes to feel a soft wind blowing and someone, probably Blessing had covered us with a blanket. Nyika had made all of our blankets in the house, she had croqueted, them lovingly in beautiful patterns and colours. They were warm and cosy. I looked through the wire mesh of the enclosure out and up into the African sky. Huge, dark clouds had formed – a thunderstorm was coming our way.

Nothing smells as gorgeous as the first summer rains in Africa. It puts all perfumes to shame. Somehow the mixtures of foliage, dust and animal scents, whipped up by the wind and mixed together, creates the perfect fragrance.

The combination of the short hairs of Guru and Bambi, the dust and the hay made me sneeze an almighty blow. This immediately woke the lambs and they were up on their hooves in a flash. I felt so bad. Their eyes were full of fear and confusion. I soothed them as best as I could.

By now the thunder was rolling like my stomach before lunch, I have been doing intermittent fasting my whole life, without knowing how good for one it was. I had never been a fan of breakfast. The lightening cracked the sky, just as we crack open a boiled egg. The sky was alive. Lightning in our country is filled with woe, our high lightning toll can probably be explained by the prevalence of granite outcrops all over the country. Granite is radio-active and discharges gamma rays up to the clouds, thus ionizing the air molecules. Abundant granite outcrops, together with soot from the numerous kitchen huts, offer the much-needed opposite charge on the ground, while tall objects offer the easiest route for electrical discharge to steer its way to the ground. Loosing up to 100 lives a year in Zimbabwe, we hold the record for the most deaths from a single bolt of lightning. Can you believe it, as if our country needed more bad luck!

Whilst cumulonimbus clouds build up over drought-prone areas, like the one we lived in, it gives you a sense of hope that there may be enough rain for the crops and for us to drink, to live. Our first rains usually break in October, turning the bush into resplendent greens, returning the lowveld to that lusciousness tempering one's mind. Rainy season ends in April. The crickets were back and they had started chirruping and the noise was growing substantially, those little critters make the most nostalgic sound. Love the little buggers.

I used to pray for the sky to open right up when the lightening cracked, hoping to glimpse the other world. Wagner comes to mind.

Guru and Bambi could definitely not stay the night out here. They huddled in towards me. I was staring at the storm weighing my options when my father arrived.

'What are you up to, young lady?'

I looked up at him.

'Dad, can Guru and Bambi sleep in my room tonight?' I asked hopefully. 'This storm will scare them so much.'

My dad gave me that look of, "Well, what can I possibly say?" Fathers can rarely say no to their daughters, if ever. So, he picked up Bambi and I picked up Guru and we walked the five metres to the kitchen.

'They can sleep in the house; not in your room.'

I have learned one thing about my father and our negotiation. He rarely said no but he moved the goal posts ever so slightly, so I got what I wanted but still on his terms.

'If you like, you can sleep with them in the kitchen,' he suggested, 'alongside the wooden stove; it will keep you all warm.'

'OK, Dad,' I replied.

'We can bring your mattress from your bedroom after dinner.'

That evening Guru and Bambi wandered around the kitchen whilst we dined. The bright lights arrived a tad later than planned but still in time for a hot shower and a hot meal. Starving and exhausted. They had fought for a tribal trust land village and ended up in an ambush from terrorists holding a brainwashing session. Their eyes were bloodshot, with red road maps. They smelt of blood and bullets.

Their camouflage of shoe polish rubbed earlier on their faces that morning had now become mixed with sand. Their lips were chapped. The nails mauled. They were called Peter and Peter. The two Pete's. They could barely talk, parched, they downed litres of water. Not missing a beat. I remember thinking they were very handsome. The fact that they had come to rescue or look after us, made it more appealing of course. I showed them to their room and offered to make them a sandwich before dinner. Or at least some biltong. The very good-looking Peter, said that he had to watch his waistline and swaggered off to the shower, towel on like a lady, shower cap and a face mask. I had never seen a man walk that way, nor talk about his waistline. He asked me where the Agric alert was. I showed P, he radioed in. 'Christmas is here!' Hand on hip, just like my mother. A reply came back from my dad in the field. 'Beers in the fridge! However, I do recall you being fonder of

Pimm's P, that is located in the drink's cabinet, please help yourselves!'

For dinner, Blessing had prepared cottage pie – one of my favourite dinners – washed down with a glass of water. Our water always tasted a little bit like mud as it was from the natural spring. My father washed it down with a few scotches. Along with P and Peter.

They looked dashing - especially the one with the swagger, he was picture-perfect like the men in the magazines. I immediately warmed to him. During his stay, he taught me to walk like a diva, to wear lipstick and how to make homemade face masks from cucumbers and avocado. We painted our toenails cherry red like my mom. He could dance like a dream; we danced every night! He taught me drag he called it. Blessing was overjoyed by this prospect and we dragged the days away. You would never think there was a war going on.

One evening we did a show for my dad and Peter. We dressed up and did ABBA, we used my mom's clothes. Blessing too, he looked awesome. They later got elegantly wasted. P could also be heard singing his heart out from the tower adjacent to the house when he was on night shift. Bob Marley and the Wailers would have been so proud of P. I lay in my bed laughing. His bedtime stories for me were also hilarious, about what happened to Cinderella after being married to Prince Charming. It all went to shit, he used to say. You see Bambi and Guru; it all went to shit. He loved the impala lambs.

As all good things come to an end, I had to say bye to P and Peter. I was looking forward to their next visit. I sat on P's knee and did his camouflage for him. He was so fussy, ending in stitches of laughter. I took my mom's lipstick and put it in his pocket, just in case. I smiled. A tear escaped his left eye. Slid down his camouflaged face. I gave it a kiss. Love you P. Then they left. P and Peter on the road again to save souls.

'Will I ever see them again Dad?'

'Maybe and maybe not, trying times Joe.'

That evening my dad decided he would educate me about whiskey. We were not a wine country. I have always loved the smell of whiskey; the clink of ice against a glass and the slosh of the first tot. So elegant. I also like the masculinity of a whiskey glass. The woody vanilla and phenolic of a peated scotch aroma were incredibly appealing to me, to this day, I almost like the smell as much as I enjoy the scent of horse sweat and polished saddles in a horse stable.

When asking for a sip, my father turned to me and said, 'Perhaps in a couple of years.'

'What does it taste like?'

'Well, Joe, on the palate it has a slight ashy character with a dry lingering after taste, it is matured in Bourbon which has a tad of tar in it and that gives off a smoky flavour.'

'Dad, I am nearly eight, it makes no sense, just give me the simple version.'

He smiled and savoured another sip.

'Learn to appreciate the finer things in life, dear.'

He lifted my chin and then planted a kiss on my forehead.

Blessing had moved my mattress from my bedroom to the kitchen and placed it by the wooden stove. The kitchen's concrete floor was painted the colour of rust. A large wooden table stretched down the centre, a collection of copper pots hanging above along with ropes of garlic. It was a large kitchen with a very high ceiling. A basket of firewood sat by the stove – this needed to be checked regularly as snakes tended to use it from time to time to keep warm.

Blessing was once bitten by a tiger snake that had been hiding in there. He had been reaching for some wood for the stove when the surprised snake sunk its fangs into his hand. Fortunately, though very painful their bite is not deadly. He had raced into the dining area, in a flat spin, snake in one hand and his other hand raised in the air. The snake was a tiger snake, flashes of orange and black stripes swung before my eyes. Just another day on the farm.

We had a large pantry in the kitchen stocked with goodies from the town. It was always a room of temptation. My sister Samantha and I discovered a way to get into this room through the outside window. I am sure my mother knew about it but she never once mentioned it.

I climbed into the crisp, cotton sheet bedding on my mattress that was placed close enough to the wooden stove to keep me warm. Bambi, Guru, Chico and Wednesday all surrounded me. Wednesday was missing Samantha- very much. She was never quite herself when my sister was not around and she kept trying to nudge Bambi and Guru away from me. Wednesday was without a doubt the boss of all the animals in this home. Wild or domestic. I looked into Guru's eyes, so gentle. I felt guilty that I loved biltong. She licked the tip of my nose. I laughed. Everyone had been fed and now we drifted off into a deep sleep.

The cockerel crowed, the sun peaked over the horizon and a new day appeared. Daring an encore. Wednesday stretched herself out over the two deer nudging them awake and Chico had already gone out through the trap door of the kitchen door. I could hear him barking outside. He had taken well to Bambi and Guru. They were now part of the gang.

Still in my pyjamas, I eased myself up and walked to the dairy at the back of our house. Sleep was still lodged in my eyes and I had to fetch them their milk. They fed eagerly. For the rest of the day between mealtimes they followed me around everywhere. They pranced around the garden, chased and mock charged Chico (especially the male Bambi).

Time passed – as it invariably does – and the deer grew strong. Soon, they had reached the age of no longer being allowed in the kitchen as they left their droppings everywhere. I would clean these up and put them in the compost heap that we used for our vegetable garden at the back of the house. Bambi and Guru got into my mother's peas, beans and lettuces one day – she was seriously pissed off. There was nearly biltong made from Bambi and Guru.

When my mother returned from Mas Vegas, she was pleased to see Bambi and Guru and happy to see me in such good spirits. Nyika was now in better spirits too, she arrived back home the same day as my mom. She had accepted her heart-breaking situation as much as that is ever possible living with pain as sharp as a needle; it takes somewhat of a certain character. I noticed Nyika became closer and even warmer than she already was to me. I enjoyed that. I also understood why. I loved her even more so. Bambi and Guru were never released into the wild. They remained with us and even moved with us to our next home.

I enjoyed the responsibility that came with animal management – the unconditional love they give back to you; the trust they have for you. It also gave my life meaning – a purpose. Being busy was taking my mind off everyone being away and I was no longer feeling sorry for myself – I was not alone now. What is so refreshing about animals is that they don't lie. In some ways they are better company than human beings – they don't let you down, and none of them would ever become child soldiers. They don't need constant reassurance, acknowledgement and attention. I say that as I need all of that desperately at times and those who say they don't are talking codswallop.

The next little critter to arrive in my growing menagerie was a beautiful chameleon. We named him Sir Chameleon Dilepis (Camo for short) and I loved him immediately. He walked in perfect rhythm to the jazz music that Blessing would play and we danced to the likes of Nina Simone and Aretha Franklin on more than one or two memorable occasions. Blessing (a bit of a distance between him and Camo though) with the odd drag move, Bambi, Guru, Wednesday and Chico accompanied me on dances on the lawn, generally giving me very puzzled stares.

Camo's arrival in our lives came completely out of the blue, out of thin air. Literally so – he landed in my lap while I was swinging on my swing under the Shepherd Tree. While I was all smiles and shrieks of delight, Nyika was quite the reverse. She turned an odd shade of grey, screamed and abruptly bolted from where we were around the side of the house. Oh, it must me another terrorist? But no...

She yelled at the top of her voice: 'Maiwe! Maiwe! Maiwe!' (translated it means, 'God, help me! Oh my God!')

Happiness and Blessing came to see what all the commotion was about, thinking naturally it was a snake or a terrorist. Blessing armed with a rifle and Happiness armed with a badza (a type of shovel for gardening). Then they all turned that same shade of grey and too ran away shouting, "Maiwe! Maiwe!" Oh my god! Oh my God! Not really the direct translation, but something along those lines.

Was I missing something? Clearly, I was. I went to my mother in her office, knocked on the door and told her what happened. She laughed out loud.

'Joe, Shona people are terrified of chameleons,' she said, still grinning. 'It's a superstition. It's said, they believe that the chameleon was sent by God to tell them that they would live for eternity. However, the chameleon took so long, as its gait is extremely slow so God then sent the lizard to tell the tribes that they would die. The chameleon is blamed for this.'

I watched my mother chuckling to herself.

'They see this gorgeous reptile as an incredibly bad omen – hence the screams and the shrieks. The poor chap is blamed for everything.'

It is a rather bizarre looking creature with its roll around eyes and always outstretched palm as if to shake your hand. Camo's tongue was so fast – like a blur – when it was reeling in prey. I tried to replicate it – trying to catch cookie crumbs with my tongue – but failed miserably, of course, the things we do to occupy ourselves.

We could always see when he was communicating (long distance calls we called it) – when he quickly alternated between bright colours. We needed phones and the Shona people needed drums. He just needed his own unique design.

African Drums served as an early form of long-distance communication, not only for ceremonial and religious functions. Surprising many a European expeditioner. A drum message can be transmitted at the speed of 100 miles in an hour. During slavery drums were banned because they were being used by slaves to communicate over long distances in a code unknown to the bastards in this trade. Talking drums as explained by Andreus Bauer in the "Street of Caravans." Drum communications are fascinating, they are languages in their own right and are based on actual natural language. The sounds that are produced are conventionalized signals based on speech patterns. The messages are very much stereotyped and context dependent. Often, they can transfer a message using the tonal phonemes alone. It's simply as so:

In certain languages, the pitch of each syllable is uniquely determined in relation to each adjacent syllable. In these cases, messages can be transmitted as rapid beats at the same speed as speech, as the rhythm and melody both match the equivalent spoken utterance. Misinterpretations can occur. But in normal speech too. In practice, not all listeners understand all of the stock phrases; the drum language is understood only to the level of their immediate concern. The next time you pick up a drum you will know a little more about what precious craft you hold in your hands. As far as I am concerned, music is the best way to communicate. The Chief had spent so many hours with Kudzai and I trying to explain to us the drum calls. We managed one. It was extremely difficult. As I was still not Shona fluent. I looked at Camo balancing on my shoulder. Sometimes he would climb onto my head and just sit there for ages.

Camo's changing colours reminded me of the perfection nature shares with us. When the brightest colours appear in the pigment cells, the miniature crystals are moved in order to reflect different wave lengths and therefore colours of light. Camo is the Wizard of Oz and possibly the Mr Bell too of the reptile world and so it came to be that Camo became my wizard (and I became Joe in Wonderland Bush Africa). He would perch all day on my shoulder sometimes venturing onto my head. One added bonus of this was that I was never bothered by flies (and especially Mopani flies that tend to buzz around your head in the heat in enormous numbers trying to gather the liquid from your eyes which is incredibly annoying).

When Nyika, Blessing and Happiness finally came home it was with much trepidation. They were calling from a safe distance of 100 metres asking if the coast was clear. After a rather tiring debate, it was agreed that Camo would live with me and he was free to come and go as he pleased. Bath times were in my favour, as Nyika supervised these and she refused to come to my room or the bathroom with Camo there. Sometimes Camo, landed in the bath, not by choice, but he did look cute with bath bubbles on his head. He would then find his way to my leg, then arm, then to his pot plant, and rock arrangement in the corner of the room.

Camo's entry to our lives was sudden, dramatic and a blaze of shrieks, shouts and colours. His exit – a couple of weeks later – was just as sudden. He fell in love, left my side and was never seen again.

My Wizard of Oz left me and bath times went back to normal. My alter ego – Joe in Wonderland Bush Africa – became a little bored not having him around to place on different coloured surfaces and cast my magic spells on the Tokoloshe. However, it wasn't long before the next character came along.

He was called Bolt. My father rescued him and brought him into our lives. Driving home in his Land Rover after cotton picking season, my father noticed a very young and very small tortoise on the road. Growing up in the wilderness you learn to see animals even when they are camouflaged. You subconsciously search the bush, looking out for animals – my father called this, "keeping your eyes peeled."

Bolt was, of course, the fastest tortoise known to mankind. Well, this is what I would tell everyone anyway, 'Bolt can actually sprint, you know.' When my father spotted him, he braked sharply causing the Land Rover to stall. Stalling, he turned the key to restart the engine but it just gave a pathetic whirring sound. This is not the sound you want to hear close to sunset and in a war. Nevertheless, he stepped out the Landy to go and see the little chap.

He was tiny, probably a newborn. My father searched the area for his mother but there was no sign. Just as he was about to give up, he spotted her being feasted upon by a crow. Crows pick up the tortoise in their claws, fly up relatively high and drop the tortoise on a rock until the shell smashes open. The rock acts as a nutcracker so to speak. Then they can eat the meat.

My father carefully picked up Bolt and climbed back in the Land Rover. It wouldn't start. He gave the engine a bit of a rest but still no life. At this point my father was feeling rather nervous – we were in the middle of a civil war and night was approaching. Not only that, a storm was on its way too. *All this for a bloody tortoise!* I'm sure this is what he was thinking, cursing his luck and perhaps his over-zealous stupidity about perhaps bringing a baby tortoise home for me.

Luckily, he had the walkie talkie in the car. He radioed home for Truth or Zuvarashe to come with jump leads to start the Land Rover. It didn't take them very long to reach my father. They jump started the car and soon they were on their way home, fortunately having not encountered an ambush.

It had been a long day in general. My father (who was always dressed elegantly on the farm, with his linen shorts, cotton shirt, neutral colours) took off his hat, washed his hands and combed his hair with the comb he carried, lodged on the inside of his long socks, all the time. It's a memory I hold dear. I had never seen my father a mess. His hair was always perfect. He used to say, we may live in the middle of nowhere but it is absolutely no excuse to let yourself go. I wish I had been given this comb, after he passed, but I got what matters most, his determination. To this day, even when I eat alone, I set the table, cutlery, crockery, glass all correctly in place, OCD playing havoc. You never know who will arrive and believe me we have had very colourful characters arrive out of the blue.

My father had earned the nickname 'Slick' because even if we lived in the 'sticks' he always appeared as a well-groomed gentleman. What a charmer.

'Joe!' he called. 'Guess what I found.'

I ran to the kitchen. By now, Bambi and Guru were sleeping and free roaming around our garden, so only Chico hurried behind me, goodness knows where Wednesday was.

'Close your eyes,' he continued when he saw me, 'and open both hands in front of you.'

I did. He placed something cold and hard in my hand.

'Open your eyes!'

I was amazed. A baby tortoise. I had never seen one before and it was adorable. So dinky. It would fit in my doll's house – it could be Barbie's new pet – and he could sleep there. Bolt and Barbie became firm friends. He also had fresh lettuce and tomatoes from our garden.

Each day, I would take him for walks. One step walks, one step of my stride to begin with as they took all day. Slowly he grew bigger and he grew stronger. He developed a fetish for the sprinkler in our garden and if I could not find him, I would turn the sprinkler on and he would bolt across the lawn to the sprinkler and bathe in it. He thought it was another tortoise. The joy of raising wild animals.

Bolt remained with us for good.

Shortly after Bolt's introduction to our family, my brother's interest in snakes increased. This was not too difficult as all he had to do was go outside with my eldest sister and they would see a snake. Crazy as it sounds, she was like a snake magnet, well so the story goes.

I can clearly recall my first incident with Jnr's python. Jnr had picked me up from the dairy in his Land Rover. It had been given to him at the age of sixteen to do errands for my dad and so he could learn to drive properly. We all had it at some point. It was compulsory that all farm children learned to drive from the age of twelve.

He told me to climb onto the front seat for the drive home. I could not move the sack that was on my seat as I had a bottle of milk in my hand. My brother didn't offer to take it, so I just sat on top of the sack. The sack was from the cotton-picking bales used when the cotton is transported to the mills. It was not a long drive, maybe 2 kilometres and when we arrived at home, Jnr was killing himself laughing. I climbed out the car.

'What is it?'

When finally, he could tell me, he muffled, 'You've been sitting on my python since we left the dairy.'

He then immediately collapsed laughing again. I was speechless.

To have a fear of snakes is called ophidiophobia; I don't have that but I really would have preferred not to have been sitting on this reptile. It's Africa's largest serpent and can grow up to six metres. It is able to attack and swallow an infant the size of a full-grown sheep, thankfully this is rare.

The python is a fascinating creature. It is non-venomous and kills by strangling you to death although you die of cardiac arrest, rather than by asphyxiation. You have a heart attack of course, who wouldn't. It mostly feeds on birds, bats and medium-sized creatures. Larger pythons may feed on chickens, warthogs, dogs and even smaller crocodiles. A big meal can take months to digest.

The Pied Python stayed with us for a number of weeks in my brother's room in a glass cage, a very large glass cage, decorated as if it was outside. My father said he could stay long enough for us to learn about him. Then, as it was a protected species, we were to let it back out into the wild. Preferably in the original surroundings that he had found the python in the first place. My father was not impressed by this new venture. Wild animals belong in the wild. So true. So obvious. Was a tortoise not a wild animal?

The day came to let Pied Python go, he was so handsome and interesting. Jnr put him back in a sack and put it in the back of the Land Rover. We would be taking him back to his original home area, we didn't drive far from the house as we were still in a civil war, and my brother had originally found him not far from our house. My brother had his FN rifle – I could also shoot with it now. We had a few cans in the back of the car and were going to do a bit of target practice after letting Pied go. I really did not enjoy this, I despised guns. I still do. Hands over ears eyes shut. Mind somewhere else, what's new. I always tagged along but never participated. After all my big brother was my hero. Maybe I thought that this "edge" I felt for guns and the noise they make would dissipate if I confronted it. It never did.

We opened the sack, pulling it back with a long stick with a hook on it. We waited and waited, until finally, Pied's tongue could be seen darting in and out – his long black fork. We had bought a dead chicken along for his farewell dinner. I was not sure if they ate dead food? Either way it made me feel better for him. Not letting him loose on an empty belly.

After setting Pied free, we jumped into the Land Rover and went to practice target shooting. Nyika was relieved. She was worried the entire family had lost their minds. First Camo and now Pied Python. However, during their stay with us, I had the opportunity to teach Nyika the importance of all these creatures in the ecosystem, from my childish point of view. She knowing way more than me already, she listened patiently and lovingly, encouraging me always. Under the shepard tree, me and my miniature black board. Nyika spread the word amongst her tribe that chameleons were not an evil spirit and that snakes were very important. Nobody listened of course.

There were a couple of snakes after Pied but thank goodness this period of Jnr's life came to an end. It didn't end though without one or two more pranks on me.

We used to "apple pie" each other's beds for fun. My brother, though, took it to another level. He had a harmless brown house snake in his room. It was totally harmless – like a big worm – probably about 60 cm long. One evening, he put it at the bottom of my bed between my sheets. I happened to be dozing off. Naturally, the snake was attracted by my warmth. It decided to sidle on up to me.

I screamed bloody murder in absolute silence as one should remain dead still whilst in a snake encounter. Naturally I could not see what species it was, so I didn't know if it was poisonous or not. It never occurred to me for a split second that this could be a typical brother prank? I couldn't move, terrified I would be bitten. I had no idea that my brother would have done this and was sure it had slithered in from outside. Surely, he was not that crazy.

The family were all in on it and they arrived in the room in fits of laughter. I had to laugh in the end as well. Thinking they were all stark raving mad. They had been waiting impatiently outside my bedroom door stifling giggles.

Later on that year, my father decided to go into ostrich breeding, so along came all the chicks and naturally some adults too. Thankfully, they mostly survived the incredibly long journey. Only two chicks died. Young ostriches are extremely vulnerable. One little guy arrived in need of nursing back to health – but it seemed all he needed was some tender loving care. They are such ugly birds when they are young. Ugly and beautiful at the same time. All legs and eyes.

After a few days of wandering around the house, my mother had had enough and said he should be returned to his friends. Nyika had been seen chasing him around the garden after he ate her lunch that she left on the outside table. Even though she was a good runner, you cannot outrun an ostrich - try as much as you like. I watched them up and down the front lawn. She gave up in a heap in the end. The chick, nicknamed Fred, was just over half a meter in size and we fed him tit bits from the table, being omnivorous they consume a variety of plants and animals. Due to the fact that they were to be released back into the wild, we had to maintain their natural diet. One of our jobs was to gather, grasshoppers, shrubs, plant roots and succulents. At night the light in their pens was put on for a while, it attracted moths, which they need to eat. Lizards, frogs and snakes were everywhere, so they wondered into their outdoor pens naturally. They never went without. They swallowed stones (small pebble's), which is part of their diet to breakdown various foods. This is because they are gastroliths, a direct translation is "stomach stones" Like many birds it does not have teeth, these stones and grit are held in the muscular part of their body called the gizzard. Stones etc are all digested they eventually break down and then are replaced by more stones, sand and grit.

Blessing and Nyika. had told me that under no circumstance, is cleaning up bird shit part of their job description, I laughed at their expressions. I knew it was my job to clean up their... guano. I had another, more pleasant job which was to turn the eggs in the incubator. I loved this job, I found it absolutely fascinating. So did Nyika. We once asked my dad if we could make a fried egg just from one egg, he was not amused. That would have been a costly egg.

Fully grown male and female ostriches arrived too and were put in their large pens as they needed a lot of space. During mating season, they can be incredibly aggressive, so we were told it was best to stay out of their pens and out of their way completely. If you think Greta Thunberg kicks ass, you should see an ostrich, nothing quite like it!

Nyika accompanied me during my egg turning duties. The rest of their turning was done at night by the next person on duty.

Finally, the day came for the eggs to hatch. Nyika and I waited eagerly wondering which egg would get a crack at life first. Then it happened. To watch life struggle through a shell and peek its tiny head out – it's very moving. We were cheering, 'Yeah push it, oh baby!' Screaming at the top of our lungs. Honestly, we laughed so hard. Salt-N-Pepa? It's the same feeling you get when you watch your child compete in a race and they win, against all the odds. We watched it slowly emerge from the shell – its huge eyes and half bald head, its long skinny neck poking out, craning to see what's around it; its animal instincts kicking in.

Then one sunny day, in strolled "Bird." He was a Ground Hornbill, he originally belonged to a Mrs Loving Hamm. My sister Susan's mother-in-law. He had broken his wing and could no longer fly. However, being a ground hornbill, that was probably not the end of the world. His wing mended but he never left. He was such a character; he would join me on the swing or he would even go on the swing himself. He loved that swing. He would walk Nyika to and from the compound. Free as a bird.

We once had a soldier with platinum blonde hair. Bird took an immediate disliking to him and chased him at every opportunity. What a hilarious sight, this grown man running away from a Ground Hornbill bird in hot pursuit. Nyika and I would collapse laughing in a heap. Bird also made himself at home in the kitchen and if Blessing was preparing a stew, he would stand alongside him by the huge wooden stove and wait for Blessing to feed him cut offs from the meat.

He even learned to knock at the back door or on the windows using his huge beak to be let into the house. He also accompanied us on game drivers perching himself on the tire at the front of the Land Rover. It never occurred to him to fly away or to fend for himself again. During locust season, my pet fear so to speak, he would snap them up in his huge beak and I would find some sort of pleasure in that. God, how I detest those creatures, they give me the heebie-jeebies and they come in swarms, sometimes covering entire trees. Eating everything in sight! I am damaged by them. To say I am terrified of them is an understatement. If I see a locust, this is probably a second occasion that you will see me able to run!

One unfortunate incident of having one stuck in my hair and having to wait for it to kick and scratch its way to death was enough to do my head in. Its legs with those tiny thorns kicking against my neck. It gave forever, an entire new time frame, it gave forever an actual meaning, because once it becomes entangled in your hair, it's impossible to get it out, your hair acts as a spider web for it, so you just have to wait to let it die, then cut it out, whilst it struggles, the spikes on its legs get tangled in your hair.

Bird lived to a ripe old age and he was always around. Sadly, one day he had an encounter with a cobra and didn't live to tell the tale. Nyika and I wrapped him in a sheet, dug a deep hole next to the shepherd tree and buried him there. We marked his grave with a Shona sculpture of a hornbill. Carved by one of the incredible sculpturing artists surrounding Mas Vegas. Under the shepherd tree was his favourite place. Close to the swing. I missed him on walks to the dairy and the kitchen felt empty without him.

There were no animals to rescue for a long time until one rather sad incident. Happiness arrived at the back door announcing that a Kudu (a large deer) was trapped in the canal that ran from a dam nearby (the Manjarenji Dam) to the farm to supply our irrigation system. The kudu had tried to jump over the canal and in doing so its hoof had lodged into the grid and it had fallen into an awkward position. We all jumped into the Land Rover and the entire family tried to help the Kudu out of the canal. We sedated him so that he would be more relaxed around humans. After a long while, and after all of our efforts, it became clear that the Kudu could not be removed. My father shot him. It was the kindest thing to do. To remove his body, we had to saw his hoof out the grid. In life, sometimes it is better to be cruel than to be kind.

Peepo – the night ape – arrived at dinner time. My father sat down at the table – we were all there waiting for him – looking prim and proper. We were taught that it was important to maintain standards of appearance, even if you lived in the middle of nowhere. Yes, you have to hear it again. There we sat, all fresh and clean, faces scrubbed, hair parted and combed, all smelling of Lux beauty soap. My mother was freshly sprayed with Blue Grass perfume – the frangipani's fragrances filling the air. This scent was combined with the wafts of the Yesterday, Today and Tomorrow plant in all its glory!

The oak wood table was set out in its usual style, sufficiently good enough china, silver wear passed down, crisp white serviettes and a tablecloth. The ice was melting in the silver water jug. Meal times never failed to make me a tad anxious. "Manners maketh a man and a woman. For what we are about to receive may the Lord make us truly grateful." We laid our serviettes across our laps, then the magic happened. Peepo peeked out of my father's shirt. I screeched with delight. We all did. We all laughed. He was the cutest and most adorable munchkin I had ever laid eyes on. He looked like a Monchichi.

My oldest sister had an enormous collection of them and she was nearly twenty-one. My father gave him a carrot from his plate. He immediately popped it into his mouth and looked up pleadingly for another one. Peepo. He was a legend. He ruled the roost. This put Wednesday out a bit. He attended every meal time till eventually he was allocated the baby chair at the table.

Peepo was never any trouble. He slept with us in turns, rode along on Chico's back, slept curled up next to Wednesday the cat, came on car journey's with us and he even had fans in Mas Vegas at my siblings' school. He was well-known at Palm Court, my grandmother's café/restaurant. He was even served his own fruit salad when we lunched there. Peepo's favourite thing was homemade ice-cream. His eyes would light up whenever this came his way.

Nyika also loved Peepo very much. I caught her once talking to him telling him about her day. Spotting me, she immediately pretended that she had been muttering under her breath and not talking to a night ape. She even made him his own croquet blanket and pillow for his shoebox bed.

'I heard you Nyika,' I said, laughing. 'And I saw you! Ha ha! Got you!'

Peepo enjoyed terrorising Blessing. His favourite trick was to jump out of the pots that hung above the long table in the kitchen. He would wait and just at the right moment he would leap out at Blessing, copper pots flying in all different directions.

He would curse him sometimes and say, 'You are going to be in my stew one day, Mr!'

Peepo even met Truth, Zuvarashe and Chief Marimba. He attended a rain dance with me. We found ourselves facing a severe drought and I went tribal with Nyika, we slaughtered the sheep, the Nyanga prepared the Chikokiyana (homemade Shona Aacohol). It is said to contain methylated spirits but the Chief assured me this was not the case, he had made it from the fruit of the marula (Sclerocarya Birrea, indigenous to the miombo woodlands of Southern Africa) trees. We danced to beckon and plead with the gods for rain. We danced every day for a week and the rain arrived. Unbelievable? We danced in that rain as if it were holy water. Once in a while, Peepo would take a bath with me but he did not enjoy it too much. He did enjoy trying to catch the bubbles from the side of the bath; more often than not that's how we got him into bath as he would inevitably fall into the bath water.

Peepo brought a great deal of joy to our lives until sadly he died of old age. He was so beloved we even carved a small coffin for him and my mother wrapped him up in royal blue velvet. The whole family attended the funeral; he was buried alongside Bird. No matter how tough a man you were, there was not a dry eye in sight at this small funeral for our adorable night ape – not even the chief; not even my father. However, more adventures and guests were to arrive.

My story of the three little pigs is rather different to the famous tale. Once again, my father was driving home when a mother warthog ran across the road with her three piglets. At the last moment my father tried to brake but unfortunately it was in vain. The mother warthog and two of her babies were hit by the Land Rover and died on impact. The other little chap, well he survived, but was squealing terribly and was obviously in a great deal of pain and distress.

After countless rugby dives and attempted tackles in the bush, my father managed to grab a hold of him and calm him down. The thought of rugby makes me smile there was never a Sunday without the rugby news or discussion. My father and brother had played the sport religiously. He administered a sedative and soon the little chap was lying on the Land Rover passenger seat and on the way home to us. It was a joy to have Pig – his name, Pig.

Pig had to have been the runt of the litter. He had so much character and he quickly became Chico's new best friend. They spent hours running around with one another. Nyika was beside herself.

'I have to deal with a Pig now too; Joe, what has gotten into you? Have you gone mad? I think you are taking your Bible stories a little too seriously, Noah's Arc in particular. What next?'

Like Peepo, he would take baths with me too. Much to Nyika's total and utter disgust. I have now seen it all, bathing with a pig who would have thought, people would do that? She laughed and kissed me on the head. She never attended bath time with Pig and I again.

'It's a pig, Joanna, a dirty, stinky Pig,' she scolded.

She refused to join me on these occasions. He was gorgeous, would wake you up with grunts and push against your face until you woke up. He was always with me during my home schooling and he allowed me to lie against his stomach under the shepherd tree. If he wanted your attention, he would give you a nudge. He grew up to be rather big and strong – overtaking Chico (our husky) in size – but they were still best buddies. Pig was allowed anywhere in the house.

This part of my childhood was unbeatable. Our family was together, we were laughing so often, we had not been attacked for weeks, the sun was shining, and my father's crops were doing well. The chief was considering allowing us to build a school for the children of the village so they could join me for school on the air with the BBC – to learn to read and to write. To give them a fighting chance in life. A head start.

Chapter Seven
The Shade of a Shepherd Tree

The shepherd tree is my all-time favourite tree in Africa officially known as the boscia albitrunca. Most of my learning and great moments of my young life took place under this tree. My shepherd tree grew at the bottom of our garden. My childhood swing hung from it made from a tractor tire by Happiness and Truth. We nearly died under this tree with Nyika when the terrorists attacked us.

Nyika and I had our tea parties religiously here. In the shade of the tree every single day at 4 p.m., unless it was raining. I would take out my play tea set with its tiny cups and saucers on its little tray accompanied by a fairy cake from Blessing or a crunchie made by my mother.

Nyika never cooked except in the compound. She had no talent for cooking, but she made the best sadza and nyama (meat, mostly from goats, sheep or cattle) that I ever tasted. To this she added tomato and onion gravy and sometimes a vegetable called rape – it was healthy but tasted bitter. I think it's part of the kale family.

At times we had sadza and nyama under the tree. It is the staple diet of the people in Zimbabwe – everyone loves it, if you don't there must be something wrong with you! What's great about eating sadza is you get to use your hands. You roll the sadza, which is a stiff porridge of maize into the size of a golf ball. You roll it up tight and then you dip it into some gravy, grab a piece of meat with that and add a portion of rape onto it, then pop it into your mouth - delicious. So tasty. Such a treat. And it really fills you up. Somehow, being allowed to eat with your hands seems to make it taste even better. After being brought up strictly British, so to speak, a chance to "break the rules" and eat with your hands is a real pleasure. I prefer it! We were brought up British but we did not have a British bone in our bodies. Food somehow just tastes better when you eat it with your hands. Citizens of a British Colony are often more British than the British themselves, even if they come from German/ Dutch or Irish descent. The French and Italians never caved to this way of life. The first time I tasted pasta I was 10. The first time I ever tasted Asian food I was nineteen. On a date with some guy trying to master chop sticks, how embarrassing truly. Out of nervousness I ordered nearly the entire menu hoping it would take forever, to avoid eating with chopsticks at all. Only to be handed a spoon by the waitron.

At home it was a staple diet, mostly following a combination of German, British and Dutch dishes. Roasts were every Sunday religiously, I only stopped having roasts when I moved to Cape Town and in all honesty preferred to have fish, fresh from the market in Kalk Bay. I do miss mushy peas though, cannot seem to find them anywhere in Europe, nor sugar bean salad. I miss my mother's food the most. I would give my back teeth to have her food one last time. My eldest sister cooks a lot like her, so at least that's a plus. Sadza does not exist in Europe or Asia. Not at all. Nor anywhere I have gone since leaving Zimbabwe, so up in smoke with that too.

My eyes drifted from up in the tower down into the garden. I loved that tree. The shepherd tree can grow up to seven metres tall. The leaves and fruit are high in protein and are enjoyed by both the birds and antelope alike. It provides a good deal of shade and hence that is why our shepherd tree was my favourite place to sit, in the shade of its branches. It's found in many countries in

South Eastern Africa – so not just in Zimbabwe but in many of its neighbouring countries as well.

One can make coffee from the roots as well as a porridge. An array of star-shaped yellow flowers form a golden crown encompassing the shepherd tree. It blooms from July to November. The star-shaped flowers are accompanied by gooseberry-sized berries that are sweet and fleshy.

The shepherd tree is drought resistant. This tree is grey when it is young and whitens as it gets older. A mass of pollinating insects inhabit this tree. My all-time favourite, the butterflies who hibernate within its make-up, thus creating their home and on top of that give it that "flyaway look." It is almost magical. It seems at any moment it could lift up into the sky and take flight.

Our shepherd tree was home to Chamo, and it was the burial ground of Bird and Peepo. It was also a classroom for me once a week, weather depending. My mother would lay a picnic blanket on the ground and Nyika and I, as well as any other children from the compound (who wished to join us). There we would learn all sorts of fun things from the alphabet to social studies. Sometimes we would bake. Our social studies explored everything in our surroundings. It was an investigation into the fauna and flora that surrounded us. It was a look at different ethnic groups and cultures in our country. Then, for fun, we would learn how to cook crunchies and enjoy eating them. During the rainy season we would make mud cakes, which we pretended to eat. However, it was much more fun to run around in the rain and get covered in mud. I revelled in running outside in rainstorms, there was something magical about it - almost meditative. The sound of the raindrops hitting the ground was hypnotic and calming for me.

There were three of us in the class. Kudzai, used to be there too, in the beginning, but now we were all girls. It was to be my last year learning from home. My father had built a classroom adjacent to the house with a blackboard, handmade wooden desks and chairs. My mother was our full-time teacher. She had also taught

Susan, Jnr and Samantha. Once they had put glue on her chair. She sat down unaware of what was going on; the three of them giggling and trying to muffle their laughter. Only when she tried to get up her dress was glued to the chair. Super Glue. No doubt they got into a bit of trouble for that stunt.

The additional two desks were taken by the two girls the same age as myself from the compound. Beauty and Joy.

School started at 7 a.m. sharp. We started with the national anthem. At that time, it was, "Rise O Voices of Rhodesia." Now days it's, "Simudzai Mureza wedu We Zimbabwe", it was written by Solomon Mangwiro Mutswairo. He was a novelist and a poet. He also wrote the first novel in the Shona language, "Feso".

We didn't have uniforms but my mother had made the three of us a sort of pinafore dress out of navy-blue linen. We also wore white ankle length socks, and black baby doll school shoes, found for nothing at the Bata shoe store, the only shoe shop in the country. Which probably explains my fetish for shoes as an adult woman. You try living your whole life with one shoe shop? Exactly!

Once upon a time, the Bata shoe store thought it would be generous. A lake was being made in the northern part of the Zambezi basin; it was to be called Lake Kariba. It was to be the largest man-made lake in the world. It was a huge project. The Italians helped design the dam wall and a number of them lost their lives to disease, sunstroke, malaria and misplacing their footing on high scaff-holding proved fatal. The Italians deserve more than a pat on the back for this monumental achievement. A church has been built in remembrance of their bravery, the people's movement and animal rescue operation during this time was called Operation Noah. For this dam to be built, a tribe called the Tonga tribe had to be re-settled and the developers had to make sure that burial grounds were not disturbed.

Well, along came Bata, with a novel idea, which was very sweet, but not at all well thought out. They generously donated a ton of shoes for the Tonga Tribe. However, they didn't do their research

– the Tonga have only two toes and none of their shoes fitted them. Was this an urban legend?

Back to our school. We arrived for lessons scrubbed clean. Nyika made sure of that – she had an obsession for scrubbing us clean. I am sure she removed more layers of my skin than I care to imagine. After the national anthem we would take our seats and begin the lessons. Social studies was easily my favourite.

It was a gorgeous day. The sun was shining and there was a light breeze. The sky was a brilliant blue. I always mention the blue sky, because I miss it so much and I took it for granted. It was neither too hot nor cold. It was perfect. The flowers of the bougainvillea trees tumbled to the ground as if they were cascading waterfalls, while the buffalo grass was abuzz with insect life all hurrying about their day in a plethora of colours.

The stick insect, slowly making its way down the trunk of the tree, was perfectly camouflaged – only the trained eye could possibly pick one out. Dragonflies filled the air as if they were mini helicopters, pausing occasionally on the bird bath for a sip or two of water, sending ripples across the dish. A chorus of birds chitter chatter filled the air, ever noted how their music never collides? Is never jarring?

I was feeling euphoric – so were my classmates. Their names were Beauty and Joy. Joy had a huge afro and the longest eyelashes you have ever seen. She had so much energy and when she ran, she threw her head right back and looked at the sky. I often wondered how she didn't run into things or fall down running like this. She was very thin with huge lips that were naturally bright red. Beauty had so many teeth, she looked as if her mouth was a mealie cob. An ear of corn. Pearly white. Quick with words. She could explode in a second and then the next all was forgiven. Joy could make you laugh as if there was no tomorrow.

Beauty was very smart – far smarter than Joy and I. Beauty had a stern way about her, form young it felt as if there were an adult in the room – she was a combination of scientist and old-soul joined together in the body of this young girl. She loved mopane worms and we got them as a daily treat – with a bit of mayonnaise they are delicious. The mopane worm is found in the mopane tree. If you collect them, squeeze out their guts, then dry them or fry them, they make a yummy snack which is also highly nutritious. We would eat them during our break time, without mayo they are revolting.

Sometimes Beauty bought along fried locusts and wild honey. I was terrified of locusts and eating one of them willingly didn't appeal to me at all. However, the wild honey still in its comb from the baobab tree on bread was scrumptious. To this day the thought of it makes my mouth water. There was a beehive in the baobab tree at the back of our house and we enjoyed the honey on a regular basis. We were bought up respecting nature, so we never took more than necessary. Well, maybe sometimes, it was just to goddam delicious.

Running through the grass outside our school were a few praying mantises. Cannibalistic creatures, the females eat the males after intercourse. They remind me of the sport karate – I called them "karate bugs." Their bulging eyes and diamond-shaped heads made me think they were from space – karate bugs from outer space.

The topic about "mating", "intercourse" or "sex" inevitably came up out of the blue. Children and their curious minds. I remember my mother explaining this diplomatically, remaining ladylike. Later on in life, it was explained perfectly through song, in the film Grease 2.

We asked my mother what they were doing.

'Making more of their species,' she replied simply.

We had many priceless moments under the shepherd tree, during our moments of learning. Today would prove to be no exception. One incident comes to the forefront of my mind.

Unfortunately, there was also the blister beetle and the stink beetle. They were running around the lawn too. If a blister beetle peed on you, you would contract blisters that become extremely itchy and irritating. I did happen to mention this earlier on in this story that I had had a rather unfortunate incident with one of them previously. As for the stink bug, it let off a scent – like cooked cabbage – if you startled it. It is the skunk of the insect world. The stink bugs were shaped like the armoured vehicles I saw in the war convoys we used to travel with.

Then there were the rhino beetles and the dung beetles. I loved these guys – so cute. If they fell on their backs, they struggled to tip back onto their legs. At times, I would just go around the garden on "Beetle Rescue." Dung beetles spend their time rolling up untidy poop and they were always very busy with the elephant dung mostly or cattle dung here on the farm.

Our garden was littered with butterflies and often when I looked up there was a flurry of them across my vision. I used to imagine playing dot to dot with them. It was also the season for the flying ant – another source of food. The best way to catch them is to leave a candle burning at night and they gather around the light. If you place water bowls close to the candles, they fall in them and drown. Or you can spend your time catching them alive, taking off their wings and throwing them in a pot of water. I spent a lot of time doing this with Nyika. We called this game round and round the candlelight.

While we were chasing flying ants, the glowworms were also out in full force. Spotting them in the evening made the myth of fairies even more real. I decided that I didn't want to rip the wings off these flying ants. I didn't want them to suffer. Yes, they tasted delicious, fried in butter and garlic but I did not like the fact that they suffered. It didn't fit with my garden of fairies. So as soon as it started it abruptly ended.

Adding to the magic was the cricket. His high pitch chirp makes my day. I used to try and replicate it but could never quite manage it. And boy, what a jumper – so elegant and impressive.

The garden was truly magical – like a fairy tale. And every fairy tale needs a villain. We had three villains. Three different types of spiders in our midst. One was the baboon spider; another was the rain spider and the last was the dreaded black widow button spider.

The baboon tarantula spider is called simply the baboon spider in Africa because it resembles the finger of an African baboon. It can grow anywhere between twelve and fifteen centimetres and like crickets, they are also good jumpers. If you are unfortunate enough to be bitten by a baboon spider, you will vomit your heart out and feel extremely dizzy. However, they don't attack unless they are provoked. Plus you won't die.

The rain spider, which often runs over your feet or body in your house, is called the rain spider simply because during the rainy season it takes shelter from the rain and more often than not in your home. They have tiny bodies, long legs and in size they grow to around twelve centimetres. They are regularly seen during the rainy season darting from one side of the room to the other. Nyika and I often had one scurry over us and your fear was so delayed it was halfway across the room before you realised what had happened. Then we would scream. Jump up onto the couch. How's that for a delayed reaction?

Finally, the black widow red button spider is small but incredibly dangerous. A bite to a child would be fatal, although the body mass of an adult can just about handle it. I never saw one in Zimbabwe growing up. I had to check my school shoes every morning to make sure none of them had taken up lodging there. Nyika always used to say, 'Empty shoes, empty shoes,' and so right she was. I have her to thank yet again for not being stung by a scorpion, they often took up residence in our gumboots, the Brits call them Wellingtons.

That day's lesson was a lesson about malaria. A dreaded disease in my part of the world. I happened to get in once when I was older. It's horrific and naturally, without the right medical help, you can die. Malaria is caused by a plasmodium parasite. The bites of an infected female mosquito – they are called malaria vectors. It kills you when the blood to your brain becomes blocked, through the likes of anaemia or hypoglycaemia. When it's really bad you may go into a coma, develop life-long disabilities or die. The big D. Stone dead.

We always slept under a mosquito net. This is a net with small gauze hanging from the ceiling above your bed. Nyika swears that it also keeps the tokoloshe away.

A few people we knew from the tribal trust lands had died from malaria. Larvae breed in still water so you have to be ridged about what buckets of water you leave lying around. In fact, you have to be careful about still water in general. Malaria does not discriminate; it does not care about your skin colour or your gender. But those without access to the necessary medicines are the ones who suffer. Like with all diseases in Africa – like with HIV, like Covid 19 – people die for no good reason. The medicines are too expensive for most developing and third worlds countries and unfortunately these people end up losing their lives.

We sat under the shade of the tree, learning about malaria, well as much as little kids could learn, apart from my eldest sister and Nyika. Nyika often sat and listened to the lessons. We were trying to absorb everything my mother was telling us. Gathered were Nyika, my mother, Joy, Beauty, my eldest sister Susan, and myself. We were going to have a tea party, shortly after this class.

There we were, all dressed up with hats and gloves, the uncompromising ladylike paraphernalia. The fine china perfectly laid out. Rather lovely if I say so myself. Elegant. I basked in moments such as these, such fine memories almost as fragile as the china tea set itself. Ever so glamorous.

Suddenly, there was an almighty explosion.

My mother screamed, 'Leopard crawl! We're under attack!'

We lay flat on our bellies and proceeded to crawl our way to the house at top speed. Hats and china flying.

Then there were more explosions. My mother was now convinced we were under severe threat and that this would be the worst attack, we would ever witness or endure. We crawled even faster; dresses hitched up and hats slanted. We must have looked a real sight.

Eventually we made it to the house and ran inside. Blessing was standing in the kitchen, his uniform covered in caramel with only two small drops of caramel on his forearms. He had forgotten the tins of condensed milk boiling away in the huge pot on the stove, this turned the condensed milk into caramel. Caramel, was our family sweet, as sweets were not readily available on the farm or the country during the war. But these tins of milk had of course exploded, as Blessing had forgotten to puncture the tins and had filled the pot with too much water.

Worried that Blessings' burns would scar, my mother immediately tended to him. Thankfully there were only one or two minor burns. However, thinking about the other explosions, she was still worried about further terror attacks. After all, two tins of condensed milk didn't add up to the number of additional explosions we had heard. She yelled for us to get to the bathroom, our safe place. We dashed off, after all we knew this routine all too well. My mother was about to radio for help on the Agric alert.

'Where are Samantha and Jnr?' she asked. Pausing as if dazed.

They were nowhere to be found. More panic.

Samantha and Jnr were found hiding under their beds. When asked what this was all about, they were trying, hard not to laugh. They had played a prank on us. My father was away so they knew it would end up in laughter. Samantha and Jnr, had collected all the empty spray cans and then, had thrown them into the furnace that heats the water, that we use for bathing. Naturally, they knew they would explode.

They knew all too well that during our lesson and afternoon tea, the chance to gain maximum effect with as little surprise as possible was the perfect opportunity, to spook us, they did, perfectly! What an afternoon including the "Adrenaline Fuelled High Tea". We all went back outside, a fresh pot brewing. Samantha and Jnr were not to be trusted alone. We drank tea laughing heartily. Pranks in our family happened often. I really do think that has something to do with having a brother. Even now that we are older, on the rare occasions we have managed to get together, this prank culture has been engrained.

Chapter Eight
Manjarenji Dam

The Manjarenji Dam was built to supply irrigation water to the farmers in the Lowveld area, mainly Chiredzi. It was about a half an hour drive from our home on very dodgy roads. This dam also became a local gathering point for farmers and their families in the area. It was very common for a couple of families to share a speed boat. We shared ours with the Mathews family. Mr and Mrs Mathew's had two daughters who were about the same age as my siblings. They were good friends and we had spent many pleasant moments with them as a family. The war was starting to become less aggressive and people were starting to let their guard down a fraction. Once in a while, we would go to the dam.

The dam had been filled with bream. In my opinion, this fish tasted like mud, however, many people enjoyed it with a splash of mayonnaise or a drizzling of cocktail sauce. The fish has so many bones that it always seemed to take a lifetime to eat. Leaving you hungry. No point. The area surrounding the dam had become a nature reserve and there was an abundance of wildlife and bird life. I am a bird person and loved spending time here. The trees sung with the likes of the yellow fronted tinker barbet, ground scrapper thrush, grey-headed kingfisher and the variable sunbird. However, my all-time favourite bird in Zim is the "go away" bird. He looks like a punk but he protects all the weaker animals at the bottom of the food chain. He will start singing, try to imagine this,

'Go away, go away, go away,' (in original tweet form people) and impala will somehow realise they are in danger and become alert. They do the same thing in gardens for small birds being stalked by domestic cats. It's magic.

The grasslands are covered in long honey-coloured grasses and trees as far as the eye can see. The bushveld signal grass – white buffalo grass – fields of gold. The grass sways much like the hips of an African woman dancing. The dam was always accompanied by a gentle breeze and the smell of muddy water. This water was filled with iron – sort of a burnt orange-brown in colour – as was our bath water at home. The perimeter of the dam, was extremely muddy. Sinking into this mud right up to your knees was common. Trying to not disturb the mud crab was also an art, along with the huge bull frogs. It was a thick clinging mud, resembling clay. Turning your legs grey once it dried. You did not want to get stuck in it, whilst launching your boat onto the water. They finally built a launchpad after some or many failed attempts of launching boats.

Sticks also pushed through this mud, so if you happened to be barefoot, which occurred on occasion, it could turn rather ugly. Sometimes, even if you wore your tackies (sneakers), they got vacuumed up by the mud, the mud somehow sucked your tackies right off. You would find yourself with a clean foot up in the air, having to confront the inevitable, however you always gave it pause, standing with one foot and shoe, mud halfway up your one leg and the other slightly clean foot leg, sort of doing a weird form of the airplane pose in yoga. The other alternative was to wear rubber shoes made from the discarded car tyres. They were so ugly; I would not have been found dead in them.

That particular morning, we set off for the dam, cooler bags packed with potato salad, cold meats, biltong, bean salad, homemade bread, homemade sausages (called boerewors), lamb chops and coleslaw. In the other cooler bag was a lot of ice, beer, tonic and a full bottle of gin or two – lemons to boot. My mother never drank her gin out of a plastic cup, no way. She never forgot her fancy gin glass, nor her slice of lemon, nor her ice. My grandmother had also come to visit – so Madam Pearls and cherry fingernails came along, with spanking brand-new swimwear from overseas. They were never the latest fashions, but they were still glamorous. After all it was the middle of nowhere. Sifting through piles of clothing sent to Africa and sorting out second hand vintage was an art.

We all were given gorgeous hats to go with our outfits or very pretty swim caps made of rubber, in bright greens, oranges and reds; eye wear to match. It was all very ladylike and an enormous amount of fun! Huge rubber flowers balanced daintily from swimming caps. We were the most fashionable family in the country, no doubt about it. My grandmother was known for her style and her shop. People travelled far and wide to buy her wares.

We all clambered into the Peugeot 404 station wagon anxious to meet the convoy of one patrol car from the army, mainly because he was a friend and enjoyed fishing – so a homemade convoy. My mother sat with her FN rifle, my brother with his.

Nyika and I crammed into the boot of the car amongst cooler bags and clutter, swimming towels and too many accessories. Off we went all in good spirits. It was as if there was no war at all we were laughing and joking. We were having fun.

My parents had started to argue and disagree on just about everything. All too often these days you could cut the air between them with a knife. They had spoken about separating. I pushed that to the back of my mind and decided to snuggle up to Nyika. Nyika also enjoyed a day out at the dam. We would fish off the jetty after everyone had gone water skiing. We all had to learn how to water ski whether we wanted to or not.

My mother asked my father not to force us. That fell on deaf ears. I really did not enjoy water skiing, I would become paralysed by fear. I did not learn at this dam as I was too young but I learned later in life at another dam outside Mas Vegas close to my playground – The Zimbabwe Ruins.

We eventually arrived at the lake and all jumped out the car. My mother used to have a reoccurring nightmare of being stuck in the reeds in a white bathing suite with a crocodile approaching and being unable to get out of its way but it always swam around her. This nightmare I can totally understand – who in their right mind teaches children to water ski in a crocodile-infested lake and a hippo-infested lake to boot – such an aggressive animal that one!

We unpacked the car, hooked up with the Mathews family, set out the BBQ (which we call a braai) and the day panned out as all other days at the dam. Off went my dad with the younger teenagers for water skiing while my mother, Nyika, my grandmother and I set everything up. After this, my mother and grandmother poured themselves large gin and tonic's and plonked themselves elegantly on the fold-out chairs in the shade of a tree. With cherry-red fingernails and ice cubes, sipping gin on the banks of the dam, legs crossed toenails perfect while Nyika and I played alongside them.

A while later, nature called, so Nyika took me to the rondavel, where the ablution blocks were. We walked hand in hand, enjoying the day, the breeze and the freedom. As we went around the footpath bend, we came face to face with a huge, fully-grown, adult female hippopotamus. It was massive. With its dumpy dark brown body and stumps for legs, it shook its enormous head, twitched its tiny ears, while the oxpecker bird balanced on its back, fearless. Probably relieved that hippos cannot fly. Its short pig-like tail tik-toking. Its hooves sunken into the muddy veld, its four toes clamped solidly. Steadfast animal this. You would think weighing in at 3,200kg it would be incredibly slow.

Well, that's the opposite for the hippo, it can be extremely fast and aggressive. Male hippos can grow to three and a half meters in length and stand one and a half meters high. What most people don't know is that hippos cannot swim. Running on land they can reach a speed of up to forty-eight kilometres an hour. They can also live for ages. It is said that a hippos skin is bulletproof? So, if you are going to want to kill a hippo when it's charging you best you have a venerable 375 be it the well-regarded HandH or the much new Ruger 375, this is the only time I would consider shooting a hippo. I felt like a toy, like a tiny rag doll next to its gigantic frame. I watched its nostrils flare. I could see its whiskers, I thought I could feel it's breath. It opened its huge mouth in a deafening honk. These honks, let me tell you, can be 115 decibels. That is the volume of loud thunder. This didn't sound welcoming. Showing its extraordinarily large molars.

'Oh no, Joanna, oh dear,' muttered Nyika.

'Is this another Maiwe moment, Nyika?' I whispered. We had disturbed the family hippopotamoid.

She squeezed my hand; I could feel the perspiration on her palm. We walked slowly backwards being very careful not to make a sound. We managed to put quite a distance between us and the mother as now we could see she was with her calf. Hippos are extremely dangerous if they are with their calf and if they feel trapped, intimidated or threatened they will kill you in a heartbeat – charging at you and trampling you to death. They have been known to topple canoes, chew people up and spit them out. Being a herbivore means nothing when anger has taken over them.

Clumsily, I tripped over a piece of driftwood. The hippo looked up and, in our direction staring at Nyika and I, It began to charge.

'Run! in a zig-zag motion!' shouted Nyika. I half ran and was half was dragged by Nyika.

Nyika was epically fast. She swung me onto her back and bolted off. I could hear the hippo's breath or maybe I imagined it – maybe it was just my own pounding heartbeat. Then I saw my mother and grandmother. In all their fashionable glory, my grandmother stood up with a shot gun and fired two loud shots up into the sky. By this stage, we had managed to scurry up an anthill and then up into a tree. We were so incredibly fortunate to have a tree in sight. Nyika's natural instincts kicking in with her bush survival skills coming naturally.

The hippo stopped dead in its tracks after hearing the gun shots, quickly turned on its heel, swung its ass in our direction and sauntered off swaying its butt as if it was a Brazilian super model. If that wasn't an adrenalin rush, I have no idea what is. It comes to mind on reflection, just how many survival skills in the African Bush Nyika had installed in me. I say installed because they have never left me. I will forever be grateful as it has aided me to survive more than once. Sheer willpower is the second "installation" I was blessed to receive.

My grandmother was incredibly chuffed with herself and felt she deserved the reward of another gin and tonic, a double this time. Nyika dressed my knee with mercurochrome, this red liquid that's a miracle drug for all cuts and scrapes, no matter how big or small. Leaving you with big red patches that resemble birth marks.

As we settled down from the morning's commotion, the rest of the gang arrived for a hearty lunch. This was followed by a nap – for an hour. As I drifted off to sleep, Nyika and I would make pictures of the clouds. A gentle breeze blowing across our bodies. The whiff of smoke wood. Then it was our turn on the boat –Nyika, my father, mother my grandmother and I. Samantha wanted to ski again, so we would let her do one round, drop her at the jetty and then continue around the lake, eager to spot deer, fish eagles, crocs and hippos. Sometimes we fished, but not very often. We caught bream, being of the right size. Mud fish yuck! I have never enjoyed fishing. Taking that hook out of a fish's mouth is just one step too barbaric for me. Although, cowardly, I do eat saltwater fish.

My father only enjoyed tiger fishing and there were no tiger fish in this lake. I was glad – I much preferred taking in the incredible sights of the lake whilst the smell of mud water drifted across my face and my hair was blown outwards from the propulsion forward motion of the speed boat. The warm sun on my skin, boosting my mood.

Samantha sat on the jetty waiting for her next water ski round. Ski's up high waiting for the last moment that they had to touch the water. We drove the speed boat out onto the water, it was a perfect day for water skiing, the water was as if resembling glass, the slack ski rope turned tight and yanked her clean off the jetty. She was lost in the water for a few moments which terrified us, well my mother and I, especially when we could imagine the crocs lurking hungrily. I go on about croc's a bit, but you should really understand that this was a very real issue, and for the life of us or maybe only me, I found this incredibly silly of our parents.

My elder sister swears to this day that once when she was waiting in the water for the ski rope to come back her way, whilst watching the boat leave you in a wide arc, that a crocodile touched her ski's underwater, she felt the ridges of its scale skin bump up and down for the duration of its length on the back tips of her water skis, that float or for a better word rest below you as you sit with the top part of the skis above the water. That must have been terrifying. Hence the jetty became the only place to take off and to land back on. In the interim best you do not fall off your ski's.

Soon though, Samantha was back on her skis and we were going along smoothly. Or so we thought. Out of nowhere, a hippo's head bobbed up in her path and Samantha ramped, went right over the top of the back of its head, its head resembling a ski ramp as if on snow. She flew across the water, up into the sky and by some small miracle, she landed with a bit of a wobble back onto the water and carried on skiing. My mother and all of us, Nyika included, yelled for my father to return to the jetty. So, we circled in a large arc and went back. As the boat passed the jetty, Samantha knew to let go of the ski-rope and grab the jetty. It is said, that crocodiles don't attack in the middle of a lake, so you are safe. Apparently, in addition, the noise of the speedboats engine's in shallow waters along the banks of a lake frightens them off. Samantha, was in no danger! Go figure.

Despite this, I was happy to see her safe and sound on the jetty. Am I traumatized by these Sunday's? Without a doubt I am! Swimming in any lakes where I cannot see the bottom, is difficult for me. Even in countries that have no lurking reptiles. So weird, it can look the same, and have no present danger, but the feeling remains.

Everyone was alive with chatter and adrenaline-fueled conversation. A few people on the shore had seen what had happened and were cheering Samantha and declaring her a heroine. What extremes. Leaves me cold and spellbound.

'In my opinion,' said Nyika, 'things happen in threes; and today we have had two incidents.'

Sure enough, a third was to follow.

For the rest of the day, we stayed at the boat clubhouse with all the other families and farmers. Everyone was in high spirits, predicting the war was to end and celebrating that no-one had been attacked recently.

As 4 p.m. approached, traditional tea and cake were served. My mother – known for her talent in baking – was surrounded by admirers, keen to sample what she had brought. My father did not enjoy the attention being diverted from him to my mother and I could feel the change in him with the attention my mother was receiving. He always had to have centre stage. God forbid my mother had it without even having to try.

My sisters and brother asked if they could stay at the Mathews' house that night as they wanted to have a teenage party. Other teenagers were joining from the other families. My parents agreed. They would be escorted home by the army guy in his tank and all dropped off at home the following day. The tank was landmine proof and bulletproof, it seated 12 people comfortably, so our parents were pretty confident there was nothing to worry about. They were in the middle of their winter holidays.

The sun was dripping behind the kopjes, as if melting butter and syrup and it was time to go home.

We have a curfew, the war is still on, quiet or not. In the tribal trust lands life was completely unpredictable. Reading something did not make it a fact. News propaganda.

We climbed into the car all packed up from the day's festivities. Nyika and I now had back seats, so we were happy. I sat between Nyika and my grandmother. Feeling safe, I do recall thinking, if I sit in the middle, I am less likely to get shot first or at all. What kind of thinking is that for a seven-and-a-half-year-old, I remember that as clearly as daylight, on more than one occasion?

To this day, I do not know what triggered the following event. I struggled with whether I should even mention it but I think it's important because in a relationship or a marriage, I think that too much water can go under a bridge and the bridge will wash away.

I once heard that eighty percent of marriages where there is a child death ends in divorce. I personally think this is the worst that can happen to a parent. I certainly do not wish it on my worst enemy. Then add a civil war to this cocktail and it becomes a recipe for disaster. I don't want to judge my father as I am by no means a saint. We all live our lives and most of us just try to do our best. When faced with challenges we do what we can.

My father's adoration for other women was his "pleasant" distraction from reality. It's not abnormal, in fact it's rather common, considering the dire scenario's surrounding us. Any distraction was probably welcomed with open arms.

The sun was behind our car, our beige Peugeot 404. The rays reflecting in the rear-view mirror. The smell of mud water in my hair. Sunburn on my shoulders, dried mud on my feet. A damp costume. We had left the boat with the Mathews. The gravel on the road was loose causing the car to slide on occasion.

My grandmother had fallen asleep, still propped up elegantly, but fast asleep. Nyika and I were scanning the bush for terr's. My parents in the front of the car had begun to bicker. The bickering gave way to yelling and in time to screaming and shouting. Granny's eyes remained shut, I was sure as hell she was trying to ignore this scene. Nyika, shifted uncomfortably. My mother could be fragile, and my father so overbearing.

The car climbed the embankment, the tires slipped then re-gripped the earth, the sound of crunching gravel and a car in the wrong gear. Grinding like teeth.

As we reached the top of the dam embankment there was a sheer drop on the passenger side of the car, where my mother sat. Below were large boulders of granite, grass, loose rock, thorn trees and more gravel, the odd tree stump and a few anthills. I looked back over my shoulder to see the sun dip softly and gently behind a kopje. The kopje resembled the silhouette of a matriarch. I turned back to face the road ahead of us, the lights of the car had come on and I could see the gravel strip road before us, with long red (themeda triandra) grass growing down the centre of it. The dry grass always made the same sound as it tickled the chassis of the car similar to that of the swishing of the Shona broom (mutsvairo). A mutsviaro is made from bristles, twigs, reeds and grasses all bound together by a piece of reed or discarded rubber. At sun rise compounds are swept to keep away the evil of the night and to announce the breaking of a new dawn, "kuchena mumweya, pfungwa nemumagariro"- which means to be spiritually clean in thought and deed. Moths danced in front of the car's headlights along with a myriad of other insects and the night jars. A spotted eagle-owl glared at us from its tree. A black-backed jackal crossed our path. A startled impala sprung into the bush wide-eyed.

My mother opened the Peugeot door and jumped out. It happened as if in a dream. Time stood still. A breath escaped my grandmothers' lips. Nyika's eyes darted in the dark. I froze. Alarmed, I did not understand? My father did not have enough time to react. I saw her tumble down the embankment. My father slammed on breaks, reversed the car at one almighty rate, put it in neutral, pulled up the handbrake, dust everywhere, climbed out the car and went running to find my mother. My mother had fallen or rolled a quarter of the way down the embankment. Nyika and I climbed out of the car. My grandmother was in shock, but her hands still managed to find her lipstick, nervously she applied it to her puckered aging lips. She muttered something about young people these days having no finesse and being too vulnerable.

'She's just like her father,' she muttered, 'too soft, too caring, too loving, too artistic and too beautiful.'

'Thank you, Granny,' I said back, 'but today you are out of whack. Going off pop like that. She is your daughter!'

We walked over to my father who was by now in no mood to talk to anyone. Nyika and I were afraid but we carried on looking out for terr's in the bush. I had switched off the car headlights so as not to attract any more attention.

My mother surprisingly enough had survived and she stood up shakily. Her hair dishevelled, her skin cut, her shoes gone, she appeared as if she were a wraith of a person. My heart was beating so fast – my mother was everything to me. Nyika held me fast. My father went down the embankment to hoist my mother up. He carried this frail bird, put her in the car and we drove home in absolute silence.

I was more than ready for the day to end. Between the hippos and my mother's little stunt, I had had just about enough. My eyelids felt heavy. I snuggled up to Nyika in the back seat of the Peugeot secure in her arms– the reassuring smell of Lifebuoy soap and Vaseline. She began to sing me a lullaby. This I think calmed everyone down and I drifted off into a deep sleep. I dreamed that I was under the shepherd tree; I felt the lightness of the swing and imagined I was able to fly.

I awoke the following morning snug in my bed as if yesterday had never happened. I woke up to the sound of tea being made. I stumbled sleepily to the kitchen happy to see things were normal. Blessing was making scones with my mother and Nyika was setting up the tea tray. My father was listening to classical music on the BBC interrupted every so often by the news. My grandmother announced she would prefer to leave a day early so she was packing up. Wednesday the cat was on the fridge. Normality returned.

Outside, my swing swayed in the gentle breeze under the shepherd tree. Butterflies gave it a golden crown. Happiness was mowing the lawn while Truth and Zuvarashe chatted at the back of the kitchen with their large cups of tea filled with at least five sugars and massive white bread and sun jam sandwiches.

I hugged my mother.

'Are you alright, Mum?'

'Yes, my darling,' she replied, 'I'm fine. We will be leaving Ngwane Ranch at the end of the crop. Your father has secured a farm a little way from here; about two hours away for us to grow wheat and cotton there. They have a community and a clubhouse where we can play tennis and golf, swim; a place where there will be life and people to talk to.' My mother missed people. I on the other hand prefer solitude.

'What about everyone here?' I asked. 'What about Chief Marimba, Beauty, Joy, Happiness, Zuvarashe, Truth and all the other villagers? What about Nyika? Bolt the tortoise?'

I suddenly felt panicked and broke into a cold sweat. The kind of sweat which runs down your back where you turn ice cold and want to visit the toilet and vomit at the same time. Apparently, I had turned white.

My mother got down on her haunches and looked me squarely in the eyes. 'The best news is that everyone is re-locating with us;' she said, 'we have organised a new compound for the chief with a local relative of his in that area. He will remain chief of the tribe but will add the rest of the family to the tribe as well, so they will grow stronger. You will go to a proper school – Mkwasine Junior School. Your teacher is from Australia and her name is Miss Scott. You will make more friends...'

I was curious, I have to admit.

Chapter Nine
Mkwasine

And it's true; the whole tribe moved with us. Everyone was in high spirits and our convoy was escorted by our friend with the armoured vehicle. Some of us had our weapons close by. The chief sat up front in the Peugeot 404 with my father, the chief in his full regalia. The leopard skin, lions tooth necklace, every charm to bring us safely to our new home. The car had been blessed and adorned with paraphernalia in the belief of the Gods of Mwari.

He also had an AK-47. My mother, Nyika and I sat in the back seat. In the two cotton bale transport trucks were the tribal people (Shona's) – all the cotton pickers, planters and gathers along with the furniture and belongings of everyone, with some of their accoutrements. Chicken's and goats to boot.

The chief enjoyed my mother's ham sandwiches with mustard that made him sneeze often and loudly … something which made us all laugh. He also insisted that we listened to the BBC. Eventually my mother was tired of the BBC and asked if he would like to hear BONEY M instead. He nodded his head in agreement and we listened to the Rivers of Babylon album for the rest of the trip. The chief adored BONEY M and from that day on we could hear it being played in the compound regularly. *A new adventure, a new house,* a school with more children and a clubhouse that showed movies. My life was about to become so much better; so much more civilized… or was it?

We arrived around noon at our new home. The windows of the house were barricaded with grenade screens. These are huge, heavy shutters that slide across all the windows. They were all closed. My father walked around the house to the kitchen entrance at the back and opened the front door for us. We walked inside. It was a standard Zimbabwean farmhouse: three bedrooms, a single bathroom and separate toilet, kitchen, lounge and dining room. My sister Samantha and I were to share a room. The spare room was to be Jnr and Susan's, although Susan had already left for beautiful Cape Town, I happen to think that Cape Town is the most picturesque city in the world. Susan was studying nursing and Jnr was in his final year at Falcon College in the north of the country.

Falcon College was Zimbabwe's finest school for young gentlemen. Here, you studied your ass off, played rugby, had chapel every morning, learned to play chess and rubbed shoulders with the country's most elite. A Christian boy's school of comradery with blazers, batons, cricket, falconry and high tea being served every day at 4 p.m. Cognac in the senior year, in a study. It was a beautiful school and the men that came from Falcon were well-turned-out, fine young chaps. St George's and Peter House were a close second.

We rushed into the empty house running from room to room, bashing into one another as it was a lot smaller than our old farmhouse on Ngwane. I had to say, this place had no charm or character.

'Mum,' I said to her, 'Mum, you're going to have to work your magic here.'

Just as I said that, a band of six horses came cantering round the side of the house. I stood fixed, as I stared out the huge lounge window. That was a sight to behold.

'Time to learn to ride!' my father shouted. He was an avid horse rider.

I was in heaven. Maybe this house wouldn't be so bad after all.

The dominant mare halted the band. I dashed out of the house as if a bull in a china shop. 'Careful,' chided my mother. Once outside, I contained my excitement and walked towards the horses calmly. They still appeared rather skittish.

There was a foal too. Standing unfamiliarly on her spindly legs. Tilting her head a tad, unsure. The band of horses had settled by now and they imbibed their surroundings as if unknowingly tipsy with freedom and beauty. Scanning the African Savannah, the umbrella trees and thorn bushes. Offering shade. The anthills and tufts of grass, jutting out the earth, resembling an alarmed nature. The "Lowveld" where we now lived in geographic terms is a name given to two areas that lie at an elevation of between 150 and 600 meters above sea level, encompassing a sub-tropical climate, where summer days are hot and humid with temperatures soaring above 40°C at times.

The rainy season is welcomed from September through to May. We have dry winters, which are my favourite time of the year, and the best time for viewing animals in the bush. The foliage appearing dry and wrinkled, twigs snapping under foot with little to no effort. Similar to a body in an exposed grave. Dust to dust. Bones brittle. Dry. Bone dry.

Animal's scurrying, hurriedly for coverage and shelter. The earth was a deep rusty red in places and an oatmeal beige in others, that boasted the ever-present baobab against a fiery setting sun. Huge granite domes if you must or Dali's marbles, was my name for them, although they were more common in the north of Zimbabwe, they appeared less frequently in our area. Balancing and pivoting at bizarre angels as if defying logic. A scattering of Msasa trees. I looked across the horizon and drank in the pure splendidness, remembering the trip here. How bonded. How young and unimportant was my opinion?

'Can I have her, Dad, the foal?' I asked. 'I'll call her Misty.'

She was a dapple-grey. I couldn't get near her but tomorrow I would try again and every day until I gained her trust. The horses were taken to the paddock at the front of the house and left to roam and graze, as they were to do most days. They were beautiful, fit and healthy. They were retired polocrosse ponies so to ride them would be easy enough once you mastered the art of riding a horse in open savannah. Unlike most other open spaces in the world, here we had to be careful of disturbing snakes in our path, whilst riding. A horse can fright easily.

My horse-riding lessons would start the following morning but not in the classy modern sense or term. There would be no airs and graces, no formal uniform and stiff upper lip. Pinkie up. I would simply learn to ride a horse. My father enjoyed horses. His horse was named Blaze.

He once crossed the Save River alone on horse-back with a 1000 head of cattle and not one was eaten by a crocodile, a lion or a leopard. Once many years later, when I was interviewing him, he said this was his biggest personal accomplishment in life. Him in the wilderness, alone, with Blaze and the wild. His dog The Fonz a Rhodesian Ridge Back. His heaven. I must get it from him. The enormity of my love for the "wild" of Africa.

All the cotton picker ladies and men from the tribe were taking their luggage down from the cattle truck. The women as usual were carrying everything mostly on their heads, their African sarongs colouring the tediousness of moving and the African men barely helping at all. Nothing new.

Our beggarly amount of furniture was making its way into the house, on heads and in hands. When I say beggarly, I really mean nothing. My mother and father's precious wedding presents now fitted into the size of a vacuum cleaner box, the old kind. I felt as if I should brace myself, as if this was surreal. The evening was fast approaching. Saying goodbye to Ngwane had been strenuous and arduous on all of us. Blessing had already set up his compound and was sorting out the kitchen. Blessing had one wife, who unfortunately had passed. He preferred to stay single from then on. Devoted to his work. His life was well lived, when I think back to it. A simple life equals a happy life. He represented that. Blessing was a profound part of our lives. Everyone that worked with us, stayed with us until their dying day or our eventual departure from Africa.

Tonight, would be the very simple dinner of baked beans on toast. It's one of my happy memory dishes. In the meanwhile, Happiness had his ten or fourteen wives running around whilst he was instructing them as to how to set up his compound. Oh, for the love of God…

Suddenly, all hell broke loose. There was screaming, yelling and shouting and on hearing this stentorian outburst, we walked outside to see Nyika and "Happiness's first and head wife Pretty" having a full-on rumble – throwing punches, tearing at each other's clothes, pulling each other's hair, biting, scratching and spitting. How dare someone do this to Nyika? She had a position in her tribe, which demanded respect! I found it simply dreadful. How could people behave like this? Literally like two wild cats. Did Pretty have the right to even touch Nyika? A catfight indeed, woman when it comes to "fighting", in my country, fight with a lot of posturing, filthy looks, tongue clicking, a cascade of bitter words and territorial gestures. In this case fists flew, which was rare. It was mentally and socially under-cutting. Everyone standing around mesmerized. Malicious and spiteful and it would not solve or resolve a thing. Catty. Each one wanting that final word, the insults stooping to the lowest levels of language! Words impossible to take back. This exchange was loaded with dynamite!

Just then, my father stormed out the front door, it slamming loudly behind him. Having nearly come off its hinges, marching over to see what all the commotion was about. I could see the steam leaving my father's ears. Not a good sign people, not a good sign at all. I have to tell you that Shona women can perform and switch on the tears and drama like no other. Italian women would be put to shame and stand no chance against a Shona woman in this regard. Even the horses had stopped grazing and were looking wide-eyed in our direction.

'What's going on?' he snapped. 'Happiness, get your wife under control. Nyika, stop.'

My father then grabbed the hosepipe which was now already set up in the garden watering the lawn and sprayed the two women. It worked a charm.

'Pretty, tell me what's going on?' I watched anxiously from a distance. Pretty placed her hand in her handbag and drew out a notebook. Trembling she passed it to my father.

He opened it and turned a deathly pale, he moved away from Pretty toward Nyika. 'Nyika, is this yours?' he asked.

'Yes, it's mine.' Nyika glared at Pretty. Deadpan. Nyika realising the magnitude and repercussions of that *precise* moment, as the enormity of her situation rushed to the forefront of her mind. She had been set up. She would never be able to explain this. The proof was in the pudding. Bare before my father in black and white. Pretty must have stolen the notebook. Always that one person.

The notebook was a ledger of planned attacks with the terr's on our home. It had our house drawn to perfection – the bedrooms, kitchen, bathroom, toilet, lounge were all marked clearly. The dining room places where we all sat were also marked clearly. Our routines after lights out, curfew all noted. Hagen Snr, in this chair, listening to the BBC, Mrs Hagen would be helping in the kitchen with Blessing, Joe would be in her bed in her parent's room. I saw all our names marked on our dining room chairs of where we sat, appearing neatly as if an innocent drawing but quite the opposite in this particular case. There was my name, above my chair, alongside my mother, father, brother and sisters. This was the real version of Goldilocks.

The lead terrorist had planned to wipe us out. Our whole family. Even Blessing apparently, and some of the head farm management. Nyika? Their finale. A major plan was to attack in broad daylight something no one suspected or expected. They were coming to kill us, Nyika had helped them and betrayed us, Kudzai was part of this group now. This was obviously part of his initiation into the lost manhood. Kudzai my friend was preparing to murder us; this information was not sinking in at all. Nyika, had known about this all along the last two attacks had maybe been target practice for them, that is perhaps why they lasted such a short time? Nyika my most trusted friend. The Chief had been right about Kudzai. The tables had turned. Leaving when we did, without a definite date and time, only to be shared at the last minute, had saved all our lives. My father's gut instinct had been right, about the timing, but surely not about Nyika. Had we just been lucky, we would never know.

There was a deathly hush. The air turned cold and not even a blade of grass dared sway in the breeze. Everything halted and rushed to silence and yet there was a loud ringing in my ears – like a steam train approaching, screeching on the tracks. My father's voice was ice cold.

'Nyika, take your bags,' he said, 'you will go back to the old compound in Zaka. You are no longer part of this family. Go! We never want to see you again.'

Nyika had turned an ashen colour and was trying to explain herself. My father just turned and walked away.

'Nyika, you are dismissed!' he said coldly. 'Now leave! Your payment package, you can collect from Truth tomorrow at sunrise. Goodbye.'

This could not have been happening. Nyika betrayed us? I ran past my father. He grabbed me and held me fast, below my shoulder, at the top of my arm. Marching me along with him.

'She is a traitor, Joanna,' he said, 'she had planned with the enemy to kill all of us even their own relatives. I am fortunate I never gave the exact time or date of our departure from Ngwane. They could have attacked our convoy if they had known. Thank, God. I had also told your mother, to say out loud to the domestic staff, that although we are packed and ready to go, we do not really know when we are leaving and at what time. Just be ready. Friend or Foe Joanna? Ask yourself every time. Nyika is a bad woman just like Kudzai, who is the enemy and we will deal with them as such!'

'No, no, it's not true,' I was shouting for Nyika, out of control and screaming. My father grabbed me around the waist. I was kicking and screaming. He carried me upstairs and locked me in my bedroom. I felt stone dead. I felt so sick. I was numb, I just could not put this puzzle together.

I rushed to my bedroom needing solace, pushing and pulling the grenade screens open. They were made of metal, an inch and a half thick and one and a half metres high with handles. They made a clanging noise. The same noise as jail doors. Loud and intimately rude, jarring! My bedroom window looked onto the driveway. The big cattle truck was parked to the side, in the driveway, as if teasing, as blue as the sky.

We had been so happy an hour ago. How can the world turn upside down so fast, without even a warning? I watched Nyika reach for her suitcase and balance it on her head. I watched her hands that had consoled me a million times over. Her fingers gripping the saxophone my gramps had given her. That she loved. I felt that horrid feeling, similar to that of when you are in the shower and that damp wet curtain touches your legs. EEK. The feeling as if in a dream and you are falling but cannot wake up.

Everyone watched, they looked on at the "criminal." They cleared a path for her as if she had a contagious disease. A deathly hush fell and she walked the walk of shame, her head down. I watched the other woman, and I saw Pretty, Happiness's wife laughing. Sneering in pleasure. It struck me as rather odd. Pretty said something to Nyika as Nyika passed her. I was too far away to make out what was said. The moment was now engraved in my mind. Nyika, was wearing her traditional clothing and the bright print of oranges, golds and browns clung to her body. She walked out the security gates. I watched her go till she was a dot in the distance. How would she get home? Walk? Walk two hundred kilometres home alone? Scared, tired and hungry.

I turned and vomited all over the new linen on my bed. I retched until I knelt on the floor and cried myself to sleep. I was alone in this big, wide world without Nyika. She had been my shadow, my other mother, my friend, my confidant and my teacher of all things African. I would be lost. I was heartbroken. Heartbreak is truly a disease and I had caught it. My symptoms – a sudden lack of appetite, a feeling of living but not functioning, vulnerability at an all- time high, cold sweats, my mind invaded with intrusive thoughts bordering on obsessive revenge and a lack of wanting to continue with my routines whilst waltzing with insomnia, one, two, three, one, two, three, one, two, three! Brushing my hair hurt – no one did it quite like Nyika. Rolling out of bed now took such a strange amount of effort – there was no soothing voice that Nyika used to coax me up. Touching my laundry, knowing the last person who had ironed and washed it so lovingly was gone. Forever, banished. I had not only lost a friend. I had lost my Momette!

How could she have done this? Why did she do this? Did she do this at all? I would in the future question these things daily and a wall of tears would form at the rims of my eyes, like a dam wall threatening to crumble. You push them back, you toughen up. You begin to realise that life is like the fragile network of a dot-to-dot puzzle and missing one number could be the outcome of the picture that is left lying in front of you. I was determined to find her one day; I promised myself that. For now, I would grow and become strong, listen and learn. Where was Zaka? How long would it take to get there? I had heard grown-up's chatter of 200kms, roughly two hours by car, give or take. It had never occurred to me before to learn about maps and where things were. Now it was imperative.

Nyika would say, 'Focus on the future, because you can do nothing about the past.' I heard her voice – gentle and calm in my heart. My mother came and fed me pea-soup. Spoon to lips, shaking. Joe, this is all too much to comprehend, take one day at a time, your father means well in this case, the evidence supports his decision. Struggling with the soup, she took the bowl away and came back to tuck me in. That night she read me the story of Judas. I recalled Nyika's words. Sometimes we are forced to do things we do not want to do. I looked up at my mother. Mom, I believe Nyika was forced to do this mom! I do too my darling, I do too… but give it time.

I dressed the following morning. I felt confused about my love for my father. I felt anxious and uncertain about almost everything and anything. Challenge yourself. I knew what I would do. Misty. I would learn to ride a horse. I finished my breakfast, surprised that I had actually enjoyed Blessing's legendary scrambled eggs and fried tomatoes, fresh bacon, baked beans, boerewors, fried onions and topping it off with deep fried bananas. He had made me an extra helping. He had given me a lot of love in the past days, so had my mom. I had spent most of the past hours and days cradled in her arms, helping her in the house, unpacking, watering the pot-plants and the garden, hanging up paintings.

Happiness was truly living up to his name once again and had told Blessing to tell me to meet him at the stables. I wandered over to the stables and felt excited for the first time in a while.

'Good morning,' I said. 'Happiness, I hate your wife, Pretty, let's get that straight. One day I'll find out exactly what happened and I'll set the record straight once more. I'll help Nyika get her dignity back, mark my words, if it is the last thing I do! Damn right I would. Damn right. My Nyika would have had a reason. My job as her friend was to figure that out.'

Happiness stared calmly back at me.

'If that is God's will, Joanna, it will be granted.'

'She did not do this,' I continued, 'I'm sure of it and if she did, then I take back my words, but for now, I never want to see Pretty again. I hope she gets eaten by a hyena and that it laughs as it eats her. I may not be able to control my actions.'

Happiness nodded at me. 'Yes Joe, you have always been a wild child. Still not wearing shoes, did you even brush your hair or teeth this morning? Joe, you are high spirited, sometimes feral. Unmistakably a child born for the wildness of this country. Your free spirit is a blessing and a curse, it's not up to me to squelch your personality or passions. You will always survive Joe; you have an imperishable ability and a resilience second to none! I am sure you will figure this out. Perhaps I may even help you?

About Pretty, I don't like her either, it was an arranged marriage. She's not right in the head, that one.' To be honest even I am a bit afraid of her.

His words were trapped like a fly in a web, in my brain. 'Odd thing to say about your wife. Yes, Happiness so all twelve were arranged marriages? You have a massive ego!'

'Miss. Joe, I am your elder, a little respect please.'

'Yes Happiness,' I muttered rolling my eyes.

'Male chauvinist pig,' I said to myself.

Chauvin the first part of this word comes from Nicolas Chauvin an extreme patriot in Napoleon's army, the second part of the word comes from the 1960s and 1970s by student activists during the American Civil Rights Movement to denigrate the police. Mashed together they give you that term.

'This is Misty's mother,' said Happiness, 'her name is Flame. She was the foal of your father's first horse when he was a young man. We brought the horses from your father's parents' home. They are old now and could not look after them.' Their polocrosse days long behind them.

We had so little contact with them, due to the war, but the contact we did have with them when it was possible, was always rich and rewarding. They lived on a farm outside Mas Vegas. What I do recall was my grandmother's voice like that of an angel when she sang; a voice as rich and warm as oatmeal porridge, drizzled with honey. My grandfather was a jazz musician. He wrote music and played the piano like a dream.

Back in the day he had a jazz club in Johannesburg called, "The Green Door." He was incredibly talented. Music came as naturally to him as breathing comes to us. He composed music and had a hit in 1934 called "Girl of the Golden Reef." After roaring around in their youth my grandmother had finally demanded they settle in what was called Rhodesia, now Zimbabwe on a small farm.

Thanks to my grandmother he found himself in the Lowveld. Surrounded by his three-farming son's. Close to Zimbabwe Ruins and the Church of St Francis of Assisi, this was constructed by the Italian Prisoners of war during the 2nd World War. 71 of them didn't make it and their bodies lie interred in the walls. He taught children music and anyone else who wanted to learn jazz.

Their home overlooked the valley of the Zimbabwe ruins the Acropolis on the hill visible, it is said that it was occupied for 300 years, spirit mediums and oracles occupied the ritual enclosure and metal craftsmen were said to have supplied the kingdom with jewellery and spears. The famous, Zimbabwean, soapstone birds are in the enclosures. The iconic tower is what you see on all postcards. No mortar holds these structures together. Speculation suggests this was the royal harem. The medieval African Kingdom in your back yard. If that doesn't inspire you, nothing probably ever would.

My grandfather would tell the story whilst sipping a whiskey, ever so elegantly in his beige linen suit, and hat. Ridgeback lying at his heels. His grand piano in the background, various musical instruments scattered around the house. Eyes twinkling, foot tapping, a tick, jazz music spilling onto the veranda, colonial décor to boot, a master unto himself. Sharing the story of the Karanga people that came from the north, across the Zambezi, finding life easy here amongst the fertile soil and appealing weather. Would begin something like this; The 13th century king was nicknamed the "Stone Man", more likely the Stoned Man, seeing weed was readily available. He was also the "mambo" responsible for building these walls. He would gesture at the horizon. Do you know that those granite blocks still stand five centuries later, you energetic young people can clamber the rocky Acropolis and wonder through the valley of enclosures? Antelope, leopard and zebra live in these hills, so keep your eyes peeled. The bell would ring for super. Traditional roast beef on a Sunday.

Herman Hagen Snr. mostly taught classical piano and had opened a music school teaching local children and children from more privileged backgrounds instruments. He was such an elegant man, always dressed well, the perfect artist and gentleman. He apparently went on to open seven schools of music in southern Africa, so I am told. Herman, mainly focused on the rhythm section. He taught them a different style of the piano, incorporating his own vision with this instrument as well as the trumpets, trombones and saxophones. He had incorporated the African drum and Mbira (African thumb piano) and had composed music with locals as well as folk who resided in the area.

Once, he had spent a whole afternoon trying to teach Nyika and I the saxophone. We were enthralled. Time past, without appearing nor reminder. Nyika was a natural with musical instruments, and wished she could learn more about the Saxophone. Realising her eagerness and natural talent, Gramps had given her his much older saxophone, with a series of exercises to master. She had applied herself diligently. She got really good at it. On some evenings she had played for guests and some afternoons under the shade of the Shepard tree. She had accompanied my grandmother in a performance to raise money for music in our local area on occasion.

I loved that about him. His complete lack of judgement and one hundred percent belief in life, that everything is possible, but only with jazz.

However, as much as I love jazz, I was not talented with any instrument. Free dance I can. Jazz in itself has a language of its own. It talks directly to your soul. You cannot excuse it or make excuses for it – it lays you bare. Jazz was a part of my soul. It grabbed me tight and never let me go. It is the only loyal love I have ever known in my life.

My grandfather was eccentric but also incredibly smart. My grandmother had the elegance of a clever woman and a stillness that ran deep. Her azure eyes continuously calm and never less than total reassurance emanated from them. My daughter has so much of her within her being. Her eyes said, 'Everything would be fine,' and you unforcefully believed it. Back to the horses:

The stable smelt of polished leather and fresh hay.

'Before I give you the reins, Joanna,' Happiness said, 'you have to earn them. Your daily responsibilities are to brush Flame and Misty, turn the fresh hay and fill their water troughs. Let's start with that. Go and get some water!' Off you go, move it! 'Trot along dear.' He laughed throwing his head back. He could be so precocious. Though I must admit, his command of the English language, was jolly good indeed.

He pointed in the direction of the reservoir.

I picked up the bucket, walked the very short distance over the gravel and bald parts of buffalo grass to the reservoir. Butterflies danced around me. I dipped the bucket into the fresh water. It didn't smell like copper and I tasted it. It tasted fine no hints of blood or should I say iron. I placed the full bucket automatically without thinking on my head. Just as Nyika had taught me.

It sloshed a bit over my shoulders, the cold water a welcome relief to the hot weather. Flies buzzed annoyingly around my eyes. I got stung by a horse fly and naturally dropped the bucket. Their bite is really quite aggressive. I swatted it hard and it splattered across my leg. Blood and guts on my hand and on my leg. Poor bugger, but you deserved it. I washed it off with the remainder of the water from my bucket. I felt, more guilty than annoyed about the waste of water. Water here was worth more than gold. I ambled back to the reservoir, and looked out onto the horizon, it was a clear day. It was going to be scorching later on. I filled the bucket, trying not to become distracted by all the beauty surrounding me.

As I walked back, an image of Nyika flashed through my mind. She had spent days teaching me to carry buckets of water on my head. How we had laughed. I stopped and heard the laughter echo around me. She showed me how to walk for miles without spilling even a single drop. She had a cloth to roll up into a baguette. Then this was made into a circle – like a halo – and placed onto your head so the bucket does not rest directly on the crown of the head but on the circle of the cloth. I would not forget my cloth next time. Carrying the bucket this way was certainly not practical.

I arrived back at the stables and poured the water into the horse troughs. Misty eyed me from behind her mother Flame. Her long eyelashes and dark brown eyes searching. She finished suckling her mother. I loved the smell of our horse stables. It brings to mind the smell of honest sweat, leather, polish and dust. It is the opposite of malodorous, it is ambrosial as if an elegant fragrance.

'Now, Joanna,' continued Happiness, 'here is the horse brush. You slide your hand under the grip.'

The horse brush was the same style brush Nyika and I had used to polish the floors at home. Another image of her came and went. It hurt to think of her for too long. Flame was a big horse – a rich chestnut in colour with a long mane. She was a specimen of pure splendour. I was to learn to ride her first. I brushed her coat from the neck down talking to her all the time, singing songs once again; words of the songs I had learned from Nyika. I told the horses how I was feeling and they seemed to listen tentatively or so I thought. Such a refreshing change from humans who seem to think you want an answer for every feeling you emanate.

Animals absorb your feelings and then they act. To show a horse fear is a big no, no, well to show any animal fear including domestic animals at times, is just a faux pas. They always should know you love them but that you are in charge. Strength does not come from whipping the shit out of an animal; it comes from quiet and firm movements and not the erratic behaviour that may startle them. It took time, patience and a day after day routine to establish my firm love for the horses. I brought them carrots and the odd stick of sugar cane. Soon they were delighted to see me knowing that I came with treats. Misty let me touch her now. I seemed to have mastered the art of looking after a horse. It had taken at least a month. These tasks took my mind off Nyika's absence.

Chico our dog sadly passed away that week but although I missed him, I missed Nyika more and the sadness I felt for him soon evaporated. Wednesday, the cat, was still around and she still remained perched on the fridge. I had stopped believing in fairies and goblins, along with Father Christmas, Easter Rabbit and the Tooth Fairy. What a bane it is to grow up.

Beauty and Joy no longer came to play. They had been married off. I had a chance to say goodbye but I was not my usual self and it just felt like another goodbye - another nail in the coffin. Their lives decided for them. A tear escaped my eyes. My mother had also decided she preferred to do the chores in the house herself since she had the time. My father had hired a full-time accountant so my mother no longer handled the farm accounts. Truth and Zuvarashe went on with their jobs as per normal - everyone did. Soon the farm was in full swing. The cotton was in bloom and it would soon be picking season. No Nyika.

My brother had come and gone. He was now studying in England at Cirencester Agricultural College - the best in Europe. Also, during this time, my father had sadly lost his brother Richard (and Richard's wife) in a horrific car accident. Their son, (my cousin) Richard junior, had come to live with us and he was going to study to become an engineer. His three sisters Joan, Elizabeth and Margaret had long since left home and started families of their own. I had just begun my first year of proper schooling. I missed my mother teaching me under the shade of the Shepard Tree. No more BBC school on the air. No-more, fresh breeze. No more jokes. Just learning the alphabet in the most unoriginal way possible. No more Nyika to chase with a chameleon, no Nyika or any familiar friend at all in sight.

My little school was called Mkwasine Junior School. Mkwasine was a shithole. It was one room with one teacher and three different age groups in the classroom (Kindergarten One, Kindergarten Two and Standard One). There were six students in KG One, four in KG Two and two students in Standard One. It was a sort of pre-school before we were shipped off to become weekly borders living with families we had never met – a family who responded to the following advert...

Seeking a loving family to host our daughter Joanna Vye Hagen for the duration of the school term, aged eight at your home from a Sunday evening until close of school on a Friday at 12 noon. Anyone wishing to assist us please contact Claire Hagen or Herman Hagen Snr on this number – two shorts and three longs. Naturally, your kindness will be compensated.

Our teacher was a Miss Scott and she came from Australia. She had a mass of curly black hair, unruly long red fingernails and ample bosom. Miss Scott could dress, I will give her that much, she did have her own unique and colourful style. She drove a bright yellow Beetle with a fantastic sound system. We could always hear her coming and going from a mile away. A bonus for any class of students. She must have had a thyroid problem as she had rather bulgy eyes. Her face contained a sprinkling of freckles and she wore bright red lipstick with a lot of mascara that clung desperately to each eyelash – sort of reminding me of grease in a car engine. Her voice was so loud, or was it just all these woman in Mkwasine, their voices alarmingly jarring?

Our lessons were pleasant enough but I did not develop a deep love for school. To make it worse, we had to all take part in a school play. I was an angel, dressed uncomfortably in a homemade sheet appearing angelic but secretly wanting to kill someone for making me dress up in this goddam thing. It was hot, no it was boiling hot.

I could not stand to make a spectacle of myself and being dressed up as an angel was my idea of torture and so far removed from my actual character. My one and only line in the play: "These mosquitoes are driving me crazy!" This notion kept me awake for days. I didn't enjoy so much direct attention. Even for that short amount of time. I had made a friend at school called Shereen, we got on well it was fun to have a friend my own age. The weekends went by with sport at the local Sport Club, true colonial style. Kiss catches, doctors and nurses, teacher and student. Playing army in the trenches, which surrounded the club house, for us to escape to in the case of a terrorist attack. Trap doors were placed in all the club rooms, with staircases that lead down to additional chambers. Each chamber had supplies. It was damp down there, and there were rats. Big ones. It smelt of mould. It creeped me out.

By this time my sister Samantha had gone to study "Wellness" in Cape Town. We spoke once a week to everyone all huddled around the telephone on a party line on the old wind-up phones. My siblings seemed to be doing brilliantly. I was happy for them. I, on the other hand, may have been falling apart with little to no expression. Joe sat on a wall, Joe had a great fall, all the tribes could not put her together again. Humpty Dumpty…

Things at home, however, between my parents were worse than ever – and hysteria frequently filled every corner of the house. One would blame and curse the other; words would be hurled, each digressing sentence inflicting unnecessary scarring. The tongue being the most dangerous weapon on earth by far. Followed by cowering and cradling. Sometimes the fights got so bad, I would hide under my bed at night with Wednesday the cat to keep me company.

Now that's really saying something as our relationship was not wonderous. Those nights were long. My mother often found me sleeping under my bed in the morning. Guilt etched in her smile. How long would she continue to pretend everything was fine?

Then, one morning something came along to put a smile on my face – a rarity such as a mars bar in my world. Happiness announced that my first riding lesson was to take place. My grandfather had taught him when he was a boy. I was soon to discover that Happiness could also play the Saxophone. That he also loved Jazz, my little world became somewhat brighter. Maybe he was not such a tosser after all.

Firstly, I would learn to saddle Flame. I was shown how this was to be done in one swift movement; the idea was not to dump the saddle on the horse but to lay it down as gently as possible similar to laying down a tablecloth on a large table, ever so gently in one swift swoop. It was difficult because the saddle was so heavy and with my limited experience, it was definitely no win. Flame neighed and bolted off. I had naturally startled her whilst dumping the saddle on her back. Ungraceful indeed. It seemed to take a lifetime to convince her to come back to the stable. I was out there for what seemed an eternity. It was hot and I was irritated and being bitten by horse flies and having Mopani flies buzzing into your eyes was enough of a negative recipe.

Happiness scolded me and sent me to harness her. I really disliked him in this moment, all the pleasant thoughts I had ever had of him dissipated in a torrent of Tourette. I cursed him relentlessly, behind his back of course. To him, I would never have dared. Horses are far from stupid, so I was out the entire morning trying to harness Flame. Eventually, I just grabbed some sugar cane which I realised I should have done to start with.

Day one over and I hadn't even managed to sit on the horse. The next day, the saddle landed like a tablecloth being spread across a large table. Flame was obedient. I tied the saddle down under her ample belly, adjusted the stirrups and tightened her reins, all the while listening to Happiness's firm instruction.

Eventually, I was able to mount Flame and, for that first week, we began walking. We walked, walked and walked. The following week, Happiness announced that we would start learning to trot. 'And Missus Joanna, not the foxtrot like your mum and dad do…' he threw back his head laughing at his wit. I laughed too realising it was a foreign sound since I had not actually laughed since Nyika had left. This included a double bouncing of your butt – with a little rhythm too. So that week we trotted and in the end the muscles in my backside hurt and burned.

Happiness laughed, 'You, feel it? Too bad you got a white butt.'

I laughed, all too true.

By the third week, I had gained substantial courage and asked if we could learn to gallop.

'I don't see why not,' said Happiness.

This was the beginning of my escape from the misery of home. To gallop through the large paddock at the front of our house, up and down the hill, freed me from all worries, energising and lifting me. To feel the wind on my face and to listen the beat of horse's hooves on soil was so gloriously monotonous and uplifting. With each beat of hoof to ground I hypnotically chanted, it's going to be alright, it's going to be alright. I was smiling again.

That evening Happiness taught me about cleaning horseshoes and horse hooves. How to heat a horseshoe till it became bright red, and to place it on the hoof of the horse. Horse pedicure. After a few failed attempts, we both agreed that becoming a farrier was definitely not my forte. Both agreeing in the end that Happiness would remain in charge of this department. I am sure the horses were secretly pleased with this decision to.

'Tomorrow, we will fly!' I said to Flame. 'Yes, we are going out of the paddock, into the veld and we will be galloping!'

I was so excited that evening that not even my parent's boring old bickering at each other relentlessly could dampen my mood. I was in another world… dreaming of flying with Flame.

The following morning, I jumped out of bed, pulled on my jeans and t-shirt, grabbed my riding hat and pulled on my boots.

'You smell like a horse,' my mother said with a smile, 'and, I think you are starting to look like one too.'

I brushed Flame, extra nicely and gave her some sugar cane and a carrot. I saddled her and made sure her water was fresh and clean. I gave Misty a hug, brushed her too, gave her fresh water and a carrot. Misty was no longer suckling; now she was on water. She was growing up and what a stunner she was turning out to be, perhaps even more so than her mother.

In class, all I could think about was Flame and Misty. Often Miss Scott's sharp voice would penetrate my vivid dreams of galloping across the veld or her long fingernail would push into my scalp.

'Did you hear me, Joaaaannnna?' her voice would twang and drawl.

Sort of similar to a record track you desperately wanted to end at a party you didn't want to be attending. Nails down chalkboards.

Happiness and I warmed Flame up in the paddock. Misty came with us every morning but today she would be left alone without her mother for the first time. Such is life, Misty. I had given her a whole pile of extra horse cubes to distract her. We would not be gone too long. Happiness demonstrated a gallop. It looked pretty simple to me.

I nudged Flame with my knees and said softly, 'Let's fly!'

Well, we took off. I had never felt so elated, so free and so full of wanting to actually be alive, to live, this is what it meant, full of life! I was truly flying. For the first time in my nearly eight-year-old life, I felt invincible. I felt like a warrior of light. A goddess. This was freedom. I loved Flame all the more in that moment. She had shown me happiness and made me laugh, like I used to laugh with Nyika. A laughter that resonated from your gut and came full throttle out of your mouth. A real laugh. Something characteristically part of my nature. No muffled laughter for me anymore.

I grew more and more confident with Flame; we started galloping without Happiness. Flame and Misty were an everyday routine now and they knew all my secrets. My secret being, that I would go and find Nyika and that she would work and live with us once again. I would go and rescue her on my horse. That was my secret. That was my dream.

My parents had joined the Mkwasine Sports Club and were sampling the colonial escapades that came along with it. This club was an estimated half an hour, give or take, drive from our house. When we drove to the club, mostly on weekends, I would try to spot monitor lizards and cane rats the size of Jack Russel's, that ran along the sugar-cane fields, besides the dirt roads and canals. Some were being toasted on coals by the cane cutters, along with ears of corn.

The sugar cane estates, cotton and wheat fields, stretched on for as far as the eye could see, past telephone poles, villages and men on bicycles, with chickens under their arms, past canals and Hiroshima-Baobab trees that were massively proportioned, outlining the skyline. The fruit of the Baobab trees tasted so much sweeter than the other Baobabs in the wild, probably due to the fact that its roots sucked sugar from the cane I imagined. Who knows? The honey supplied by the bees that made these trees their home was unparalleled. Swarms of bees inhabited these trees.

As time came to pass, we found out inevitably, that there were a few "undesirables" in this Mkwasine Clubhouse. Like every small town in the back end of beyond, small-mindedness is literally a disease. The sheer amount of it at times was jaw-dropping.

Mkwasine Club life was one long party with a bunch of adults who forgot they were still in a war, save for a few level-headed people, such as my mother.

Life ebbed and flowed like that of the tide, and I found friends in the strangest of places for example, Jim the barman was a great guy, looking after us along with our nannies, or lack of, whilst our parents golfed, played tennis or squash. As children were not allowed in the bar, we would use a side window that ran alongside the bar counter, where Jim would serve us packets of salt and vinegar or tomato sauce chips made by Willard's'. As Willard's Chips "make music in your mouth," the advert on television kept blurting out. Served along with a cream soda, the boys had this awful habit of "backwashing" their chips into their drinks. Revolting. Chocolate Fredo Frogs and gob stoppers. For dinner we were religiously served jaffels, these are rounded toasted sandwiches with a mince filling and cheese or just cheese and tomatoes, or chicken and mushrooms.

After dinner, whilst the adults showered and dressed up for the clubhouse, for an evening drinking, flirting and fighting, we spent hours inventing games that involved the trap doors and trenches surrounding the clubhouse. These trenches were made as a means to escape and hide in the case of a terrorist attack. They ran for quite a few kilometres around the clubhouse, sports spots and various T's on the golf course. When we were not fighting off imaginary armies we would put on shows, for instance we formed a group and pretended we were ABBA, performing for those unfortunate adults who would be forced to endure a terrible rendition of such songs such as "Waterloo." In fact, ABBA became a religion in Mkwasine.

It blasted from the clubhouse speakers constantly like a Chinese raindrop on the centre of your forehead.

It was on one of these party evenings that I was proposed to in the children's playroom. One of the boys got down on one knee and asked me to marry him, producing a ring from a Christmas cracker. I also had my first kiss. I remember thinking that was rather sweet of him.

The clubhouse also offered Movie Night on a Friday evening. Children got to watch Disney cartoons after which we were sent to the car, in the car park. Since I had no Nyika, I went alone. In the

171

back of the Peugeot, there was a mattress with a sheet and blanket and also a small picnic in a basket, which my mother had made with care and love. A lot of other kids we sitting in their Peugeot 404's and land rovers too, all probably being fed the same thing, only they had supervision, which limited their scopes really. I certainly had an advantage here. Freedom, not to go to sleep on time for example.

In the cubby hole of the car, in-front of the picnic basket (which was positioned on the passenger seat, next to the driver) was a small handheld revolver in case it was needed. Some kids play with revolvers and some kids play with the Rubik's cube, depending on where you grow up. I am relieved that I never had to use it. I am forever grateful not to have had blood on my hands. I say play with a revolver, because as a kid you really do not understand the magnitude of self-defence. In the end, you would probably trust an untrustful adult.

My picnic or as it was more commonly referred to as a "midnight snack" religiously contained two boiled eggs, with a little salt wrapped in tinfoil, cheese and tomato sandwiches, chopped tomatoes, cucumbers, and a "liqui-fruit," either guava or apricot (this was an absolute treat as you could only buy these in South Africa). If there were no liqui fruits there was either a pack of jelly tots, a chocolate log, a local chocolate called a Fredo Frog or black sweets called Nigger Balls. These were eventually renamed in 1980 and called Black Balls. There were also gobstoppers – apricot and peach flavoured hard sweets with a soft marsh mellow filling.

One evening, I heard the adults mention that the film JAWS would be showing. I was thrilled and nervous because I planned to sneak back to the clubhouse to watch it. When I heard the Universal introduction through the windows of the Peugeot, with the drumbeat after the trumpets, my heart quickened. I climbed out the car and snuck through all the plants and trees to the front lawn of the clubhouse. I would have to sprint across ten metres of open lawn with no protection so if I was seen I was busted. I'd have to return to the car with a warm backside, courtesy a la Mama.

I made it. Inside, I could see the big screen and I was just in time. I peeped around one of the huge pillars, got as comfortable as possible and had my eyes glued to the screen. Hiding between the elephant ear plants and the pillar. Naturally, I did not know what to expect and when the child got knocked off the plastic floating dingy, I screamed. All the adults turned around in the direction of the scream, however, they were so engrossed in the movie that no one was willing to investigate the source.

I watched wide-eyed for the entire movie. I was riveted. Naturally, the truth came out when I was too afraid to get into the swimming pool the following day at the Harris' house. These were friends of ours. My mother's best friend actually, who did not frequent the clubhouse ever. She played her tennis and then went home. My father insisted on staying after a shower and his round of golf, tennis or squash at this House of Horror Club House.

It would be Christmas the following week and Christmas at the clubhouse was a real treat. The only good thing about the place. My father directed a show every year involving lots of women doing the "Cancan." The signature dance from France. I wonder why? I have to admit they looked amazing. With their bright-coloured outfits, high heels and kicking their legs high into the sky, I was mesmerised. So was my father. Miss Sherry and my mother naturally were the best by far and, naturally, my father was not looking at my mother.

All the families gathered at the clubhouse as Father Christmas was arriving. We were all so excited that he had managed to find Mkwasine having travelled so far from the North Pole. Even though I no longer believed in him. Our Father Christmas, though, arrived in a Huey Helicopter, escorted by two army soldiers with rifles sort of like a gangster Father Christmas, which landed on the practice putting green to the side of the clubhouse surrounded by eucalyptus trees.

When the helicopter landed, and had switched off its engine and the blades had stopped rotating, Father Christmas climbed out of the chopper and strode across the putting green, chest puffed out, huge belly, with an enormous sack on his back and one in his hand. Two soldiers had jumped out of the chopper just before it landed – about a metre from the ground – like ninja turtles. They had quickly positioned themselves to sight terrorists and shoot them if necessary. Dressed as elves, absurd, quite obscene.

Father Christmas walked into the breezeway at the club and took his place on his stool at the foot of the almighty Christmas tree decorated with crepe paper and soap-scudded homemade snow made from LUX beauty soap, that you grate and mix with water, till it forms hard peaks of artificial snow. My mother made this, then transported it in a cool box and threw it at the tree with a wooden spoon, half aggressively, for the love of God, religion and her situation. The Christmas tree was made from asparagus fern and spray-painted silver propped up on a piece of spray-painted gold driftwood. All the children had made handmade drawings of Father Christmas and coloured them in with wax crayons. They now hung from the tree – the colours running from the melting soap snow in amongst the tinsel.

We took turns receiving our gift and a packet of sweets from him alongside the tree whilst we sat on his lap. That year I received a doll. The first doll I had ever owned, it was called the "Walkie Talkie Doll." What was I supposed to do with a doll? Such an innocent present for such novice times. She stood in my world as if another piece of shrapnel. Facing the corner of my bedroom. She creeped me out.

On this particular day, my best friend, Joshua Harris, informed me that this year, 'Father Christmas was his dad!' He was so proud!

I spent so much time with Josh that he became like a brother to me and I found his company refreshing. I was the only girl allowed to play with his boy group which was made up of Columbus and Captain Cook, Da Gama, Peter Pan, Sir Francis Drake and Halvah Hudson.

There was no girl group and eventually my friend Shereen joined the boy group too, not to be outdone, I pretended to be Isabella Bird (183-1904) an English explorer, writer, photographer & naturalist, she was the first female to be inducted into the Royal Geographic Society of London and Shereen pretended she was Annie Smith Peck (1850 – 1935), one of the greatest mountaineers of the 19th century. We pretended we were in the army, fighting our imaginary wars. I was in charge of keeping the ledger and my friend drew routes of our treks, through imaginary terrains in the conjured-up mountains. We had an enormous amount of fun as children. We were allowed to camp out at night (only after the war), with our bushfires and our own tents. Making it all very real. The Harris' house became my second home and my mother and Josh's mother became firm friends – Clare Harris and Claire Hagen. The Claire's/Clare's. We were at the Harris' house every Sunday without fail. That particular Sunday was as if God himself was going to make an appearance, everyone was shocked and speechless, pink lip-sticked mouths agape, saliva stretched as if chewing gum between lips, catching flies. Then very verbal, hysterical and gobsmacked. Mr Jackson, no way, his poor wife, oh no God no. Gasps, tennis match forgotten and scandal at breakneck speed.

A cracking whip and a shot in the dark. People were left reeling and speechless. Mr. Jackson had run away with the maid! Good Lord. You could hear the gasps falling like expensive china sliding off a tea tray. Welcoming the shrill sound of female scandal. Scandal bags lacking in imagination.

No one had the full story but it was the talk of the high tea. Never, had whispers been so tantalizing and at the same time ludicrous. Most ladies took the stance of, "Thank, God, it wasn't their husbands." However, they were ignoring the very real likelihood that their husbands were not perhaps as devoted as they may have liked to believe. Those trenches around the clubhouse exposed dark secrets. I had seen some of these woman down there, panting and not because it was hot down there. Colonial times, in such an uncertain war-driven situation, is a recipe for such behaviour.

However, there are different views about our farmers, and one you cannot ignore was that they were the backbone of the country's success. Our country was reeling from war. A stagnated future was the only dish on the menu. Everyone was fed up and confused. The farmers and the farm workers had made sure Rhodesia and Zimbabwe were the bread baskets of Africa, and so it came to pass that the country was turned into a basket-case country instead, and you question my sanity?

The war started in Rhodesia on the 4th of July in the year 1964 and ended on the 12th of December in the year 1979. I was eight, going on eighty. You can grow up rather quickly under these circumstances. Rhodesia's Unilateral Declaration of Independence was signed on the 11th of November in the year 1965, in the capital which was then called Salisbury, now Harare. The signatories were Ian Smith (Prime Minister of Rhodesia, Clifford Dupont the Deputy Prime Minister of other cabinet ministers).

Ian Smith was a nonconformist. He truly believed that we could be a great country working and progressing alongside one another. It was his hope, his dream, like so many of us who wanted to see equality for all races and tribes in Zimbabwe. I include the word tribes because tribal warfare soon took place after independence. So independence was available but only if you supported the Zanu PF party, if you didn't and you supported the other tribal party, you were tossed aside, Gukurahundi in force! A dictatorship fresh for the picking! Smith was exhausted by London's quibbling, niggling, cavilling and old-fashioned approach. He was particularly annoyed by the continuous quell and repression of the Zimbabwean Majority. Ian Smith did not want to encourage colonialism, quite the opposite actually. He truly wanted the best for everyone in our country. In our country there were more than black and white races, there was more than one tribe and, in the confusion, other races and tribes were swept aside.

Ian Smith walked to work, or he cycled on his bike, he was never in a convoy loaded with protection. It is said that the war took 30,000 souls, I beg to differ, I think it was significantly more. Regardless, one soul is one soul to many. After the Gukurahundi Massacre scenario created solely by the dictator, there are said to be another 20,000 souls added to this heap of soullessness and complete lack of vision and empathy for our Zimbabwe.

Zimbabwe's new leader pressurized and persuaded at the same time his own people to treat themselves impecuniously. He wore the best designer clothing and rallied his people to remain barefoot. That sort of wraps up his vision for his people and as a unit for our country. Here and no further.

Zimbabwe could've been one of Southern Africa's most lush, fortunate and blooming countries, if handled correctly, able to stand on its own feet barefoot or not, given half the chance. Our one wonder of the world, Mugabe, no of course not, yes, Victoria Falls, majestic in its vastness and plunging waters, its transfixing motion drawing you into a natural embedded trance. The Smoke that Thunders, apt. Not only the Zambezi River but the entire Zambezi basin displaying an abundance second to none of plant life and wild animal life alike. Zimbabwe's soil, a desire of many a country. It is said that Zimbabwe is the richest country *per square meter* in mineral wealth in the entire world.

In 1997, Zimbabwe had the fastest growing economy in all of Africa; now it's the fastest plummeting. Dimming away bit by tiny bit. The all-weather friend having a field day! A onetime net exporter of maize, cotton, beef, tobacco, roses, protea's, wheat and sugarcane now exports only its scholarly and lettered, non-manuals and manuals alike, who are fleeing by the tens of thousands, along with all our minerals such as gold, nickel and diamonds. Gold and Tobacco being of the highest scorers. In amounts of four to five billion US dollars a year. Is there a light at the end of the tunnel? Your guess is as good as mine. Although Zimbabwe has some of the richest farmland in Africa, children with "kwashiorkor" bellies are parading the streets. Kwashiorkor is a severe form of malnutrition. It's most common in some developing regions of the world, where babies and children do not get enough protein or essential nutrients in their diet. The main sign of kwashiorkor is too much fluid in the body's tissues, this will cause swelling. A honest sign of a country where good food is not readily available.

As foot in sock, the new government began stifling the throb of the very productivity for which our country was celebrated, asphyxiated we began to tumble.

Any facility that crosses your mind, from schools to cinema's, sports clubs and so forth, everything, suddenly bearing an abstemious resemblance of an empty carnival arena. With only the clowns remaining. Smiles not reaching their eyes. Public toilets sinking in their own waste. Farmers and business people once discussing in elation cotton prices, now they could barely afford clothing. Sports results were now pushed aside and a sudden migration as if we were birdlike was becoming the norm.

Getting one's money out of Zimbabwe was a further challenge and creativity was at an all – time high.

The first couple of years after independence, people were known to re-invest in the country. Our family certainly did. We believed in our country! We even believed in our leaders. People had hope. It dwindled and was left to the wayside. The shrub of the yesterday, today and tomorrow plant dying in the aftermath.

An increase in the illegal wildlife trade is rumoured. It's difficult to establish the truth, simply because no one knows what to believe anymore. Once again abusing souls without a voice. The sheer scrapings of what remains, a pot left to long on a fire. When there is no more water and you never bothered to fix that dripping tap!

The dictator in his paranoia and panic due to his subsiding popularity, decided to eradicate all the farmers. He played the race card whenever his position was challenged. With no plan at all.

The farmers were forced to leave. If they were not killed first. Unproductive, weeds began growing in fields. Some farms he gave to his cronies. The farms were never given to "the people". His people once again left out of the mix, the lost ingredient.

For farmers, farm workers and their families, this was no easy task. They made sure no one went starving in our country – all races. Farm workers lost their livelihoods, lost everything in the hope they would be given land. Farm workers did not want to attack farm owners, some of them were forced to commit atrocities that they did not want to have anything to do with. They were never given anything. Far too many of them, later on, farmers and farm workers alike were killed by bloodthirsty teenagers and other unemployed individuals...

Brainwashed. This band of "angry army" were not even born when there was the struggle for independence. They had too much time on their hands and too much time leads to one thing – trouble. People were burnt alive in front of their wives and children. Fires running across mowed lawns.

Everyone lost someone they loved in the late 1990s and early 2000s. I was left with an extremely disturbing image of US dollars blowing in the breeze on washing lines, hanging on wooden pegs, a dollar a peg. Left to dry and only then to re-enter the market. Packets of one dollar-bills, tattered and torn. A dollar bill escaped a peg, and landed on the street, a child ran to catch it, this gave a whole new meaning to autumn leaves. I watched the washing line fade in the rear-view mirror. It began to rain.

The Mkwasine clan, despite its personal hang-ups, the odd back-stabbing and rife promiscuity, would invariably stick together. Whether there was a family emergency, a farm attack or someone needing a lift, families would always look out for each other, in this "particular" respect, as not to would only be completely stupid.

With the fear of terrorist attacks always in the back of our minds, it was a comforting thought to know that there were others looking out for you.

I had finished Standard One at Mkwasine Junior School. I was turning 8 and I was to be sent to the nearest town, Chiredzi to become a weekly border.

Chriedzi was the town where I had apparently been born, at 10p.m. at night, my father assisting in the delivery since he was no newbie to delivering babies. Chiredzi hospital. It has recently been in the news, as a large crocodile had been spotted wondering down it's corridors after the recent floods in that particular area. Still remote people, still remote.

Nyika came to mind, and I pushed the painful thought aside. When I was a toddler Nyika had come into my life. I also missed Kudzai, but the memory of him was fading. I couldn't think too much of her, or them. I had decided that if I did, it would only be to remember the good things about her or him and to imagine that they were at the end of the rainbow. Even if it was probably, not the case. Only then did I not feel too guilty. The guilt weighed heavily on my heart. Oh, hurry up and get older, so you can do as you wish. I had foolishly told Happiness in a moment of trust that I was planning to ride to Nyika on horseback, to find out the proper story.

Incredibly gullible of me I believed he may help me. He had told my parents. My horse-riding days became monitored. That plan went out the window. My mind drifted to Chiredzi and what I was to expect from this dorp.

My mother had told me the story of her rushed delivery of me and the very bumpy car ride from Ngwane Ranch to Chiredzi, on the dam awful roads, it probably served in a healthy and helpful delivery. She reminisced of the moment my brother and sisters were waiting patiently in the car for my birth. They had also had to endure the tedious journey in the war years of charging out in the early evening, guns blazing literally, to get me into this world. No convoy. Then on top of it all, sit in the car and await a new sibling. Directly outside the delivery room window. As I was coming into this world my mother and father heard my brother say, if it's another girl I am leaving! Still a family story to this day.

Chapter Ten
Chiredzi

Chiredzi was more or less a one-horse town. Naturally I have a soft spot for it having been born there. I am sure that most individuals reading this book have never heard of the place. Not to worry.

Chiredzi is a small town in the Mas Vegas Province, in south-east Zimbabwe. It is located near the Runde River and its tributary is called the Chiredzi. Its rural council was established in 1967.

It has a population of 30,197. The Chiredzi, also includes the famous Gonarezhou National Park with Malilangwe. International celebrities at one point flocked there. Its wildlife consisting of carnivorous, herbivorous and omnivorous animals, such as the red-billed quelea and the Zimbabwean Cheetah. Chiredzi, although small, is very important. It serves the area's irrigated agricultural industry. Although its mostly in a natural region, it is marginally suitable for dryland cropping and it is suited to extensive livestock production or game ranching. Primarily, the sugar estates are in need of irrigation. My father was the chairman of The Zimbabwe Cotton Growers Association. Chiredzi also has a small airport called Buffalo Range, where I often flew to with my father in our plane.

Chiredzi means, "a place where a fish can be caught by a line or a string."

In the town's centre there was a grocery shop, a bank (Barclays), the famous Bata shoe shop, a chemist, the post office and a takeaway. That's it. In the industrial area was the cold storage. Which I visited on one occasion and vowed never to return. There was only one car park in the middle of all these shops.

A letter had arrived in the mail; a response to the advertisement my parents had posted. Remember the advert:

Seeking a loving family to host our daughter Joanna Vye Hagen aged eight at your home from a Sunday evening until close of school on a Friday at 12 noon. Anyone wishing to assist us please contact Claire or Herman Hagen on this number – two shorts and three longs. Naturally your kindness will be compensated.

The headmaster of the school I was to attend and his wife a teacher at the school were to be my hosts. They were the Paterson's and they had a daughter, Elina, who was two years my junior.

The Christmas holidays soon came to a grinding halt and it was now time to start weekly boarding with the Paterson's.

My father drove me to my new host family that coming Sunday afternoon. I had tried every trick in the book not to become a weekly boarder. I had made a glass of soap and water, drunk it in the hope it would make me ill, only to burp bubbles. I had acted a starring role in saying I had a stomach-ache. I had held my hot water bottle on my forehead for ages to create a temperature. I had held hot tea in my mouth for a thermometer, but had choked on it and given myself up. I had begged Blessing to talk to my parents and persuade them not to send me away from home. 'If we did it, Joe, you can do it,' my father and family said firmly. My mother looked away, onto a horizon of uncertainty and disdain. Her dislike for my father was beginning to increase by the minute.

My suitcase was packed. A week felt like eternity, not to be with my parents, Blessing, Happiness, Blaze and Misty. I had a small tuck box filled with treats. A big packet of homemade biltong and crunchies. I had asked Blessing to please make sure I would not starve, as I had no idea what this family I was going to cooked like.

I also had a present for the Paterson's: a tin of Colcom Gammon Ham (pure gold). This was the ultimate gift from a Zimbabwean to another Zimbabwean or a South African family originally from Zimbabwe. Like spaghetti is to Italians or liquorice is to the Nederlanders.

We arrived in our upgraded blue 504 Peugeot Station Wagon. The Peugeot 404 now a museum piece. The Paterson's were diligently waiting for us on their patio. The father looked like a headmaster. He had dark hair, cropped very short. A large nose reserved for intelligent people. He always wore matching veterinarian outfits, with long socks and city shoes perfectly polished. He was a kind man. His wife had a mass of bright, raw-red hair representing the colour of a bright copper and her freckles stood out on her pale skin. They were both above the average height. She had a distinct elegance. She wore '70s dresses with bright floral patterns and came with an easy laughter. My father definitely ruffled her feathers, and she would blush deeply, and spluttering politely 'oh Hagen, how wonderful,' head bowed and eyes a flutter. She was not the only teacher in my school career that had developed a crush on my father. She could be fiery within a second though, turning the colour of a ripe red tomatoes. She drove us to school every morning in her beige Renault. As it turned out, she could not cook and therefore surplus supplies had been a good idea.

Their daughter Elina was the spitting image of her mother, a missed opportunity of a Loretta Lux potential portrait. She took every inch of my patience. Forever the tell-tale girl.

My father parked the car, got out and pushed his door closed. It was my opportunity. I moved as fast as a pouncing cat and locked all the doors by pushing the black doorknobs down. The boot was already locked as there was always a fear of being robbed when travelling through town.

The keys to the car were in the ignition. I was as pleased as punch with myself. *Take that, Daddy! I don't have to be left with this crazy bunch. What are you going to do now?* My father was greeting the Paterson's and he turned to check if I had followed him. He stared at me as I remained sat in the car and I could see as he walked to the car that he was annoyed. I could literally see his face crumbling in anger. He reached for the door handle. It was locked. I just looked at him. He walked around the car until he had tried all the doors and realised they were all locked and the keys were in the ignition. He turned to tell the Paterson's that he would have to deal with me and they were welcome wait or he would give them a shout when all was in order again.

It took a lot of coaxing and negotiation through a small gap in one of the windows but eventually I emerged. Of course, nothing that my father promised me during that negotiation ever materialised. Oh, for the love and belief of a parent.

I greeted my new "rent a family" and was shown my room. It consisted of two beds with baby pink eider downs with that classic diamond sewn shape on the cover made from polyester. The same shape was on the pillows too. My mind screamed prison cell. Pink on top of it – baby pink. Lord have mercy. There was clunky white furnisher scattered all over the place and a carpeted floor in an awful shade of mauve. No taste at all it screeched. These people ate bubble and squeak for God's sake. Happily, I was not to stay with them for too long as soon my life took a turn for the better.

I had been going to school at Chiredzi Jnr School for six months. The school in itself was rather pretty, it had a beautiful garden, miniature tennis courts made from clay to help us tiny tots learn to play tennis. Great athletic, rugby, hockey and cricket fields. Nobody played football. School started at 7:30 a.m. every morning and finished at 5 p.m. Sport was compulsory, so learning to be competitive from an early age was built into my make up. There was music school, so I joined the choir. I preferred swimming and tennis over every other activity. I excelled at swimming. I had made two friends, Clint Robin and Dirk Mathews. I was secretly in love with Clint Robin. He however didn't give me the time of day. It was the first boy that had had that effect on me. Suddenly, school became a better place to be. He sat next to me in maths because he was so bad at it and I was so good at it.

My main tutor's name was Mrs Dunoyer. She was a great lady; she made me fall in love with school and she radiated class. She developed my love for storytelling. She encouraged and praised my runaway imagination and did not criticise it. She had two sons at my school, kind boys, very clever. I had joined an art school program for after school as art was my favourite subject. It was during my art class that the little bit of the world I had tried to hold together fell apart.

My father had informed my mother and I that he would be attending a farmer's conference in Durban (South Africa), that it was to be a business trip and that wives and children had not been invited. It was unfortunate, he told us, but it was their rules not his. He promised to bring "Hello Kitty" stuff on his return and groceries with all our favourite goodies. He was to be away for three weeks.

I was in my art class after the Easter holidays. I had not seen my father very much anyway, and for the fourth week he was home, he was always out in the fields or playing golf or tennis at the Mkwasine Sports Club. So, it came to be that I found out about my father's girlfriend.

An art classmate asked me out of the blue, 'How was your holiday?'

I said, 'Fine. Nothing special. Spent all my time with my horses and my mum.'

'Oh,' "it" continued, 'because we went on holiday with your dad to Durban.'

'That's not possible,' I replied, 'my father was working at a conference in Durban.'

'Your dad is my mother's boyfriend. For quite some time now. They met at a tennis match in Triangle.'

My cheeks burnt. Hot tears stung my eyes.

This happened so fast. I didn't know what to start thinking or how to react. The art teacher picked up that something was out of whack and called me to his desk. The pieces fitted, one of her kids, was in my year class. Interestingly enough, her child had the exact same Hello Kitty stuff as me, just in other colours. Only available in South Africa, that is where Durban is. The puzzle came to an end. The picture, clear.

'What's troubling you, young lady?'

'I just found out that that my father is having an affair,' I replied in hushed tones, 'that he lied to me and my mum and said he was on a farming conference in Durban.'

The teacher looked at me dumbfounded for a split second.

'Let's go for a walk.'

We walked to the rugby field, he put his arm around my shoulder. I loved my art teacher. He was wonderful, the best teacher I ever had. Mr Yend. It all made sense now. All those Friday afternoons waiting for my dad to pick me up at noon.

Instead, he used to arrive at 3 p.m. or 4 p.m. I was left alone, sitting on my suitcase waiting outside the locked school gate to go home. I used to watch the last kid being collected. Sitting on my wooden suitcase, pushing my shoes awkwardly into the sand, eyes cast down, trying to avoid judgement, questions that I could not answer. My Tutor, Mrs Dunoyer, would wait for as long as she could. Not wanting to intrude, but wanting to at the same time. Eventually leaving. She would wave goodbye reluctantly. She knew what was going on. Why had no-one informed my mother? How was I supposed to tell her this? I thought that if I didn't then it would all just go away. I kept my mouth tightly shut.

The security guard became my friend. His name was Lovemore. A strong Zulu and Shona man. Mixed blood. I felt protected by him. He had long dreadlocks and huge kind eyes. He kept me company, we played drafts with rocks and sticks on the sand or we would look for twirly-whirlies.

These are little animals the size of 2mm. They look like sand tanks, out of the war in Afghanistan, their homes are in the soft sand, in an upside down and hollow pyramid. With a stick of grass, you mix the upside-down pyramid ever so gently, as the object of the discovery is not to destroy its home it is only to expose them gently and briefly. Then you watch them borrow down again. Oh, my goodness, what one does to pass time. During the rainy season we would look for the baby rain spiders and rescue them from the rivers of rain. He shared his umbrella with me. He also shared his hot sweet tea.

He told me stories of Matabeleland in the north of our country how the Zulu's conquered every other African Tribe and how the Matabele were tougher, smarter and stronger than the Shona's. He told me how he hated being half Shona and half Matabele how he didn't fit anywhere. Mixed marriages were frowned upon in those days between the Shona and Ndebele. Well, I told him you fit here looking after us kids at school, if that helps you? All Fridays were spent this way, wasting time that I could have had with my mom, Blessing, Happiness, Blaze and Misty.

It happened on one occasion, my crush came to me in the playground, why are you always the last to leave school? It's me and then you, or Mrs Dunoyer then me then you, do you, want to come home with us one time? I smiled. That's very kind of you but I never know when my father will arrive. The following week, my crush stayed with me, he bought extra lunch, and we both played draughts with the security guard. When my father arrived, he was surprised. He knew the family. My crush stayed every Friday after that. I soon began looking forward to Friday afternoons after school wound up. He was the kindest boy I had ever met. We played marbles all afternoon, rain or shine.

Today was Friday. I once again sat till 4 p.m. waiting for my dad to collect me. He arrived, late as usual, full of bouncy energy. We climbed into the car. I knew his secret now. Weeks had passed, me knowing his secret, watching his behaviour at home. My sibling's knew nothing either. However, I was not going to say a word. I was not equipped.

I said I didn't feel well so I didn't have to speak. The truth is I did not feel well at all. The art teacher had asked if I wanted to say anything to the headmaster or have a meeting with my parents.

To which I replied, 'I need some time to digest this all, thank you, and no I don't want a parent meeting with teachers.'

Home life on weekends was awkward. Fortunately, however, this weekend, after about six months, we were invited to the Harris's house for a barbeque and tennis. I would see Josh and tell him all the news. Maybe he would have some advice for me. I doubted this, however, all he wanted to do was behave like a hooligan and throw water bombs.

We arrived and the get together was in full swing. They had a Spanish gazebo overlooking the pool, rambling lawn and at the far end of the garden was the tennis court. They always had water scorpions in their swimming pool and spiders in their toilets. The buggers in the pool meaning the water scorpions could fly and sting. However, the daddy long legs in the bathroom they were harmless but hid in the spare toilet rolls and an unexpected tickle on your fingers would often rattle you.

The Spanish gazebo had a dance floor and a bar with an amazing stereo system. ABBA blasted from the speakers. Then after that, STARS on 45. Not to be outdone, Mr Harris himself took out his trumpet reminding me of when he played outside our home the morning after the attack all those years ago.

The war had come to an end today. It was the 12th of December, 1979. We had one more week of school before the Christmas holidays.

Result: Majority rule introduced under the Lancaster House Agreement. Zimbabwe granted internationally recognised independence.

Some adults were jiving and us kids followed Mr. Harris like the Pied Piper. We all knew the drill and thoroughly enjoyed this part of the day; it had become tradition. We marched and sang at the top of our voices.

In the excitement we decided to go for a swim and changed into our costumes. My mother suggested that I show Clare Harris how well I could dive. I don't know what happened but I dived straight down and hit my head on the bottom of the pool.

Apparently, someone jumped in to pull me out and I came out of a minor concussion spluttering and saying, 'Mum, Dad has a girlfriend. Her child is in my art class. Her name is Molly Reed.'

My mother cradled me in her arms and took me inside to the Harris's lounge where she burst into tears.

'Clare, did you know about this?' she asked.

Turning to her best friend.

'Yes. We did. We've all met her.'

'What?'

'I didn't know how to tell you,' Clare continued. 'She is part of the tennis crowd in Triangle.

'How long has this been going on to your knowledge, Clare?'

'Roughly half a year,' replied Clare, clearly embarrassed.

My mother placed a pack of frozen peas on my forehead and laid a duvet over me.

She walked outside. She returned with her handbag. We left the party. She cried a lot. It was the last day I saw any of the Lowveld people. On returning home, she told Blessing the news and said we would be leaving at the end of the week. She made a phone call to my father at the Harris's to tell him to find other accommodation whilst she packed up the house and divided everything equally among them. That she would file for divorce. It was game over. She drove me the one and a half hours to school, that Sunday telling me she needed to pack alone and it was too emotional having me around. I said goodbye to Flame and Misty wondering if I would ever see them again. Wednesday had been bitten by a cobra and had died a couple of months back.

School passed that week in a haze. That Friday, after school, dead on time, my mother arrived at noon to collect me from the last day of my life in Chiredzi and my last day at Chiredzi Junior School. The Peugeot 504 was piled high with our few belongings. Blessing was in the car with my mother. I was so grateful, to see him and I felt cheerful to know that he was coming with us. We were returning to my mother's hometown, previously called Fort Victoria and now Masvingo, or as I call it, Mas Vegas. I said my goodbyes to the security guard, Lovemore. I was sad to say goodbye to my pash. He kissed me on my cheek. You're tough he said. No need to worry. See you around. Giving me a bag of marbles, he spun on his heel and ran to the playground. I never saw him again.

My mother had dressed for this occasion and was wearing a flamboyant summer dress with a hair headband, big plastic earrings, bangles, heels and her seventies glasses. Blessing was dressed in a suit with his ever so famous bowler hat and bow tie. His cravat in his jacket pocket. They hugged me tight. I said goodbye to everyone I knew. I felt downhearted to say farewells to my art teacher Mr Yend, Lovemore of course, and Mrs. Dunoyer. I said my cheers to the Paterson's. They had been sweet enough.

We drove through the school gates looking like gypsies. New adventures. Mostly I felt confused. I didn't know how to feel about my father and some time without him around would be welcome. Then I heard the smallest meow, repeatedly. I grinned, yes it was a kitten. Black and white and looking like a powder puff. I named her Puppet. I felt a certain sadness lift from me. My mother slid a tape into the tape deck. Blessing rolled his eyes, and rolled a joint then lit it, took a deep toque and relaxed smiling, my mother pumped up the volume and yes ABBA blasted through the speakers. We were on the long drive to Mas Vegas and the war was over. No more convoys, no more late panic, no more bunches of keys falling to the ground and grappling nervous hands trying to pick them up to put them in the ignition to gain time. Blessing started singing along to ABBA as well. A new chapter once again and I was filled with optimism as I had not felt that in ages. Puppet curled up into the top of my neck. I leant against my pillow propped up against the window. I was to be a day scholar again, to be with Blessing and my mother. Rumour had it that my sister Bell would live with us to, how wonderful. Joy mine for the taking. Where the hell was Nyika?

Chapter Eleven
Mas Vegas

Mas Vegas is situated smack bang in the heart of Shona Ville. It is where all the best Southern African Art, especially sculptures, come from and originated. The majority of artworks you see in South Africa are from Zimbabwe. Apart from the bead work. In my opinion, we have the best sculptures in Africa.

The Mas Vegas area I grew up in was literally surrounded by natural artistic talent. I was blessed by beautiful and majestic surroundings and dramatic images from the get-go.

Shona artists are becoming rather popular, mainly known for their finely carved soapstone sculptures. There are five main Shona language groups Kore, Zeseru, Manyika, Ndau and Karanga. To know about their history is imperative. At the end of this book, there is a specific document, for a thorough look into the Shangaans, it's a very good read in order to fully understand the migration and changes of the African Tribes of the region. I grew up in the South of Zimbabwe. The Ndebele (which are currently these days mostly situated in the north of Zimbabwe), absorb the last of these groups, when they moved into western/northern Zimbabwe in the 1830's. Shona's, prefer to live in isolated settlements usually consisting of one or more elder men and their extended families. A Shona's religion is a blend of monotheism and veneration of ancestors. Their god being Mwari the creator. Ancestors and intermediaries are used as connectors to Mwari.

As we drove along the tar road towards Mas Vegas, I watched the thatched huts and hills pass by out of the car window, my kitten Puppet curled up fast asleep on my lap. Blessing played the mouth organ whilst we listened in silence. The sadness in its notes moving us. My mother wiped tears away from time to time through-out the journey. After all they had been married for twenty-five years, they had built a life and family together, gone through a war together, lost a child together and built a business together. My heart hurt for my mother; she was fragile during this period but not broken. How much more was this world going to ask of any of us, I wondered. Blessing sang the blues on this journey. It helped process some of our emotions. Blessing our true Blessing.

I missed Nyika a great deal, and I could really have benefited from her company in that moment. I wanted to grow up as fast as possible and go and find her. Now that my parents were divorcing it would have been incredibly comforting to have her here around with my mother, Blessing and I. Had Nyika left Zimbabwe? had she gone to live in SA, like so many other Zimbabweans fleeing this country. We were barely out of one war and there were talks of another? I had asked Blessing and Happiness where she was, but to no avail. I had asked the whole tribe; I had asked the Chief. He totally ignored me and had banned me from the compound. Saying I was a nuisance. He had no idea where Nyika was and that she and Kudzai were dead to him and to his tribe. He said he was too old for all this commotion!

As of 2019, a count showed 12 million Shona in Zimbabwe and in neighbouring South Africa a count of two million Shona's. At the hands of the tribes of South Africa the Shona's suffered terribly, due to the fact they were seen more favourably when it came to hiring employee's, naturally because they were educated, we never had apartheid. So many Zimbabweans had left for greener pastures, only to risk their lives once more to xenophobia.

South Africans abhorred Zimbabweans for their higher level of education, the Zimbabweans endured horrific tortures, xenophobia rife. I just hoped and prayed Nyika was not one of them. Blessing had told me a million times to let it rest.

I started my life in Mas Vegas. To get some perspective, here are some distances, so you may understand the magnitude of the area and so forth.

The distance from Chiredzi to Mas Vegas is 200 kilometres. If, you drive at 120km/ph. you are likely to arrive within two hours. The likely hood of this was pretty unreal as the roads were and still are tainted with potholes, donkeys, cattle, goats, chickens, the odd person, dog or scotch carts laden with goods for the market. In the meanwhile, bus drivers tend to overtake on blind corners and blind rises that are located on the verge of a bridge. These buses tend to be over laden, may I add, not only with people's luggage but also with bicycles, mealie-meal bags, bread, goats, pigs, chickens and whatever you can imagine. The odd person sitting on the roof of the bus amongst the luggage, a familiar sight... The only thing missing was the kitchen sink.

People drive with no lights at night, only guided by the moon, the god Mwari, Chibuku beer and the strong smell of the herb drifting out the windows of the huts. The lights of the cars probably do work they just forgot to switch them on. Small holding fires burn brightly at sunset in the compounds, and the smell of sadza on the boil mixed with wood smoke, fried onions and garlic fills the air. Tonight, would be a killer sunset. The drums were beating rhythmically as the women went about their chores. Each passing moment appeared and faded - similar to a projector of slides, filtering through my mind.

Mkwasine to Chiredzi is 40 kilometres, it is incredibly close. Mkwasine was the farming Estate we moved to after the Ngwane Ranch House in Zaka, where all the terrorist attacks took place. Chiredzi was my third place of schooling and Mas Vegas Junior school would be fourth, the first being Ngwane school on the air brought to me by the BBC, then Mkwasine Estate Junior School, then Chiredzi Junior School.

Mas Vegas to where Nyika lives is 87 kilometres apart. In Mas Vegas, I went to Fort Victoria Junior School for a year, whilst my mother and father figured out their new lives. Once they had done that, all communications went through me, which was an absolute bane. No emails or WhatsApp's back then and they preferred not to talk on the phone either. My father was officially not allowed on my mother's property. They really despised each other for years. He had to make his appearance known, by hooting at the front gate. I was a day scholar. Which meant I slept at home in my own bed day after day, week after week, month after month for a solid year. I loved this life. I thought it may even last. Masvingo was called Fort Victoria before the war, named by the Brits. Mas Vegas was mostly known for tourism for Kyle National Park, Sculptures and art/crafts, Mushandike National Park and the Zimbabwe Ruins.

We arrived in Mas Vegas at 4 p.m. on the dot. We were perfectly on time for traditional afternoon tea at my Aunty Joyce's house. She was my mother's younger half-sister. For the next couple of months, we would be living with my aunt until we moved into our own home. I looked up the rambling lawn, towards my aunt's abode. They were all playing gin rummy outside, I could hear the shrieks and bet placing from a mile away.

I once saw my father out and about with his new family in Mas Vegas. It was the oddest experience, as if I had never known him. Wondering through Meikles Department Store buying clothing for his new wife and her kids. I just stared at them. A deer in headlights. They had not seen us. Come on said my mom. It will get better over time. He had turned his back, and I watched him laughing and joking with them. His new family.

I watched him pick up his novel three-year-old, ruffle his catechumen son's hair. The other daughter was from my epoch. My stomach knotted and stayed knotted for years. His new wife was a whippersnapper. Cliché. His hand slid down her back, landing suggestively on her very young ass. He hadn't seen us.

After tea, we were to view our new home. I was looking forward to this, full of enthusiasm. Finally, my very own bedroom, and if things couldn't get even better, I was allowed to decorate it as I saw fit. For the first time ever, I would not be sharing a bedroom with my sister. Peace for the both of us at long last.

The only downside was that I would not have easy access to her clothing and make-up, (which I sucked at), but loved to try out regardless. Something she loathed me for. Later on in life, she got me back though. I got to feel the blunt end of the stick. I could listen to my own music full blast without her screaming at me to turn it down. As much as you can love your sisters they can also get on your nerves at times. She had the room alongside mine. I decided to decorate my room, in burnt oranges, beige, greens and golds, the colour of wheat. Fawns all over the curtains in a monotonous pattern. A clown hung from my ceiling a present from an ex-girlfriend of my brother's. As if masking my thoughts.

I had inherited my mother's dressing table. How I adored that piece of furniture. So many memories came along with that dressing table. I sat on my mother's lap there, whilst she got dressed every morning, and she placed a splash of perfume on my wrists. Through the various perfume phases; Blue Grass, then Opium, then Red Door. My mother had styled and cut my hair in front of this mirror whilst I sat on the dressing table stool, on more occasions than I could recall. I had taken out her curlers on Sundays in front of this mirror. We polished our nails here. I watched my beautiful mother intently as she applied make up to her Sophie Lauren eyebrows. I smiled.

Auntie Joyce's house was cheerful and coruscating, always full to the brim of delicious food. Cakes, cheeses, breads, all types of desserts the best potatoes you have ever tasted, roast lamb to die for, a tonne of Greek food, Portuguese peri-peri chicken and garlic or peri-peri prawns, the best coleslaw, cold meat cuts and chocolate eclairs that I would sell my left arm for.

The atmosphere was literally drenched in laughter. On a daily basis. My mother's entire brood was hell bent on making sure everyone was listened and heard (two different things) too and taken care of. "Children were to be seen and to be heard". Unlike the very old-fashioned idea of "Children should be seen and not heard". Refreshing to say the least. You never, not on any occasion felt out on a limb with her family. They embraced you, celebrated your faults. Rejoiced in your successes. A real family indeed. It was with them that I have always felt most secure. It's the closest I came to being wrapped in cotton wool.

I was to sleep in my cousin Christiana's room until our home was available. I really adored my cousin. She always made me feel so welcome and shared everything with me. She had a head of unruly black curly hair, and really long legs, she was as quick as a whip and as bright as a button. She helped me considerably during this time. On one occasion, the school bully, that gaggle of geese, punctured my bicycle tyre's. She happened to be a prefect at Fort Vic Junior School, at the time. She made sure that they didn't get away with it!

There were two girls and one boy in this family and two additional boys, who were cousins from Joyce's Greek husbands' side that lived with the family. These boys were full of energy being typically Greek in their ways. Their love of food, fashion, wine women and song. Education was of such a high standard in Zimbabwe in the beginning, so much so that people sent their children from overseas for schooling in Zimbabwe once known as Rhodesia.

My cousins' names were Christiana, Andri, Eleni (Jack), Lambros and Alexandro Angelopoulos. Samantha, my sister, would join us in a month or so. She had moved from Harare (as I mentioned back in convoy times) and was in Mas Vegas already, but at boarding school, she would finish this particular term at her boarding house. Then come to us, as a day scholar for a year and then she would go off to Cape Town to study, Wellness. My eldest sibling had finished up her nursing in Cape Town. The love of her life had, been shot during the Chimurenga and she had returned to nurse him back to life. They have not been apart a day since then.

Auntie Joyce's home was alive with the promise of Christmas; which meant the best food ever, as my mother, Blessing, Anna; the chef in the house and my grandmother would all be cooking up a storm. We, the children, all helped cook, I opted to design the look and feel of the Christmas table settings and the décor. This was my job year in and year out. The tea bell rang and Anna appeared with the tea tray and fresh chocolate cake. Everyone gathered round.

Anna was not a Shona. She was an Ndebele. She was enormous – every part of her, from her hands to her ears and eyes, nostrils and nose everything was huge. No one messed with Anna. She ruled that house. One slap on the backside with those almighty hands and you would live to regret making the mistake in the first place.

Plus, Anna could run, so you could never get away from her. Well, she couldn't swim so if you made it fast enough to jump into the pool, you were lucky. She was respected and adored! We all sat around the tea table and discussed the divorce. When it came time for court, I was to tell the judge which parent I preferred to live with. That was far off, as divorces can drag on unless you live in a country where you can do this at an ATM. Very forward thinking. This divorce was like a plaster being taken off slowly. The thought of choosing which parent to live with was easy. It was my mother of course. However, how to say that straight up to my father in front of a judge was going to be heavy. No matter the situation, he was still my father. I loved him.

The subject of the fact that I had blamed myself for the latest happenings came up. Like that of an unwanted meal. How I blamed myself personally for the divorce. The simple reason being that if I had not had a concussion, then my mother would not have found out? Guilt ridden. My secret would have been safe with me, my art teacher, her children and the security guard at Chiredzi Junior School.

I was reassured that it was not my fault and it would have all come out anyway. My father, to our surprise, had bought a mansion five blocks from our humble Spanish looking abode, with its terracotta clay tile roof, white stucco walls, soft arches and hand carved doors. He would be living in his manor with his new family for the next year or two. His pristine life spread before him, as if it were a red carpet. None of us felt as if we were on the guestlist.

The reason being is that he was to start a new project with a certain Frenchman who was well-known in the country. He had decided to re-invest his hard-earned pennies, back into the new Zimbabwe, for the benefit of the youth. They were to build The Save Valley Conservancy and turn thousands of hectares of an existing cattle ranch called "Devuli", (the size of what most people would call a country) back to its original natural state, introducing certain species that were once originally form that area. Devuli would be turned into a wildlife conservancy, taking it back to its natural state. Valorous. Heroic even. That was definitely a bold move. It would be a lie, if I didn't say, this made me extraordinarily proud of my father. One thing my father never did was run people down, nor did he ever talk negatively about them, when they were not in his presence. His idea of a gentleman was one that did not blow his own trumpet.

The main negotiations would take place in Mas Vegas for the first two years and then they would move to The Save Valley Conservancy which we normally referred to as "The Ranch" or "HQ" or "Devuli" and later Chishakwe. We never ever called it the conservancy amongst us in conversation, it mostly remained The Ranch. They had divided the land into around ten different sections and sold them off to potential investors both local and international. My father had bought one and he had called it Chishakwe – which in Shona means, "Place of the Lions." The ranch was 225 kilometres from Mas Vegas. The same road you start off on to go to Zaka, where Nyika came from.

We were halfway through tea when we heard my grandmother's car drive up. It wasn't the engine we heard; it was the music. Ella Fitzgerald blasted from the speakers; blasted from her Citroen.

She parked the car and checked her lipstick like she always did. Granny Rita, what a legend. She lived until the ripe old age of ninety-two and only stopped working and driving a year before she died. The driving stopped because she left her car handbrake off on a very steep hill. After searching for the car for a couple of hours and assuming it had been stolen, she called the police who found it lodged in the canal at the bottom of the hill. In all honesty though, that could have happened to anyone. Her age played no part.

She stepped out clad in the newest fashions. I adored her fabulousness. My mother was the same. My aunt was more natural and down to earth but still so beautiful. Good looking sisters and respected in the Mas Vegas community. They were not boring either. They ran the show just like their mother did. From acting at the theatre to organising sports days and black-tie events. My mother later became golf captain four years in a row.

Their brother resided in Mas Vegas too. His name was Harry. My mother had a different father to her siblings but he had left when she was around six or seven and she had never seen him again. She tried visiting him once in Cape Town with my father, but he had made it clear that he had never wanted children. She had left heartbroken.

Their brother, Harry, was the youngest of the three. He was a loving chap. He was a fabulous chef. Loving food came naturally to him. He was always talking about food, eating food or preparing food. That was Harry in a nutshell.

My mother's family all came from a cooking background. How could I have not acquired this very important gene. Although these days I do enjoy cooking, it is by no means a natural talent. My grandmother opened her first café when she was eighteen. It was halfway between Fort Victoria (Mas Vegas) and the Great Zimbabwe Ruins. It was called "The Stop Over". There you could buy all types of flavoured milkshakes, toasted sandwiches, steak and kidney pies, and fish and chips. Fish was bought in via Mozambique by her mates who went there on deep sea fishing trips; so, it was seasonal. Her fried calamari became known all around the region and so did her peri-peri prawns. After all, Mozambique (our neighbouring country) had once been a Portuguese colony, hence some of their dishes had remained. Peri-peri chicken being the other popular remaining meal.

She met my grandfather during this time and soon after marriage realised it was going nowhere. She divorced him – scandalous in those times – it was unheard of then for a woman to divorce her husband. He left for Cape Town, never to be seen again.

Being the strong-willed individual, she was, however, she got on with her life and rented a shop in the main street of Mas Vegas (well actually the only street in Mas Vegas). Mas Vegas was positioned superbly. It was the first town after the South African and Zimbabwean border post. Her new place was called "Palm Court," and it soon became the "in" place – the place where the town gathered. During the war years, it was a source of news. If you wanted to know anything, you went and asked Rita. Rita smoked as if she were a chimney. She talked as if she was a New Yorker. Nobody messed with Rita, ever!

Not to be outdone, or to sit still for a second, she opened her very own vintage shop next door to her café and persuaded the only hairdresser in town to open on the other side of her shop, naturally the hairdresser obliged. Business boomed. Fashion for us during these times, was probably not what we would call fashion in a developed country, but it made us feel glamorous and "all womanly" nevertheless!

My Grandmother sorted through markets, bags, and other people's throw outs, at times converting them into her own design of fabulousness. Between the Salvation Army, her immense creativity and the Rotary's generosity she carved out her vintage corner. I am sure it made many people in Mas Vegas appear and feel just like a lady. Palm court became the place not only to get news but also to show off your latest outfit. I wish more photographs had been taken from this time, they would have been masterpieces your vision caught in their rapture. Soon, a Bata shoe shop arrived and opened its doors two shops down. Everything anyone needed was on this side of the street.

Palm Court was made up of square tables a meter by a meter in size, there were about twenty tables in total. All in rows. A long homemade rack made from wood separated the dining area from the till and counter area. The entire room was about 180 square meters, a huge white high-ceilinged room, with large heavy concrete columns. The kitchen was to the back of the space. It wasn't a restaurant and it wasn't a café, it was both. Everything and nothing always happening at the same time. Alongside the counter and till, stood a single table for family only. The waiters in the maroon suits and pill box hats with black tassels hanging down from the middle of them. Somewhere between British India and British Africa, this style of hat and waiter uniform had been conjured up. Each table covered with a white-and-red-checked tablecloth. As if we were Italians and nobody was. On the counter, sat the most ancient and old-fashioned till you could imagine. Orders were written down, put on a spike at the till with one copy taken to the kitchen. There were four waiters. They were called Memory, Restless, Telephone and Obey. The chef was called Chief. Palm Court was loud. All day long, it was loud. Busy and brisk. The smell of fried chips and garlic forever present, but not unpleasantly so. We spent many meaningful and bonding times at Palm Court.

We literally lived there. When school finished, we cycled to Palm Court, spent the afternoon doing homework, buggering around, arranging the songs for the Lyons Maid Top of the Pops listing, helping out with the cash up or playing cards. My toasted sandwich of choice was cheese and tomato followed by a delicious strawberry milkshake. We hung out mostly at Palm court unless we had a sports activity in the afternoon. Knowing that I was safe helped my mother focus on her baking and her job at Polar Refrigeration. Cycling home around five in the evening, together, my cousins lived two blocks away from us.

We worked as waiters on weekends and monitored the till. Our uniform was a maroon pair of trousers accompanied by a maroon jacket with black trimming and black buttons up the front. Sort of similar to a bell boy. We could wear Bata black tackies (sneakers) to finish off our uniform. I really enjoyed waitressing. We all enjoyed helping my grandmother at Palm Court. My aunt eventually worked there daily, helping my grandmother, the shared workload was necessary. Palm Court was busy!

Fish and shellfish arrived from Mozambique weekly at Palm Court and the town residents flocked in for crab, lobster, calamari and king prawns in peri-peri sauce. Everything was served on a bed of curried rice and raisins and a generous dollop of garlic butter. My grandmother cooked everything in butter, enough to give you a heart attack.

The menu was made up of the old favourites: toasted sandwiches including the popular ingredients of; cheese and tomato, chicken and mayonnaise, cheese, tomato and ham and any variation of these a customer wished. The milkshakes were delicious and I loved a "Brown Cow" (coke float) on occasion too. The only three desserts on the menu were jelly, ice cream or banana split. Uncle Tony used to have his gambling room for cards and horse race betting in the back of the restaurant where the smell of cigars and whiskey flourished, laughter sounded, the lamp above the table swayed and Vicky Leandros sung her lungs out.

Our family table was for listing the charts and hits from the radio, doing our homework, eating and talking! My eldest cousins, Eleni and Alexandro, argued non-stop over which song deserved more credit. Lyon's maid hits of the week. Which became a religion to my cousin along with him becoming the towns one and only DJ.

I never saw my grandmother sit down once. I am sure this is what kept her going and gave her such an upbeat personality. She loved people and people gravitated towards her.

Anyway, as she walked up the driveway to us, with a swing in her step, I felt more secure knowing she was beside us now. She truly ruled the roost. No one dared give her lip!

She apprised my mother, 'Better late than never, you woke up!' Well, bully for you! Your ex was way too much work! Come to think of it he's a bit, too much like me, sorry love! Thinking of taking your own surname back then, darling?' Claire Reagan sounds so much more compelling and elegant than Claire Hagen, don't you think? Everyone?' Glasses raised in agreement! Clinked. Rita was extravagantly fanciful and she lived life to the brim. She was far from ordinary and paleness would never be her friend.

This year we would be with Joyce and Tony for Christmas. Tony was an awe-inspiring character. He loved music and filled the house's every corner with it. You could hear him singing in the shower to Vicky Leandros. "Après toi," her voice in the house daily.

'Whomever doesn't know her music should be ashamed of themselves,' he would say.

Tony was never without a cigar. His 70's rimmed reading glasses, Gelled hair and heavily scented aftershave. Every bit a character. A perfect character for a Guy Richie film.

Years later, I was standing at Tegel Airport in Berlin only to discover that Vicky Leandros was standing in front of me in the check-in line. What a lovely moment.

Along with Vicky, we were also introduced to Mikis Theodorakis's Zorbas music and dance which showcased at the

Greek club in town every weekend. People naturally assumed I was Greek. My sister too.

The family opened several restaurants and take-aways. One was in Cape Town - a student seafood and steak place - it was a roaring success, in Muizenberg, a suburb there, then there was "The Cottage Shop," which specialised in my mother's baked goods. "Snacks" – as the name suggests – served wholesome snacks, also thanks to my mother. Finally, there was "Beauty's in Bulawayo". All of these restaurants did home and event catering and were very popular. Naturally don't forget the legendary "Palm Court" and "Stop Over".

Tony loved his cards, gambling, cigars and whisky. There was a table and private room for him at every venue. Eventually, he started a horse betting business and between him and Alexandro, it took off. Alexandro, later became a famous race caller. Lambros became a high-flying lawyer in London. He even has a chauffeur. Eleni continued with restaurants and stayed in Zimbabwe. Always successful. Christiana and Andri ended up in South Africa and England respectively having families and training champion children in show jumping.

As my grandmother sat down to tea, we continued our conversations. Everyone speaks at once in my family but we all manage to hear one another. Unlike my father's intellectual family, you never had to prove who you were with my mother's family. If you did well, great, but the most important thing was that you were happy, and that you loved food.

Life took place around a table full of good homemade food. Zimbabwe is not a wine country or I am sure that would have been there too. Instead, there were G and T's as sundowners or a whiskey – Bells or Jameson – depending on the occasion. When wine was available, it had been dropped off as a gift at Palm Court. It came in five-litre boxes secured in aluminium with a tap. Which on completion you blew up and used as a sun-tanning pillow in the swimming pool. Scorching your face in the meanwhile.

Later on, two wines became available in Zimbabwe: Green Valley White and Green Valley Red. Simple decisions. How I miss those easy moments of clarity. Either this or that; not millions of choices.

The best way to transport a large amount of wine, without breaking wine bottles on ill equipped roads, was in two-litre cardboard boxes. This and as many Julio Iglesias albums as possible and the one and only Sugar man. Which later became a religion just like ABBA.

The best part of everyday was hearing the ice cream man ring his big cow bell and as soon as you heard it you ran down to the gate to buy your Eskimo Pie, Lyons Maid pies or Green Mamba or Space Man Cream Soda. The ice cream guy was a friend of ours by now and my grandmother had put his daughter and son through school.

The whole family would go out to buy an ice cream and have a chat with him, find out how the kids were doing and so forth. I learnt to be kind to people less fortunate than myself from both my parents and I learned a lot about how to manage money from my grandmother. When I was forced to leave Zimbabwe, after a near death experience and the unforeseeable future of the country, I managed to leave only because of my grandmothers advise on finance.

I escaped by placing hundred dollar bills between sandwiches, disguising them with lettuce shavings. Money sandwiches at the bottom of the Tupperware, real ham and cheese sandwiches at the top, to offer border officials. As border controls were tight. That is how I got my money out of the country, positioned neatly in Tupperware's on my front passenger seat. In my Golf One, Baby Blue, arriving at 24 years of age in Cape Town after driving 3000 kilometres alone, with Lenard Cohen, Natural Born Killers, Talking Heads and Sugarman to keep me going. I had to turn Zimbabwe dollars into US dollars on the black market, to get the best rates. I bought them from a friend of a friend who knows a friend, and so it went and so it goes.

The evening progressed and it was wonderous. Days turned into weeks and time slid by. Mercury smoothly. One morning, we were all in my grandmother's car; Blessing in tow. Blessing had his own house adjacent to my aunt's estate. We were to go and see our new home. Excitement rained down on us and we scurried and rushed around like an ant family.

I had been carrying Puppet the cat everywhere so naturally she came along too. It was not far from my aunt's abode. We neared the corner and turned right into a street called Mukwa (which means; a tree's name. this tree is used to make the famous mbira, the famous thumb piano from Zimbabwe, as well as for medicinal purposes, ring worm, blackwater fever, and to increase the supply of breast milk). The house was of a Spanish style and looked like an '80s wedding cake – the way the icing used to look as if it was trying to escape the cake. Or the top of a clover ice cream cone. It really was the perfect home for us at that time. Bougainvillea spilled over the balcony in a genus of thorny ornamental vines as if belonging to a four o'clock family. A Bright fuchsia. The thought of having my own room came to the forefront of my mind and I felt elated. Oh, where was Nyika? Blessing was already out of the car singing with his hat on and Sunday attire. Singing Marvin Gaye. I ran up to him and we sang hands in the air, running toward the house. Our new home. At last, a place to call home a place to call ours.

Each bedroom had a patio and an outside door leading onto the patio. My father had put a deposit on the house and my mother was to pay the rest. We would be baking non-stop in this new home; I was sure of it. Just to pay the bills. I felt elated. I was so happy. As simple as that. All my anguish had been stilled.

These years were the best years of my life; the best of my childhood. We had hardly anything to move into our new house but it didn't matter. The most prized possession was the briefcase record player with about 20 records. Those years I would take back in a heartbeat. Happy memories. Dancing and smiling, whirling and twirling, we hardly ever had any money but we were so fulfilled and joyous.

My mother, Samantha, Blessing and I had a blast. My eldest sister also spent time with us, but not long. It was an epic time. We just all got on so well. There were hardly any quarrels, if there were, they were short lived.

Bliss really. I got to know my mother far better, realised she liked the odd smoke (but choked her lungs out in the process) and that she had an opinion on just about everything. I also learned that she could dance like a diva; that she loved dancing more than anything. I learnt she was not only a mother, that she too was a person of her own personality.

She learned to reverse out the driveway at a hell of a rate. She taught me to ride a bicycle and drove behind me the whole way to school – to make sure I got there in one piece. She dropped so much weight, started playing golf and walked for miles. Of course, she was baking like a maniac. We all helped, without fail. When I woke up there was always music playing. I do this to this day too unless there is someone sleeping in late of course. That would usually be me. A morning without music is not a morning.

The months came and went with games and lazy Sunday afternoons at my aunt's swimming pool. My mother gave us room to breathe. She was so kind – our best friend. Blessing looked after us like a good uncle would. He introduced me to the African tradition of the herb, as I said he was a good uncle and from time to time, we would smoke and philosophise about everything and nothing simultaneously. He was also a champion at math! Always there to help me with my homework. Not once did I go to bed hungry. He made sure, when my mom had a golf competition or had to work late, he made me dinner, and sat with me in the kitchen with big mugs of sweet tea, until my bedtime. Happiness made me oats porridge every morning, with paw-paw on the side.

Grown in our garden. Yes, we had our own vegetable garden at the back of the house, iceberg lettuce, tomatoes, peas, sweet potatoes, cauliflower as well as strawberry and pine apples plants, paw-paws, lemon, avocado and loquat (you can also make a herbal tea from this fruit tree) trees. Happiness made my lunch box for school, which always included a sweet or two.

My mother was enjoying her job at Polar Refrigeration as a secretary. The owner, Mr Whyte was a family friend. However, she wanted more, so she began making plans to open her own – "Cottage Shop"!

Finally, the day came for me to go to my new school. Fort Victoria Junior School (or Mas Vegas Junior School). Blessing cycled alongside me on my first day of school, just to make sure I didn't fall off my bike, and my mom, as I mentioned earlier drove behind me. The ride to my school was roughly 5kms. Navigating traffic after living in the wilderness for so long was a feat all of its own. He also walked me to my class. My teacher was to be a Mrs Venda. My school life fell apart. I started writing words and letters two lines at a time until I had filled whole exercise books. In maths, I wrote a letter to the teacher explaining why it was not important in my life and gave a number of different reasons why. The final straw was when I slapped my teacher across the face. She dragged me out of her class by my ponytail and marched me to the headmaster. Things improved dramatically after that.

'Joanna, what do you think I should do with you?' he asked kindly.

'I think you should transfer me to a teacher I am able connect with,' I replied. 'Someone who is not dragging her personal relationship with my mother into the classroom. That's what I think.'

'Couldn't agree more,' replied the headmaster.

I was speechless.

'You will be moved to Mrs Chapman's class.'

Mrs Chapman turned out to be a dream and I began to excel at school. She also gave me some additional counselling and encouraged me to write about my feelings. She had a teenage daughter called Anne who became my sister's best friend and she soon became part of our family.

I finished at the junior school that year and was fully expecting to carry on to Mas Vegas High School. This was not to be the case, however, as my father had enrolled me at a boarding school in South Africa in a village called Pietersburg. It was around a six-hour drive from Mas Vegas. I was to join my step-sister and brother at their school – P.E.M.P.S – Pietersburg English Medium Primary School. Much to my chagrin, I was to remain in primary school; but only because they start school one year later in South Africa.

As this was yet again me having to change to suit my father, I saw it as a perfect chance to strike. I would ask for Nyika to come back. My plan was to point out that no-one was perfect, that everyone makes mistakes and that he should be willing to forgive. I called and asked him if I could come over to his house to see him about an important matter. We met an hour later.

His house was intimidating. He called me into his office where he sat behind his large wooden desk, which was a further menace. Mostly working on the Save Conservancy Project. They were all going to move there in a year.

When we were alone in the office, I began:

'Dad, I have an important matter to discuss with you,' I began. 'I want Nyika to come home, to come back.'

'No, that's not an option,' he replied. Deadpan.

'Oh, but it's an option for you to go on holiday with your girlfriend, when you already have a family?' I snapped. 'Well, here is your option from me… either Nyika comes back or I don't go to boarding school with your new family. I want to hear her side of the story. No one gave her that option. Either Nyika comes back to work for you in this house or I will never again set foot inside your home.'

I was terrified.

'That's enough!' he replied. Slamming his hand down on his desk. My heart shook.

'Fine, I will give Nyika a job and she will retire after you leave home for college. I would also like to hear her side of the notebook events. This record will naturally need to be set straight. That's the deal. But you will have to go and fetch her yourself. Make a plan with your grandmother or your mother.' He spoke, as if he had never spent twenty-five years with this family, they were referred to as your grandmother, your mother, your mother's house and your family. Weird. Just too odd. It annoyed me. Ridiculous. Made my blood pressure rise!

I left and rode my bike as fast as I could, straight home to twenty-one Mukwa Street to tell Blessing, my mother, my sister and my grandmother the good news. They were thrilled. Blessing said he would send the good news immediately to Nyika, so she could get ready. I hoped she would agree? 'Really?' I thought, 'so you have been in touch with her all this time? Blessing, have you been in touch with her all this time and never told me?'

'Of course, Joanna, but what good would it have done you, be still child.' I listened, which is rare. I smiled at him and gave him a huge hug. Blessing also said reassuringly, "This will be the news Nyika has been waiting for, she is dying to come back, to be by your side, she will be surprised at how much you have grown and matured". Thank you Blessing. Ndinokutendai zvikuru kubva pamoyo wangu, (thank you very much from my heart). We would leave this coming Saturday at dawn. It was only an hour in each direction. I was so excited I could only blabber and bounce around. Just like a loose cannon.

When Saturday came, we left in high spirits while it was still dark. My mother loved to drive before the sun came up. She said driving and watching the sunrise was a direct prayer from Christ.

Blessing agreed but said it was from Mwari. The fresh light spoke directly to your heart. Jazz playing, we set off into the African Tribal Trust Lands of Zaka, in the bright blue Peugeot 504. Jnr Hagen was still studying in London and Susan was getting married in a month's time, to the young man who had been shot in the war, the one she had returned to Zimbabwe for, to nurse back to health. Our uncle Smurf.

The sun rose over the Great Zimbabwe Ruins as we listened to Nina Simone. I opened the flask of tea and poured us each a cup. Welcoming steam rose from the plastic cups. Sacrilege my mother joked, tea out of a plastic cup. She naturally did not have a plastic cup, she had a proper tea cup especially for long-distance driving. Blessing, smoked his cigarette and we all sang and drank our tea along with the music. On road trips with my mother, we always sang with the music on full blast and when we had run out of music we simply sang some more. Blessing always brought his mouth organ.

It was a terrible time, however, in Zimbabwe. Awful things were happening. The Gukurahundi Massacre's had begun to take place. It was hair-raising. Further agitation and trouble.

During these times trying to navigate through a conversation was taxing. It had become exhausting just to try and make it through a dialogue without offending someone. Dodging bullets of tete-a-tete and potholes of emotional blackmail, making sure your facial expressions matched your speech. Everyone was nervous and on edge. What would be our future prospective? Did we have a future here at all?

Whilst recently living in Dubai, I came upon a number of race conflicts; with the Zimbabweans abhorrence for the Kenyans and the Kenyans detestation for the Nigerians, in both directions etcetera. It was a deep dislike, they bullied each other badly in the hostels they lived in. However, they all stood together against an Indian, go figure! Most people cannot even tell a Kenyan apart from a Nigerian or Zimbabwean. As Africa is so often referred to as one whole country, people assume we all have lions running around in our backyards. I have known individuals that are not able to follow an all-black cast in a film unable to tell an actor apart from the other actors and they were born in Africa to boot.

The leader of the Zanu PF being Robert Mugabe and the leader of the Ndebele being Joshua Nkomo. I met Joshua Nkomo at my father's house on occasion. I liked him. He was real. I enjoyed his company; he spoke to us about our country not his country our people not his people. I once even asked him if he could be my godfather seeing as every time, he visited I had to give him my bed, and that we had the same vision for our country?

Both were imprisoned together. Shona and Ndebele alike. Both suffered the same capture. Both invariably promised to never let the other one down and behind bars lies took flight when nothing else could.

Robert Mugabe was the most qualified president in history some say. He was no one's fool. However, his dark side was alive, kicking and willing to do anything at all to win anything at all. Not in his defence but my personal analysis on his background (I am not a shrink) was that he hated his own people. Growing up, he was forced to study all day and all night, based on some priest telling him that he was the next messiah, that he was to lead his country into the next century and to make it a better place for all, I suppose. Or was that just some dream conjured up by a witch doctor after one-to-many cups of home-made brews? He did not have a childhood of adventure and play. I can imagine that children in his village may have teased him about this and therefore day after day, year after year being teased may have planted the seed of hatred and decay, directed towards his people. This blossomed when he became the leader of poor Zimbabwe. He improved nothing for his tribe, he made it worse. He threw them under a bus and, on his deathbed, gave our country to his all-weather friends.

There are still people in tribal Zimbabwe that have never seen a non-black person. They are always intrigued by our hair, loving to touch and play with it. Children gather excitedly around me, tugging at my hands and inviting me to play football. Feet covered in dust and huge welcoming smiles. Rows of perfect white teeth. Rolling laughter carried on the wind as if a song. Unjudgmental. We are all taught to hate. We don't come into this world hating and wanting to kill. Love we do come with. Love is our go-to. Even the worst of the worst need love and who are we to deny them that?

There is so much blood drenched into our home soil, no wonder it is only fertile for short periods of time. I mean that metaphorically. It was white-owned farms, then minister-owned farms, then all-weather-friend-owned mines and farms. At what point will it be Zimbabwean soil, that means no conflict with Shona and Ndebele, no more conflict of white and black, black and Asian and no more dictatorships? What is the likelihood of that outcome? It's nowhere to be seen, it's never going to surface simply because then Africa would become too powerful. The west would lose its grip on the world's riches. So, they are kept at bay like a bad-mannered child. Speak when you are spoken to.

There is such an enormous number of souls leaving airports and border posts going to support far-off lands whilst our people are dying of starvation and disease. How in God's name is that possible? In a land that is filled to the brim with resources.

When the Chimurenga war was over, brothers in arms celebrated. AK47's silhouetted in sunsets no more. Pambere fists at sunrise instead. However, it was short-lived. People were free or so they thought. It was time to move forward. My generation were the ones able and ready to do this. We joined classrooms eager to learn, to listen and to be one. We joined assembly. We assembled.

Then like a creeper, the ugliness reared its monstrous nostrils and flared them, breathing fire, wrath and havoc over its brothers and sisters. No comradery here, brutality back again. Devil's mischief. A gentleman did his utmost to put an end to this "killing disease," let's call him "The Priest". He died a hero and he lived as a hero. He met numerous times with the powers that be demanding peace and change. To no avail. It fell on deaf ears. He fought with all his breath as a human rights activist and a true man of God. Being at the front of the army of good.

The Gukurahundi Massacres took place in Matabeleland, the place and home of the Ndebele tribe. Together with other bishops in Zimbabwe, some churches, civil society activists, diplomats, humanitarian groups and the very brave journalists, The Priest, opened up the most atrocious and disgusting post-colonial killings of black people by a black government led by none other than Robert Mugabe. Exposing exactly what was going on. Robert Mugabe was a Catholic himself educated by Jesuits. How is this Christ-like behaviour? War hiding behind religion once again.

1983, March 16th – A meeting was held at the State House in Harare (Zimbabwe's capital) with Mugabe and The Priest to discuss the horror killings. The ethno-political military unit formed and were trained by North Koreans (later assisted by operators from Tanzania), the fifth brigade. They were deployed on January 20th 1983 in Matabeleland North, Ndebele homeland. They rampaged the region in three months. Using intimidating tactics, beating people, attacking woman and children alike, slaughtering, raping, maiming and torturing massive amounts of people up to thousands at a time. This insaneness was worse than even colonial security forces had ever displayed or taken part in.

The Priest and other priests confronted Mugabe over the gumption of the animal-like killings that were raging across the south-western region like a rapacious tornado, leaving only destruction without apology or acceptance. As usual, Mugabe's reply and attitude was one of paranoia and absolute fear, which was like a card he played at every opportunity it was required. Saying he was under threat by the Ndebele. Maybe he was mad, truly mad after all. Mugabe also took on a bluffing strategy with apartheid. He would castigate this when it suited him and consort with it against the ANC/Zapu alliance when it was advantageous for politics. Mugabe developed a lily-livered approach to avoid confrontation with apartheid leaders PW Botha and later FW De Klerk. Apartheid agents killed a man in a shopping centre in Harare Zimbabwe under circumstances of collaboration by Mugabe. Moments before being under the watchful and permanent eye of the intelligence services. This was certainly not for the fellow's protection. This was to make sure certain undesirables did not have bases to fight from within Zimbabwe.

Mugabe used the excuse of saying he deployed the fifth brigade to fight imaginary dissidents. He was asked on occasions 'Why is the army killing civilians and not going after these dissidents you so vehemently protect?'

There was so much going on between what was called Zapu/Zipra, Super-Zapu, Operation Mute and Operation Drama. That was a whole new war at play. Unless you actually grew up around this, it will be a little difficult to fathom. However, it was all to make money in the end. To have total power of Southern Africa's abundant wealth. A number of men were arrested and the keys of cells forgotten and misplaced. These men who had so willingly given their lives for the Liberation Struggle. Some of them died as a result. Nkomo, the opposition leader of the Ndebele people survived an assassination in the dead of night at the witching hour, so it is said, who knows? It was supposed to be staged at his home in Bulawayo. He had received a tip off and was not there. He fled to Botswana and later to London.

A gentleman, sitting next to The Priest in the meeting said to Mugabe:

"If anybody is going to attack, rape and then kill your mother, sister or your daughter, you would have to be a good Christian not to seek revenge against them in future."

He was warning Mugabe of the real-life consequences of the killings and the untameable circle it might create.

Quoted from text:

A certain person concluded the meeting, saying, the bishops would release a statement making their position on the massacres categorically clear. To which Mugabe reacted: "You can go ahead!"

The facts are there for all to see. It was a calculated reign of terror. Killings, wounding, beatings, and brutalisation. Homes were burnt down and children and adults alike were left to starve, no drought in sight and food supplies being cut off to them. Witnesses saw 22 people killed at Minda Mission and a priest in Lupane saw 52 people being massacred. Overall, 22,000 people were killed.

So, it came to be a one-party state. With the emergence of the MDC in 1999, a decade after the collapse of the Berlin Wall and the crumbling of the Soviet Bloc, there is compelling evidence about this massacre if you would like to research it in a deeper level. An all too sad and devastating reality in the midst of a win-win. Black and white tears alike watering barren lands. This county is not fit for any man; this country is only fit for criminals. (thestandard.newsday.co.zw) April 12, 2020.

Chapter Twelve
Nyika's Return

Since then if you see the latest news things are going towards a brighter light, a forgiveness one hopes, The Herald.co.za, there are some positive steps being made for us all to heal to move forwards. Freedom of speech would be a wonderful start, woman's rights, free education and medical aid for those who cannot afford it and other basic needs that we take for granted in developed countries would be a God send!

African women are the way forward for Africa. All these thoughts of history running through my mind as I watched the landscapes slide by from the car window. I felt I had aged 8 going on eighty, right?

After our tea, we stopped and had a pee in the grass alongside the road. Trying not to drown the ants. We climbed back into the car, wiped our hands and faces, refreshed ourselves and by this stage we were not too far from Nyika's home, our old home too, we were in good spirits.

We were nearly there. I knew the hut. It was behind the old farmhouse at Ngwane. First we had to drive past our old farm house. It had been bombed to pieces and the only remnants that a home once existed was the toilet seat. I wondered briefly why no one had taken it for their long drops? Ghosts of conversations and laughter echoed across a stage of ruins. A theatre playing in my mind. I smiled inwardly, gently and whispered to myself, "it's alright, everything is going to be alright!" It's the past, it's behind us. My heart felt sore, for a moment it fluttered. For a fleeting moment my soul felt vacant.

No more garden, no more fencing and no more swing. The Shepherd Tree had been cut down; probably used for firewood. It looked like a burial ground. All of the memories, everything I remembered, was gone: placed out of sight. I stared and stared. Felt deaf. Watching laughter and scenes in a play gone by.

I blinked back tears, then remembered why we were here; and that made me smile. Never mind if the gooks destroyed our home, so what? I would see Nyika and Nyika was coming home. She was coming back to be part of our lives.

I glimpsed Nyika as we parked and I literally aviated out of the car, the blue Peugeot 504. As reliable as a wax teapot. I ran as fast as my legs could carry me and fell into her. Her familiar scent, I felt a genuine "faire bon accueil" welcome immediately at home, in her embrace and all the past years of severance slid wordlessly away. I had grown. I could look her directly in the eye now. Ndine urombo, (I am sorry in Shona). I would have my protector. I would no longer be circumspect in my father's house. No longer bested, no longer solus. I had most of all felt acute nostalgia when Nyika my companion was not around, the person who could understand all my sentiments. Nyika had championed my side on more than one ground come rain or shine. She was dear to me. The void once so prominent, had been pervaded, just as much as a Jasmine fragrance in bloom captures your nostrils. Even though so much time had slid by, it was as if it was yesterday once more. Only the fundamental things will apply, as time fly's by. Nyika had grown older and grander in stature. An element of wiseness, her halo. That absolute quality of being prudent and sensible. Her steady gaze. Our family had once again reconvened! All of us, embraced one another with fondness and warmth. We broke it up because Blessing kindly offered a cup of tea. Of course, right!

We bundled Nyika's carryall into the boot of the car and Blessing climbed into the front seat. My mother put the car in first and we glided – well more like bumped – along the dirt track, leaving Ngwane behind us in a flurry of dust. I sat curled up in Nyika's arms. I could not let her go unless this was just a dream. I looked over her shoulder at our old and ruined home. I watched the rail dust cover it, until it past from sight. (The term rail dust originated when cars first started being delivered by train, small particles from the tracks would fly up and land on cars). That had once been our family home. That is where we had last had life as a family, and just like that it vanished, as if life itself was just a game.

Nyika informed us that Chief Marimba had passed on to the next life and a new chief had taken his place. Like his predecessor, he was also a good man. All these wonderful people caught up in propaganda and politics. I always felt as if I just managed to escape a flood, a drowning of sorts lifting my legs up just in time. Before a raging river passed on down below. At least I would have more people to welcome me on the other side. I would love to meet Chief Marimba at the gates of Peter... if I got there!

We chatted and sang along in the car and on the way back we stopped at the takeaway, halfway to the Zimbabwe Ruins, which was also owned by my grandmother. It was called "Stop Over". We clambered out, surprised to find my grandmother there. It was unusual for her to be at this store, since Palm Court took up most of her time. The Stop Over would be closing soon, as Palm Court was just too busy and making too much money, whilst Stop Over was not turning over as much as it once had. She was going to sell it to a local man to turn into a shebeen. He had decided to keep the name, you do the math.

Granny was so pleased to see Nyika and we got her best welcome. We had toasted cheese sandwiches, Brown Cows (coke floats) and a big plate of deep-fried calamari with a smattering of sandwich spread alongside it, cabbage salad and beetroot salad.

We ate as only kings can. Nyika ate for two kings. Surprisingly so did Blessing, my mom and Bell. So, did I. At the end of the meal, we licked our fingers clean of the garlic butter dip. Satisfied, we hugged Granny Rita goodbye and left for the last 30 kilometres to Mas Vegas. All of us in complete sync with one another. True family, a genuine household.

Nyika was to stay the weekend with us at our house, then start work that Monday morning at my father's house. Naturally she had a few questions.

Her salary would be a good one. Medical covered. Learning to read and write was an option if she wanted too.

'Joanna,' she said to me, 'what's an old lady like me going to do with reading and writing?'

"Reading is a wonderful sense of company, Nyika,' I replied. 'You get to create all the images of the characters, situations and landscapes. It's a treat. My, all-time favourite treat, anyway.'

'Who would I write to? My only son was betrayed by this country and I know I'll never see him again.'

Her eyes filled up and spilled over. Have you ever noticed your tear drops can be exceedingly large at times? The memory as vivid as if it were yesterday. "But where are the fruits of yesteryear? Of war?' I hugged her tight, for a long time. Nyika had aged quite a bit. she was greying at her temples. However, she was still as strong as an ox. My Nyika was back. I would look after her from now on.

That evening, Nyika and I were sitting alongside the fireplace in our lounge, the fire crackling. We were roasting marsh mellows.

'Nyika,' I began, '...what happened? Why did you tell the enemy about our home and about our life? My family, Nyika, we are your family, who you were a part of. Who you are still a part of? Why had your father not defended you and come to speak to my father, after all he was the Chief? I was too young to understand, but I would like to understand now, please Nyika, tell me everything!'

'The terrorists came to the compound, two days after they took Kudzai. I am not sure if you remember me reading you the story of Judas, the night you last saw Kudzai? I had got wind of what had occurred in other compounds, inevitably our turn would come. Other woman in these villages had lost their sons to the same fate. I needed you to understand that story, I was afraid something would happen and you would not understand because you were too young. People were forced to betray one another at gun point. Them or us? You or me?. What would you have done?'

'They had warned us they would come back, funeral and goodbye's or not! I had, had a premonition that awful things were going to happen to all of us. The night the troops arrived; I had a gut feeling that unwelcomed events were going to start to occur. One after the other, until they got what they came for. Call it a mother's intuition. Call it war paranoia. Maybe just call it fate, coincidence or superstition. I have tried to recall the events but I have also tried to forget them, otherwise I would have become demented from pain. I couldn't believe they had bought Kudzai with them. My child, another part of his initiation perhaps? Threatening to maim him in front of me unless I told them the way the inside of your house was laid out. What your routines were. Where you all slept. They dictated what I should say. What I should draw in the notebook. I had no choice. They beat me. The beatings were harsh, however less than the first occasion. This took place during my grieving days off; you remember you did not see me for quite a while? I had felt so much hope when the soldiers tried to find him. To no avail. That dreadful day. After the festivity we had, to bring closure to Kudzai's disappearance, I was woken by force. The whole compound suffered. That was by far the worst night of my life.

The opposition brought him back to me and tortured me further. What kind of world is this? They did not attack your house that particular evening as they wanted precise information about your locations and movements etcetera. They wanted all of you dead. There was a rumour that your father had already received a warning from them the day they shot at us on the swing. He had received a letter, so it is said. I do not know if that is true? I never saw the letter.

Perhaps, they thought, your father ignored the warning and he was taking too long to leave, that is why they needed more information from us. A back up plan? Your father on this occasion orchestrated the move perfectly and in the end his plan worked. It is said that your uncle Andre's name saved our lives. It was our last chance, our only chance, if we had not left when we did, we would all have been slaughtered. Looking back, it was also smart to not have given an exact time or date of departure and instructed to just to be ready as we could leave at any moment. A good move that was, to keep it quiet until the last minute, because if we had known, maybe it would have been beaten out of us too. Respected uncle or not. One pardon. The terrorists parting words, "Leave, and leave fast!".

In my heart, I like to think they did not kill us because of your uncle. One pardon remember. I had no idea that they had left the notebook behind. I was far too upset. Pretty saw the opportunity, she had been waiting for all along she must have picked the notebook up during all the commotion. I cannot even recall having it. Did they hand it back to me, throw it at me? I cannot remember. I was way to traumatized. Pretty just made it appear the day we arrived in Mkwasine. I had tried to snatch it away from her, knowing what that notebook would cause. She worshipped power, either she wanted my position at any cost or was she part of the enemy all along? We just didn't see it? I honestly have no idea! So much time has passed, apparently she has already died, so she will meet her master. Revenge is not my style.

Only because of the drawings in the book. My life was turned upside down and inside out. All fingers pointed in my direction as if we were conspiring with the opposition to destroy you as a family. Perhaps one big attack before we moved. The grand finale attack by Nyika, the enemy and Kudzai. Maybe we had all overstayed our welcome?'

'It's so complicated Nyika, lost in translations, a recipe for a disaster,' I muttered. Indeed it was. "So let me get this straight, it was something like this?"

'The, terrorists came to threaten you all to get the information about our home, as a back-up plan in the case we did not leave fast enough, they would attack the house kill us, then kill you. You had no choice to lie to them? To draw incorrect drawings?'

'No, Joe, no, I was so terrified, I did what I was told to do. I did not chance a lie! Life is not a theatre play that we listen to on the BBC radio,' she said.

'It did not even cross my mind to not do exactly what they were telling me to do.'

In the same position, we are all too eager to give our opinion of what we would have done. It no longer mattered. I loved Nyika. She was safe with me now. An envious woman had tried to destroy Nyika. Here we were alive. Pretty was six-foot under.

"A pardon perhaps and a secret kept us alive!" As in Zimbabwe we have sayings; Just now, which means in a while, or a time that suits the person stating that. Now-now, which means sort of immediately and so on. All one huge misunderstanding in complicated times! I offered my young interpretation of adult events. Nyika carried on.

'I had no idea how to tell your father or, your mother... I was too ashamed, mostly to face you, simply because you still had the element of innocence. I didn't have the words, and the evidence was laid bare. No story could protect me, there it was in black and white. Interpreted as it was seen. There is no fairness in love or war. It is what it is.'

'You see,' Nyika continued, 'your uncle was a very special man indeed. He had a big influence amongst local African people. He had a close relationship to the Senior Chief of the Shangaans, and

226

this resulted in the Shangaans (of the extensive area), eventually initiating him into their tribe in secret ceremonies, which he apparently would never divulge, it meant a lot to him throughout his life. You must realise this great honour was never bestowed on any other white man. My heart swelled with pride for him. A hero indeed, a man who embraced everything Africa gave him. He was an African, skin colour did not play a role in his theatre of life. I found it all so confusing, though at the same time, I would never truly understand it all. I had had the opportunity to meet my uncle on occasion. He was no doubt a hero, it emanated from him. He was so comfortable in his own skin. He carried a certain aura. That's the only way I can describe him.

'Did Blessing know about this?'

'Yes but what could he do?'

'True. Did, Happiness, know?'

'They all did. Everyone knew but no one could do anything about it. Everyone was beaten and tortured that night, even Blessing, but not so badly. No one escaped that terrible night, mentally nor physically.

You asked why I did not ask the Chief to get involved. He simply had been through too much, he was aging, and I wanted him to die with dignity. It was my choice he say nothing. Happiness also managed to not get beaten too badly. They were all tied up and made to kneel in the dirt. AK47s pointed at their heads. The unwelcomed guests were menacing and affrighting concurrently. We were caught like a rock in a hard place. One woman though saw it as an opportunity, that one woman being Pretty, the woman who turned the notebook over to your father.'

She had always been jealous of Nyika's position within the tribe and the advantages she had being the Chief's only daughter. Jealousy drove her to expose Nyika. It would have all been water under the bridge if she had not shown my father the notebook or made such a commotion to attract attention. She definitely

227

thought she had won. However, Nyika has principles and is not one to seek revenge. She believes Mwari takes care of the dishonest, the jealous and the devious. Pretty, had tried to knock Nyika off her pedestal out of her position, in some ways they had succeeded, however in the Chief's heart and eyes they had not. Pretty, died from a snake bite, not so long after causing the commotion and turmoil in Mkwasine. Was it fate? Or was it that she just happened to mess with the wrong woman!

He was present that evening he knew the truth. However, he was older and did not have the energy for battle any longer, and now he had passed on. Nyika, was tough, Nyika was a leader. Nyika would survive, to see more than just another day! It was a time of trial and terror that never seemed to subside. Believe me, there are more than twelve hours in the dark when things become so calamitous. I never thought I would bear witness to the beast unleashed from the pits of hell among us on planet earth. Let alone in our compound. This fiend, demon and savage ripped our lives apart and found humour whilst torment played out, eventually giving way to its crescendo.

A mortified sorrow will fill our souls in one way or another for a lifetime. That feeling is inevitably etched in your subconscious, shake it off as much as you try the images will not perish. 'The last time I saw Kudzai, Joanna you would not recognise him. They had brainwashed him and drugged him; they beat him up in front of me to an inch of his life. Then those bastards,' I had never heard Nyika swear before, 'dragged him by his feet out of the village. His head was bouncing on the gravel over rocks. I don't even know now if he's alive.'

'The war is over now, Nyika; you could find him. I could help you.'

'Don't be naïve, child. He is up there with the criminal politicians stealing money from this country and entertaining the fat cats. If he survived. That or he is stone dead. I have never received a cent from him. This is a relief. I would not want blood money.

He probably spends his days sleeping with prostitutes, drinking and getting high. What a terrible life he was forced into, I would do the same. I would spend my life drunk. I think I just might kill myself. What other kind of life could he live? Knowing what he has done? He was so young when he was taken. Taken from me. Taken by his father, already a terrorist, who raped me when I was a young girl. You never asked me where my husband was?'

'I am sorry, Nyika,' I continued, such a useless word for such an enormous misinterpretation. I was grateful for an explanation. It confirmed what I already believed, that story of Judas had resonated, but I had been unable to put the two stories together being 7 years old. I had thought it just a hunch. My hunch in the end was right. Nyika had not stood a chance, I felt deeply sorry for all the parties involved, the time would come when it could be explained clearly. Nyika would get her reputation back, against all odds. I would make sure of it!

Nyika nodded slowly and looked deep into my eyes.

'No one is born bad. We are taught to lie, to cheat, to hate, to be racist, to murder and to steal. All these things we are taught so as to survive. Just to survive to have a life we didn't ask for in the first place. Come here, child, and rest your head in my lap. Your life is going to change. Those Africans in South Africa are from Zulu descent, they are very strong and tough! You will find your path. Those Afrikaner girls – good luck with them. There is no calling home, except for maybe once a month. I hope you will talk to me. Tell your father. I want to hear the news. I will guide you through. We will live to see another day, Joe, but from now on together again! Never think for one moment you are alone. You are not!'

'How about tomorrow we wake early and go for a picnic at the Zimbabwe Ruins?' I suggested eagerly to Nyika, 'and drink a coke at Lake Mutirikwe? At the boat club? Let's go and see Norma Jean's house and have tea and scones? What do you think, Mom?' She had just arrived home from a golf tournament, and had plonked herself down on the couch with a stiff G and T.

'I don't see why not,' she replied. 'Bell, are you coming? Blessing?' They had come into the lounge from their various corners.

That day was a dream. Blessing and my mother woke early to bake scones as my mother had a few orders and didn't want to run out. She would make extra to drop off at Norma Jeans. It was Sunday after all and their high tea was very popular. My mother's baking, the gorgeous setting of Norma Jeans and the wonderful staff meant that Sunday especially was a very busy day there.

Norma Jeans guest house, it was hidden up on a hill surrounded by lush vegetation. It was fabulous, such a gem. It had such a picturesque view overlooking the lake. That Sunday, I couldn't wait to go.

The Lake Mutirikwe: Once Known as Lake Kyle.

We dressed up in our Sunday dresses. Like every Sunday it started with church! We met the family there without fail every Sunday.

The happy clappers were back to jiving and throwing their hands up in the air. Speaking a foreign language called tongues. As hard as I tried, I was never able. Hallelujah! Amen to that. Life carried on and everyone found themselves back at Palm Court having milkshakes, laughing and fighting as families do. Playing cards, smoking cigars, eating prawns and listening to Vicky Leandros.

After church, we set off in the Peugeot 504 still in our Sunday best. Hats to boot. My grandmother had decided to join us as she wanted to be there to drop Nyika off at my father's house. She wanted to see the new wife of course and secondly to make sure Nyika went off alright. Nyika, my mother and my grandmother had discussed Nyika's misinterpretation to great lengths, they had fully grasped the magnitude of the moment. Nyika was welcomed back with open arms. Let bygones be bygones! It is possible to make up for lost time, you just must be willing to do so, and we were all more than willing to do just that!

Great Zimbabwe is a wonderful children's playground to entice your fantasies of having your own fort and fending off armies descending on the left and right of you. To be a princess, thrust into the arms of a dashing prince, who rescued you. A place where you become queen and reigned over the land, making the people prosperous or perhaps an evil queen rendering the people helpless.

Nyika and I would play there for hours on end playing these games of make believe. We would chase one another along the narrow and steep corridors of ancient stone, later taking time to have a picnic pretending it was a feast. We had played this game over and over again growing up during the war years when we visited my grandmother. Only we had been escorted by troops thanks to my grandmother's connections. It was delightful.

Zimbabwe Ruins was not far from the Stop Over, where we could rest at some point. Today, we would climb the ruins once again and feast in the cave that overlooked the smaller ruins. We had the usual picnic: cold roast chicken, potato salad, coleslaw, cucumber salad, peaches, watermelon and chocolate mousse for dessert. Blessing had been singing for us the whole trip and we all joined in.

We drove along the strip tar road to the Zimbabwe Ruins. My mother was driving, Samantha (Bell) and I were on the back seat with Nyika in the middle. Blessing was in the boot stretched out on a mattress and propped up on pillows. My grandmother in the passenger seat singing at the top of her voice, and smoking at the same time. Nyika – I talk about her being my Nyika – but she was also loved dearly by the whole family.

Halfway to the ruins, my mother asked Samantha if she would like to practice her driving as she was doing her learner's license. They swapped places. Samantha took her place in the driver's seat. After stalling twice, we bunny-hopped along the road till finally she gave the car some gas and we veered off the road just missing goats, chickens, cows, people and stray dogs. Samantha was screaming trying to hang onto the steering wheel while Blessing was clutching the support handle above the boot. My mother yelled at Samantha to hit the brakes and Nyika was clinging to me. Granny had turned white. I was laughing so loud, because I knew, Samantha could not drive to save her life. So hopefully, Mwari would save ours.

We came to a halt in a compound. Granny had woken up to the fact that she could pull up the hand break. Rather embarrassing. In a cloud of dust. Needless to say, we were suddenly surrounded, as was the compound tradition, by half-naked children pulling my clothing and touching my hair. Samantha, paralysed by shock, clutched the steering wheel tightly. Knuckles white.

Blessing was having another smoke. This time with a tad extra. 'Care for some Granny?' he asked.

'Definitely' she replied. Granny smoking the herb. That was a first for me to see, but I guess she was a grandmother already so she could certainly decide what she wanted.

'Mrs Claire! Mrs Claire!' A distant voice came from the middle of the bush. 'Mrs Claire.'

My mother's head followed the sound of the voice. A lady was running toward us. It was Anne – Joyce's head chef– she was on vacation.

'Are you alright, Claire? Can we do anything?'

'Well, how about a cup of tea?'

Typical Mum. Typical African Zimbabwe.

'Anything stronger Anne?' Granny asked.

'Oh, there's Granny' she exclaimed. 'Of course, Gogo, come sit, let me pour you a stiff one!'

We had a cup of tea at Anna's Kaya (hut). Granny had a stiff G and T and more herb. By this stage, Samantha's colour had returned. The whole compound came for tea. It was wonderful. We decided to share our picnic with everyone and it was a blast. It was too late for Norma Jean's but not too late for a coke at the boat club at the lake. All the scones had been devoured; they had been a welcome treat in the compound. I had also bought a sculpture from a well-known sculptor in the area – Anna's husband. He was called Emanuel. A Shona married to a Ndebele hardly ever heard of. He was so incredibly talented. All the sculpturing artists were and this Mas Vegas town rained down talent.

We left the compound in high spirits and continued down the winding strip road to the lake. It had been a big part of my later childhood. Learning to water-ski. Learning to drive a speedboat. There was no such thing as having to do a boat license. Attempting wind surfing and failing miserably, more worried about being eaten by crocodiles than concentrating on what I should have been. I do not miss Zimbabwe for the crocodiles one bit, nor the swarms of locusts that appear as if tree's and crops take flight.

We arrived at the boat club for a much-needed coke. Everyone knew everyone and their business too. Sunday was in full swing. The players were putting on a show for everyone. The in-betweens were trying their best too – trying to keep up with the players – but not quite managing. The money makers of the town, trying *ever so* hard to not be seen spending their money lavishly. Their wives were ever so sweet but ever so fake.

The hairdresser was still there – having tried to shoot herself the week before. Luckily for everyone, she had not been successful, for the simple reason that she was the most interesting person in town and without her, quite frankly, the women would look shabby, as she was bloody good at her job. The former terrorist, with blood shot eyes from one-to-many drinks was sitting in solitude, he liked it that way. We waved; he lifted his raspberry beret. Slugged his beer. Smoked his Madison Reds, laying by the hundreds in the unkept ashtray besides him. We town folk had arranged for him to have a chalet every Friday, as not to drive blotto and kill himself on the roads nor anyone else. He staggered across the bar floor, fell down the stairs and some fellows sitting close by, picked him up and walked-carried him to his chalet. It was a weekly occurrence, he didn't fall down the stairs every week, this was a particularly drenched Friday. He had been checked for injuries. Nothing except a slight graze and bruises in the morning for sure. No judgement here. His life had been hard enough, let him be. Drunk town folk were playing darts, drinking Castle or Lion beer. Everyone and their grandmother smoked – and they all smoked Madison Reds. Everyone wore boxer shorts and was barefoot while all the women seemed to be wearing blue eye-shadow. Music blared from the speakers. The Ramones. Billy Idol – "Nice Day for a White Wedding." The song reminded me that my father's wedding date had been announced. The invitation sat in my bedroom dustbin.

We greeted the various groups. The fake, the not fake, the players, the by goners, the nutty hairdresser, the bowls captain, the brick layers, the policemen and women, the Palm Court crowd, the Greeks, the Indians, the Italians and the decedents of Germans, Dutch and Irish and the Gook who lost it every Friday. He was a security guard in town at "OK Bazaars". A grocery shop. A colourful group, in a small town in the middle of nowhere. Oh, and not to forget, the mad Frenchman (the theatre director), who drank Zimbabwe's terrible wine and never complained, who ate our two types of cheese and smiled. The gooks, terrorists and freedom fighters who conversed only under drunken conditions. Mas Vegas even embraced those who were gay when the rest of the country frowned. Our "queens" were fabulous. Loud and Proud.

The car ride home was quiet and we were listening to "Perfect Day" by Leonard Cohen. Deep orange colours, pale yellows and magnificent golds danced across the sky as I looked up out the window leaning my head against Nyika. No matter what kind of day it was, Zimbabwe without fail gave you a killer sunset.

We drove into Mas Vegas down the one and only main road past Palm Court. Everything was closed, it being a Sunday. My mother had given Nyika half a pill to ease her nerves for meeting my father. I needed a whole pill.

We passed all the grocery shops: OK, N. Richards, Bata, Spar, Ali and Co and Bon Marche. The sun was setting.

We arrived at my father's huge house. My mother honked the horn. He came out together with his new family, her son and two daughters. A foreign sight for us. Off, just off.

My father greeted Nyika; he even hugged her. A remarkable moment, erasing years of pent-up misunderstandings, tensions and actions. All this happened as if in slow motion. It was intense, to say the least. He held her shoulders and looked at her squarely, telling her it was high time he heard her side of the story about the notebook and the events leading up the that terrible day, all those years ago. He reassured Nyika and I there was nothing to worry about, it had all been sorted out, so we could all get on with our lives. So much lost time, ravelled up in a heartbeat. Forgiveness. At long last.

'What do you mean, it's all been sorted out Dad?' I managed.

He told us that Happiness had heard about Nyika's return. Happiness, had gone to my father with the truth, and told him what Pretty had done. She was not there to tell her side of the story and Happiness, could no longer carry the burden of Pretty any longer. That her envy and jealousy had gotten to her in the end. She had not been part of the enemy. The truth was spoken after nearly a decade. Instead of being angry with Happiness, my father embraced the situation and decided to make both parties rest. We had all been through too much. The less drama and the more peace the better. My father was not getting any younger either. He was sick to death of war too. We all were.

Finally, we were all able to let go of our grief. Nyika looked at me. She was so proud of me in that moment, it shone in her eyes. I will never forget that particular exchange.

'Thank you Doobs,' my father said. 'You are a Henningway after all!' We laughed, the sadness moved away from the encounter. We all breathed a sigh of relief. We were not going to be prisoners of our pasts.

I said hello to his new family and her children. I offered a handshake. My grandmother and mother stayed in the car. Blessing was in the car too. He waved.

My emotions were torn – love for both my mother and father; memories of our home together, past life and the reality of what we had now. Nyika was safe and back with us. For this I was grateful.

Samantha and I climbed back into our mother's car. Everyone waved goodbye. Nyika would be living down the road. She was safe and just like that, as if a finger snap, all was forgiven. We were moving on!

We drove home in silence, but a good silence. An exhausted silence, but a happy one!

Chapter Thirteen
Boarding School and Bells

Some children love boarding school. Not me. I never quite got the hang of it. I didn't hate it, I loathed it. I was so miserable there, I excelled. I excelled in everything ridiculously so!

The good news, though, was that Nyika was back and I saw her every weekend before leaving for boarding school. She spent her days off at our house – we had made up a room for her. Sometimes during the week, if I didn't have sport in the afternoon, I would join her for tea, in her lodgings at the back of my dad's house. Not visiting them necessarily either.

For the weekends I had to spend at my father's house, Nyika would be there too. Her presence helped me profoundly.

I noticed that my father had changed. He was happy and always smiling. For him, I was grateful that he had found his true north. It's true, I did so desperately want to feel that for him. He deserved happiness in massive dollops. He was incredibly kind to her children and he was so calm and content. He was indeed a completely different man, in this environment they had created, and for that I was grateful. The old saying so clear to me, some people could bring out the worst in you and some people could bring out the best in you. My parents had run their race. Their parting had been for the best. Both were much happier in their new-found love. That would eventually trickle down the inevitable layers of hurt and pain.

Me on the other hand, I felt like a complete stranger in his home. Not one photograph of me and my siblings hung in the house. The one and only photo of me, never changed, I just stayed eight for years and years. We did not connect on any level and I found myself always being overly polite. As soon as I arrived, I wanted to leave. I was given the spare room, which was fine. However, every time I tried to make it a little bit "mine" by sticking up a few posters - as teenagers do - or leaving something behind or bringing my own duvet cover, I returned the following weekend or shared holiday and it was back to its original and formal state. What a welcome. Never once did it occur to his true north, that it might be nice and kind even to have something I liked to eat in the fridge. It's really the small things that matter for children.

Later on, she would often make snide remarks when no other adult was around. One that sums her up in a second is this... we had just moved to the Save Conservancy and we were swimming in the pool.

She turned and said to me, 'Joanna, you look so much better lying down in your bikini than walking around in it.'

What kind of comment is that? What kind of person would say that? I was grateful that she made my father so happy. But that was my only positive feeling towards her.

One morning, my mother had begun to explain what boarding school was about. She said it was such a shame that I had to leave and go to the school in South Africa (the school my step siblings were at) but that I should do the best I could and that I should remember it was only for three years. After that, I would return and enrol in a different boarding school in Zimbabwe. The school in Zimbabwe was in a village called Mutare, which was only a two-hour drive from Mas Vegas.

'Just keep your head down, Joanna,' she said. 'Do your work and do your sport. You're an excellent swimmer; go for gold!'

My stomach felt queasy.

'Mum,' I replied. 'I won't see Samantha, Blessing or Nyika for three months at a time. Then I have to split the holidays between you and Dad. So theoretically for the next three years, I see you in total seven weeks in a whole year. Mom, I am a kid, it's too long. Her kids will see her and Dad because they will visit over long weekends. The distance to come home on long weekends to you guys is just too far, six and a half hours to drive to you and six and a half hours back again, some 500km or so. There were trains but you would not risk them. I'm only allowed one phone call a month. Well two – one to you and one to Dad. Dad's one I have to share the time with my step sibling, as she has to speak to him and her mother, so it will be very brief.'

Each phone call home was only fifteen minutes to allow all the children a chance to speak to their parents. Every Sunday evening, after homework, we would also write a compulsory letter home.

Meanwhile, Samantha would be starting her first job at Glen Livet Hotel on the banks of Lake Muturikwe (Lake Kyle). She would be managing a resort there and setting up the wellness sector. She was saving money to travel the world. At the same time, she would be sending money home so that my mother could open "The Cottage Shop." My mother worked tooth and nail to make this a reality. She did not have the time or the capital to visit me in my "forced Afrikaner Ville" school in Pietersburg. The school was supposed to be English but the teachers were predominantly Afrikaans, well, let me rephrase that, they were all, Afrikaans. Not my cup of tea, people, not my cup of tea! I despised everything they stood for as a country at the time. How the hell could I be sent to school here, clearly this was a completely disturbing reality for me.

Bell really looked after my mother during this period making sure she never missed a hair appointment and that she never went without. The Cottage Shop eventually opened and it was a hit. Now Mas Vegas had a place to buy decent coffee – even a cappuccino. Miracles do happen. My grandmother and my mother had the two hippest places in town. Unfortunately, Palm Court would soon be closed down as my grandmother wanted to move to the north of the country with my Aunty Joyce and Uncle Tony. Here, they were to open a horse betting business and takeaway alongside it. It was to be called Maria's. In Bulawayo. A lot was changing and change is good... apparently.

'We need to go shopping and prepare your trunk for boarding school, Joanna,' announced my mother and Nyika.

First thing the next day, we hit the *metropolis* of Mas Vegas. First, we went to a shop called Meikles. This was the place to buy perfume and the type of goodies that only a girl needs. My mother took extra care to buy me suitable lingerie and perfume.

After that we had tea in the Meikles Lounge - toasted chicken and mayonnaise sandwiches. My mother lifted her pinkie as she drank her tea, smiled and said she would miss me. I asked what she would miss the most. She said she would miss my cuddles and she would miss us dancing around in the lounge to jazz. After all I had been her closest companion during her divorce.

Once we finished our tea, we went to Balmain to shop for what boarding school calls "tuck" - sweets and treats placed in a Tupperware box. In this tuck box, I included biscuits (tennis biscuits and my mother's crunchies), four bars of chocolate (Kit-Kats and chocolate logs), a couple packets of jelly tots, a tin of milo, a box of black tanganda tea (my all-time favourite) and biltong (courtesy of my brother-in-law). Susan and Uncle Smurf as we call him, had since got married. A rather stylish affair. I also snuck in a packet of rolos, a packet of rosemary creams and a bottle of Mazowe cream soda mix.

The tuck box was completed, wrapped up and eventually laid on the one side of the trunk. My trunk was one and a half metres long and half a metre deep. Made of tough metal. Black. On the top, in big white bold capital letters, was my full name and address and the house I was placed in. The "houses" in the school compete in sports events and academic achievements. At the end of the year, all of the house points are totalled up and one of the houses wins (to extremely loud cheers). It's great fun.

I was to learn that I excelled in this competitive environment. I like to compete. I enjoyed beating the "rocks" (Zimbabweans nickname for Afrikaners), one at a time!

The day came for me to leave. The night before, my mother had made me my favourite dinner – cottage pie. I was even allowed to have tomato sauce with it. This was a rare treat as it was normally banned in our house – my mother firmly believing it overrides all other flavours. Which it does.

My father picked me up at the crack of dawn from my mother's house. At the gate, hooted. It was an awkward goodbye as my father and his new family were waiting in his car. My father was not allowed on my mother's property. We had to drive to Pietersburg. This took 6 hours. I climbed into the car, hating to be there with these people in such close proximity. I put my headphones on and pushed play on my Walkman. I had my own lunchbox and water. Not a chance I was eating all-sorts of their food.

On the drive I had seen so many sign boards each one making me a little more homesick. I would be alone. I planned to just study like a maniac.

I felt as if I was stifling hot for the whole journey. The landscape changed as we drove over the tropic of Capricorn. It was a lot flatter looking and no large boulders loomed out of the earth. We were definitely in South Africa.

The first week at boarding school was the worst. Without fail, at the beginning of each term, every time I opened my trunk there was a letter on top of all my clothing from my mother and Nyika and that just made me miss home like hell. After some time, I would immediately throw the letters in the dustbin just because it hurt too much to read them. My step-sister and I shared a dormitory. It was made up of four beds, two each side of a wall divider, – each bed one looked like they had come directly from the prison. Each bed had a very thin mattress with a bottom sheet, top sheet and a grey prickly blanket. One hard pillow. I bent to smell the sheets, no love in that, just sterile. Washing in mass. Mass washing. It made me lurch. A wooden chair accompanied the bed. Our cupboards were two shelves, each a metre long and half a foot deep with a metre hanging space. We had lugged our trunks upstairs and these were positioned at the end of our beds. My step-sister was rallying with her friends, clearly comfortable in familiar surroundings.

It came time to say goodbye to our families. Then we would have a meeting with the headmistress in an hour. She was to inform us about the rules. Above each bed was a window. I opened it so that I could get a much-needed breath of fresh air. Shortly afterwards, my father announced that they would be leaving. I walked with him and his new-found love down the stairs. I waved goodbye. I felt in some way relieved that they had left. They had no sooner left when the bully made herself known. There is always that bully, the most insecure person in the group.

Her name was Jade Van Der Merwe. She had to be the world's least well brought up individual to cross my path. Certainly, I am yet to meet one to surpass her. Her art in manipulation was award winning. She managed to turn people against one another with immense skill and ease through scandal and her corrupt imagination. Hours wasted on plotting and planning to make other people's lives, who her challenged her miserable. The other girls seemed to fear her. Naturally we did not hit it off at all. Her other two friends – Elly Maggot and Beth Wright – were fortunately tolerable enough.

A bell sounded and a thousand footsteps in unison stumbled, ran, tripped, walked and paraded to the meeting of Miss Jagger. Our headmistress, Miss Jagger. Miss Jagger turned out to be an amazing lady who took extra care of children whose parents were particularly useless or non-existent and of children like myself, whose parents lived in another country. I was the only Zimbabwean at this school. I had no idea what citizenship my step-siblings held. However, shortly afterwards, other families from Zimbabwe began sending their children to P.E.M.P.S. too - believing that the Zimbabwean educational system had taken a turn for the worst. I did not support their idealism.

Miss Jagger took us out of the hostel on some weekends to her private home with special permission from the school and she would sometimes buy us our favourite goodies and sweets, sometimes a dress or T-shirt and she would rent out the best video cassettes. At her place we watched Ghostbusters, the entire series of Hammer House of Horror, American Werewolf in London and numerous other horror films. All I wanted to watch were horror films – anything to distract me and take me out of this reality. The more horrific and mentally whacked the better. Unfortunately, these weekends had to be shared with the Van Der Merwe sisters. This Jade chick came with a sister who had a very similar attitude. Clearly a very dysfunctional family. Elly Maggot went home every weekend with her mother but Beth Wright came along with us from time to time. She had a sister here too. Beth was really quite nice and I wondered why she hung out with these girls. Miss Jagger also had a pool at home and I happily spent most of my time in it.

I missed my Zimbabwean friends and school a great deal. I missed Palm Court. I yearned for my family and my cousins! I missed Nyika and Blessing every day!

Being in the belt of Afrikaner Ville. This school was exclusively white. It was a shock to my system. Not one black person except the personal cleaning. South Africa was still wrapped up in the cling wrap of Apartheid. Man, this was going to be one hell of a long year (or two or three). I detested being here.

After our parents left on the first day, we sprinted up a flight of around forty steps where we all huddled in the prep room to meet with Miss Jagger. Two hundred of us. The youngest children were five years old – weekly boarders, except for three of them who were long haulers. I felt so penitent for them – most of them were crying or had been crying, red-eyed and dishevelled. Noses dripping snot. The entire hostel age group ran from five to thirteen, some were older that had previously failed their last exams and had to remain behind and repeat the year. Miss, Jagger rang the bell and silence gripped the air.

'Welcome back, ladies!' she began, 'and a warm welcome to our new girls and young ladies. The rules are as follows:

'Every mealtime there will be a bell.'

'Shower time in the evening, a bell.'

'Shower time in the morning, a bell.'

'Beginning of prep, a bell.'

'End of prep, a bell.'

'The start of school, a bell.'

'Break time at school, end of break time, a bell.'

'End of every lesson, a bell.'

'Beginning of assembly, a bell.'

'There will also be a bell just for scholar patrols. This is when they will prepare the roads for the crossover from hostel to school.'

'At every wake up there will be a bell.'

'Every inspection – which happens every single day except Saturdays – there will be a bell.'

'What does inspection mean?' asked one of the girls.

'Inspection means the following…' Miss Jagger replied. 'Freshly polished school shoes every morning. You must polish your shoes before you go to bed. Fresh white socks according to winter or summer uniform. If your hair touches the collar of your uniform, you are to tie it up.'

'No hair is to hang on your face or over your eyes; it is to be clipped up or tied up. School underwear only! This too will be checked so do not think you will get away with it. No nail polish – short and clean nails only. No makeup.'

'When the bell sounds your cupboard should be in order and your bed made – I expect hospital corners. Seniors in charge of the "wings" are to help and supervise the little ones. If they are late you will be punished, not them.'

'Here are the other rules…'

'No running in corridors.'

'No running up or down the stairs.'

'Lights out at 8 p.m. during the week.'

'Lights out for the senior year at 9 p.m.'

'Head girl, deputy head girl and prefects have lights out at 10 p.m.'

'On a Friday and a Saturday everyone goes to bed one hour later than their given time.'

'No talking in prep.'

'No talking when you line up for tuck. Tuck is only on Saturdays and you can have one sweet a week.'

'No talking during meal times.'

'You may take a weekend out with a friend if your parents have given permission. Signed permission.'

'On Saturday mornings, after breakfast, you may go outside into the garden till lunch time. After lunch there will be compulsory prep time to do your weekend homework. This is from 2 p.m. to 6 p.m. with a tea break at 4 p.m.'

'Every Sunday, you will wake up at 6 a.m. hours for church service and breakfast for everyone is at 6:30 a.m. You will wear your full uniform and blazer for church. You will walk to your respective churches – either New Born Christian, Catholic, Methodist or Presbyterian. Find out where each group leaves from. If you don't know what religion you are stay after this meeting and I will inform you.'

I had been told that I was Presbyterian. My father had been Presbyterian his whole life. He had converted to Catholicism for my mother so they could be married in a Catholic church. My mother was not a staunch Catholic; despite being raised as such. Eventually she became a new born Christian. She was open to all religions and later on – after my time at boarding school had finished – she said I could choose whatever religion suited me as "they are all the same at the end of the day." I chose to be Catholic simply because I found the churches so beautiful. I am not a believer in religious dogma. It's clear there is a God.

Later in life, I have found that I am not "religious," in terms of rigid religion following all the rules, so to speak, no thanks. I took a bit from Buddhism and I certainly have an affinity with Christ. In my most difficult and life-threatening moments, he has never failed me. To each his own. Religion and beliefs are personal and I will leave it at that. I respect everyone's choice as long as it was their choice.

'Uniform is worn every day except Saturdays,' continued Miss Jagger. 'If you are sick there is a sick bay. If you have a temperature you will be admitted. No temperature, no admittance. No bunking off. We know all the games children can play.

'If you do not adhere to these rules, you will be punished in the following ways:

'No tuck for up to a month.

'Writing lines.

'Picking up stones off the sports fields.

'Slapped on your hands with a plank, three times.

'You can choose your punishment.'

I would always opt for the three hand spankings. However, I discovered (painfully) that one particular teacher would make you wet your hands before he smacked them with a plank.

The second day at boarding school arrived and sure enough I was woken by a loud bell. I made my bed, checked that my cupboard was in order and tried not to run to the bathroom because I needed a pee so badly. There, I brushed my teeth and showered. Then I walked back to my dormitory, brushed my hair, dressed in my uniform and polished my shoes. I remembered to slide on my granny underwear (my grandmother would not be caught dead in these things). They were a punishment all on their own. School rules, honestly, the underwear we had to wear was by far my worst punishment of my schooling years. To this day, I splash out on underwear. As you can see, trauma affects us all differently. Finally, I sat in my chair with my hands on my lap and my feet together – no slouching, up straight. My hair was so short – due to a depressed hairdresser in Mas Vegas – so I had no need to worry about the tied hair rule. I looked just like a boy.

The next bell sounded. This meant no talking and await your inspection. I waited. The teacher on duty came in. I think her name was Mrs Greene. She was kind enough! As the teacher walked in, you stand, hands behind your back, and say, 'Good Morning Ma'am.' Then she would check if your closet was perfect – all stacked at right angles. Then she would check your hospital bed corners give you the once over. 'Panties,' she would say and you lifted your dress slightly. 'Fix your socks, Joanna, you are showing to much of your lower ankle.' That was it. Inspection over. Another bell rang and we walked to breakfast. Here, we would line up silently then enter the huge eating hall.

After grace, we would be instructed to sit.

'Be seated!' the headmistress Miss Jagger would say. We then lined up again table by table to be served our breakfast exactly like in Oliver Twist. Breakfast was either baked beans on toast, scrambled egg on toast, French toast or (on Sundays only) fried-eggs, bacon and tomatoes.

After breakfast, yes, another bell. In my first year I was made a scholar patrol, so at least I got to leave breakfast early.

The days and nights flew by. I went home for my first holiday after three months. My father had bought a small plane – a Cessna 172. The Save Conservancy was in such a remote location that it was a necessity. He had completed his pilot's license and he was flying to Pietersburg to pick us up from school. This excited me a great deal. It would be my first time to fly and it would be in our very own plane.

My father and his new-found adoration were to have their wedding in Mas Vegas this holiday and were to move to The Save Conservancy directly afterwards. This was the last vacation at the mansion. Nyika, was moving to the Conservancy with them.

We packed our trunks in good spirits. The dormitories and the rest of the school were alive – children and parents coming and going. Everywhere, the thunk and clatter of trunks and happy chattering.

We took a taxi to the airport – me and my two step-siblings – we would be meeting my father there. I sat in the front. I announced I would be doing the same in the plane.

We were all very happy to be going home. I couldn't wait to see my mother, Samantha, Susan, Nyika and Blessing. My brother Herman Jnr too. He had finished his studies and was coming home from London. My sister Susan had married her boyfriend and they had moved to The Save Conservancy and lived in one of the houses at the headquarters – at Chishakwe – which my father had bought. Also on Chishakwe, lived Mr and Mrs Loving Hamm - my brother in law's parents. His father, Mr Loving Hamm was one of the best cattle men in the country and the conservancy was originally a cattle ranch called Devuli before it was turned into a conservation. He was also incredibly informed on the nature and wildlife of the area so he stayed on. He had a humour second to none. His laugh was contagious and he always had time for me and his brandy and coke. Every time I saw him, I also learnt something new about the bush or cattle.

Mr. Fuller had been hired to harness cattle on 3442 kms squared of wild land. This must have been a rather taxing job! Considering the heat and the sheer magnitude and wildness of The Ranch. Alexandra wrote *Let's Not Go to the Dog's Tonight, Leaving Before the Rain Comes* and *Under the Jacaranda Tree*. In *Let's Not Go to the Dogs Tonight*, she also mentions The Ranch.

She describes The Ranch (Devuli) and (The Save Valley Conservancy) as follows; This was from her latest book – Travel Light, Move Fast, she has inspired me, and I am grateful for her words;

"THE MIRACULOUS RANCH in southeast Zimbabwe was the wildest land we ever lived on, the least scarred. It wasn't a complete cure for what ailed, for the shocks and the aftershocks of the war, and for all that had come with the war, but I think it was the beginning of the cure or the cure was ours for the metabolizing, if we knew it or not." – Page 62

AND words from her father who had worked on the ranch

"That was the wildest place we have ever lived, Bobo. You could really fall off the map out there." – Page 64

– in Alexandra Fuller's own words from her book "Travel Light, Move Fast"

There was another family there too – the Gosling family. Everyone living there had some part in making the conservation possible. Some, however, did leave before it was fully realised as their passion was cattle farming and not wildlife.

We saw the plane touch down on the tarmac. As usual, my father was late. I have never known him to be on time once in his life. It can really get under my nails when people are late repeatedly, my father was no exception. Probably because most of my life I was ordered around by a bloody bell. The little plane bumped along the airstrip and came to a whirring halt just to the left of us. In those days, at small airports, you could wait to the "side" of the tarmac, alongside the airstrip.

The plane came to a spluttering stop a few metres in front of us. The propeller finally stopped turning. It sounded like a VW Beetle. It looked that sort of size too with just a tail and two wings. Once the plane was fully stationary, we loaded our trunks and clambered into the plane. My father put on his headset. He gave me mine too and told me I was his co-pilot. It was our first real connection in years. Things changed from that day; our relationship improved. He did his checks, then his fuel check and finally announced our code. 'Yanky Yanky Tango,' came the reply, 'you have permission to fly.' Permission for take-off.

The little plane shook, rather like a dog shaking itself after a bath, then my dad accelerated and we sped along the runway. It was exhilarating. I felt goosebumps all over my body. The thrill was magnificent. Then we suddenly lifted up into the sky and watched the earth drop beneath us. The world from up here looked like an entirely different place. Dinky cars drove along snake like paths; some on dirt roads with a puff of rail dust flying behind them. Cotton candy clouds were all around waiting for us to fly through. I imagined I was a bird – a hawk – watching everything. I thought about the first female pilot. Today I would pretend to be Amelia Earhart.

The flight took us two hours – we were heading back to Mas Vegas. *Why would one ever want to land?* I thought. My father could see how much I was enjoying this moment. Not only because of flying but it was my first time alone (well semi-alone, upfront) with him in a very long time. I was never offered alone time with him, nor had he bothered to make time with me alone and I had always craved it. I always had plenty of time usually with my mom. Which was equally important to me, but our relationship was solid. My father and my relationship needed work. However, I really missed time with just my dad and I.

'Dad,' I remember asking, 'Will you fly me from the Conservancy to Mas Vegas when you move there?'

'Of course,' he replied.

'Can it just be you and I?'

He looked over at me and said, 'Yes let's do that.'

'One more question,' I continued. 'Can, Nyika, fly with us too to Mas Vegas, for one week of my holidays too?'

'I'll check with Molly.'

It was a start. The sky was a brilliant blue. Kopjes were scattered beneath us. My father pointed out sites I knew very well.

'There is the turn off to Zaka. That is our old house – Ngwane (toilet seat left only and no Shepherd Tree). There is Nyika's village. Over there is the Zimbabwe Ruins and look, there is Mas Vegas.'

It was beautiful; as far as the eye could see. I didn't want to lose this moment. Seeing things from this perspective made distances between my mother's house and my father on the conservancy relatively minimal. It was no longer an "astronomical distance" in my mind. I wanted to be in this moment for an eternity. Right where I was.

'This is Yanky, Yanky Tango,' my father said into the radio, 'do we have permission to land?'

'Permission granted, Herman,' came the reply, 'How are you?'

'Doing well. Is that John?'

'Yes, sir. How's the family, Herman?'

'All wonderful. How about you?'

'My youngest is sadly not so well – malaria. But the rest of us are fit, fat and flourishing.'

'Has your daughter seen a doctor?'

'Yes, she is at the Mas Vegas Clinic.'

'I'll drop a bonsella.'

'Thank you, Mr Hagan. Yanky Yanky Tango has permission to land.'

I had seen my mother, Blessing, Samantha and Nyika all standing alongside the Peugeot – a bright blue dot of a car. They were waving their hands above their heads. My dad dipped the wings, it became our inside joke. We sort of kangaroo hopped on our landing – the wings of the plane wiggling. We landed at quite a speed simply because the tail wind (the wind behind us) was particularly strong that afternoon. We stopped a few metres from them and waited for the propeller to come to a standstill. Then I opened my door, climbed down from the plane and with fresh air in my heart and lungs I galloped towards my family. I dived into my mother, Nyika, Samantha and Blessings' arms. It was a massive and wonderful group hug. You may have gathered by now that I am that hugging person, who needs physical contact, pretty much all the time.

As if she could read my mind, I saw my grandmother's Citroen come flying up the road. Naturally, she wanted to see me but she also wanted to see if the story about the plane was true. She fully exited her car and sauntered over with her pearls, gloves, bag and polka dot dress.

'Oh, how fabulous!' she shouted at the top of her voice, 'How dinky. Herman, oh, do take us for a flip?'

Knowing his former mother-in-law never accepted no for an answer, he skilfully obliged. Molly was waiting by her car; her children were already with her. No goodbye's, no hello's. The usual tolerance slicing through the air, between us and them.

So that day, off went Blessing, Granny and Samantha for a flip with my father. My mother, at that stage, could not bear the sight of my father longer than necessary. She said goodbye to him curtly and drove Nyika and I home. Nyika said she would fly with me when we flew from the farm. Granny Rita would also drop off Blessing and Samantha at my mother's house later. It was a weekend after all and Nyika was with us for the next two days.

I was so happy and relieved to be home and was looking forward to spending time with all my family and both my parents. Christmas wasn't too far off and I was already feeling sad that I would not be spending it with my father. This would be my first ever Christmas without him. When the judge asked me which parent I wanted to live with at their divorce hearing, I had chosen my mother. Then I thought about some of the perks of being a child of divorced parents and the sadness faded a little. I would get two sets of Christmas presents and seeing as they were not talking, it would probably be two sets of Christmas and birthday presents for quite a while.

Dinner that first night of the holidays was cottage pie and yes, tomato sauce. I fell into my own bed that night and only woke the following morning at 10 a.m. Nyika woke me up with a cup of tea and sat on the edge of my bed. My room was bright with sunlight and dust ballerina's, I was taken back to Ngwane for a split second. I had a four-poster bed. Curled up at the end of my bed was my cat Puppet. My brother was due back home that evening and from what I'd heard, he had a very good time in Europe. He'd been running with (or away from) bulls in Spain and drinking too much Guinness in Ireland. I had not seen him since my parents had divorced and I was really looking forward to catching up and spending some time with him.

Nyika and I sipped our tea together. She munched on her favourite sandwich – white bread, two pieces, each piece four fingers high smothered in Sun Jam.

'Joanna,' Nyika said, between cement mixing her food, 'tomorrow is your father's wedding. You need to be on your best behaviour.'

'How is his future wife with you?' I asked. 'Is she kind to you, Nyika?'

'She is definitely not like your mother at all. She is just lukewarm water. Why don't you take her just at face value? It would make your life so much easier. Now get up, the day won't wait for you. We have to go and get you a dress from Granny Rita's shop for your dad's wedding. Let's bike into town, then go to your mum's coffee shop, (The Cottage Shop) for a cappuccino. After that, we'll go to Bata and get us both a pair of shoes. Your Granny Rita already bought my dress and she bought Blessing a new suit. Happiness will be there too and so will Truth and Zuvarashe.' All looking fine!

The crew would be back together after so many years. The wedding just got so much better. Is Samantha, shopping with us?' I asked.

'Yes, Joanna,' Nyika replied, 'she will join us for coffee. As you will see she has a boyfriend.'

'A what?'

'Yes, a boyfriend.'

'Do you like him, Nyika?'

'Not at all. Lazy ass young man. Sits doing nothing all day. Doesn't rise before 12 p.m. She runs around him like a mother hen. I warned her. She gives him money too. She must have been born blonde for a reason.'

'What's his name?'

'Douglas.'

'Well, if you don't like him, then neither will I.'

'Typical African man, that man. Sitting on his backside doing nothing,' she went off muttering. 'Someone needs to light a fire under his ass!'

I could smell fresh scones baking in the oven. I was home.

Nyika screamed at me, 'Get up! Get up! Otherwise, you'll become just like that lazy ass Douglas!'

I rolled out of bed. Those boarding school bells were a distant memory. If only she knew. I had managed to speak with her for only about three minutes so far on the long-distance calls home. My mother had filled her in with the rest.

'Joe!' she shouted once more. 'Remind me to talk to you about that bully at school. I have a remedy. You will love it. It will be our little secret; works like a dream, every time.'

I made a mental note to remind her and looked forward to whatever she had in mind.

We wolfed down Blessing's homemade scones with fresh strawberry jam (courtesy of my mother). Then I brushed my teeth and checked to see if Samantha was in her room. Apparently, she had not come home the night before. I would see her later. I made my bed; it was second nature these days. Then I folded my pyjamas and threw on a dress. The weather was glorious. Zimbabwe had such perfect weather.

We jumped on our bikes, asked Blessing if he needed any groceries for the house (nothing needed) and sped into town. It took about half an hour. We parked our bikes outside my grandmother's vintage shop (simply called The Dress Shop). I hugged my grandmother's assistant good morning; we had a brief chat and she suggested I try on two or three dresses. I chose a shell-coloured dress just above the knee with a high waist. I also chose an elaborate hat with a dashing rim. It was broad and so very Monaco. At that age I had no idea what or where Monaco was. I just liked the idea of what I had seen in fashion magazines that arrived in our country rather dated. I would match it with a pair of my mother's earrings and seventies sunglasses.

Next, we rushed off to Bata. I chose a pair of black ballerina shoes; Nyika chose the same.

'What colour is your dress, Nyika?' I asked. 'Mine is a bright blood orange and I have a leopard print box hat to match it. Granny has lent me a string of pearls and gloves with an extra gift of my first handbag,' she replied.

'Wow, I can't wait to see you in it,' I replied, 'you are going to look beautiful.'

'Is my mother going to the wedding?'

'Don't be daft, child.'

Nothing more was said but she had some news of her own.

Next, we stopped briefly at Palm Court. I took my last look around it as it would be closing the following day. The vintage shop was to remain open. It would be strange without my grandmother around. A lot was to change. We then peddled to my mother's Cottage Shop. It was so quaint and so pretty. I was incredibly proud of her – standing behind the counter – she looked so alive. Divorcing my father had been the best thing for her.

She was wearing a canary yellow, halter neck dress with low slung heels, big bangles and big earrings. She tottered around the tables, smiling and serving. Fresh cakes and scones filled the countertop. It was beautiful.

'Well done, Mum!' I said and gave her a big hug.

We had bought her a fresh bunch of yellow roses; her favourite flower and favourite colour rose.

The yellow rose - long associated with the sun and its life-giving warmth, yellow is the age-old spokes-colour for warm feelings of friendship and optimism. In many Eastern cultures, the colour represents joy, wisdom and power. But, while any yellow flower will send a light-hearted message, the history of the yellow rose in particular has an optimistic and serendipitous character that really makes it the complete package.

My mother was the full package too and she deserved all the happiness in the world. At the back of her Cottage Shop was a table for family and old friends only - sat there today was my godmother, Mrs Vye Glover. On a cloud she was. She had the look of a gazelle with a pinch of peri-peri. Vye had a chauffeur and a Bentley and played golf with my mother. She spent every Sunday after church with us in our swimming pool sipping gin and tonics with my mother, grandmother, Samantha and I. I didn't start on G and T's till I was sixteen. Vye spent her days playing golf and shopping. In her spare time, she arranged fundraisers to help educate children in the tribal trust lands.

My family and her family would hire a ten-ton truck and fill it with old and new clothes, used toys, bikes, lots of food, reading glasses and books - anything you could imagine. Including specific packages that they had asked for on our previous trips, items they were in dire need of. Then they would drive the truck around Zaka and the Bikita area giving the families Christmas presents. No one went hungry at Christmas time. We decorated the truck in tinsel and we dressed up as Santa Claus and elves. What a sight we were. Not only did my mother do this, she took the "snotty" out of golf and in her spare time gave golf lessons to children and caddies who could not afford the sport. She was golf captain at the club for four years running.

'Joanna,' my mother said, bringing me back to reality after catching up with Vye, 'I have met someone. He is lovely; very gentle and kind.'

'Yes,' I replied, 'and?'

'You will meet him after the wedding,' she continued. 'We plan to get married this coming Christmas.'

'Do you love him?'

'Yes, I do,'

'Well then,' I said as I adjusted the yellow roses in the vase, 'that's all that matters. What's his name?'

'Tom Mathews.'

'Nice surname; sounds proper. Will you change your name to Claire Mathews?'

'Yes, I will,' she replied.

'Then let's have some Brut (the only drink vaguely resembling champagne or prosecco in our Zimbabwe)!'

I popped the cork and the whole tearoom turned to glance in our direction.

'A toast,' I said, 'to my mum – soon to be Claire Mathews.'

I lifted my Marion Antoinette Champagne glass to clink with my mother's. Even Nyika had a glass – that was a first.

Vye reappeared and bought Brut for the whole tearoom. Soon a party was in full swing and ABBA blasted out the stereo. Oh, for the love of ABBA. Everyone was dancing and we joined in. It was a fabulous, spontaneous party.

My father's wedding came and went. A few chosen friends and family. Happy to be with my crew at our table!

Nyika and I spent a lot of time together during the holidays. We rode out to the Zimbabwe Ruins on our bikes and camped at the dam for the weekend. Samantha came by car with her boyfriend to join us.

I soon met my future step-father – Tom Mathews – and was happy to see he was a gentleman. He came with two children who were a lot older than me. He had a son and a daughter. So now, I had three step-sisters and two step-brothers.

Eventually, the day arrived to return to school in Pietersburg. Knowing that we would fly there made it exhilarating and I was not feeling so bad about leaving. I was excelling at school and was top of my class. At the end of the year, it was announced that I was to be head girl and sports captain of my house Orion. My swimming continued to progress well and I soon had my national colours in butterfly.

The trick with the bully worked too. Nyika had given me grounded buffalo beans. I had rubbed the powder in Jade Van Der Merwe's clothes and she got such a rash. From then on, every time she gave me (or someone else) a hard time, I just put buffalo beans in her clothes and watched her scratch herself near to death.

I also made sure that she was caught out for forcing me to do her homework. Originally, I had agreed just so that she would leave me the hell alone. But eventually, I had enough. I wrote the exact same essays in my book and hers for geography. The teacher understood immediately. Her standard in class meant it was obvious that she had not written this essay. Silly girl.

I never had trouble from her again and my time at school was that much better for it. The last I heard; she had become a policewoman. Go figure. If you know anything about the former police in South Africa, you will know it was mostly Afrikaners who were total racist pigs. Now she probably uses a uniform as an excuse to bully people.

Soon it would be the Christmas holidays and I would be leaving this school for good. I was delighted to be joining a new school back in Zimbabwe in Mutare.

A new life on The Save Conservancy awaited me and a new school. I would fall in love; I would become a woman and I would master the art of flying. May the zest for life always remain in my blood and heart. Zimbabwe, I am coming home – where people speak proper English, return smiles and make proper tea.

Chapter Fourteen
Place of the Lions

This would be a dream part of my childhood and early teens. One I will look back upon with great fondness and deep unshakable love for Africa and my father. My father and I were gradually bridging the gap; however, I never felt welcome in his new home. I felt like a guest. I decided therefore to behave like a guest. It was so much easier and thus it worked.

When I was staying with my father, I would spend most of my time out of the house or I would bring friends home from my new school in Mutare. Christmas had come and gone; I was to start school in Mutare – formally known as Umtali. Nyika was at my father's house too so that was an added bonus.

At school, I joined the tennis, hockey and swimming teams. I made it into the first teams for all of them and this involved a lot of travelling for inter school competitions. I excelled in these sports – I made province colours in tennis and national colours in swimming, adding to my swimming accomplishments at my South African school. In hockey, I played left half or centre forward. In my last year of school our team won the competition, "Golden Girls," meaning our school team was the best senior hockey team in the country. However, I found hockey a bit too masculine and gave it up immediately after school.

Back at the ranch, or should I say the conservancy, they had a new chef – well, cook-boy – called Reckless and an additional maid called Fifi. Happiness was working in the garden and Truth and Zuvarashe had moved to the protea farm that my father had bought up in the Bvumba Mountains – the place he had decided to retire to one day. The Bvumba Mountains were roughly a two-and-a-half-hour drive from The Save Valley Conservancy, in the opposite direction to Mas Vegas. The farm in these mountains was an additional project to bring in money for the family. My father was growing king and queen proteas on this farm for export to South Africa and to Europe.

The additional bonus to having the Protea farm in the Bvumba was Antoinette's Coffee Shop. It's also a reason in itself to live in the Bvumba. The woods and mist in the area invited fantasy.

On the conservancy, I was allocated the guest room. I had long since given up trying to make any room in my father's house my own. I spent equal amounts of time in their houses but only felt at home in my mother's house. The Save Valley Conservancy was now in full swing. I had officially started school in Mutare at Hillcrest College (a three-hour drive away or a short plane ride). The hostels for the boarding school section of the school were still being built so I had to board with an elderly couple for the first few months. They were very sweet and looked exactly like they came out of a rusk packaging commercial.

During this time, each morning, I had to catch a ride in a truck with metal benches with a man called Mr Hocks. He owned a car repair garage. He would drive his son to Hillcrest every day and a couple of us other kids would hitch a ride along with him for a fair price.

It was on one these rides that I found a kitten who I named Pandora,

and gave her a home on the conservancy. Pandora went on to mate with a wild cat, a civet and produced two kittens, Garfield and Forget, who in turn grew up and produced a number of kittens themselves. Cats were a necessity on the conservancy due to the sheer number of venomous snakes, most notably the spitting cobra. They also helped to keep the vast number of creepy crawlies in check. I do not miss these bugs and spiders in the least. The feeling of an insect walking up your face in the dead of night is terrifying. If for some reason you had simply forgotten to use your mosquito net. We had a generator which was turned off in the evening, so you could not even switch a light on to see which insect it was. You would slap it hard and hope to hell it was not a scorpion. I took to sleeping permanently with a mosquito net. I would imagine so as it was also an area rife with malaria during the rainy season.

My class were Hillcrest's first students and we all helped to some degree in building and establishing the school. We spent many an afternoon clearing the sports fields – students today still benefit from our hard work. It was great fun and it meant a lot to all of us. For those of us with a touch of the mischievous spirit we probably cleared slightly more of the field than others.

The girls' lodgings were not so glamorous and we always had a shortage of hot water! The boys were given a bus ride to school while us girls had to walk.

The same rules applied at this boarding school with the bells for absolutely everything. However, there was no inspection. The headmistress in charge had lost her marbles eons ago and the smell of a urinal followed wherever she appeared. Her teeth were askew and half rotten. Her mottled hair, grey in patches, looked like it had never seen a comb or a brush. Forever losing her glasses and calling us whatever name came to her mind, as she was then as blind as a bat. This helped especially during bunking out sessions. You could literally say you were anyone. She looked like the female version of Catweazel – the mad wizard.

We walked to school which was strangely awesome (although not in the rainy season). I had gumboots (wellingtons) and on more than one occasion I would pull on one of my gumboots and feel a frog nestling there in his new home. You can imagine how unpleasant this is – for both parties. I would yelp, then tip it out and it would hop off. I never remembered to check each time forgetting to turn my gumboots upside down to see if anything was inside. I heard Nyika saying 'Told you so.' The walk to school was along a dust road that turned to sludge mud in the rain. You arrived at school after about a two and a half kilometre walk with your gumboots full of mud. Naturally, you had your clean polished school shoes in a bag which you slid into with much more confidence, no surprises in these ones.

My school days flowed pretty easily at Hillcrest. I enjoyed my art, as we had the best art teacher this side of the equator. He was my favourite teacher at Hillcrest, by far. He was also our house teacher. He had a certain craziness about him which I appreciated. He was an artist and had a lovely air of eccentricity. He was totally non-judgmental and he encouraged you to use the open mind that God had granted you with. He encouraged my "craziness" instead of hindering it. I didn't fall apart as a teenager because of him, he cared!

At the end of every term, which usually lasted around three months, I would return to my parents for the holidays. Half of the holiday was spent with each parent. My mother had since remarried and I was relieved that there would be no more parental weddings to attend. There was a time when weddings seemed to be contagious – they were happening all the time. It was spreading as fast as Covid.

I had, at that time, firmly decided not to marry. Or if I did, it would be later on in life. First, I had to live alone and discover as much of the world as possible. I enjoyed my own company and I really needed to have it.

At school, I did not have a best friend or a friendship group. Instead, I sort of flittered between an array of fellow students, never really getting particularly attached. If anyone, I would have to say that, my art teacher was my closest friend. Art class was my escape. An escape from a reality that I found all too consuming.

Which leads me to escaping everyone on the conservancy. On 3442kms squared you can find absolute solitude; it gives you the opportunity to get to the very marrow of being human.

We had a warthog (wild pig) here who resided under the table in the kitchen. His name was Cork. Naturally, the conservancy came with an array of animals – all types of species, colours, sizes and sounds.

The ranch house was beautiful in its authenticity, it didn't cry out to be the latest in fashion "African Safari Getaway" and I rather liked that. It was positioned in the Northern half of Devuli (SVC). They were real homes, gorgeous. I adored the ranch homes. Built by the first settler there. Unique in every way.

At this point, I would like to introduce The Save Conservancy to you. What my father and family and the other hands involved, they know who they are, achieved is one of the greatest gifts to this planet. I was fortunate to have been part of it. However, my brother, Herman Hagen Junior, was right by my father's side helping him every step of the way. What an achievement for a father and son. What a feat. I have a tremendous amount of respect for my brother in completing this project with my father. It is never easy to work alongside a parent and he did so admirably. During this time, in 1992, we suffered a severe drought and my brother and father decided therefore to build a dam. The dam site, positioned on Chishakwe, was chosen for three main reasons:

1) The granite rocky outcrop on the one side made for an ideal spillway design and the other side was steep enough so the dam wall could be of sufficient length.
2) The rainfall catchment area for this dam was 500 square kilometres which meant it had a very good chance of filling every year
3) It was the best location in reasonably close proximity to headquarters

4) My brother and father built it with a team of guys from the ranch, three tractors, 1 grader and it took two years to build.
5) During this time, they were also building the safari camp and they discovered some dinosaur bones and fragments of dinosaur bones.

My work on the ranch was allocated per holiday with much delight to me from my brother, cheeky bugger – checking the fence around the property was my main job during the holidays. The fence surrounding the Conservancy was a 400km double fence, so 800km's of fencing in total. This was built specifically for foot and mouth disease, bought on by the buffalo. Fortunately, my job was just to check the fencing around Chishakwe. It took me a solid week to manage this task. Perfect! We would camp in a tent and sit beside an open fire. This was before the Chishakwe Lodges were built, otherwise we would have had five-star accommodation. It's not five stars because it's luxurious; its five stars because it's exactly the opposite. You feel nature, you see nature, you smell nature and you interact with nature. It is just how it should be.

I was accompanied by two others to help me. We would gather firewood, open a tin of baked beans, heat them up attach the homemade dough, wrap it around the end of a stick, cook it over the fire, dip it in the baked beans and swallow it down in un-lady like chunks, with a cup of sweet hot black tea – Tanganda – grown in our very own Zimbabwe. The best tea on earth – one which should be served with lots of sugar and milk. Then after your ablutions you would climb into your sleeping bag alongside the fire (which you had to keep burning all night to ward off predators – lions and hyenas and such like). You would hang your mosquito net from a branch and tuck it into the base of your sleeping bag. You made damn sure you did not need the toilet in the middle of the night simply because it was such a bane to get comfortable again, and you certainly did not want to run accidentally into a predator taking a night stroll.

Lying there, a blanket of stars would open up above the roar of the lions, the nightjar, the bark of the kudus (antelopes), the rustle of the grass and the crackling of the fire – and the hard crackling once every so often, louder than the rest, the chirping of the crickets. Then there was the smell of the bush and the freshness of it, so clean.

In the morning, the dawn would peek over the horizon and a gentle orange glow seemed to whisper in your ear – *rise and shine, this day is mine*. The silhouettes of the hills surrounding us would have made Dali proud. Boulders balancing on one another in such peculiar ways, sort of boulder yoga. You just cannot imagine rocks being able to balance like that. Up in my mosquito net, the various bugs would now be flying away and the fire had died down to only embers with just enough life to be able to start it again for our morning cup of tea.

I would brush my teeth with a stick and ash just like Nyika had taught me. Nyika refused to come on these trips with me. She said she had grown too old and preferred the luxury of her bed, a flush toilet and running water. Then I would wash out my mouth with just a small amount of water. When you experience a drought like the one we had in 1992 you learn to respect water that much more. How essential it is and just how much we depend on it. Leaving it running while you brush your teeth was never an option for us. It was an incredibly frightening time watching the earth dry up all around you. I rolled up my sleeping bag immediately as it had been known for snakes to like the warmth of a sleeping bag and to have crawled into one or two, giving quite a fright to the roller upper (most snakes are venomous).

So here it is for you. The official document of The Save Valley Conservancy. Enjoy! I will share more stories about me and Nyika after this taste of where we lived.

'There is not one person to gain gratitude for the Conservancy, there were many. A great idea may begin with one person but a brilliant idea takes many people to realise it.'

The Save Valley Conservancy was formed as a result of the coming together of a number of circumstances. The first was that an epic drought brought an end to cattle ranching and agricultural endeavour in the area and with it, the realisation that wildlife was the only viable future for the area.

This dovetailed perfectly with the arrival of the first black rhino which had been moved from the Zambezi Valley where they were being poached to the point of extinction. The SVC is large, it is 3442km squared. SVC is located in the semi-arid South-East Lowveld of Zimbabwe, boasting a woodland savanna.

It has a low rainfall. The soils are not rich in this area therefore not good for crop farming at all. An attempt at potato farming was once toyed with to no avail. The SVC is surrounded by communal land. The area was called Bikita it is now called Nyika.

Once long ago the conservancy was enjoyed by the Bushmen or the San, we have a gallery of their work etched in rock paintings. As a child, I would climb up this kopje on the main road (if you can call it the main road, it was the road that ran from the two gates of the conservancy). I would run my fingers over them, compelling their speech their wisdom and their story. I found it fascinating. You see I had happened to see the film "Gods Must Be Crazy" – and I so wished to meet the bushman, guess I was a little too late. Then along came the Bantu, who took over the place. The first known Europeans passing through is documented in the 1800's. One of the wagons of these "voortrekkers" is positioned at the entrance of the main office on the Head Quarters called – Chishakwe, our home, back in the day.

Explained in maps as "not fit for white men", with that along came an enormous number of leopards, which did not help cattle rearing. Dense vegetation, malaria and a lack of water. These pioneers,ill-equippedd had a rough time, it was not a walk in the park, I can promise, you, that. Even with modern-day facilities we as a family had our fair share of hardships. Hence, a little history for your perusal, for your imagination, because these days there are very few places that take you off the grid, this is one of them. Visit whilst you can. Thanks to the efforts of many people the SVC became a reality.

In addition, a few enormous ranches were subdivided and sold in lots. These attracted local, regional and international investors; all keen to be a part of the new conservation vision that officially became The Save Valley Conservancy in 1991 when the constitution was signed by all parties.

All internal fences were removed from an area totalling 3,442 square kilometres and a 400 kilometre double perimeter fence was constructed. Approximately four thousand animals of fourteen species were reintroduced, including elephants, in the largest translocation of that species ever undertaken.

As a result of the size of the area and the enormous habitat diversity contained therein, the conservation of the full range of indigenous mammals was possible.

The ecological value of the area was considerably greater than that of most game ranching areas in southern Africa (most of which were fenced into small compartments). Wildlife populations increased rapidly, including those of several threatened and endangered species and The Save Valley Conservancy developed into a conservation area of global significance.

The Save Valley Conservancy now contains a viable population of critically endangered black rhinos, a healthy number of endangered African wild dogs, a rapidly growing population of African lions and significant populations of other threatened species, such as southern ground hornbills, lappet-faced vultures, elephants, cheetahs and white rhinos.

Plans to involve surrounding communities in the conservancy were initiated early on with the formation of The Save Valley Conservancy Community Trust.

During the Government of Zimbabwe's fast track land "reform" program in 2000–2001, approximately thirty-three percent of The Save Valley Conservancy was settled by subsistence farmers and eighty kilometres of perimeter fencing was removed in the process. The government has since made the decision to retain conservancies for wildlife production but the partial settlement of

The Save Valley Conservancy remains for now, resulting in a mosaic of human habitation and wildlife habitat. This mosaic creates conditions conducive to intense human-wildlife conflict, illegal hunting and habitat destruction: essentially, a microcosm of the key conservation threats facing wildlife in Africa.

Unfortunately, the drought of 1992 was emotionally crumbling and crippling. Animals, and plant life were dying left right and centre. "Want not, waste not" reared its head once again. We had to cull so many impalas. It was probably a life-altering moment for me and so many others. It was best to shoot at night (although not on a full moon), the darker the better. For the most effective shot, as to avoid spoiling the meat, one should aim directly a third or so higher above the foreleg angling slightly towards the rear of the Impala. I used a 2.2 rifle. After dinner, which I could barely eat, knowing I was going out to cull these beautiful animals, I went with my designated team. These were long nights – we would often only return home at sunrise.

We packed flasks of water and tea and some chocolate. I had to shine the hunting torch standing in the back of the Land Rover. There was a rail in the back of the car for me to hold on to. Torch in one hand, rollbar in the other.

Two other conservancy guys were with us too. By shining the torch into the bush, we would see the red eyes of the animals staring back – blinded.

Looking back, I am sickened by what I had to do. However, this is a job that had to be done. I still have to keep telling myself that. The impala would have died anyway and the people on the conservancy had to be fed. If we had left the impala, we would have had rotting carcasses everywhere, leading to disease and sickness, as there is only so much that scavengers (jackals, hyenas and vultures) can eat. Everything was dying. Vultures circled the sky non-stop during this time. Their shadows moving around the earth eerily, their cries beckoning other vultures for what represented to them a feast. To us, a baren existence. There is no one side to any event or story, there are always two. Hear both. Try to see both. Bones lay scattered around and dry winds scratched the backs of our parched throats. All of our throats; all of us animals. Experiencing a drought of this magnitude is life-altering. It is worse than any horror film you may have seen or twice as scary as you may have ever felt. Its achingly slow, its silent, its death, and there was nowhere to go. Day after day, dry winds blew, and day after day you look to the sky. Even the hardened atheists began to pray. Some days as a family we barely spoke to one another, that's how scared we were. There were no words, not even soothing ones simply because the truth was right in front of us. There was no way to cotton-wool it.

After picking up the eyes of the impala, you would drive towards them, then stop the Land Rover – you had to be dead quiet. It haunts me to this day. So quiet. No crickets were chirping; my heartbeat was like thunder in my ears. I remember the panic in the eyes of the deer. Then crack! The sound of the rifle piercing the jet-black night; the thud against the impala's flesh. The bleat of its last breath, then the gentle fall to ground. Eyes wide open, dying an unexplained, unnatural death. The other two conservancy guys shot as well, so in a herd of impala of say twelve, we could cull up to six or seven at once – blinded by the light.

After the shots, we leapt out the Land Rover and ran to the impala. The conservancy guys had to help me push the impala's neck back while my legs straddled its back. Then, with a very deep, precise cut, I would slit their throats. We all had our turn at that. Didn't seem to affect anyone but me. Each time, I would turn and wrench to the side. The men laughed at me.

The next step was for two of us to pick up an impala – one would grab the two back legs and the other grabbed the two front legs. As we carried them back to the car, their heads and necks would, bounce on the dry earth; their dead eyes stared back at you in the darkness partially covered in sand. Then we hoisted the impala on to the back of the Land Rover. This was repeated until there was a pile of them in the back of the Land Rover.

There was nowhere to stand on the ride back so I had to sit on top of that pile of dead impala's. Some were still jerking and bleating while others were excreting. There I sat with one conservation guy called Sadza, who was my brother's best friend on the ranch. My blue overalls were now purple with blood; my face full of dust. Stinking.

We had to cull many impalas – the four of us – and it took a couple of weeks. I was looking forward to going back to school. I do think this event changed how I saw life – I seemed to become less fragile afterwards. The last cull took place just before sunrise. As the sun came up that morning, we parked the Land Rover and we all leant against the bonnet. I opened the flask of tea with my bloody hands, leaving behind fingerprints of blood and let the warm and sweet liquid – so welcoming – ease the guilt I felt. It was for the best.

This drought was life and death staring straight at you saying fuck you. You just wouldn't listen, would you? Nature – you cannot mess with her. She will beat you every time. It made me feel better knowing that the meat went to the entire neighbourhood of the surrounding area of the conservancy. Delivering this meat balanced the guilt I felt in the pit of my stomach. To see the families overjoyed to receive the food. The meat, the skins and the horns – all parts of the impala were used.

We were standing, drinking our tea and talking about the night's escapades. Suddenly, one impala jumped into the front seat of the Land Rover by accident; its horns had nearly ripped out the eye of one of the conservation guys. They only just managed to escape the sharp hooves of the impala too. This one had managed to escape. Escape to a certain death. It had slid from the heap, it was alive. As it stumbled away, certainly wounded, its throat slightly open, I lifted my gun and shot it. Stone dead. I watched it lying on the ground, flies covering its eyes. I was not cut out for this. The tea turned sour in my mouth.

We all know that death is inevitable but we continue living as if we are never going to die. Living consciously is the hardest task of all. What am I really doing with my life? What are my goals? What are my aspirations? Publishing this book was one of my goals, helping to leave some kind of legacy for my family. To leave a record of our families passion for the African Wilderness. For my daughter to understand her mother's past. To thank Nyika, to try to make sense of a war that I never fully understood. A way of healing perhaps.

The Save Conservancy was up and running. What an enormous project. As children, we were brought up aware of our surroundings. We had such a rich upbringing and acquired a deep knowledge of the African Bush. Nyika had helped me scrub the blood and dust out of my matted hair.

'Look at you, child,' she chided, 'it has to be done. Just look at it that way.'

Tears rolled down my cheeks. I bit my nails.

'Stop that,' Nyika muttered more than once. Slapping my hands away from my mouth.

One day, Nyika came to me and said, 'I want to learn to swim and I want to learn to drive before I die.' Nyika was not getting any younger and she had mentioned she was thinking of retiring when I had finished high school. She had made that decision and I totally understood. All I cared about was that she retired as comfortably as possible. I could still see her if I visited Zaka (her compound area) and she would come to town and stay with us from time to time in Mas Vegas. However, those plans changed.

'No problem, Nyika,' I replied. 'We can learn to drive this afternoon on the airstrip.' It would be a superb distraction. No sleep would come my way anyhow. The airstrip directly in front of our house. So that afternoon, after lunch (the standard potato salad, cold meat and homemade bread, courtesy of Reckless the cook boy– I do miss these lunches), Nyika and I headed off to the airstrip in my Land Rover. Normally after lunch everyone took a siesta as life on a conservancy starts at sunrise. However, I never enjoyed siestas.

My Land Rover had been owned by all of us at some stage. It had a short wheelbase and was a faded green. I chose the airstrip for Nyika's driving lessons because there was nothing to hit or drive into. I had also learned here – mostly through trial and error. We all had. I decided firstly to explain the basics of the car engine and then how to change a car tire. After that, I showed her how to fill up with petrol or diesel and the difference between these two fuels. On the first day we did not even manage to get behind the wheel.

Day two arrived and we set off after a hearty breakfast. I asked Nyika to sit behind the wheel. I explained the functions of the brake, accelerator and clutch. We went through this for such a long time – it felt like an eternity. Then the gears: first, second, third, fourth and reverse. Then finally, it was time for her to drive. Nyika was looking extremely nervous. To loosen her up, I decided to give her a scare. I shouted "Nyoka!" (meaning "snake"). She yelped, jumped out car and started running. I let her run a while, then I called after her, 'Nyika, I'm only joking. Now we are rid of your jitters, can we get started?'

She returned to the car laughing and slapped me playfully across the back of my head. 'OK,' I began, 'clutch in, gear in first, then let the clutch out slowly.' I compared it to checking bread in the oven – the slowness of easing the clutch out. 'Now, Nyika,' I continued, 'ease the petrol in with the accelerator. Gently. Like you're stroking a cat.'

Nyika moved the car forward beautifully and smoothly. I smiled. All was going well. Then she changed second gear. I thought she was a natural. 'Brilliant, Nyika!'

Then the panic started. We were coming to the end of the air strip and running out of runway. Nyika accelerated. 'No!' I shouted.

'Slow down! We need to stop!' Not Nyika. We were going at full speed, in second gear, about to head into the bush at the end of the runway. I pulled up the handbrake just in time. The Land Rover kicked up a cloud of dust.

Nyika's mouth was wide open in astonishment. 'It's OK, Nyika,' I assured her. 'You did great! Now let's turn the car around and go back down the airstrip.' Slowly, off we went. We got into third gear this time, when suddenly, out of the blue, a family of warthog decided to cross the airstrip. Nyika took her hands off the steering wheel, her feet off the gas and the clutch and we came to a grinding halt. Stalled.

We went every day to the air strip and Nyika mastered the art of driving after about a week. After that, we went on longer drives on the dirt roads. We had a petrol and diesel pump at home. (however, no wasting it). Nyika would now drive the Land Rover to help my father pick up and collect whatever was needed from the camp they were building so it turned out to be extremely useful her learning to drive. Nyika enjoyed it thoroughly. She revelled in her newness.

Time came and went like that of the ocean tide. Nyika and I remained firm and steadfast allies in a house that expelled us. By keeping a positive mind all things can be realised in God's time, she offered me on a regular basis. The Conservancy was blossoming; even anti-poaching units had been set up. It was fascinating.

Anti-poaching – not letting criminals get away with it. Hats off to all these guys who put their lives on the line daily to save our wonderful and natural wildlife. Thank you. Saving the rhino, elephant and wild dogs from these human atrocities. One practice that really gets to me is killing these magnificent animals to satisfy some ridiculous cultural beliefs. One of these is the belief that consuming a rhino horn increases the size of your manhood. I mean, seriously – there are no words.

The conservancy is made up of other lodges and homesteads – not just Chishakwe and the headquarters. If you are planning to really experience Africa and understand its challenges in conservation, this is definitely the place for you to visit. If you just want a safari, it's not the place for you. The conservancy allows you to understand the dance of nature at its best – sheer perfection. My advice – visit the conservancy.

Time had moved fast as time does. Nyika had noticed the swell of my breasts and mentioned to me that my life would soon be changing. 'They may be mosquito bites now, Joanna but not in a couple of years, I am sure they will be mountains.' I laughed, I tried to hide my embarrassment but she knew me too well. 'I may have some explaining to do for your future, young lady,' she said. Half smiling and half laughing.

Womanhood needs a different camouflage. The change from child to woman represents a change that will come whether you like it or not. Of course, not everyone has a luxury of choice; for some, the only choice is will you survive or not? I was fortunate in my country not to be taken to elongation and to be sold off to a man that I couldn't stand.

I was in full puberty by now and Nyika had decided to explain to me the ins and outs of womanhood. I had one more year of high school to finish. Nyika invited me to her compound one evening to tell me about the joys of becoming a woman and what it meant. She had lovingly prepared our sadza (the staple meal in Zimbabwe made from maize), nyama (meat), rape (green vegetable), tomato and onion gravy. We sat outside her thatched hut and mudded walls barefoot and eating with our hands. It was delicious. It was kind of Nyika to make this time for me. She had watched me grow from a child; she had been through everything with me. I found this extremely touching and caring of her. I left her compound feeling good; ready.

She also informed me how fortunate I was to not have had the unfortunate "Elongation of the Labia" procedure which was the norm and compulsory in Shona culture when she was growing up. Elongating the labia means pulling the labia with your hands till it stretches. Sometimes it tears – so incredibly painful. This tradition started when Shona girls had their first monthly cycle – the average age being twelve. This is still practiced to this day, even for Shona girls living around the world. Old habits die hard. Some mothers even send their children back to Zimbabwe to have this performed on them. It is meant – or it is believed – to give men incredible pleasure and your husband will be so satisfied that he will never stray. For me, it seems to be in conflict with another Shona tradition, whereby a man can have as many wives as he wishes.

The years passed and during my holidays from high school, Nyika and I would visit other parts of the conservancy. Sometimes we would camp and at other times it would just be a day visit. During our camping time, which had become rare as Nyika preferred her necessities. Nyika never failed to remind me of what a favour she was doing for me by giving up her bed. We loved to go to one clearing teeming with yellow acacia trees. If we sat quietly, we would see a world of birds come alive in front of our very eyes. It was surreal… mesmerising. Whenever I listen to *Follow the Yellow Brick Road* from The Wizard of Oz' I'm always transported back to that spot.

We would take a picnic along with us with freshly squeezed orange juice from the orchard at home. Nyika had her sun jam sandwiches while mine were filled with cucumber. The brilliant combination of emerald-green grass and yellow bark sparked the imagination. This was one of our quiet moments, just happy to share one another's company. I called it our "Canary Calling Time." It was also our code for "let's get the hell out of here" without being impolite.

It was here that I was reminded how important Nyika was to me in my life. That she had come back into my life and protected me. How she made me feel there was at least someone who wanted me back in my father's house.

'Joanna,' Nyika began, 'You finish school this summer and you'll be having your farewell party with all your friends.'

I would be turning nineteen and would soon be moving to Miss Patel's Secretarial School in Harare.

'Watch out for the men in the city,' she continued. 'City slickers. Don't trust them too readily. Don't be loose. Remember, women have the power in the end. Oh, and you still have to teach me to swim – just like you – well... at least to keep my body afloat.'

Nyika drove us home. I watched the African Bush slide by. I felt a great deal of contentment. On the way we passed a herd of elephants; the calves were close to their mother's sides. Did you know that elephants bury their dead? They have funerals. And on their natural migration paths, they pay tribute and respect to their dead. The elephant is my all-time favourite animal. Its intelligence surpasses many a human being. I could quite easily lose myself in a life without humans. Their huge ears flapped gently. Nearby, a few zebras crossed the road.

At home, the smell of mashed potatoes filled my nostrils. It was particularly warm – a dry heat – and the sunset was strikingly pink this evening. The cry of the fish eagle echoed over the endless terrain as I sat with Nyika. Our friendship felt deep and endless. Nyika was an intricate part of my family of my heart. I knew she missed Kudzai terribly. I knew she had permanent heartache from this terrible snatch of life out of her clutches. I looked over at her and smiled. Nyika was my hero.

My school term came to an end and my school days were now behind me. My father dispatched a cattle truck to collect me. It was my last day at Hillcrest College. All my friends had prepared their rucksacks and bags. They would be spending five days with me on the conservancy. We would camp at the camp site. Everyone had brought along with them a bag of food and drinks.

All of my friends had met Nyika. A few who had been to the house more often may still remember her now. She always welcomed them with love and care. Later, she would give me her opinion as to who I should not bring home again and who was welcome next time.

This get together was an event that none of us will ever forget. It cemented friendships that would last a lifetime. We spent days driving and tracking in the bush, learning which spore belonged to which animal and laughing at our sheer lack of directional skills without a compass (there were certainly no Google Maps then). Nowadays, there is just dodgy internet reception. As I said, off the grid peeps off the grid! Fantastic!

Where I was brought up you learn to take stock of your surroundings. To this day, when giving directions, I use landmarks; preferring these to street names and numbers. This backfires on me in every city I live in.

Every day we swam in the river watching out for crocs. Two people were allocated to "Croc Watch." Similar to Baywatch, just a little more rustic. We tubed on the Save River on big tractor tire rubbers bouncing over rapids screeching with delight. Some virginities were anointed during that time while others were kept intact. However, stringently, my father tried to maintain security between male and female tents; where there was a will there was a way.

We sat around fires at night listening to bushfire fairy tales that my father loved to tell and we all loved to listen to. We cooked and made tea over the fire. The age of innocence coming to a gentle finale.

We took night drives to find leopards. We took the time to breathe in the stars. We took the time. We learnt to exhale when it was time to say goodbye. In the bush at morning light my eyes never flicker open in a panic. They open gently and take the day as it comes.

It was over. The next chapter in my life awaited me. I had packed my few belongings that were at the house on the conservancy. Nyika was then to fly with me to my mother's house in Mas Vegas. It was not her first flight – that was some time before with me and my father – but the flight to Mas Vegas would be the last flight I would ever take with Nyika.

We had dressed up for the occasion in our Sunday best. The flight from the conservancy to Mas Vegas would take roughly an hour and a half.

Usually, it was my father and me alone during these flights. I had grown to really appreciate this time as it was the only occasion I could be really with him, without steps and halves and god knows what else getting in my way. He had a cushion for my seat so I could see over the dashboard. We didn't say much during these flights but to spend this time with him, quiet, peaceful time, with only the gentle hum of the aircraft was a privilege I will always look back on with great comfort and pleasure. My father my beacon. Slick, (his nickname) liked to nap during these flights. He would say, 'Joe, keep the compass! Just there. And wake me up in twenty minutes.' It was here I found my love for flying. Between his snoring and the whir of the engine, my heart soured.

Nyika was so excited. She climbed into the plane with a dash of trepidation and a dollop of thrill and excitement. Happiness cleared the runway of warthogs, impalas and rabbits shooing and shooshing animals out of the way. With his staff shaking curses in the air, he marched up the airstrip. Happiness was eventually given a monkey bike and a megaphone. What a sight that was. It makes me keel over in hysterics just thinking about it.

The plane's engine booted up with a shiver. We accelerated down the airstrip. 'This is Yanky, Yanky Tango,' came a voice over the radio, 'and you are cleared for take-off.' It was such an exhilarating feeling, an addictive feeling, like suspense and danger combining in unison. Nyika's eyes reminded me of an owl – large and keen – as if spying prey on an empty stomach. She grabbed my shoulder. She was sitting in the back seat while I was up front. I had to sit here because sooner or later it would be my father's nap hour and I would have to fly the plane.

First, my father decided we would have some fun. He wiggled the wings just as he always did when he dropped me off at school. Just to say I love you. The plane sounded like an amped up mosquito. We lifted up into the African sky. I turned to look at Nyika. Her mouth was open and a hypnotised expression covered her.

I smiled at her and we shared a moment of "If only Kudzai was here too."

Africa's bush fell below and we could see the herds of buffalo and elephants. The Save River was snaking slowly through the endless blanket of green. Rainy season was upon us and the cumulonimbus clouds hung heavy, fat and boldly on the edge of the sky becoming angrier by the minute and starting to egg crack with bolts of lightning on the horizon. The thunder drowned out the noise of the mosquito humming plane. The trees looked like shoots of broccoli and paper cocktail umbrellas that are served in Holiday Inns at sundowner time. The sand shone as if it were pure honey. The sky to our right was a bright luminous blue – like a wizard's eyes with the odd stroke of a painter's white brush. The kopjes were rising and falling resembling the scales of a crocodiles back while boulders appeared to be caught off guard. Close by, a circling flock of vultures cried out into the abyss. Herds of impala scampered across the plains and my heart became an African drum beat. My rhythm forever altered to the call of the wild.

Nyika's absolute thrill lay exposed upon her expression – frozen. Pure joy. It was time to land in Mas Vegas.

'Yanky, Yanky Tango,' my father said into the radio yawning, 'requesting permission to land.'

'Welcome back, Mr. Slick,' came the reply, 'Good to see you again. It's been a while, sir.'

I was to spend a week in Mas Vegas packing up my belongings and spending time with my mother. I would then be ready to leave the Lowveld Region to attend Miss Patel's Secretarial College. I had joined a lift club (by car) to make my way to Zimbabwe's capital city – Harare (formerly known as Salisbury). I would share money for fuel and driving. Harare, with its Jacaranda archways, came with a little more freedom and responsibility. I was to stay in an all-girls hostel, yet again! A dam hostel. With bells… for meal times only. I was, to say the least, slightly peed off.

Nyika was to help me pack my meagre belongings. No more school trunks. Instead, a snazzy suitcase, a rucksack and my make-up bag – my vanity bag – which my grandmother had prepared, of course. We didn't have many brands available in Zimbabwe. The only places to buy the few we had was at the Meikles Store in Harare and my grandmother's shop in Mas Vegas. She had filled my vanity case with Lancôme, Yardley and "Beautiful" perfumes for day wear and Opium for evenings. There was jungle red lipstick. Also included were several packs of chewing gum – Wrigley's and two pairs of sexy lingerie. Then there was a one-hundred-dollar bill – not to be used ever – only to carry in my purse and for use in case of an emergency (like a man leaving me high and dry at a restaurant. I could still pay for my meal and grab a taxi home). "Emergencies only" was written in BOLD on the envelope. Finally, there was a nail set, tweezers for my inherited wild eyebrows, some wax strips and a little black book, for people's phone numbers. Scribbled inside this, my grandmother had written, "Make the *first* time count." I smiled and laughed to myself. My grandmother was such a character, unlike anyone.

We had one last meal together – Nyika, Blessing, Samantha, my new step-father, my mother and their dog Buddy. Puppet the cat had passed on. We had cottage pie – with tomato sauce.

My lift arrived the following morning at dawn. Goodbyes were nothing new to me. I took a deep breath, rolled into the car and announced that I should drive the first leg of the journey as I was wide awake – they all looked a bit sleepy. Oh, the controlling person I am. I hugged everyone goodbye, told Nyika and Blessing I would see them soon (as I still had to teach Nyika to swim, and we as a family had promised Blessing a scotch cart for his compound) which would be one of his retirement presents. My mother looked happy and for that I was grateful. Tom seemed to have been good for her and good to her.

The car was a Land Rover. Piled to the hilt, snack basket for the trip intact (with my mother's crunchies inside, tea and sandwiches), I started the car, put it in gear and drove down the driveway, watching everyone in the rear-view mirror waving. God, how I hated it when they did that. It made me so incredibly homesick. A lot to look forward to. I had my array of bangles, my hair in a high pony and I was wearing my stone washed jeans and a Wonder Woman t-shirt. I wasn't wearing shoes of course – they were in my bag for later. To this day, I prefer to drive barefoot which is usually frowned upon but it just seems natural for me.

I tooted the horn, goodbye everyone and we hit the road. Well as much of a highway as Zimbabwe had. I turned on the tape deck and slid in my tape with songs recorded from the radio. Prince – *When Doves Cry* – blasted out the tin speakers. Yes, I was on my way to what I thought was freedom.

During our first weekend in Harare, we would be going to the Human Rights Concert. Half of South Africa would be there. I was dying to see Tracy Chapman live on stage. *Fast Car* was the next song on the tape. Too bad the Land Rover's engine was not up to driving fast. I smiled. My friends were already asleep. I would wake them up in Chivu – halfway to Harare. We would buy a Fanta and some of them would need a smoke. Madison Reds.

Chapter Fifteen
Harare Hangouts and Growing Up

My all-girls hostel in Harare was called George Fleming.

As I drove and listened to my music, my friends slept deeply. They had apparently had a rough night the night before, typical. Graham had just got back from Cape Town. He was a well-known photographer already. A hippie at heart. Looking like a typical surfer. Mark on the other hand was in advertising, but it wouldn't last, he was going back to med school to study to become a surgeon. By far the best mind for coming up with creative ideas that actually work. I have yet to work with someone more brilliant.

He was also a surfer. Mark had a solid manner, people gravitated toward him. We had been good and reliable friends for years, we still are. I would have to say these two are my best friends if that word exists. We have been through most growing experiences together in our early adult years. I looked over at Mark in the passenger seat, how could he sleep in that position? Graham, the shorter of the two by far, was sprawled over the back seat. I cared about them a great deal.

The first part of the drive was uneventful. Thoughts drifted through my mind and left my mind just as easily. That's why my favourite past time are road trips, when I am driving that is. In open lands, not between cities in small countries, but long-distance driving when it's just you, the road, good music and the horizon.

I watched the bush slide by, watched the young children run along the side of the road on the way to school, probably averaging five kilometres to school and five kilometres back home. They were around six years old with no adult supervision and no shoes. They did this Monday to Friday. No wonder they went missing. These days when you stopped to give them sweets notebooks or footballs or pens, they scampered into the grasslands, afraid. I totally understood that. They were waving, I waved back and blew kisses. They laughed. I smiled looked in my rear-view mirror. What a beautiful photograph I thought (short-lived though) as I over-took loaded buses pouring out exhaust smoke. That exhaust smoke destroying the beautiful image behind me.

I was relieved that Nyika, would be working in Mas Vegas with my mother at her Cottage Shop Café. Instead of retiring, she opted to work alongside my mum and to live at my mom's house. That meant she would be safe. That also meant that my mother would be looked after by Blessing and Nyika. My eldest sister, Susan, had moved from the conservancy to her own farm, just outside Mas Vegas. She was always bringing fresh produce in for my mom from her mandarin plantation. Whether it be meat, eggs or vegetables and mandarins of course. We call mandarins naartjies.

I had, in addition, been thinking of getting a side job. I had seen some girls waitressing in films. Maybe I could babysit? Hell no! Bar work sounded like something I could do.

I also thought – glumly – about having to go to this secretarial school. I had no enthusiasm for it at all. I just had to get through it for one year. Maybe then I would start my own company. Doing what? I had no idea yet, that would come.

I drove into Chivu and pulled up outside the town's bar. Not for a drink, it was the only parking place in this one-horse town. Dust devils blowing along the streets. Lingering stares whilst chewing a piece of long grass. Mealie cobs lay scattered as if pebbles.

Chickens crossed the road everywhere, so did goats and donkeys. The old Coca-Cola signboards hanging on a worn-out piece of wire. Flapping and banging in the breeze. The scotch carts cow bells and whip sounds drifting on the wind. Despite Mark and Graham offering to drive, I preferred to drive the whole way – roughly another two hours. Plus, they would probably have a Lion beer (or two), so I would drive.

They woke up, yes, had a beer and smoked a couple of Madison Reds. Then they bought a beer for the road. I drove. The inside of the bar had turned into a brothel and hookers leant up against walls in their best attire. Zimbabwean hookers are not thin ladies. They are mufuta (big). To be thin in Africa, as you are probably aware by now, means one of two things: you are either poor or sick. Hooking in Chivu – you need a gold medal. There is a ton of traffic passing through so they make more than a decent living.

The woman even asked me if I would like a favour. I smiled. One lady, called Black as the Night, sidled up to us with her whiskey, sloshing it on the table as she sat down, her bra strap hanging off her shoulder and her tight leopard skin dress stretching over her African butt like cling wrap. African butt's make J Lo look like Bambi.

'I'm going to be a lawyer,' she slurred.

'Good,' I replied, 'Because every time I drive through here, I'll stop and check that you are doing just that.'

I respected these women a great deal.

Another woman spoke up, 'You know, white men stop here too?'

'I'm sure they do,' I replied.

Jungle fever.

'You like Africans?' she asked.

'Black as the Night,' I replied, leaning forward, 'I am an African; and you are clearly intoxicated so let's talk next time.'

'I'm an artist,' said another woman, 'I sculpt.'

'May I see your work on the way out?' I asked. 'Come on guys' I chided; 'we really need to keep going!'

285

'Yes,' she replied, 'I have some pieces at the front of the hotel.'

It was rare to meet a female sculptor in Zimbabwe. Most of them – well ninety percent – were male.

Another hooker piped up, 'And my name is Ebony Everest!'

There was no need to ask why.

'I'm a mother.'

'I'm a wife.'

'I'm a lover.'

'I'm a cook.'

'I'm a provider.'

'I'm a daughter.'

'I was sent here by wife number one to make money for our compound.'

'Make sure you look after yourself,' I said.

'Guys, let's go!'

'One for the road, barman, please,' said Mark, 'Lion beer number three.'

The lady sculptor walked me out to show me her work. I bought one – mostly just to be kind. I didn't have the heart to tell her that her talents probably didn't lie in sculpting. However, I did congratulate her on her allure like a spider catching a fly, of intriguing me. That was her talent – her power of persuasion.

'Are you interested to study at all?' I asked her. She was so young, maybe 19.

Her name was Midnight Caress.

'Yes, I'm on my way to South Africa,' she replied, 'and from there to Dubai. I heard I could work in Dubai if I get a qualification.'

It crossed my mind, in that moment, what a spoilt brat I was being, complaining about a secretarial diploma. I had everything compared to this lady. I decided that I would do my best rather than cursing my luck.

'What are you going to study?' I continued.

'I want to be a nurse. If that doesn't work, it's Dubai – as a maid, a security guard or cleaning lavatories.'

'You will make it, one day at a time, you would be a good nurse and our country needs nurses. There are help centres in Harare, you should try to check them out.'

I kept the sculpture – a reminder to be humble.

We clambered back into the Land Rover and continued our journey. My two friends were in high spirits. We were discussing the human rights concert we would be going to that weekend. We had decided to inject lemons with gin instead of taking or trying to smuggle alcohol into the concert. Which we clearly could not afford, bar prices and student bank accounts. It crossed my mind that my mom had placed a huge box of groceries and snacks in the back of the Landy. For sure she would have included a bottle of gin, and a packet of lemons. I would do the same with oranges. Mark could organise the syringes. The Landy we were driving in to Harare belonged to Graham, it was called Baldric. The colour Mother of Pearl.

As we drove into Harare, I saw clouds of pollution. Devious and devouring. Menacing. A deep blanket of filth. Looking like a huge earth cappuccino with too much cacao on the froth. Through the pollution, Jacaranda trees exploded, natures fireworks, with their brilliant violet bouquets of flowers, thrusting forwards and upwards as if soldiers in deep violet velvet cloaks, hoarding the demons off, pushing the negativity away and arching over roads to protect the being's living underneath and in between. Our shelter, our luminous violet world of serenity, a pathway before our eyes. The loud popping sound of the flowers as the tyres of the Landy crunched down on them. It was almost surreal. The petals that had fallen creating a purple carpet to drive upon. It felt as if I may have fallen down a rabbit hole. Pinch me someone?

The boys dropped me off at my George Fleming All Girls Hostel (not again, yes again) with my few belongings. We said goodbye. They gave me my much-needed bear hugs. Oh, they knew me so well. Hugs as you may have gathered are my life source. I would see them tomorrow for the concert. They'd pick me up. I stood on the street for a while just gazing at my surroundings. Graham shouted out the window, hey farm girl put on some shoes, glancing down at my feet, I realised I was still barefoot. That would be no way to greet the headmistress. There were my father's words, it takes a lifetime to build a reputation and a few seconds to destroy it. I slid on my Bata Specials.

I gathered my belongings and walked through the doors. There, I met with the headmistress who showed me my room. Why do all headmistresses in charge of girls hostels always look the same? They all have that stale taste in clothing, hair and make-up! Mouldy. I don't think I will last here that long, I am done with that look, that tone, that unnecessary sternness! I watched her hard-no-nonsense approach at climbing the practiced staircase, the all to natural arch of the brow and hand on hip. 'Welcome young lady, we are a responsible hostel for ladies.' There was a long pause. 'You do understand that, don't you?' Her eyes giving me that once over, spelling it out slowly verb by verb with her demeanour. The question hanging there as if from a bad breath. Halitosis perhaps? Would you like a mint Madame? What a perfect dominatrix I thought, fleetingly.

My roommate was already there. She had dated my step-brother for a while and we had been good friends in our first two years of high school but that ship had sailed. We looked at each other, I unpacked awkwardly. She had asked to share my room, I had agreed but here I was knowing it had been a mistake. We had nothing in common. Except the past, and even there we had differed. The final straw inevitably breaking the camel's back. Her hairdryer at dawn every morning drove me nuts, waking up at 05:30 a.m. to do her bloody hair. I definitely needed a change of scenery urgently. I desperately wanted to get as far away as possible from this mountain of unnecessary rules. The unspoken ones in friendships to. I didn't dislike her. One just outgrows people and visa-versa.

I soon found a side job waitressing at a restaurant called Home Grown. I was officially sorted for rent money, food was sorted as the restaurants fed me, and with the money I saved, I could furnish my apartment. Home Grown Restaurant was located downtown all the way downtown almost right in the shutteen as we say in Zimbabwe. In amongst the hustle and bustle of Harare's bus stations and flea markets. It is partly what gave Home Grown its edge, its charm. It was not a restaurant only trying to make it in the "white" areas of the city. The boss, arranged transport for me to and from work, including weekends as it was a tad dangerous downtown.

Unfortunately, Zimbabwe was not taking a turn for the best, the country was beginning to come undone. The roadworks were cracking and not being completed, potholes started appearing everywhere, bridges being washed away and not mended. Telephone lines failing, postal services became hugely unreliable and people stopped sending parcels as the postal services just opened the parcels and helped themselves. Corruption had crept in and you were able to buy everything now: from your driver's license to fake ID's and passports for non-citizens.

I phoned home weekly as if clockwork to keep abreast of the ins and outs of everyone I cared about. Blessing invariably answered the phone.

'Hello, this must be Doobsie.' This was my nickname for as long as I could remember. Blessing and Nyika would give me the updates as my mom who had since become golf captain and was hardly ever home. 'Good for her,' I thought. It had become a rarity to get her on the line, golf competitions being an almost a weekly occurrence. She also coached the caddies at the club, one of them became a pro-golfer sponsored by corporates.

I imagined both Nyika and Blessing huddled over the mouthpiece of the phone positioned alongside the fireplace, overlooking the sunken lounge. An 80's fashion feature of modern homes. I could just picture it. Nyika's expression if Blessing gave the wrong advice or altered story, making him the hero.

My mother was satisfied with the way the takeaway and her businesses were running and Nyika as well as my eldest sibling and elder sister Bell (the one working at Glen Livet Hotel), pitched in on occasion helping when they could. Blessing was always knee-deep in scones, crunchies and whatever new diet soup my mom was drinking. It was around this time that Nyika had mentioned that she was not feeling a hundred percent. Not her usual "spot on", she chuckled making the statement less glaring. She said she should feel fine after some rest but she just could not seem to shake this flu or cold, and chest pains. I thought nothing of it. I felt sorry for her, imagined it was just that time of the year again. For sure, she would be looked after very well by the team back home.

Before leaving George Fleming All Girl Hostel (Hell Ville), I would have to stay with my cousin and her husband for a while until the apartment I had found was ready to move into. It was not to be too long, so they said. I handed in my notice at my hostel, the very next day! Thanks to my cousin and her husband I had a home for a while. I was so relieved that they had agreed. They were chill and easy-going. It was a breeze really for me, gotta laugh here.

I bought a second-hand race bike. The brakes were mostly non-existent. Now I could ride to Miss Secretarial College. I did this every day except Friday. I had tried to make myself invisible at the back of the college teacher's class but before she greeted us her opening words were, 'Back seats swap with front row seats.' We were all still in puberty, wet behind the ears, she definitely had some experience. After all, this was not her first class of secretaries right out of High School. I have to give it to her, she churned out the best secretaries this side of the equator. If that is what you wanted, she was definitely getting you there.

On Fridays, I went straight from secretarial college to work, taking my outfit for clubbing later in my bag. We had worked that "hiccup" of transport out with Cole (the owner of Home Grown) as well. The other two nights in the week I worked at Home Grown, College finished midday and not late. Friday was, a long day, simply because we had shorthand, typing, business English, accounting and a test in shorthand to top it all off. All in one day, like a wrap party for the weekend, yes ma'am!

The lady who taught us was a stick of dynamite, she was tiny and petite but absolutely nothing escaped her. When I say nothing, I mean nothing! She even followed girls to night clubs in the city and dragged their asses out of there in the early hours of the morning. In my opinion, that is taking it way too far. Her choice, she felt compelled to protect farmers daughters. I, on the other hand, was at a gay club where she was not on the guest list! Angel by day, Delightful by night!

Friday was party night and, naturally, riding home wasted was not advisable but boy oh boy my gay friends put the P in party and I never got home sober, ever! My lift home from waitressing was also organised for Saturday 3am from Sarah's night club. Talk about service! That's the upside of small communities and fabulous gay friends!

Bike riding was not exactly my biggest skill. Balance in general seemed to be a problem. Bank balance to boot. There were two things I noted off the bat, white people only rode bikes in suburbs and in the gondasha's (out of town mountain bikes or when they were in a triathlon). White girls waitressing was as rare as a zebras fart at a zebra crossing in New York City.

The looks I got, as if they were embarrassed for me, Questioning? What had gone so horribly wrong for me in my life that I had to waitress? Poor girl, wrong side of the tracks…shame. I let it slide. It was at around this time I started dating this guy who was unbelievably wealthy, ridiculously so. He had a golf course at his house for goodness' sake and he was in his mid 20's.

He did work, gotta give him that. It was not from mommy and daddy. However, when he found out I waitressed he lost it.

'My girlfriends don't waitress!' he screamed at me in the car park. 'Really,' I said, 'so who standing here is your girlfriend?' He was like '…what?'

Cheers, keep walking mate… Goodbye.

I had a lot of fun at Home Grown Restaurant where I worked permanently now, well on weekends and on Wednesdays. What a lovely family, their mum and dad were full of fun and energy too. It was not only a restaurant – the people working there became family. Being so far away from my own family, I certainly needed one in Harare. After working on a Friday night and having served more than enough Moussaka's, which was the dish the restaurant was renowned for, I would head off to "Sarah's," the nightclub across the street with its pink neon flashing sign and fabulously enticing staircase. Nyika would so not approve. She would have dragged my ass out of there given half the chance. She would have been on the secretarial college teacher's side without a doubt!

I thought, 'Well, she has to let me grow up and make my own mistakes at some point. I don't have to tell her everything.' Her mouth would have been agape if she saw how short this skirt was, it was sidling up my hips. Her comment probably being something along the lines of 'Gonna stop at Chivu on the way home. Put some clothes on young lady!'

Naturally, not everyone could get into "Sarah's" of course. The doorman, named Pope Francis, dressed in his catholic get up week in week out. Decked out in that fabulous house dress (in this case meaning "her deep house attire"), with its white cassock and attached pellegrina, girded with a white fringe fascia, its own "Coat of arms, enough to make you blush," embroidered on it. A massive pectoral cross suspended from a gold cord and red papal hung around his neck. His hair under his bright purple zucchetto (hat) which looks a bit similar to a beanie, he opted for purple as if a bishop and not a pope, was immaculate, and his perfectly square jaw cut to the chase. I would have given this pope a whirl, sadly he would not have given me the time of day.

His shoes perfectly polished and manufactured by Prada. I do honestly believe that any designer brands that existed in Zimbabwe at this time, that I am now familiar with, was only worn by gay men. As straight men in my country wouldn't have had a clue and, honestly, I certainly had no clue either. For all I knew, Gucci could have been a delicatessen or a fancy brand of chewing gum.

The club was an underground gay phenomenon so you had to know someone to get in. Raids were not unheard of and not something to look forward to. Unfortunately, a lot of my friends suffered due to brutality from all the homophobia that was rife in my country. Similar to finding your way through a minefield at midnight. Disgustingly so. In a country that to be gay was illegal.

Makes my blood boil. Can you imagine that? Ridiculous? Inevitably I would bump into the owner from Home Grown Restaurant, Colleen Rupert, after she had changed and emerged again as a totally new beautiful and stunning being. Heads turning, everywhere she went. She always bought me my first drink then we would dance the night away. Wearing her tight hot pants in various colours, tight tank top and whistle. I loved this club simply because gay clubs are always the only clubs that I have the best time in. Especially when its illegal! Cole had a partner who would by no means go unnoticed.

Oh, she opened the dance floor but believe me she closed it too. She was as enticing and hypnotising as a spitting cobra. A Cleopatra and Marylin in one face and body! Demand an audience she did with just a battering of her eyelashes. She went by the name of Madones!

I hardly knew anyone besides the girls from my old school, who quite frankly I was happy to never see again, and then there was Graham and Mark, whom I saw regularly at a rugby match or a beer festival. Which I had to force myself to go to, finding them so cave-like. I only went to these things for them. I did find them a tad boisterous. It was time to start expanding my network.

By now, I had stayed with my cousin Lynnette and her husband Vincent for a while in between leaving the hostel and moving into my own apartment. However, being in puberty and wanting to find my place in this world, I soon left to spread my wings. I am sure they breathed a sigh of relief. No more teenager to look after! One incident too much I guess, teenagers can take the blood from your nails. One scenario comes to mind, I had stayed in their granny cottage along the side of their main house. In Zimbabwe, the houses are mostly all big.

My boyfriend or ex from that time had visited me at the cottage, climbing over the wall at the end of the garden. From time to time, he would tap at my window, then I would let him into the cottage. All a big secret. Anyway, to cut a long story short, I had left a few weeks early and as I mentioned before broken up with my boyfriend in the car park because apparently waitresses were not good enough for him. Incredibly relieved that my apartment had become available sooner than expected, I had left the cottage and moved into my new home.

Well, the word on the street was he was heartbroken, more like ego broken. Anyway, I moved out early. My cousin had a friend come and stay. He was lying on the bed one evening in the cottage, he had the window open but the curtains closed. Seeing the curtain move then a hand come through it, he shot off the bed, gun in hand, pulled the curtain back with the gun, shouting, 'What you want?' This is a fact, Zimbabwe is a fairly dangerous country, way less than SA, but still robberies are very real. It's not rare for someone to react this way, nor is it unusual to have a gun. Nearly everyone had at least one gun. What a master card moment, apparently, he ran, fell, and scrambled over the wall. Since I was privy to this information, I laughed till my sides hurt. When I saw him again, instead of blowing him a kiss from behind the bar, I blew him a revolver kiss. Oh, rich boys who cannot buy "waitresses" must drive them to the brink!

Sooner or later, I was going to study clothing design and technology in Cape Town, probably at the end of the year. I had not decided. Then come back to Zimbabwe and work from here so I would keep my apartment. Rent it out.

My cousin and her husband definitely breathed a sigh of relief when it came time for me to leave. Waved and smiled bye-bye. I think I may have given them a few grey hairs. To this day. We're tight!

My apartment was slowly becoming liveable. My sister Samantha had given me her fridge, stove and bedroom suite as she was moving to Rio and these really helped. I went to markets and bought kitchen utensils. Harare had no IKEA so I hunted for furniture in old antique shops. I had to collect the fridge from a friend of my sisters but I had not tied it onto the back of the truck I had rented properly. Hence, as I rounded the corner a tad too fast, the fridge went swaying off the back of the truck and landed on the curb. I literally felt cold sweat drip down my spine. For the love of God, please let this fridge work when I get home, and please don't let me bump into any of her friends right now. Luck was on my side that day. Everything worked back at home, a few scratches, nothing that TiPX cannot hide, and a bust handle. I could fix those little mishaps in a jiffy with a bit of imagination.

In the meanwhile, I had managed to get another job at a cocktail bar called Aguila's and was making quite a lot of money. I called home once a week from a pay phone in the park across from my apartment. I got to speak to Nyika, Blessing and my mother every so often. Nyika never failed to remind me that my womanhood was gold and that I should remain respectable. Between her less than subtle message and my grandmother continually mentioning that I should remain intact till the day I married, despite her note in my make-up bag, I had begun to believe that was the way it was supposed to be for me.

I had been on a few dates but no one really sparked my interest. At sixteen, I had already had my heart broken by a navy guy in Cape Town. So once bitten, twice shy. I had burned all his cards and letters before leaving home. Letters had arrived on a weekly basis without fail for a full year. 'Dear Monkeyface...' The last one confirming he would be on a bus to Mutare at this time and that date. I had waited at the bus stop until the last patron of the bus climbed off. Then sat down on a curb for what felt like eternity. Years later, I heard from a travelling barman who worked at Aguila's with me that my navy guy had had a terrible accident in Angola. They had been in the navy together. Tragically, he was now in a wheelchair and preferred to be a recluse. However, as my wonderful gay friend always says: "Pick yourself up, dust yourself off, and get moving!" Darling, darling the world does not keep turning only for you!

I spoke to my father every other week. He was on a party line so it was difficult to get through. A party line is "one" telephone line that belongs to a number of people in any given area. As children we would try to listen in to grown up's gossip. They were those wind-up telephones – two shorts and three longs was our number.

I was still at secretarial school. I had really tried but it just didn't resonate with me. The idea of sitting across from a male boss and taking shorthand notes. It somehow seemed so dated. I am just not that chick that looks like she will make you breakfast. I did benefit from business English and accounting which were taught at the school – these two attributes really helped me when I opened my own business later on.

Chapter Sixteen
When Spirits Take Flight

I had not been home for a year. It was Christmas time and this year, I was to spend it with: my mother and stepfather, Nyika, Blessing, my grandmother Rita, my aunt and her crew, my Godmother Vye and her driver Charles who drove her around in her Jaguar, my eldest sister, her family and Samantha. I wished my brother would have been here too. A full bustling house, alive with little footsteps this year. Our eldest sibling had by now a daughter of three, a son of one and a brand-new baby girl. They were adorable.

I had borrowed "Baldric" Graham's landy to drive to Mas Vegas and Christmas came with all the bells and whistles (Christmas has to be my all-time favourite festivity of the year you may have gathered this by now). The weather was fantastic, everyone was in good spirits and my mother's kitchen was ablaze with treats, delicious delicacies and rich aromas. We didn't have the snow and the cold. Instead, we had sunshine and we hung out at our swimming pool, sipping gin and tonics in long glasses with lots of ice and twists of fresh lemons from our citrus trees in our garden. Nyika, Blessing and Charles also joined in and had one. Blessing preferred his beer, but it was religion to start festivities with a G and T.

Nyika and I went Christmas shopping in the Metropolis of one-horse Mas Vegas. Stopping to catch up with everyone and their mother, dog and brother! It was really awesome. I miss these people. I thought they'd be there forever, that Mas Vegas would be part of my life till eternity. Nothing like having a carpet pulled out from under your feet.

That Christmas we all taught Nyika how to conquer her fear of water and how to remain afloat. Granny Rita had bought her the most fabulous swimsuit and cap. Aside from the laughter, we were very encouraging. Nyika had a chequered past when it came to water.

As a child, she had grown up alongside the Sabi/Save River. The area was prone to torrential rainfall and the overflowing riverbanks were inevitable at times. This river was completely unpredictable and, on more than one occasion, I had also been stuck on the other side of it. The river ran through the ranch – it was between the main road and the main headquarters at Chishakwe. The Save River once called the Sabi River.

When Nyika was a child she had been playing hide and seek along the river bed using the trees, long grasses and reeds as hiding places. She had slipped on the sand bank and fallen into the rushing river. She had been carried along the rapids like a rag doll and miraculously was spat out onto the banks after roughly a hundred metres. It was just pure luck she survived – just not her time.

Naturally, water terrified her after this and she had avoided the river completely. Whenever she did need to approach it, she would treat it as if it was the Tokoloshe itself. Or like a deer knowing it's thirsty and knowing that crocodiles were lurking, ready to snap it up. Fragile necessities, that you cannot avoid.

It is said that crocodiles do not attack in a raging river or a flooding river. As children, we believed this and would tube down this same river without a care in the world. Happily, we would bounce over rapids, fall out of the tubes and swim long distances in the still water between. It simply was not our time either.

On this terrible day that Nyika had been playing hide and seek with her friends and was swept along by the river, one of her friends did not return. She swears he was taken by a crocodile. I don't doubt her words – either he was taken by crocodiles or he drowned and would eventually have been eaten by crocodiles.

Crocodiles only eat you when you have rotted. They take you down to their caves and push a rock over your body to weigh you down. At this point, you are already dead. They twist you with such force, snapping your neck, just like we pull the wish bone after a roast chicken. Then you rot and then they feast.

It's not the first death I heard about where crocs were involved. I am terrified of them along with both Nyika and my mother. I have had many a nightmare involving this monstrous creature. Passed down to me by my mother. My father too was nearly taken by a croc. The only thing that saved him is that he stepped right instead of left. The croc came from behind him to knock him over and pull him into the water. But my father unwittingly stepped aside and the crocs momentum in the other direction meant it missed him. My father was able to escape and quickly get back to his car. It was just pure luck. Gotta love that "luck."

During my parents' marital years, they had to poison some crocs as they were coming inland to eat the cattle. Ngwane (if you remember) had a dam. They went out at night on a rowing boat and with a torch, spotted crocs and dumped rotten meat overboard. You can tell the size of a crocodile at night by the gap between its red/yellow beady eyes, when you shine a torch on them. How romantic, 'What do you want to do tonight darling? I was thinking we go and get rid of the huge monster of a crocodile that is eating the cattle. You know, the one making a nuisance out of itself. You in? No, not that dress, maybe something a little less, you know glamorous.' My mother marrying a farmer, what was she thinking?

If the width is small between its red/yellow beady eyes, it's a small croc. If the width is large, then you have a monster on your hands – a monster growing up to seven metres long. They had to maintain the number of crocs in comparison to the size of the dam. Otherwise, things became unbalanced. Crocs bred like roaches.

Relocating crocs was not an option during these times. The largest lake in the world is the man-made Lake Kariba, also in Zimbabwe, and it was said to have one crocodile per metre of the perimeter of the entire lake.

By the end of the Christmas holidays, Nyika had managed to master the art of doggy paddle. She was beaming with pride. She had overcome her fear of water and overcome her fear of drowning. I had fulfilled my promise – one more tick on my to-do list. I sometimes get so carried away and plan to do a million things and never get half of them done on time. But I get them done eventually. African timing, I guess. I have a bucket list that I am still working through.

Christmas Eve came and we all went to midnight mass, sang our hearts out, had my sister Susan's legendary gluhwein and ate homemade mince pies. We sat outside with our treats under a blanket of stars.

The following morning, the cattle truck was decorated with Christmas tinsel and laden with gifts for the children in the Tribal Trust lands. We were dressed as elves and Mother Christmas's. This year, Nyika was at the wheel. She was beaming. I was so proud of her. She had mentioned she was still not feeling one hundred percent. However, she looked just fabulous today! We had our grass basket of tea and Christmas cake. We set off. Nyika, made a few bunny hops, we lurched forwards and backwards, in fits of laughter.

This was an all-day experience. I say experience because every year it touched me deeply and reminded me of how fortunate I was and how I should not take all I had for granted. It's necessary to have this intact in Africa or any developing country. Sharing the privileges, you have should become second nature. The children, on seeing the truck, ran out from the compounds across the open savannah plains, dashing out from under the umbrella trees and thatched huts. Screaming with joy at the top of their lungs. Christmas, Gogo Christmas!

We had speakers attached to the truck and we were playing Christmas carols. What a sight to behold. We went from one compound to the next, each one equally joyous. Christmas is not Christmas without children. To feel their open-armed hugs around your neck, the sheer joy in their eyes, full of hope, intrigue and genuine happiness – no fakes here. Alive with promise, alive with fairy tales and allure. Dancing with the children and their families in the dust, to the sounds of merriment, even if it was a thread of hope, it was still hope. It really costs so little of one's time to help to bring joy to others, less fortunate than themselves.

Nyika and I danced around with my sister Samantha, my mother, my godmother, my grandmother and all the villagers. We sang along to *We Wish you a Merry Christmas* and danced to Boney M's *Christmas Delights*, along with good old Bing Crosby and all the jazz greats. Not forgetting the ever so famous George Michael's*, "Last Christmas!"*

We always ended the drive with a sherry under a shepherd tree and another slice of Christmas cake. Then we would head home, dive into the swimming pool and have a G and T (or two).

Soon it was time to start preparing Christmas lunch for the following day. What an occasion everyone got involved willingly, even myself in the kitchen. It was by no means a small job, it was a tremendous feat, and magic materialized. Mince Pies, melba pudding, roast, chicken, pork and beef. Roast potatoes, roasted vegetables, all from the garden. The meat all from Susan's farm. Fresh green salads. The unfailing prawn cocktail starter. The avocado's from the trees in our garden. The prawns fresh from Mozambique. Bean salads, cold slaw, mint sauce, gravy, you name it.

After our Christmas lunch slightly stuffed, we went and lay by the pool. Pretty much unable to move. My godmother on the other hand relaxed elegantly in the pool doing sort of leg lifts, chatting away to no one in particular but to everyone in general. When I think of her, *Driving Miss Daisy* comes to mind. She was in every meaning of the word of stiff upper lip and undoubtably refined, a perfect lady. Leaving no question about class, but she knew how to let her hair down and be part of the gang. Years later she married the town's Father Christmas. He then became my godfather. He was a wonderful man and was gifted with a sense of humour second to none.

My godmother would ask if we all had our dresses for the Club Christmas Annual Ball. We did of course and (as was traditional on Christmas Day at our mother's) we were prepared for a pre-parade of dresses for her. We had to walk the length of the pool, turn elegantly under instruction of course, hand moving just enough by your sides. 'Head up, chin up, confidence, Joe, you are not on the farm!' Every year without fail. That year, I wore all gold – it was an eighties thing. I looked dreadful but I had convinced myself I was the splitting image of Olivia Newton John in Xanadu. My mother wore a shade of purple (as usual), gorgeous. My mother turned heads all over the world, everywhere she went and whatever age she was. Samantha was wearing gold and white, Nyika was wearing shades of green and gold, granny was wearing jet black velvet suit with a smattering of expensive jewellery, Susan was wearing navy, white and also gold, she looked so striking and my godmother, well, we all had to wait to see her outfit (as was traditional). The men all wore tuxedos – Blessing, Charles and my stepfather looked particularly dashing.

The evening of the ball arrived with Mas Vegas' finest ready to party. The hall had been beautifully and badly decorated and tinsel was everywhere. Waiters dashed here and there breathlessly while spotty teenagers and hardened alcoholics hung out rapaciously in a corner. Crystal glasses clinked and the rock 'n rollers hit the floor. Sadly, my mother's new husband could not even keep a two-step but kudos for trying though. Blushing, he negotiated his way back to his chair while my mother – being a good-looking woman and a great dancer – did not have to wait long for an invitation. Everyone, took to the floor in a mirage of colours. One thing for sure, these people new how to let their hair down and have fun. The town, put their differences aside this one night a year, and we had an absolute jawl.

The theatre director was watching on and drinking it all in, no doubt a new play being born in his mind. He was a fine fellow. A friend of mine who worked alongside him had announced that evening to everyone (after way too many shooters) that he was as gay as a coot. I was so pleased for him – finally, honesty at long last. It took so much courage to be openly gay in a small town like this. Although once out, you were adored more for it. Mas Vegas filled with Madison men, real men you know?

Everyone was there. Even those bats and their battering eyelashes, you know the ones, there are always "those ones," but tonight they could go to hell! Their lizard tongues split with gossip, clutching their invisible egos and treacherous fantasies. The hairdresser sat in her finest in the furthest corner of the room.

I had avoided a sweaty hand teenage dance by saying I was on my way to talk to the hairdresser. I found myself stood right in front of her, not knowing what to say.

Completely at a loss, I spurted, 'Why did you try to shoot yourself?'

She looked at me, startled.

'Everyone's talking about it,' I continued, 'so, I just thought maybe I would ask you myself. I also want to know if you are lonely or just depressed. Can I help you? Can I do something for you?'

All the questions that are always asked too late.

She looked up at me with vacant eyes.

'Get me another drink, will you?'

'Certainly!'

As I turned to go she added, 'And don't be stingy with the good stuff, make it a triple! It's goddam Christmas after all.' I smiled. She had vuma!

I saw wandering hands and car keys in a bowl. The swingers and twirling cocktail sticks, old Olives and young Popeyes. The town butcher, baker and candle stick maker, sailing out to sea on the one night of the year they got to mingle with the small-town elite. The mechanic was there with his greasy nails and his ruffled tuxedo – unshaven, leering over a girl who would never be able to leave this town. She would wind up living on the wrong side of the tracks with too many kids and no time for a hairdresser... asking herself how she got there, listening to Dolly Parton from her trailer remembering the good old days before gravity set in and poverty ate her heart right out.

I watched on as the one of the town's leading men slid his hand up and down the ass of the black barman pretending to help behind the bar. Clearing his throat as his eyes met mine – that moment of sheer panic – I smiled at him.

'It's cool with me,' I said, 'I happen to think you have good taste.'

'Oh, Joanna,' he replied, clearly relieved, 'he's divine!' They both grinned.

Thumbs up. Now I knew why he remained a charming, good-looking singleton.

I walked to the lavatory only to see two pairs of high heels poking out the bottom of the toilet and hearing moans of pleasure emanating from within. I stifled the giggle rising in my throat. There was definitely something in the water in this Mas Vegas.

Nyika had followed me and seeing my fascination with this indiscretion dragged me out of there in a hurry.

'Come on, girl, you owe me a dance.' We marched onto the dance floor and woke these white people up a tad. My family naturally joined in.

All too soon, it was time to go home. We strolled, well some of us staggered with my stepfather, who barely drank at all, looking after us. I liked that about him – his responsibility.

The next morning, we all woke with hangovers. Nyika had prepared bloody Marys and we sat quietly – very quietly. In the next three days, I was to go back to Harare.

As tradition would have it, we rose early the following morning to the sound of Christmas carols - the church choir at the door. We all gathered round, sang and ate mince pies. After which, we went inside and all sat in the lounge. Huge tea tray on the centre table, laden with more mince pies and toast with various toppings, fish paste or marmite.

Usually, someone was voted to hand out the presents. Nyika was voted that year. Everyone was sitting around when there was a loud hooting of a car at the front gate. We all dashed to the lounge window. My brother had arrived, as a surprise. Christmas could not get any better. My heart exploded with joy. 'Nyika, Blessing, Herman's here,' we bolted out the front door, and knocked him over.

Between tackling him down to the ground and my sister's dog Cujo (a St Bernard), we lay in a heap in the driveway. We had not seen my brother since Agricultural College in the UK and since coming home, he had been working non-stop. He was in high demand as he was not only my father's son, but a dam fine agriculturist to boot. With a deep knowledge of farming and the bush around farming so he knew how to work alongside with nature. Naturally plans changed to accommodate my brother's arrival. He had bought a girlfriend. He had loved her since junior school and she was also from Mas Vegas.

Mindy, she was gorgeous, she looked exactly like the dark-haired Charlie's angel (Jaclyn Smith) but so was my brother! I happened to think my big brother was the most handsome man in the world. He got all my mother's looks and my father's charm.

When I was little, he protected me from my crazy sisters and any boy who gave me a hard time. He was the first person to teach me and encourage me to swim. My love for swimming came solely from him. Whenever I was in a major competition, his voice of encouragement was the last voice I heard before the starting gun. 'Nail it Doobs.' He also taught me to ride a motorbike, a Suzuki scrambler 125. He taught me about Chishakwe and to love the elephant. When my father and him organised the largest translocation of elephant known to mankind at The Save Valley Conservancy, he rescued four baby elephant. Tiny being his favourite. He taught me so much about their nature, we used to take them for walks to the dam on Chishakwe which he built with our father. It wasn't a short walk either. It was also sometimes quite tough, ellies can push your buttons in their juvenile years too. He always stood up for me and by my side without fail. We of course had our differences and argued, sometimes really badly, but in the end, he was my big brother and sibling love is unconditional.

They came inside and were swamped by the family. Questions flying. Mas Vegas was, as you know, a small town so Mindy already knew everyone. She was by far the best girlfriend he had ever had. In every aspect! I thought it cute that they had loved one another since junior school. Additional presents were rustled up, my mother always managed at the last minute, golf prizes go a long way!

We opened our presents along with shrieks of delight and oh no's! Once we had cleared up the lounge, we went for our traditional walk around the village suburbs, bumping into other families and sharing good wishes. On arriving home, we toasted with good old Zimbabwean Brut out of our Marion Antionette glasses and put on our Christmas cracker hats whilst my brother carved the roast pork (no one had touched it at the large lunch the day before), with its famous crackling and apple sauce. Avocado ritz starters, melba pudding with custard for dessert. Crackers and cheese, chocolates, you know the traditional Quality Streets, bowls of nuts and sherry or cognac. Christmas carols blasted from the new Bonny M Christmas carol special album. Nyika and Blessing of course joined us as always. Blessing had got his scotch cart. Nyika had got an envelope to help her acquire her official driver's license. The L number plate may finally be taken off all our cars? Now that my brother was home, my mom organised a second seating of Christmas late afternoon/lunch or dinner. A firm believer in never wasting food, for obvious reason.

The table was always beautifully decorated. that was mostly thanks to my mother, and her daughters (us three)! We had a knack for it. Christmas at my mother's house was outstanding! Christmas carols started to play, we started to dance and sing. Everyone in my family danced. Even my step-dad, as badly as he did, he still participated. Mindy could also dance really well. We partied all day long, swimming, talking, laughing, eating way too much. We all retired early that evening. Full, exhausted, sunburnt and grateful!

The next morning arrived to soon as always, along with sad goodbyes. Our next get together would be my twenty-first birthday party at the Glen Livet Hotel in six-months-time. My sister Samantha worked there and she was organising it all with Nyika, my mother, my grandmother, Susan and my godmother. It was a forty-five minute drive from Mas Vegas in the same direction as Zaka and The Conservancy.

We were all getting older. I had noticed that Nyika had aged but she still seemed so full of life.

My cup truly overflowed in so many areas of my life, except perhaps my love life, but I was not really bothered about that to be brutally honest. Marriage, babies and a life with a man was not the be all and end all of my existence. If it happened – great! If it didn't – great as well!

I was happy to get back to my regular life in Harare – Miss Patel's Secretarial College, Home Grown, Sarah's, Aguila's and my own apartment (with no one to tell me how to run it). I had rented out my spare room to one of Aguila's managers. He was a good guy and a lot of fun – never short of a joke. I thought I had rather liked a friend of his for a while but that idea faded just as fast as it arrived. Naturally, I was just too young to fathom the depths of the laws of attraction.

After this apartment, I shared the next with another woman; her name was also Joanna. It was the two Joanna's and she was such an awesome person. We had many a laugh and she made the best pasta salad ever.

My year at Miss Patel's Secretarial School came to an end and I was pondering my next step. I had seen a gap in the entertainment scene in Zimbabwe. I thought about opening a club. Or maybe a club that staged festivals.

Thoughts turned to reality and soon enough I had started my own business – Smile Surge Productions. I was turning twenty-one and was opening the business with nothing. I took a deep breath and dived right in – making sure I had a brilliant accountant with me. His name, The Brain – an absolute magician with money. He was forever patient with me and was the complete opposite to a stereotypical accountant – such a wonderful character. I also asked a friend of mine to work with me as art director and she created a wondrous world of *fantasy minds*.

Our first *"Rave"* (as they called it in those days) made the Zimbabwe 8 p.m. news broadcast. We could have not hoped for better – and free – advertising. We called it, *Smile Surge Presents: DICE ONE.* The press lamented the rave as "Dancing with the Devil" and I had overzealous religious types demonstrating outside my new home – a little house on the hill in Avondale with purple shutters situated on ten acres of unkempt garden.

I bought a dog – a Jack Russell called DJ – and he went everywhere with me. He also sat at the front door of all my raves with a bow tie on. I had also bought a pick-up truck (post box red). Part of the proceeds of the parties and lingerie auctions (a sideline of mine) went to building waterholes for animals in dire need in the game reserves situated north of Harare.

The raves attracted the *"Queen"* crowd and the energy was palpable. The newspapers ran with the headlines *"Dancing with Death"* and *"Dancing with the Devil"* - clearly I wasn't too popular.

The entire country descended on my first rave. This is no joke, it's the absolute truth. The tobacco barn I had hired downtown had warned me they would sue me if there was any ecstasy-type catastrophe. I tried to explain to them that I had nothing to do with selling ecstasy but this fell on deaf ears. On top of all this, a rumour had started that I was not only the one selling ecstasy but I was also taking it in copious amounts. This was a vicious rumour started by a former family member.

This was not a party for me, it was work. I was crazy and flamboyant enough. My focus was to create an arena where the world of fantasy embraced people and gave them the opportunity to let go and be who they wanted to be for the night. For me, it was a business. I ran it as such. What I was not aware of and what I only found out this year – 2020 – is that my raves were considered second best, first place going to London.

A frequent party goer and acquaintance of mine informed me of such at a get together we had in Cape Town to celebrate the Queen of Queens – Madone's fiftieth birthday.

What was even better is that the gay community in Harare were free to be whomever they wanted to be at my parties.

These parties were not patrolled by the police – I had my own official security. These *queens* told me I was an intricate part of their lives back then – being gay was illegal in my country. It was the gay community that made my parties in Zimbabwe work. All of them, were and still are spectacular! My friends, Queen B & Madones, made sure all the beautiful people arrived in splendour, leaving jaws dropped wide open in their wake. The gay community opened my eyes to what was possible and embraced me when no one else did. I owe a lot to them.

Along with my brilliant art director and with our minds working together, we created spaces and atmospheres that captivated our audiences and transported them to places they only dreamed about.

Queen B, Madones, Layla Love Child, Gayle the Gorgeous, Sage Khan and Saul, Colleen Homegrown, Luca de la lucky, Sheer Surely Sexy and the crew were smack on the money – dressed by the one and only "Psycho" clothing label. Latex purple flare pants, tight luminous yellow shorts and whistles. Drag that could never be dragged off any stage. Heels and then seriously high heels. The saunters and the sways, heavy eyelashes flirting with the dancefloor – they really did have the moves. The after parties and the after after parties. Harare, thank you for a tremendous time and ultimately a learning curve, professionally and personally. Visitors for my raves came from all over the world; they flew in especially for them on airlines and private jets. I held three a year. That was my business. On top of that I opened a club called Sahara's and another called Picasso's. I held the monopoly on escapism.

Even Nyika had come to check up on me and what I was doing. She came to the party just to make sure I was not behaving too crazily. With her driver's license. She had even dressed up and danced on the stage. At first, she had been shy but after the second tequila she was just fine.

Nyika approved of my home and admired the neatness. Complementing herself on how she had installed good values in a young woman. 'Too bad Blessing never installed that in you for your cooking skills' she muttered on opening my fridge.

We had gone shopping and I had spoilt her. I even bought a first perfume for her – she chose Poison. I had also insisted we buy her some lingerie as you need this with or without a man. We did *ladies who lunch* and she met the old crew from Home Grown. She learned that to be gay was not a sin; to be gay was not a crime. She left fascinated. As I watched her drive out of my driveway in her new car (well second hand – six different owners), her new red Renault, I felt a certain surge of pride. A real Smile Surge. We had come such a long way since Kudzai had been captured. Since we had been attacked almost daily. Through the bright and not so bright days. We had gotten through it all. There goes my Nyika. I waved, she hooted and was gone. She also had a tape deck in her car... Nina Simone of course who else!

I drove home a week later for my twenty-first birthday party.

The Glen Livet Hotel was located on the lakeside of Lake Kyle (or Lake Muturikwe). The whole family had been invited and by that I mean the entire family. Aunts, uncles, cousins, grandparents, brothers, sisters and best friends. A twenty-first in Zimbabwe is very important, just like an eighteenth in Europe. You are given the key to the world – but in all truth, I already had a key. However, this was a tradition and I love tradition. I am steeped in it.

We had managed to get this hotel for the party simply because my sister, Bell, worked there and she had arranged a massive discount. Thinking back, my sister Bell has always been there for me, right by my side every step of the way. I could not have asked for a better or more loving sister than her. All my siblings had been there for me, just a rapidly declining country sets up personal borders one tries to demolish in hours after years of not seeing one another, an impossible task.

The twenty-first was a huge success and the party went as all parties in the Lowveld went – *hell for leather*. It was a wonderful time for b0onding and the last get together for both sides of my parents' families – I was the youngest and they were now officially divorced.

The entire Hagen and Reagan clan descended on the Glen Livet Hotel. The party was to last for a whole weekend with croquet, walks up the mountain, breakfasts, cricket, rugby, tennis, dinners and afternoon colonial teas arranged. There were countless fabulous outfits and endless fits of laughter. Not to go unnoticed, my uncle, after being put to bed by his wife, appeared in the bar in nothing but his underwear. Never a dull moment in my family.

The weekend ended with a speech from my father and then one from me. Moving and profound, he was an excellent public speaker – and I didn't do too badly myself actually, as I really do not like public speaking at all. My friend, Johnathan but went by the name of Jono, then helped me pack all my presents into my new car and we headed back to Harare, in convoy. It had been my parents twenty-first birthday present to me. It was a yellow blue bird Datsun with a white roof. Jono had driven me to my twenty-first initially to give me a lift. He fitted into the family just like a piece of a puzzle. He was a hoot, in addition we had spent a few months canoeing down the Orange River in South Africa as official guides, unofficially.

Arriving completely stoned to meet our clients. We had not been told we would meet them the same day of arrival. In our defence. However, they had not noticed. We then rode on horseback after canoeing down the river for about another three days. We nearly lost a school teacher who capsized her kayak. We nearly lost the same teacher, whose camel decided to bolt and took off into the sunset. After racing on our horses to stop the camel, she asked if she could ride the horse rather. I had to ride the bloody camel which stank.

The camel was called Brookjies. It only understood Afrikaans tonnes. A fantastic trip which I look back on fondly. Jono was always around and about in my life one way or another and at Aguila's. He was my flatmate's closest friend along with another guy called Scotty. Scotty was the most hilarious of them all. He had a character and humour unrivalled. They basically lived at my apartment seeing that Tony my flatmate was part of this band of merry men. Fun in your twenties!

Back to the twenty first, Nyika, Blessing, Happiness, Truth and Zuvarashe had all joined in the festivities and had a thoroughly good time. Truth had danced the night away with my uncle in the bar – they both looked the worse for wear that morning. Happiness too. Zuvarashe had decided to taste all the whiskeys in the hope of gaining some knowledge – he was struggling too.

Nyika was complaining of a headache that morning. I didn't think much of it – I thought perhaps she might be coming down with a cold. She had been having a lot of problems with colds over the last couple of years. Particularly her sinus's and lungs. I went and took her a cup of tea and some food for the rest of the day leaving an extra slice of chocolate cake that she loved. She was fast asleep, so I tucked her in. I felt her forehead – she had a slight temperature. My sister would check on her every so often. I gave her a kiss, made a new hot water bottle and placed the Vicks vapour rub on the side table along with cough syrup, Panadol and throat lozenges. I would be home in a couple of weeks again for a long weekend and looked forward to seeing Nyika then. I kissed her on the forehead goodbye.

The Msasa trees were in full bloom as we drove along the lake out past the Glen Livet Hotel and onto the dirt road. The sound of gravel against the car tires – the crunching sound – is just like that sound between your ears when you eat a deep-fried bitter ball (only found in Holland). It's the biting down and grinding of the crumbed exterior. The burnt oranges and dirty yellows combined with the emerald greens of the Msasa trees gently coaxed me all the way to the main road. Jono in his car ahead of me.

Then we were off. Packed with all the usual treats and goodies. Except this time in the basket there was a letter. I noticed my mother's handwriting immediately. I had not had a letter since boarding school. My stomach contracted. I tore the envelope open – inside was a cheque. I smiled. Best letter from my mother ever. Joking of course. It was a cheque made out to me – the savings my mother had put aside for my adult life for when I had left home. Something to help me set myself up properly.

For the love of a mother, I made a mental note to call her when I got to Harare. I really did have a truly amazing mother, one of the best I could have ever hoped for.

The music was on. A gentle, rhythmical jazz piece.

Jono driving responsibly ahead of me. On arrival in Harare, we pulled into a petrol station. Let's have a drink at my apartment I suggested. Sure, good idea. Jono always chuckled. He never laughed, he chuckled for real. As we pulled up at my apartment, our friend Tony waved from the balcony, him and his friend Slayed were having tea. I was happy to arrive to someone at home! Wig Wam Bam playing, The Sweet!

I had been home about a week when I got the news. I had phoned home like I did every week. I remembered to thank my mother for her gift then she passed the phone to Blessing. He told me. My mother was too worked up to be able to tell me herself.

'Blessing, what is it?' I asked.

I didn't want to be rude or abrupt. I just wanted the answer.

'Joe,' Blessing replied softly, 'Nyika is very ill. She has pneumonia. She appeared older and frailer when I left her sleeping in the hotel room at Glen Levit. I had pushed the thought aside. She wants to return to her homeland and compound,' continued Blessing.

That Nyika wanted to return to her homeland meant only one thing. She was dying.

'Blessing,' I replied, 'I'll drive home tomorrow morning at first light and will take her home to her compound myself. Make sure you pack everything of hers. I should be with you – in time for tea – at 11 a.m.'

Always time for tea.

'In the meantime,' I continued, 'order the best coffin and headstone there is in Mas Vegas.'

Tears began streaming from my eyes as I made this request. I leaned against the pay phone, my forehead on the glass. I felt so alone. I had no idea who sold coffins in Mas Vegas – the thought had never crossed my mind that I may need one or more one day.

'Then pack a white linen sheet,' I said, 'and make sure Nyika's favourite dress – the red/orange/gold's and green ball dress – is packed and ironed. Perfectly. Just like she has done for you for all these years, Blessing. Thank you. Love you. God bless. Please make mum some tea and pour her a stiff whiskey, have one or two yourself. Tell her I'll arrive tomorrow.'

I walked out of the phone booth and sat down. I felt numb. Nyika wanted to go home because she knew she was dying. My life without Nyika – was this really happening? I sat there for what felt like years but must have been the best part of an hour. It was not until I noticed that the streetlights had come on that I forced my legs to take me home. I didn't even pack. I had clothes at home. I just took out my croquet blanket that Nyika had made me, I still have it, goes everywhere with me. I made a packed lunch for the drive home. Then I laid down and sobbed.

I rose at sunrise. Little to no sleep. I got into my car and drove to Mas Vegas purely on instinct – my mind elsewhere. I didn't stop in Chivu. I pressed on. I arrived in Mas Vegas at 10:45 a.m.

Nyika looked so beaten – so small, so frail. I pushed back the tears that I knew were coming and held her hand.

'I'm taking you home tomorrow, Nyika,' I said softly, cradling her in my embrace. 'I'll stay with you until the end. I have taken time off work and all my team know their duties for the next month or so. It will be you and me at your compound. We will leave tomorrow at first light.'

She looked up and smiled weakly at me.

The doctor had come to our home for dinner. He had given us the news that Nyika would probably only survive for another two to three more days – maximum. I cried that night – streams came pouring out. I vowed those would be the last tears till the end – I had to be the strong one for her. I slept next to her, holding her hand. I had to be the strong one for Blessing, for my mother, for

Samantha, Susan and all of us. For Jnr and even for my father, he had come to rely on Nyika and grown to care a great deal about her. They had long forgotten their misinterpretations. They had moved on. Amendments made.

Samantha had left for Rio. My mother and Blessing had been taking care of Nyika. Her pneumonia was worsening and there was nothing they or anyone could do about it.

We drove out of Mas Vegas at sunrise. I had put a mattress in the back of my truck for Nyika. We carried her from her bed to the mattress in the back of the truck. It was a Toyota. The ambulance men helping me, administering the last drip. The weather was beautiful and a cool gentle breeze blew. She was dressed warmly with a hat and tucked in well. Very comfortable, cosy. I glanced in my rear-view mirror, adjusting it, and turned back to look at her ashen face. Her eyes had become hooded and she had lost so much weight. Her headstone had been sent ahead to the compound and against tradition she had chosen to be buried in a sheet and not a coffin. Like her mother had been. She was not a big fan of modern tribe-hood. She was looking up into a bright blue sky. I had given her sunglasses and she had her drip in. A bottle of water was next to her and I had placed my Walkman on her ears and put her favourite music on – Nina Simone: *Ain't Got No, I Got Life*.

I smiled at Nyika; she smiled weakly back. She had a bell to ring if she wanted me to stop. I had a window at the back of the truck which lay wide open. She rang the bell once on the journey. I stopped the truck and climbed into the back.

'Joanna,' she mouthed, 'I love you so much. You were the daughter I never had. Your family was my family.

'I love you so much too, Nyika,' I said gently. 'We're nearly home.'

'Stay a soul, child,' she whispered.

'Yes, Nyika, yes.'

I knew that part of me had hardened and I didn't think I could keep this promise.

I tucked her back in, puffed up her pillow and kissed her forehead. I gave her some water and wiped her brow. Her high fever was causing hallucinations. She was mumbling, strange stories. The sun was just peeking over the hills – the ones that Nyika and I had named the Jumbo, the Rhino and the Monkey.

I climbed back into the car and drove off gently. We were maybe an hour away. I drove slowly. Afraid of time, for on this occasion it was running out. As I took the Zaka turnoff, I waved at the buses of people driving and passing by, passing the mealie patches and the cobs of corn strewn across the dirt. Children were running around selling packets of Mopane worms and packets of ground worms for fishing. The smell of wood smoke filled my nostrils, the sound of the Shona people whistling and the Shona mamas, balancing bowls of tomatoes on their head with babies wrapped in towels on their backs, shouting at one another, laughing and singing in their deep soul voices. The odd donkey wandered by; the men in their scotch carts heading out with fruits and vegetables to be sold. The spoils of their land was thanks to their African women. Day in and day out. The women toiled while men were planted outside the beer hall at the turn off spending money that their wives and children so desperately needed. Stumbling out of the bar, a man fell. Nobody moved to help him. I carried on driving. I loved my country. I loved it more than anything. Why in the hell was it falling apart? Farm attacks had begun further north of where we lived. Ugly and disturbing.

Every so often I checked on Nyika. We soon approached her thatched house; her compound where Kudzai and I had played. Shona children are given both English and Shona names. Often the English names are unique – Blessing, Beauty and Knowledge for example. One gentleman I met was called Telephone. Ironically, he worked on the switchboard. Thinking about it made me smile.

The compound had not changed one bit. The majority of Nyika's family had adapted to modern day society. There was no longer a chief sitting in traditional wear. The memory of Nyika's father drifted briefly over my thoughts. The days of Kudzai and I running around the compound playing innocently. I heard us laughing, calling, shouting. I saw us eating, sadza faces. Spitting sugar cane. Chickens squawked and roosters crowed. The fire burnt in the centre of the compound. Stray dogs squabbled and barked. Goats grazed sand as the roots of whatever the imagined they were eating was gone. Boys steered oxen in the fields. Mielie cobs were piled and scattered. The chief, now donned a suit and tie. He was a good man, just as all the chiefs in Nyika's family had been and would come to be. He saw me and waved. He was sitting outside his hut; his youngest wife was close to him. I saw this particular part of culture had not changed. The younger the woman the better so it seems, men can be so vain. I resisted the urge to feel annoyed. I had bought more than enough food for the funeral festivities and mourning. The plastic bags that flapped in the wind were all branded OK. *What a crazy name for a supermarket chain, only in Zimbabwe*, I thought, and everything was far from OK.

I stopped the truck and parked it under a shepherd tree making sure Nyika was lying in the shade. Kissed her forehead. Whispered, you are home. I went and greeted the chief. He had heard I was coming. He told me the headstone had arrived. He ordered his wife to make tea. She did so immediately. Ordered being the correct term here.

I walked back to the truck to check on Nyika. Picking up her hand it felt heavier than usual. I felt for her pulse. Her temperature had come down. No pulse. I checked again. Nothing. I looked at her eyes and shut her eyelids. I couldn't breathe. Nyika had passed looking up into a bright blue sky. She had died on a clear day with the sounds of the Shona - her people - calling in the background and Nina Simone in the beginning. She had died with the smells she was used to. Her own surroundings. Her home. Her Zimbabwe. I heard the cry and echo of the fish eagle. Of life.

I looked at the ruins of my old house, further down the hill. The dam, vertially empty. A million visions running through my mind in milliseconds. Still the toilet seat remained. I saw Kudzai on the shoulders of Mr Harris, I saw us taking lessons under the shepard tree, saw us playing on the swing with Nyika pushing us. I saw Nyika holding me as a child, reassuring me. Nyika was gone. Kudzai was gone. The Chief was gone. Grass and foliage had covered the memory of what used to be. No shepherd tree. I took a deep breath.

I walked back to the chief. He read the signs. He ordered Nyika's relatives to take her body to her hut. I joined. They laid her upon her bed. It would be a long night; she would be laid to rest at sunrise tomorrow morning.

The chief prepared the village for the occasion. Nyika had been a respected woman in her family and society. The chief would dress in traditional wear and so would the women. I bathed Nyika with the help of the elder woman of the village. They gave me my African traditional dress. We wrapped Nyika in the crisp white sheet that Blessing had packed. We washed and cleaned her body.

I did not sleep that night. I sat next to Nyika and talked with her into the night accompanied by the elders transporting her spirit to the ancestral world. She had helped me become the woman I am today. We prayed.

The following morning, we carried her body wrapped in her white sheet to her grave, only woman carried her, including me.

During Shona funerals emotions are welcomed. There is no such thing as trying to push tears aside. You are encouraged to howl and wail, to shriek and scream – anything, as long as you get the grief out.

As the first soil hit the stark white sheet, my heart broke and tears flooded my cheeks. The women were singing. I looked up and on the hill behind the house where I had sat the night Kudzai was taken, there he stood again. In the not so remote distance. Close, but far enough away. I looked at him, not quite believing what I saw after all it had been a long (sleep deprived) couple of days. Through rain window eyes, I saw him wave. Everyone saw him. They carried on singing. I wanted to run to him, to hug him, to ask him a million questions but I stood frozen. It was all too much. I saw him walking away and I bolted towards him. I ran down the dirt road as fast as the wind (and believe me I am no runner). I rounded the corner only to come face to face with four black Mercedes-Benz, all with dark tinted windows. In front of them leaning on the bonnet was Kudzai. He looked like a rapper from a New York music video.

I half expected him to say "word up," or something along those lines. Here in front of me was standing Bobby Black. A river of emotions ran through my body. My childhood friend – a brother back then.

'I don't have much time, Joanna,' he said (his voice so different to the one I remembered), 'I shouldn't even be speaking to you. But after you looked after my mother so well, I feel I ought to. I loved her. I loved you like a sister. You were my sister. I thank you from my heart for looking after her when I could not do so. I respect that. You still are like a sister to me but we aren't kids no more. This is the real world. Bad times are coming. You will have to leave. I suggest you leave. It's all I can do for you and your family is to warn you – it's time to leave. You must go immediately.' That word again. Immediately, stone dead and gone!

I ran towards him. Two bodyguards climbed out the car and aimed guns at me. He lifted his hands.

'Don't shoot.' We looked at one another. A million worlds apart, but souls still connected. He slid his sunglasses on. For men in my country do not cry.

With that, he climbed into his car with his driver and left me in the dust.

I turned and went back to the funeral. I needed to get back to work, to clear my mind and to get perspective. I declined further festivities. Nyika's headstone read: *There are two sides to every story.* Then there was her birth date and her date of departure.

I paid my last respects. Then I put the truck in first gear and drove back down the dirt road. I had to stop briefly as too many thoughts were making my head spin.

I would leave Zimbabwe. No choice in this matter at all. I had been warned, once again. My soul felt shattered. My home, all I had ever known everything I had ever loved. I would implore my family to do the same.

The End

As you will see after reading this book the synopsis of Alice's life, hers was an up bringing which was arguably the envy of any number of people.

A life worth living and her world full of adventure, excitement and enjoyment, at times overwhelmingly sad lessons. She has contributed to this planet, indeed making it a better place for Zimbabwean Wildlife & her people. Her cup truly overflowed in many respects and she has very few regrets. Alice clearly has a will of her own. Her love will always be the African Bush, specifically the Zimbabwean Lowveld and Chishakwe, The Save Valley Conservancy. Alice (referred to as Joanna in this book), is currently based in Bangkok, Thailand. She is writing her next novel, "*The Flamboyant*", *a story about her families arrival in Africa at The Cape of Good Hope before the 1850's, her uncle (who is a published author in his own right) will be assisting her with the history of their families great trek.*

<u>Therefore, I leave you with this thought:</u>

The well-being and secure future of nature and human communities are inextricably connected. In Zimbabwe many subsistence farmers surround and border nature reserves. We need to assist these people in the face of climate challenges that are upon us, as they need firewood, land for their farming and so on. As these populations increase it puts pressure on those resources, transgressing into poaching, damaging behaviours and the eventual and inevitable destruction of the fauna and flora (the habitat). By assisting the surrounding communities, we can make Zimbabwe a positive example to the world.

<u>Climate Change Impacts in Zimbabwe</u>

Climate records show that Zimbabwe is already being impacted by the effects of climate change. Zimbabwe lies in a semi-arid region with limited and unreliable rainfall patterns and temperature variations (Brown et al., 2012). According to the Zimbabwe Meteorological Service, daily minimum temperatures have risen by approximately 2.6°C over the last century while daily maximum temperatures have risen by 2°C during the same period (ibid). There is a strong interaction between climate change and poverty which impacts other political, social, institutional and environmental factors. Climate change will further adversely impact agricultural production and exacerbate the problem of food security (Points et al., 2014). The IPCC (Intergovernmental Panel on Climate Change) states that in Zimbabwe, "Climate change will exacerbate risks and in turn further entrench poverty *(very high confidence)* (ibid.)." Zimbabwe is also one of the countries identified by the IPCC where climate change will increase the frequency of extreme events which are overlaid with considerable poverty (ibid). Extreme events will be harmful as

Zimbabwe and its urban areas are dependent on its lands for critical resources such as water, food and energy (ibid). A further problem is the insufficient availability of information for suitable adaptation options and behavioural issues that may further lead to suboptimal adaptation decisions. Zimbabwe has experienced the impacts of climate change mostly through rainfall variability and extreme events (Brown et al., 2012). Their impacts are expected to render land increasingly marginal for agriculture, which poses a major threat to the economy and the livelihoods of the poor due to Zimbabwe's heavy dependence on rainfed agriculture and climate sensitive resources (ibid.)

Climate change will highly impact the economy and the livelihoods of the poor in Zimbabwe, especially due to their heavy reliance on rainfed agriculture (Brown et al., 2012). Climate change has already altered rainfall patterns which has led to substantial declines in agricultural production and thus GDP since 2000. In 2007, for example, only 45% of national cereal requirements were produced in the country leading to a high deficit and reliance on imports (ibid). Increasing droughts are expected to exacerbate declining agricultural outputs, further compromising economic growth and stability, employment levels, food insecurity, demand for other goods and poverty reduction (ibid). Farmers (62% of the population) will bear disproportionate impacts which poses a major threat to sustainable development at the micro and macro levels (ibid). Extreme events (e.g., tropical cyclones and droughts), which are likely to intensify will impair the existing natural hazard burdens for at-risk populations and damage and destroy infrastructure (ibid). If current conditions continue to prevail, current traditional agricultural systems will become increasingly unsustainable (ibid.) Adaptation options are decisive for further agricultural development – if no measures are taken – yields are expected to decrease by up to 50% by next year (ibid).

Persistent drought in Zimbabwe has severely strained surface and groundwater systems contributing to the country's deteriorating water supply (Brown et al., 2012). Zimbabwe has and will experience climate-induced water stress which threatens to decrease the quantity and quality of drinking water, reduce the run-off necessary to sustain hydro-electric power supply and contribute to declining agricultural productivity. Zimbabwe has experienced periodic urban water shortages over the last few decades which have been triggered by rural droughts (Points et al., 2014). Droughts have in the 1980s already led to price shocks which resulted in physical stunting among children and reduced lifetime earnings (ibid). Run-off (the main source of water in Zimbabwe, 90% of supply) is projected to decline by up to 40% with the Zambezi Basin worst affected. At the same time, annual rainfall levels are projected to decline by up to 20% by 2018 (Brown et al., 2012).

Evidence suggests that climate change will affect human health through increases in floods, storms, fires and droughts. It will, for example, increase the geographic range of infectious disease vectors (e.g., malaria), which will be especially harmful among vulnerable people (e.g., living with HIV/AIDS). In addition, climate change will intensify the gender dimensions of vulnerability which specifically counts for female-headed households (Brown et al., 2012). The above-mentioned erratic water supply situation in Zimbabwe has already contributed to an increase in water-borne diseases (ibid). According to the IPCC, changes in temperature and precipitation are likely to alter the geographic distribution of malaria in Zimbabwe with previous unsuitable areas of dense human population becoming suitable for transmission by 2100 (Meehl et al., 2007). Disease epidemics in addition to food insecurity, chronic malnutrition and HIV/AIDS are eroding the resilience of households rendering them less resilient and more vulnerable to hazard shocks (Brown et al., 2012).

Increasing extreme events will also impact Zimbabwe's infrastructure which is already currently limited (Brown et al., 2012). The African Development Bank estimated that Zimbabwe requires approximately $14.2 billion to rehabilitate existing infrastructure. Climate related hazards, such as severe floods, will worsen this situation. For example, rail capacity utilisation has dropped from 53% in 2000 to 15% in 2009 (ibid). The right policy choices are critical in ensuring that future infrastructure is climate resilient and able to reduce risks among vulnerable groups (ibid). Climate change is also likely to compromise energy development, especially hydropower, which represents 45% of electric power in sub-Saharan Africa (ibid).

The mentioned threats demonstrate the fragility of Zimbabwe, calling into question its ability to cope with minor emergencies, which can easily turn intro crises (Brown et al., 2012).

References

Brown, D., Chanakira, R. R., Chatiza, K., Dhliwayo, M., Dodman, D., Masiiwa, M., … Zvigadza, S. (2012). Climate change impacts, vulnerability and adaptation in Zimbabwe. London.

Meehl, G. A., Stocker, T. F., Collins, W. D., Friedlingstein, P., Gaye, A. T., Gregory, J. M., … Zhao, Z.-C. (2007). Global climate projections. In S. Solomon, D. Qin, M. Manning, Z. Chen, M. Marquis, K. B. Averyt, … H. L. Miller (Eds.), Climate Change 2007: The Physical Science Basis. Contribution of Working Group I to the Fourth Assessment Report of the Intergovernmental Panel on Climate Change (pp. 747–845). Retrieved from http://www.ipcc.ch/publications_and_data/ar4/wg1/en/ch10.html

Points, I. F., Affairs, F., Ii, W. G., Review, G., Draft, F., Fifth, I., … Spm, F. D. (2014). Climate Change 2014: Impacts, Adaptation, and Vulnerability (WGII-AR5). 2–4.

The short scientific summary of climate change risk in Zimbabwe was written by: Scientist; Nicole van Maanen.

Appendix - The Tribal Story of my region,

written by my uncle, Rob Beverley

THE VADUMA (KARANGA) AND HLENGWE TRIBES OF THE SOUTHEAST AND THE LOWVELD

The first people of the southern African sub-continent were the Bushmen, or San people. They left a legacy of the extent of their area with numerous rock paintings throughout the southeast.

They were few and they lived amongst another people who were also few in number. These people were small, very dark and were exceptional hunters. It can be assumed that these were late stone-age people, the Banyai. When the Duma people eventually arrived in this area they came across the Bushmen and a people with a clan name Shoko, which must have been these hunters.

The Vaduma or Duma people originated from Tanganyika and the Great Lakes region. *Tanganyika* means "The Beginning Country". They also referred to their ancestral home as *"Guru Uswa"* (great grass plains) or as *Dumbu Kunyuka*.

Portuguese historical records however, note no mass migration across the Zambezi and it may be assumed that the migration south was a slow, gradual process over a long period of time. Documents written by Diego de Alcacova in 1506 record the main influence as being the Mutapa, Karanga and Changamire tribes, who were placed mainly in the northern areas of the highveld plateau. Until recently there was no universally accepted name for the Shona people although they were tied by culture and language. Their system had no single leader or state organisation. It refers rather to individual hereditary leaders and their relatives within their own territories.

The Vaduma people are dominant in most of the southeast. When they arrived they found the Shoko people who were easily overcome in tribal fighting, some fleeing back to Mbike, while the remainder were absorbed into the Duma people. Remnants of Shokos are still identifiable among Sadumhu Bgwazo's people. They are regarded as Mutorgwas. Kraalhead Chivamba and his clan are true Shokos.

* *

Legend has it that the original Duma ancestor was Zinyakavambe, who came from the sea with a burning firestick. It is not known if "by sea" it was meant the Indian Ocean or one of the great lakes of East Africa. There is one version presuming he came across a lake by boat from another land. Nobody knew his tribe or his name or who his wife was.

One version of the legend has it that Zinyakavambe travelled down the coast and stopped at a place call Uteve, now Dondo. Apparently his son Chimanya was born there, and eventually died there. Chimanya had a son called Chikosha, who ultimately left the area for a place called Mbire. Chikosha fathered a son called Zimutswi, who was made Chief on the death of his father. Zimutswi referred to the Bushmen as Zvidumbuseya (big stomachs).

The other version has Zimutswi living in Tanganyika when he sent his sons Mtindi and Fupajena south to look for new land. Mtindi became fearful and returned but Fupajena continued his journey down the east coast, eventually entering what is now the Bikita area. Satisfied that it was a good place to migrate to, he returned to Tanganyika to fetch his father, brother and their families plus Zimutswi's brothers Rineshanga, Nechirorwe and Rukweza. On the journey from the coast to Bikita, Rineshanga drank water from a pool with a dead body in it. This shocked his brothers who wanted to leave him behind. However, Nechirorwe stayed behind with him, they being full brothers from the same mother. They became known as Mupfumba from Neshanga.

Zimutswi and Rukweza travelled on to a mountain called Chidumana, from which they derived their clan name, Duma. They found a large cave in the mountain, which had a narrow opening, which could be closed with a flat rock, an action known as *duma*.

After Zimutswi settled he had a son Mtindi who would eventually father the first Mukanganwi. Zimutswi then fathered Fupajena.

Zimutswi died while his sons were still relatively young and their uncle Rukweza made their lives very unpleasant until they ran away and he took on the chieftainship. The two brothers eventually arrived at Mandara Mountain, which would play a big part in Duma history. Mtindi helped Fupajena to raise an impi, after which Fupajena travelled the area killing and looting. He became very famous as a warrior and leader. Rukweza eventually died and the chieftainship was taken over by his son Mudunguri. Fupajena by now felt powerful enough to challenge Mudunguri to regain the chieftainship for Mtindi, which he did successfully. It is not known if Mudunguri was killed, as he is not mentioned again. However, his son Mabika, fled to Matsai where he resided for a number of years until Mtindi recalled him to his home. Although Mtindi resided at Mandara, Fupajena was continuously away warring with other tribes. He eventually claimed all the land from Bikita to the Limpopo. His land was known as Vasina Muganu (land with no boundaries). He travelled as far south as the Orange Free State and then to the Natal coast. For the first time he saw white men whom he called Vasinamabvi (people who have no knees - because of the long trousers they wore).

It is of interest to note that another ancient name for the Limpopo River was Ngulugudela.

When he returned from this epic journey, Mtindi had songs of praise sung to him. One famous one was "Bayawabaya, mukono uno Baya Dzose" (stab and stab, my brother stabs all the people).

When Fupajena discovered that during his absence his wives had given birth to children from other men, he took them all to a big rock and slaughtered them including all people accused of witchcraft.

* *

Whilst home, Fupajena heard of the great Musikavanhu who had a beautiful daughter named Mhepo who was greatly sought after. Mhepo had taken a vow of silence to put off all these unwanted suitors. Musikavanhu had promised her as a wife to anyone who could make his daughter speak again. Fupajena travelled to the eastern mountains where he tried in vain to get Mhepo to speak to him. One day he went with her to her maize fields and while she was hoeing weeds he was digging up the maize plants and planting them upside down. This so infuriated her that she cursed him breaking her vow thus allowing Fupajena to take her home as his new wife.

Her one stipulation was that her new home had to be built where she could see the eastern mountains from where she had come, and the banks of the Sabi River. Mandara was suited for this purpose and Fupajena built a hut with two doors and dug a well inside the hut.

Mtindi had three stone seats constructed. One for himself, one for Fupajena and one for Ziki. He eventually made a fourth for Mabika when he returned.

Mtindi eventually took the name Mukanganwi and became the chief. Fupajena became paramount chief with the name Mazungunya. This remained so until recent history when a rearranging in the tribal system split the original chieftainship into various other chiefs, with their own jurisdiction but still owing allegiance to Mazungunya. Traditionally any blood relative of Mazungunya who is given a chieftainship or headmanship relinquishes his right to the Mazungunya chieftainship as it is felt they have already been fairly awarded. A chief's area in which he lives is known as his *Gadzingo* or land of the chief.

* *

In the meantime, Nechirorwe and his brother who had been left behind had accumulated a small band of people. They then moved to an area south of Bikita in the Sabi Valley where his descendants are still headmen.

All chiefs and headmen from Bikita, Zaka, Ndanga and surrounding tribal areas pay allegiance to Mazungunya chiefs. This includes the Hlengwe chiefs and leaders Gudo, Marozva and Masuka Budzi.

Fupajena's first son from Mhepo was called Nemeso. He was born with four eyes and Mazungunya wanted him killed. However, Mhepo took him to Musikavanhu to be brought up. His eventual return to his home years latter brought about his Nerumedzo clan, which is still resident in Bikita.

One of Mazungunya's praise names is Maputsura Zvose (one who attends to everything).

The chiefs of Ndanga, Zaka are Nhema, Ndanga, Nyakunuwa and Bota. They all claim descent from Mazungunya except Ndanga, who came from Gutu.

Note on name sources:
Ndanga comes from Ndatanga, Zaka comes from kuDzika or kuDzaka, , Bikita comes from Chibukutwe or can mean ant bear, Gutu comes from MuKutu weMuseve.
Chikekerema and Chibvumani are two major ruins left.
Hanyana is the highest point

* *

BOTA CHIEFTAINSHIP

Mutupo - "Moyo" - Chidau "Gondhori" Tribe Mujena of Vakarango.

The final appointment of Mujena on 27 September 1959 was celebrated by "Zibaba" Mapanje, a Sadunhu, in the traditional way. A Zibaba is responsible for going into family history to make sure the correct person is selected. Mujena was not a popular choice and was not nominated by the Zibada, although he officiated. Mapanje had nominated Ruzembera, a descendent of the Mtatawigwa clan and grandson of Nenjana the fourth Chief Bota. Ruzembera is Sadunhu Rudhanda.

Mujena's son Wilson took over the chieftainship but was killed during the civil war. There are said to be two Svikiro's in Chief Bota's area, Svikiro Mariro was Tandari, son of Matonodzi

Muwadzi. Svikiro Manjanjanja was Magenga, son of Muchemwa Munadzi.

Headmen under Bota are chiefs in their own right although not recognised as such by the authorities. They are Dzoro, Ruvuyu, Dekeza and Mushaya.

The early westward migration of the tribe is said to have reached Zimbabwe Ruins. There the eldest son, Nyajena set up his chieftainship whilst a younger brother Mariro Mazungunya and Nhema's ancestors moved to their present areas.

PATTERN OR AUTHORITY

SADUNHUS AND HEADMEN

Under Bota
Bgwazo, Rudanda, Mawadze, Chipumo, Madzivire, Mapanje

Under Dzoro
Mapuwa, Muzondidya, Dabgwa, Machiva, Chifunde

Under Ruvuyu
Makukmire, Tukununu, Zimonde

Under Dekeza
Mamutse, Mushava, Makonese, Chireva

Under Mushaya
Gorimbo, Chivuru, Mutirikwi

Disputes go as follows:-
First Kraalhead, if not satisfied, Sadunhu, then Chief
All land is settled by Chief or Sadunhu representing him

Spiritual power, and therefore to a lesser extent, political power is vested in the Svikiro. In many areas the Svikiro's influence is more powerful than usually assumed.

The Shangaan (Hlengwe)

The Nguni swept through the southeast, heading northwards in about 1840. They were led by Shoshangaan and Zwangendaba having fled Zululand after challenging Shaka and being beaten by Shaka's impis. After defeating the Rozwi people Zwangendaba went north to establish the Angoni nation and Shoshangaan went east to establish his Gaza nation with his capital Mandlikazi, established thirty miles southeast of Espungabera and five miles northwest of old Gwerudo, otherwise known as *Gwendo* or *Gwarau*. Eventually the Gaza-Hlengwe nation controlled all of Gaza and a substantial area of the southeast. The Gaza chiefs were Keshla, meaning ringed chiefs, by the headring they wore, an honour granted to veterans by Shoshangaan when they were permitted to marry. Kukeshla means to put on the headring. The Hlengwe of the Lowveld belong to the Chauke Fire clan. They say it is not customary to lick a burnt finger but to dip it in water as an act of reverence to their totem.

At the death of Shoshangaan in 1856 his body was taken for burial at his ancestral home in Tshaneneburg. The chieftainship should have gone to his fourth son Chuone, but it was usurped by his half-brother Mawewe who attacked Chuone and in a particularly violent battle in which twelve thousand people died, Chuone was murdered.

Another half-brother, Muzila, sought protection from Joao Albasini in the Soutpansberg. Muzila, later persuaded Albasini, the Boers, and the Portuguese to help him oust Mawewe, which they did in a violent battle when Mawewe was defeated and killed. Muzila's son Ngungunyan succeeded him to the chieftainship.

However, when he connived with Rhodes about giving him all mineral rights in Gaza for the Rhodesians in exchange for rifles, ammunition, and a yearly stipend, the Portuguese sent General Albuquerque to attack him and chase him out of Mocambique to an area north of the Kruger Park, which they were to call Gaza Nkulu (Great Gaza).

THE HLENGWE

The Hlengwe people are derived from the Tsonga group of people, being the ones resident in the Lowveld. The Hlengwe language is a dialect of the Tsonga group of languages.

The vast majority of non-Hlengwe Africans and Europeans refer to Hlengwe and Tsonga groups as Shangaans. In fact, many Hlengwe and Tsonga may refer to themselves as Shangaans or Changana, or Vaka Shangaan, or Machangana. Strictly speaking, the name Shangaan should only be applied to the Nguni followers or descendents of Shoshangaan, Manukosi, founder of the Gaza Empire.

The Hlengwe appear to have originated to the east of the Limpopo in Mocambique and to have been there for the greater part of the last millennium. The last common ancestor of all Chiefs and Headmen is Matsena.

The following Hlengwe chiefs claim ancestry from Xigombe, Matsena's descendent. Sengwe, Chicualacuala, Varumela, Chitanga, Mpapa and Magudu.

Chiefs and headmen mainly from the eastern areas, Chilonga, Mahenye, Chitsa, Tsovani, Magatsi, Ngwenyene and Masivamele do not claim descent from Xigombe. It is therefore presumed that Matsena being the last common ancestor, two Hlengwe groups entered the Lowveld. One group under Xigombe entered the

Nuanetsi area, while the other group entered the Sabi-Lundi and Bikita area.

Matsena was chief in about 1751. So the Hlengwe were established prior to the rise of the Gaza Nation.

* *

Hlengwe legend, as with the Duma, says they found a VaNyai (strange) people of the Shoko totem resident when they arrived. The Hlengwe people existed as a separate people before the advent of the Gaza, and they still exist as a people with their own identity. However, the Gaza had a great effect of the Hlengwe and many of them served in the Gaza Mangas (impis).

Chief Sengwe paid tribute to Muzila (Nyamande) as did his descendents. Other Hlengwe chiefs at times paid tribute to Shona or Gaza chiefs. They were not averse to using Gaza or Ndebele impis to violently sort out personal problems of inheritance or grudges.

* *

In more recent history, the location of the various tribal groups was Chief Tsovani in the Triangle/Hippo Valley area. Chief Chitanga and headman Mpapa in the Matibi II area. Chief Sengwe in Sengwe tribal area and Mateke Hills Chief Dumbo, related to Chitanga lived in the Nuanetsi Ranch headquarter area.

These people were moved at various times. Chitanga to Matibi I, Mpapa to Matibi II, Chitsa from the Sabi-Lundi junction to southern Sangwe, and Ngwenyene to Sengwe.

Ngwenyene is related to Chief Muvuve's people in Mocambique. Chief Sengwe is related to Chief Chicualacuala in Mocambique. The Shangaan dialects of Sangwe and Sengwe tribal areas are quite different. The Sangwe people are a mixed Ndau and Hlengwe. Most children in the southern Hlengwe go to South Africa, to Gazankulu to further their education after Standard 4, as they feel this is their ancestral home. They have roots there with their own traditions.

In Hlengwe tradition, chiefs and headmen have equal rights and only for administration purposes is a chief looked on as the senior leader. The chief cannot give orders to a headman, as is the Shona custom. Present day Hlengwe headmen pay allegiance to Chief Sengwe as the senior chief, the other chiefs being Tsovani and Gudo. Chief Sengwe crosses the Limpopo frequently to Gazankulu to maintain traditional ties and to be involved in all the traditional ceremonies. He pays tribute to the Gazankulu chief, who is a descendent of Ngungunyan.

Hlengwe chiefs are greeted "*Vinyachisa*" by their followers. It is interesting that they do not "*Uchira*" (Hombera) by clapping hands as the Shona do. They merely rub their hands or clasp them together at the chest when greeting. There is no audible clapping.

Chiefs are nominated by a "Ligota" the Shangaan equivalent of the Shona Zibaba.

It is said that the Tsovani chieftainship will forever remain in the Muteyo house because the Magatsi house has been honoured by the creation of a headmanship and Mahike is a Sadunhu under Magatsi.

Furthermore, they are resident in Ndanga whilst the Muteyo clan live in Sangwe.

Mahike is the hereditary name for Sadunhu Mahundlani, under Magatsi and lives in Headman Dzoro's area under Chief Bota.

Palm River Ranch, Triangle, Zimbabwe March 2000

Whilst I have made every effort to get as close to the true story as possible, one must bear in mind that the recording of this sort of history, is a verbal history.

Within a tribe, different stories are told about the same incident. Although similar they could be different experiences. All verbal history is suspect in many regards.

However, I believe this will help people to understand the people we are dealing with a little better. The knowledge of another man's history gives you a better understanding. It would also be an advantage to get to know how some of the more important names and clans fit into the present day situation.

This will make the picture clearer.

Rob

Appendix: Gazaland

Jump to: navigation, search

Gazaland is the historical name for the region in southeast Newcastle, in modern day Mozambique and Zimbabwe, which extends northward from the Komati River at Delagoa Bay in Mozambique's Maputo Province to the Pungwe River in central Mozambique. It was a district of the former Portuguese East Africa. Its name was derived from a Swazi chief named Gaza, a contemporary of Shaka Zulu. It covered most of present-day Gaza and Inhambane provinces, and the southern portions of Manica and Sofala provinces.

Refugees from various clans oppressed by Dingane (Shaka's successor) were welded into one tribe by Gaza's son Soshangane, his followers becoming known as Shangaan or Mashangane. A section of them was called Maviti or Landeens (i.e. couriers), a designation which persisted as a tribal name. Between 1833 and 1836 Soshangane made himself master of the country as far north as the Zambezi and captured the Portuguese posts at Delagoa Bay, Inhambane, Sofala and Sena, killing nearly all the inhabitants. The Portuguese reoccupied their posts, but held them with great difficulty, while in the interior Soshangane continued his conquests, depopulating large regions. Soshangane died about 1856, and his son Umzila, receiving some help from the Portuguese at Delagoa Bay in a struggle against a brother for the chieftainship, ceded to them the territory south of the Komati River . North of that river as far as the Zambezi, and inland to the continental plateau, Umzila established himself in independence, a position he maintained till his death (c .1884). His chief rival was a Goan named Manuel Antonio de Sousa, also known as Gouveia, who came to Africa about 1850. Having obtained possession of a crown estate *(prazo)* in the Gorongosa District, he ruled there as a feudal lord while acknowledging himself a Portuguese subject. Gouveia captured much of the country in the Zambezi valley from the Shangaan, and was appointed by the Portuguese captain-general of a large region.

Probably the first European to penetrate any distance inland from the Sofala coast since the Portuguese gold-seekers of the 16th century was St. Vincent W. Erskine, who explored the region between the Limpopo and Pungwe (1868-1875). Portugal's hold on the coast had been more firmly established at the time of Umzila's death, and Gungunyana, his successor, was claimed as a vassal, while efforts were made to open up the interior. This led in 1890-1891 to collisions on the borderland of the plateau with the newly established British South Africa Company, and to the arrest by the company's agents of Gouveia, who was, however, freed and returned to Mozambique via Cape Town. The border between the British and Portuguese colonies was set by the Anglo-Portuguese Treaty of June 11 1891. An offer made by Gungunyana (1891) to come under British protection was not accepted. In 1892 Gouveia was killed in a war with a native chief. Gungunyana maintained his independence until 1895, when he was captured by a Portuguese force and exiled, first to Lisbon and afterwards to Angola, where he died in 1906. With the capture of Gungunyana opposition to Portuguese rule largely ceased.

In the early 20th Century, Gazaland was one of the chief recruiting grounds for laborers in the <u>South African gold mines</u>.

History

In the 1820s, during a period of severe drought, Nguni armies, southern African ethnic groups that speak related Bantu languages and inhabit southeast Africa from Cape Province to southern Mozambique, began to invade Mozambique from what is now South Africa. One Nguni chief, Nxaba, established a short-lived kingdom inland from Sofala, but in 1837 he was defeated by Soshangane, a powerful Nguni rival. Eventually Soshangane established his capital in the highlands of the middle <u>Sabi River</u> in what is present day Zimbabwe. Soshangane named his empire "Gaza" after his grandfather.[2]

Soshangane died in 1856 and there was a bitter struggle for power between his sons Mawewe and Mzila. With help from the Portuguese, Mzila eventually gained power in 1861 and ruled until 1884. Soshangane's grandson, <u>Gungunyana</u>, took over the Gaza Empire from his father Mzila and moved the capital southward to Manjakazi, putting him in closer proximity with the Portuguese.[3]

With the prolonged drought, the rise of Gaza, the dominance of the slave trade, and the expansion of Portuguese control in the Zambezi Valley, the once-mighty African cheiftaincies of the Zambezi region declined. In their place, valley warlords established fortified strongholds at the confluence of the major rivers, where they raised private armies and raided for slaves in the interior. The most powerful of these warlords was <u>Manuel Antonio de Sousa</u>, also known as Gouveia, a settler from Portuguese India, who by the middle of the 19th century controlled most of the southern Zambezi Valley and a huge swath of land to its south. North of the Zambezi, Islamic slave traders rose to power from their base in Angoche, and the Yao chiefs of the north migrated south to the highlands along the Shire River, where they established their military power.[4]

People

The Shangaan are a mixture of Nguni (a language group which includes Swazi, Zulu and Xhosa), and Tsonga speakers (Ronga, Ndzawu, Shona, Chopi tribes), which Soshangane conquered and subjugated. Soshangane insisted that Nguni customs be adopted, and that the Tsonga learn the Zulu language. Young Tsonga men were assigned to the army as 'mabulandlela' (those who open the road). Soshangane also imposed Shaka's military system of dominion and taught the people the Zulu ways of fighting.[5]

For centuries, the Nguni peoples are thought to have lived in scattered patrilineal chiefdoms, cultivating cereal crops such as millet and raising cattle. The current geographic distribution of Nguni peoples largely reflects the turbulent political developments and population movements of the 19th century. In the 1820s the cattle-herding Zulu, led by their king Shaka, embarked on an aggressive campaign of conquest and expansion known as the mfecane. Shaka's large and well-armed armies conquered a number of neighboring peoples, and sent others fleeing. Some Nguni groups adopted the Zulu's methods of warfare and used them to subjugate the peoples in whose territory they ultimately settled.[6]

Invasion

The Gaza Kingdom comprised parts of what are now southeastern Zimbabwe, as well as extending from the Sabi River down to the southern part of Mozambique, covering parts of the current provinces of Sofala, Manica, Inhambane, Gaza and Maputo, and neighbouring parts of South Africa.[7] Within the area encompassed by the Gaza Empire, Nguni armies invaded the north

346

and established cattle-owning military states along the edges of the Mozambican highlands. Although not within the borders of modern-day Mozambique, these military states nonetheless served as effective bases for raids into Mozambique.[8]

Soshangane extended his control over the area between the Komati (Incomati) and the Zambezi rivers, incorporating the local Tsonga and Shona peoples into his Kingdom. The waves of armed groups disrupted both trade and day-to-day production throughout the area. Two groups, the Jere under Zwangendaba and the Ndwandwe (both later known as Nguni) under Soshangane, swept through Mozambique. Zwangendaba's group continued north across the Zambezi, settling to the west of contemporary Mozambique, but Soshangane's group crossed the Limpopo into southern.[9]

Another army, under the command of Dingane and Mhlangana, was sent by Shaka to deal with Soshangane, but the army suffered great hardship because of hunger and malaria, and Soshangane had no difficulty, towards the end of 1828, in driving them off. During the whole of this turbulent period, from 1830 onwards, groups of Tsonga speakers moved southwards and defeated smaller groups.[10]

Despite their eviction from the highlands, the Portuguese gradually extended their control up the Zambezi Valley and north and south along the Mozambican coast. In 1727, they founded a trading post at Inhambane, on the southern coast, and in 1781 they permanently occupied Delagoa Bay. However, Soshangane's army overran these Portuguese settlements at Delagoa Bay during the time of the Gaza Empire.[11]

Decline of the Empire

After the death of Soshangane in 1856, his sons fought over the chieftainship. Soshangane had left the throne to Mzila, but

Mawewe felt that he should be chief. Mawewe attacked Mzila and his followers, causing them to leave Mozambique and flee to the Soutpansberg Mountains in the Transvaal. In 1884 and 1885 European powers carved Africa into spheres of influence at the Berlin West Africa Conference. As a result of this scramble for Africa by the European States, the territory of the Gaza Empire was designated as Portuguese territory.[12] Gungunyana fiercely resisted the encroachment of the Portuguese but was eventually defeated. Gungunyana was exiled to the Azores where he died in 1906. The cause of the collapse of the Gaza Empire was its defeat by the Portuguese in 1895.

The Reverend, Dr Martin Luther King, said it best:
"Injustice anywhere is a threat to justice everywhere."

Zimbabwe will forever hold my heart. It was where I was born, it is my home, it was my home. The love for all my fellow Zimbabweans is paramount. There is a reason why this world is called Mother Earth and her make up is called Mother Nature. Specifically, women and children. Education is the only answer to moving forward. Education for everyone. Free education. This book has had some political passages; however, they are my personal views and no one is responsible for that but myself. They are not shared with everyone or anyone in particular. In saying that I respect all constructive opinions. No one has had any influence over my choice of words, circumstances create opinions so does life experience, (unless publishing required this) and naturally not everyone has to be of the same opinion. I respect that some experiences were personal feelings and not facts. Nyika, did not have a son and I did not have a chance to say good-bye to her which I regret to this day. However, fate dealt the cards, as I had just escaped a near death experience myself and was leaving Zimbabwe at that time.

Thank you to all the people who helped me write this book, you know who you are. Your encouragement and guidance was unrelenting and showed me a clear path. My deepest regret is that due to past references, many people cannot bring themselves forward to me to create a marketing platform through this read.

CRY FOR YESTERDAY
BY
CYNDI BARKER

I cry for yesterday
I cry for yesterday and what you meant to me,
I cry for that eternal sun
Which we thought we would always see,
I cry because of everything we have lost
And what could not be,
I cry for a land we loved
And special time we shared
And the pearl we held in our hand
And i cry for the past
For the golden dawns we woke to
The dusty winters
Our bare feet on bush paths
And how we rejoiced at the first rains

And danced for the joy of it,
I cry for the pain we carry
In this racksack called life,
And our grandchildren who will never know the real me
Or the real you
And who see us as old people
Wrapped up in nostalgia
Never knowing the magic
We saw
When we sat under the stars
Listening to the sounds of the night hunters
And the fireflies that danced in the dark
I cry for our children who were torn from their roots
And had to grow in a foreign soil
I cry for their futures
And what they were denied
I cry for abuntu
We were never supposed to live apart from our kinfolk
to learn new ways in our adopted countries
I cry for precious memories
And hope I can hold on to them till the end of my days,
I cry for the times I feel so lost
So displaced,
But most of all I cry for you
For our paradise lost
For our happiness
For the distance
I cry for the love we shared,
And how we dared to go
Where the angels feared to tread,
And wonder how we endure
When our spirits are exhausted.
I cry for all of us
And for what we didn't know we had!

Paul van Maanen, Kate Nyika van Maanen, Jane, Nicole van Maanen, Thiemo Williams, Cecile van Maanen, Lisanne van Maanen, Fabienne van Maanen, Pinio Alberto Grabbe, Blessing, Isabella Dzuke, Chikwama, Truth, Zuvarashe, Fiona, Wine, Reckless, Gustavo Montero, Derek Rudolf Henning Jnr, Kimberley Dianne Henning, Lesley May Henning, Amanda Henning, Jonjo Coleman, Mieke van Maanen (Snr), Paul van Maanen (Snr), The Family De Boer, The family De Waal, Harm van Maanen, Nadine van Maanen, Paul (Jnr) van Maanen. Dieter Lehsten, Ulrike Lehsten, Annelise Soros, Ullie, Ricardia Bramely and London Lee, Suzanne Kaiser, Bonnie Kaiser, Steffanie Verring, Morris Hosseini, Nina Houwer, Patrick Houwer, Lynn Booth, Vernon Booth, Russel Harrison, Mike Donald, Isabella and Stoffel Gras, Farnaz and Frank Riedel, Jin and Afon Guang, Fritz Neumeyer, Hani Taha, Sara Albarguthi, Ghida Shaar, Geraldine and Gwendolyn Dunnoyer, Justine Dunnoyer-Montero, Tim Cooper, Karin Schulz, Kelly Edwards, Marcus Wiest, Anja Niesing, Brenda Justine Brenninkmeijer (My Dutch/Zimbabwean mate!), David Diallo, Helen Gail Searle, John Leon Lambert and Imogen May Lambert, Emina Benalia, "T," Nelly Paula, Elijah Paula and Kiki Paula, Trisha Jones and Rees Jones, Julia and Sergey Karlovac, Michael Alexander Lindsay, Nunthinee Tanner, Nicoleta, Mara and Marion, Heidi, Andy and Cecily Sylvia Liebenberg, Mutetwa, James.

The Pikolis Family, Kim Meaden-Kendrick, Elke Kerkhoff, Shane and Pelly Stockhil, Louise-Erica and Michael Moffet Furmston, Ulrike Krischke, Jason Young, Johannes Cornelis, Jonkheer Hendrik Merkus de Kock, Mauro Santi, Michael Joseph Hayes Auret, Dan Jawitz, Paul Cohen and Azhar Khan, Heike Gabriel, Martina New, Femke Goossens and Family, Alexandra Rambaud-Measson, Tracey and Peter Maltman, Liam Du Preez Paterson, Colin William Roberts, Jigyasa and Yashita Mohit, Jonathan Symmonds, Hisham Taha, Tracy Piper, Luke West, Tricia Pahl,

Ayesha Ibrahim, Nicole Lewin, Stevn Vos, Ralph & Tao Tooten, Jo Pooley, Mike Donald Frank Vollbehr, Hans-Ulrich Suedbeck, Edward Tauscher and last but not least to Michelle Camps & Peter Galli, my husband, Paul, who has stood by my side through thick and thin and whom I love and adore without question, and my parents who were always a beacon in my life – In my tribe I trust!

Would you like to make a difference?

It takes no time at all.

Participate in our online challenge

It's simple.

1) Film yourself in slow motion on your mobile phone, throwing a ball up into the air and catching it. Maybe get creative, convince your sports teams or your family or your dog?

2) Accompanying your "video of throwing and catching the ball" include the line;

#Don't Drop the Ball; Nyika (the earth) I love you ;www.endpandemics.earth

Post it to your social media platforms.

2) Then challenge your friends to do the same so the "ball", makes its way around the globe.

3) Please think carefully, about where, or how, you decide to throw and catch the ball, safety first! Be safe! I/WE take no *responsibility for any dangerous challenges or ill thought out plans or any vindictive or inappropriate language or behavior toward or regarding this challenge and campaign!*

For more about helping our world, please have a look at the following sites:

www.dontdroptheball.org

www.endpandemics.earth

Special thanks to Michel Granger for his artwork and dedication to his expressions of our home planet earth. Jonathan Symmonds (A fellow Zimbabwean, with a worldwide reach, a 3D Digital Animator, he is recognized as the "Father of Dragons" – Game of Thrones. He has his own company and online academy!) He animated the works of Michel Granger's artwork; L'état des Lieux; The inventory of the mentioned work is; 1986,acrylic on paper 60x80cm.

In addition, a special shout out to;

Paul van Maanen, my husband and soul mate, without whose unconditional love and support this would not have been possible. *To my daughter and stepdaughters*, thank you for your constant credence in my potential as a writer. To my uncles, *Vernon Booth and Rob Beverley*, to my cousin *Stuart Beverley* and my sister *Bell,* for helping me with important documentation of past events, with steadfast accuracy. To Geraldine Dunoyer and Ghida Shaar, two of my closest friends, who have been with me every step of the way. Through all the highs and the lows. For additional support in pre-promoting my work. Legends till the end! To *Steven Vos* for being the lover of nature, reminding me about how the small things matter!

Alexandra Rambaud-Measson, one of the most wonderful souls, that I was fortunate enough to encounter along life's path and the reason that *Michel Granger* came on board. *Peter John Galli,* a former journalist and communications director extraordinaire, who has worked for the world's biggest corporate guns, often having encouraging words but more often critical ones, keeping me grounded and never giving up on me! To my production coordinator for being that reassuring voice on the other end of the line and to the other employees at AM Publishers, thank you for your positive go getter attitudes.

Daniel Swid, for developing the tech savviness we required to jump start; Don't Drop the Ball!

Michael C. Mitchell (The mind behind the logistics and many hats of "LIVE AID")

Thank you, Michael, for putting your weight behind – Don't Drop the Ball!

Steven R. Galster, a big thank you for being the voice of reason.